A NOVEL OF NAVAL ____ ____ ____
BY THE AUTHOR OF ____ ____

D0051993

JOINT TASK

FORCE

LIBERIA

DAVID E. MEADOWS

BERKLEY

$6.99 U.S.
$9.99 CAN

ISBN 0-425-19206-7

9 780425 192061

50699

EAN

Praise for *THE SIXTH FLEET* novels by David E. Meadows

"Rip-snorting, realistic action-adventure from a man who has been there. David Meadows is the real thing."

—Stephen Coonts, *New York Times* bestselling author of *Flight of the Intruder*

"An absorbing, compelling look at America's future place in the world. It's visionary and scary. Great battle scenes, believable heroes, plus villains you'll love to hate."

—Joe Buff, author of *Deep Sound Channel,* *Thunder in the Deep,* and *Crush Depth*

"If you enjoy a well-told tale of action and adventure, you will love David Meadows's series, *The Sixth Fleet.* Not only does the author know his subject but [his] fiction could readily become fact. These books should be read by every senator and congressman in our government so that the scenarios therein do not become history."

—John Tegler, host of the syndicated talk show *Capital Conversation*

"Easily on a par with Tom Clancy, *The Sixth Fleet* provides an awesomely prescient picture of the U.S. Navy at war with terrorism and those who support it. It has the unmistakable ring of truth and accuracy, which only an insider can provide. In the aftermath of September 11, this is not just a good read, but an essential one."

—Milos Stankovic, author of *Trusted Mole*

"Although the U.S. had not been attacked when Meadows wrote this series, he was apparently only too well aware that some of this country's enemies would not rest until American blood was shed. Such foresight, in the aftermath of September 11, gives the books even more impact."

—Angela Webster, reviewer, *The Newnan (GA) Times-Herald*

JOINT TASK FORCE
FORCE
LIBERIA

DAVID E. MEADOWS

BERKLEY BOOKS, NEW YORK

This is a work of fiction. Names, characters, places, and incidents either are the product of the author's imagination or are used fictitiously, and any resemblance to actual persons, living or dead, business establishments, events, or locales is entirely coincidental.

JOINT TASK FORCE: LIBERIA

A Berkley Book / published by arrangement with
the author

PRINTING HISTORY
Berkley edition / September 2003

ISBN: 0-425-19206-7

BERKLEY®
Berkley Books are published by The Berkley Publishing Group, a division of Penguin Group (USA) Inc., 375 Hudson Street, New York, New York 10014.
BERKLEY and the "B" design are trademarks belonging to Penguin Group (USA) Inc.

PRINTED IN THE UNITED STATES OF AMERICA

10 9 8 7 6 5 4 3 2 1

While Amphibious Group Two, Norfolk, Virginia,
is the outfit in *Joint Task Force: Liberia,*
this book is dedicated to all those who sail
as United States Amphibious Sailors and Marines,
ready to project power ashore
whenever and wherever called upon.

ACKNOWLEDGMENTS

It is nearly impossible to thank everyone who provided support and encouragement when writing a novel such as *Joint Task Force: Liberia*. But I would like to acknowledge some who were kind enough to encourage, provide technical guidance, or many times just answer questions unique to their professional skills and qualifications: Ms. Sharon Reinke, Mr. Art Horn, Colonel Bridgett Larew (Doc), Lieutenant Colonel Ken Gill, Commander Scott Fish, Ed Brumit, John Tegler, Admiral (Ret.) Tom Stevens, Sharon Stevens, Mike & Nancy Shank, Bob Gensler, Tommy Grunwell, and members of the VQ alumni and the Naval Cryptologic Veterans Association with their great wealth of knowledge. And, of course, the comments from the many fans who corresponded via my website at http://www.sixthfleet.com are much appreciated. My thanks to all of you.

I have two brothers, Wesley and Douglas, who have always been inspirations to me. I am very proud of the success they have enjoyed in their chosen careers and as family men. We Meadows brothers all wear uniforms. Wesley is Fire Chief of Southside Savannah, Georgia, and Douglas is Police Chief for Newnan, Georgia. Since September 11th, the importance of their vocation and dedication has never been more apparent and, to me, they represent all the firefighters and police who risk their lives as our first lines of defense against terrorism throughout our great nation.

I am blessed with the encouragement and suggestions that my better half, Felicity, continues to provide. Without her, I would never have become a writer, and neither would we have been blessed with such great children as Sara and Nicholas.

My thanks to Mr. Tom Colgan for his editorial support, and to his able assistant, Ms. Samantha Mandor. Where would an author be without a publicist? Ms. Tina Anderson and I have had the pleasure of growing together in the world of publicity.

Bottom line is that I have learned a lot from the association with The Berkley Publishing Group family.

While I have named a few for their support, rest assured that any and all technical errors or mistakes in this novel are strictly those of the author, who many times wanders in his own world.

CHAPTER 1

ULLMA PULLED THE CHILDREN CLOSER. LIBERIAN-ACCENTED
English, mixed with slaps from flip-flops hitting the wood floor
overhead, caused the three to huddle closer. A burst of gunfire
caused Ullma to jump involuntarily. Oh, why, oh, why did she
ever listen to that fool of a husband of hers and come here?
Ullma's huge arms, rolls of fat hanging beneath them, enfolded
the two children. Dust dropped onto their heads and shoulders.
Shadows flickered through the planks of the floor overhead,
blocking and unblocking the light from the faint bulb in the
dining room.

"Momma, you're hurting me," Selma, her six-year-old said,
trying unsuccessfully to push Ullma's arms away.

"Shsss," Ullma commanded. Ignoring the girl's protest, she
whispered, "Listen to me, children." She pulled Jamal closer
while pressing Selma against her side. Selma gritted her teeth,
but kept quiet. "Jamal, you're twelve years old. You know the
way to Uncle Nathan's. You gotta take your sister and work
yore way to his house. You hear me?"

Jamal leaned back, trying to see his mother's eyes in the
dark. The faint light from above reflected off two rivulets of
moisture running down her cheeks. "Uh-uh, Mom. Dad said
stay here with you." He glanced briefly at the small ground-

level basement window a few feet away. Tropical bushes blocked the moonless view of the backyard.

More gunfire erupted from above, followed by shouts and screams that caused the three to huddle closer. The cry of *"Allah Alakbar"* rose above the cacophony of noises. Three—maybe four—automatic weapons, thought Ullma. Somewhere up there . . . she didn't want to think about it.

"Jamal," she whispered firmly, her voice shaking as she glanced again at the floor a couple of feet above her head. Like an icy cold hand, a deep fear rushed through her. The man she loved, the man she followed, and her oldest son were going to die up there, trying to protect them.

"Mom, I'm scared," Selma said.

"We all scared, honey," she replied. She pushed the young girl away, holding both her arms in her massive hands. Looking into her daughter's face, Ullma continued, her voice trembling. "But you gotta be brave and go with Jamal. Now, you listen to me, Selma. You do what Jamal tells you to do. I don't wanna hear about any arguing with him. You hear me?"

Shouts drew their attention for a moment. Bits of African dust rained from the floor above as more running footsteps pounded by overhead. She was scared. *Holy Lord, He knew how scared she was.* She released Selma with one hand long enough to wipe the tears from her eyes. *Why in the hell did she ever agree to this asinine idea of Jerry's to emigrate to Liberia? Never should have left Mobile.* She should have stood her ground and told him that if he went, he went alone. Should have kept the children with her in Alabama.

She looked over at Jamal, who was staring at the floor above them. The fight up above wasn't going to last much longer. Then, those nasty God-baiting rebels would start to loot the house. Eventually, they would reach the basement. She knew from stories she had heard from other American expatriates what was in store for them. She hugged Selma closer. It was better her daughter die than be taken by the Liberian rebels—followers of this Arab bastard they called Abu Alhaul. This Arab proselytizer had issued a Fatwa to clean Africa of the American infidels, proclaiming the Arab and African people were all one, and that those who called themselves African-Americans were not African at all.

There was so much hatred against America out here. It had surprised her to discover just how much. Sure, they were Africans—African-Americans. This Abu Alhaul wasn't. He was another Arab religious nutter trying to kill his way into whatever heaven he could. Why couldn't her family come back to the land of their ancestors who had been forcibly taken away? But Ullma's friend, Christina, had answered that question. *"Honey, you can't no more go back to where you ain't never been than you can teach what you ain't never learned."*

"Listen to me, Jamal," she said, taking his chin in her free hand and turning his face toward her. Sweat soaked the loose dress she wore. She reached up and wiped the thick perspiration and the tears away from her eyes. Ullma cleared her tightened throat a couple of times, praying she was hiding the fear she felt from Jamal and Selma. She pointed to the dark entrance of the circulation pipe that led away from the basement. "You've gone through this thing before, Jamal. I know you know how to do it. You take Selma and go through it again."

"I don't want to go with Jamal," Selma whined.

She stroked the little girl's hair. "I know, sugar, and if Mommy could she would keep you here with her, but I need you to help Jamal go get Uncle Nathan. Think of it as a game."

"I don't want to play this game, Mommy. I'm scared. I want Daddy. I wanna go to my room," she cried softly, throwing her small arms around her mother's large neck.

"I know, but you're going with Jamal. You hear me?" she asked, pushing Selma away slightly and looking her in the eyes. "Momma loves ya. Mommy loves both of you. And when Uncle Nathan and his vigilantes get here, you can go back up to your room. Okay?"

The darkness of the basement hid her daughter's face. She saw the shadow of the girl's head nod.

"Good." She put Selma's hand in Jamal's. "Go. Be careful out there and avoid everyone you see until you get to Uncle Nathan's. You tell him about the men in the house. He'll come. He'll bring the other vigilantes with him. Tell him we need the vigilantes."

Jamal leaned down toward his mother's squatting figure and kissed her on the cheek. "Come with us, Momma," he said.

A burst of gunfire, followed by laughter, drowned out her reply.

"What?"

"I said, I wish I could, but yore Momma ain't small enough to get in that thing. You and Selma have used it. You know where it goes. I'll be all right here until you return, Jamal, but you gotta tell Uncle Nathaniel to hurry."

"I will, Mommy." He pulled Selma toward the lip of the shaft. "Stop that, Selma," he said.

Ullma reached out and touched her daughter. "Selma, you stop that, you hear? You do what your big brother tells you and you keep quiet. You don't want them bad men up there to hear you."

Jamal felt Selma's hand relax. He lifted her up onto the lip of the two-foot-by-two-and-a-half-foot aluminum shaft that allowed cooler air from the small copse of trees out back to circulate through the one-story house. He pulled himself up. He couldn't see her, but he heard his sister scrambling ahead of him. She'd be as scared of being in the pipe at night as she was of the men above them. He pulled himself up and into the pipe, effectively blocking off what little light there had been. The soft sound of her whimpering reached him. He should never have kidded Selma about snakes sleeping in this thing.

Jamal crawled after her, hearing the sound of her shoes scuffing on the rusting metal. All the houses along this street had these underground shafts as part of a natural ventilation feature.

Ullma listened for a few seconds until the sound of them moving away faded. Then, she reached down, picked up the fan, and pushed it back into the opening. They would never know Jamal and Selma had escaped through the ventilation shaft.

A scream echoed from above. "No, don't!" shouted an American voice. It was Jerry. The rebels must have him, and if they had him, then they had her eighteen-year-old Abdul.

Ullma put her hands on her knees and forced herself upright. She braced against the cement side of the basement for several seconds to give her legs a chance to adjust to the change. Reaching over against the nearby wall, she picked up the ax that they had brought all the way from Alabama when they shipped their household goods to Monrovia. Trailing it after her, Ullma shuffled to the narrow stairs that led up to the kitchen. "Yea, though I walk through the valley of death, I shall fear no evil, for the Lord God Jehovah, he is with me," she prayed softly, the words trailing off as she started up the stairs.

A horrible scream broke through laughter of the Liberian rebels, bringing forth a chorus of *"Allah Alakbar"* from those she imagined surrounded her husband.

Ullma put one foot in front of the other as she moved up the stairs. It was almost as if she was standing outside her body watching what she was doing. As if she truly believed that armed with only an ax, she could rout these African fanatics who believed that only by killing Americans could they go to paradise. She stopped on the next-to-the-top step and ignored the tortured screams of Jerry as she finished reciting the Psalm. She bent her head. "Our Father, who art in heaven . . ." A minute later, finished, she looked up and with her free hand, opened the door.

The kitchen was dark. The top step squeaked as she put her weight on it and leaned her head into the kitchen. One hand gripped the door facing, while the other held the ax about halfway up its handle. Faint light from the open door to the dining room revealed an empty kitchen. Ullma pulled all of her 250-pound-plus weight into the kitchen. Seeing a nearby kitchen towel, she grabbed it and wiped her face, shifting the stinging sweat away from her eyes. The fear was still there, but buried down deep beneath what she knew she had to do. *The Lord commanded. He gave and He took away.*

The rebels' celebration in the dining room drowned out the creaking of the floor as she waddled slowly to the open door. Standing to the side in the shadows, Ullma could see into the room. Her son's body sat on the floor with his back braced against the far wall. His opened, glazed eyes stared back at her. The torso tilted slightly to the right. Both hands lay palm up on each side of him. A puddle of blood surrounded her oldest son.

The rebels had Jerry tied by his arms to one of the family's pinewood chairs that they had bought at an Ethan Allen's just outside of Mobile.

Blood ran down the side of his face. One of the rebels leaned forward with a razor cutter and slid the knife down the skin of Jerry's face. She had heard of others skinned alive by these radicals. The scream broke through her inertia.

Ullma took a deep breath, hoisted the ax, and moved forward, picking up speed as she burst into the dining room like a locomotive emerging from a tunnel. She swung the ax, nearly decapitating the nearest rebel on her right, and with the return swing Ullma broke the kneecap of another African who had frozen at the sight of this unexpected apparition. His comrade tumbled lifeless to the floor, his head hanging by a stretch of skin. The laughter and shouting stopped abruptly as the huge African-American Amazon turned on her heels and bore down on them. They stood paralyzed just long enough for Ullma to bring the ax down on the head of the man with the razor, splitting his skull in half. That was enough. A couple of the rebels ran for the door. She must have seemed a mad African spirit sent to kill them.

Two men, wearing long flowing robes, busy breaking the bottles of whiskey and brandy on the other side of the room, stopped what they were doing. They brought their AK-47's up and fired. The bullets hit Ullma. Her body jerked as the bullets entered, but her momentum carried her forward, the ax coming up. It came down, slicing through the shoulder of a third attacker, who had tripped, his feet kicking as he tried to back away. The ax sliced through the shoulder, stopping as it passed through the genitals, digging into the floor beneath. The man's flip-flops jerked spasmodically, slapping the floor, as his screams drowned out Jerry's.

Two more bullets hit her. Still moving, she turned, and rushed the men firing. They were not Africans. They had the short beards, light features, and black headdresses of the Arabs. The Africans were either dead, dying, or making new roads into the jungle. The two men with the weapons stood with legs slightly spread, firing into the huge demon rushing them. Their lips curled beneath narrowed dark eyes that burned with hatred. The words *"Allah Alakbar"* flowed from their lips.

She couldn't feel her legs. All the noises and screams started to fade. Her upper body moved forward a few more feet, and in the next moment the floor rushed toward her. Pain shot through her chest. Ullma tried to roll over, but her hands and arms were numb. As if a curtain was dropping, light faded. For a moment she seemed to be looking down at her body, spread-eagled across the floor, her dress up around her buttocks, two massive thighs touching each other. The ax lay useless, a few inches from her twitching right hand.

One of the men put a combat boot under her and tried to turn her over, but her weight was too much for him. The other said something she didn't quite understand—sounded Arabic. He leaned over and put the weapon against her head. A bright white light was the last thing she saw, and before she died, she wondered for a brief second why she hadn't heard the noise of the gunshot.

"IT'S DARK. I DON'T WANT TO GO," SELMA SAID. SHE LEANED her head out of the shaft and looked both ways down the small ditch that crossed the opening.

"Look, Selma. I can't get around you to go first. You've sneaked out this way before. Just jump down. You aren't gonna get hurt," Jamal said. He pushed her on the butt. "Go on."

"Don't push me!" she shouted.

"Be quiet, Selma," Jamal said. "You want those men to hear you?"

"What about the snakes?"

"Ain't no snakes. I was just kidding yesterday."

She kicked back, her white sneaker catching him on the shoulder.

"Selma!"

"That's for scaring me."

The noise of the explosion reached them a second before the concussion blasted the two out of the shaft, sending them rolling into the bushes beneath the trees. Jamal tumbled over Selma, who started screaming. His left shoe hit her on the chin bringing the screaming to an abrupt halt. The left side of his face slammed into the dirt, causing his legs to catapult over his head, carrying his body into the thick bushes beneath the copse of trees.

He lay there a few seconds, blinking. He touched his chest, straining to take a full breath. After several tries, the effects of the concussion wore off, normal breathing resumed, and Jamal sat up. He rubbed his eyes, blinked rapidly to clear them. Squinting, he put both hands on the ground and pushed himself up, using a nearby tree to steady his shaking legs.

Faint starlight filtered through the leaves of the trees reflecting off the green-patterned dress that Selma was wearing. He stumbled toward the crumpled heap that was his sister, and breathed a sigh of relief when he heard whimpering.

He squatted and shook her gently. "Are you all right?"

She moaned. "I told you not to push me," she whined through tears. "I'm going to tell Momma."

"I didn't push you."

"Uh-uh, and you hurt me."

"Can you stand, Selma?" he asked, taking her by the arm and pulling her up carefully. He rose to one knee.

She jerked away. "I can get up on my own."

"Keep your voice down, Selma. I didn't push you. Something blew us out of the shaft."

His sister rolled over and moaned. "That hurt," she said, sitting up. An orange glow flickered across her face.

Jamal scrambled to the edge of the ditch and looked toward the house. Flames leaped from the wooden frame, licking through the roof and through a large hole from where the back of the house had been. Looking right and left, Jamal saw the houses along the row with his burning. Another explosion, this one a few blocks away, caught his attention. He watched as flames and debris shot into the air.

"Look at the house," Selma complained. "I want Momma and Daddy."

"Come on, Selma. We've got to get to Uncle Nathan's and tell him."

Jamal, holding Selma's hand, led the way as they leapfrogged over jungle debris, keeping to the edge of the American expatriate suburb of New Carrollton. The two stumbled along the jungle curtain that abruptly separated the dwindling jungle on the outskirts of Monrovia from the growing presence of Americans. His eyes roved back and forth. He was expecting at any moment for someone to jump out and grab them.

They sneaked along the back of the houses, all of them in flames. He saw the home of his friend Sam as he and Selma hurried by it. He pulled her down abruptly as a group of shouting men ran around the side of Sam's house. One of them was laughing and waving something that looked like a head.

Jamal pulled Selma farther into the jungle, crouching there until the men disappeared toward the front.

Satisfied they were gone, Jamal tugged her up and they continued toward Uncle Nathan's house. He glanced back and saw a group of men standing in a circle kicking at something on the ground.

The two siblings moved through the jungle, sometimes hiding as Africans appeared on their right. Groups of men running from the front of one house to another, silhouettes breaking the shadows for a moment before they disappeared, blocked by the next house. Periodically, bursts of gunfire broke the jungle quiet from the nearby housing complex. Each time, Jamal increased their speed, wanting to put distance between them and the fighting.

Selma's patterned dress and Jamal's blue jeans helped the two blend with the maze of grays, blacks, and shadows along the edge of the nighttime jungle. Jamal's white shirt had long ago been camouflaged by the dirt, vegetation, and clay the two had fought through.

The rebels never saw them even as, unknown to Jamal and Selma, searching eyes roamed the jungle edges looking for Americans who might have escaped the massacre. Even if the rebels had seen them, it was doubtful the Africans would have passed up the opportunity to loot the more affluent American houses before their Arab masters torched them.

Eventually, the fighting and fires fell behind as Jamal and Selma circled toward Uncle Nathan's. Four hours had passed since they left their Mom in the basement when the two weary children saw the circle of homes, one of which belonged to their uncle Nathan. Jamal stopped and squatted.

"Why are we stopping?"

"Be quiet, Selma. Need to make sure it is safe to go."

She jerked her hand away. "I'm tired and I gotta pee."

"Then pee here."

"No way. You'll peek."

Jamal sighed. "Okay, come on. It's dark and we haven't seen anyone for a long time."

He stood, reaching down to take her hand. The body slam hit him hard, knocking him onto the ground. Selma started screaming, shouting for Uncle Nathan. The man who hit him put his knee on Jamal's back and pressed down. "Shut up," the American voice said.

Selma continued to scream.

"Selma, that you, honey?"

Jamal felt the pressure from the knee in his back ease up.

"Sorry, I didn't know who it was," the voice said, standing up, freeing Jamal.

Jamal fought to keep the tears back. Selma's dress flapped as she ran toward the figure of Uncle Nathan. The person on top of Jamal moved away. Jamal pushed himself into a sitting position and put his hand against his chest, taking several deep breaths. A pair of hands reached under his arms, lifted him, and then released him. He nearly fell. A wave of fatigue rushed over him. His eyes shut for a moment before he opened them, realizing he had nearly fallen asleep standing up.

A hand reached out and steadied Jamal. "Whoa, buddy," the person who had tackled him said, holding Jamal by the arm. "Sorry about that. I could tell you were a kid, but didn't know you were Jerry's boy."

Jamal jerked his arm away and headed toward Uncle Nathan.

Selma had her arms wrapped around her uncle's legs. Uncle Nathan stood there patting her on the back with his right hand. In the left, he held an M-16 rifle. Thomas had seen the weapon in his uncle's bedroom closet. His dad had one also.

"Jamal, are we glad to see you, son," Uncle Nathan said, his eyes roving the darkness behind Jamal.

The sound of gunfire to the south drew their attention.

"Kafla," Uncle Nathan said, speaking to the young man who had tackled Thomas and who was now dogging his steps. "Take Jamal and Selma to the cars and find them a seat."

His uncle let go of Selma and reached out for Jamal. "Jamal, where's your mom and dad and Abdul?"

"They're back at the house, Uncle Nathan. Mom says for you to come quick and bring help. There are people inside,

Uncle Nathan, and if you don't come quick, they may kill—"

"I understand, Jamal," his uncle replied, a hint of sadness in the answer. "You remember how to shoot a rifle?"

"Yes, sir."

"Kafla, give him a gun," he ordered the man standing behind Thomas. "Jamal, you go with Kafla and listen to him. You and Selma stay with him."

"Uncle Nathan, Mommy says—" Jamal said, thinking maybe Uncle Nathan hadn't understood what he had said.

"Jamal, we'll try to check before we go," Nathan said, his voice catching.

"Go?"

Nathan shook his head. "Son, they've either made it and are working their way this way, or . . ." Nathan stopped, leaned down, and unwrapped his niece's arms from around his leg. "Selma, you go with your brother and Mr. Kafla here. They're going to take you to a car and find you a seat. We're leaving Monrovia tonight."

"What about Momma and Daddy?" Jamal asked falling into step beside Uncle Nathan as they hurriedly walked through the dark toward the front of the houses that circled this small cul de sac in the suburb of New Carrollton. "Momma and Daddy were there when we left, Uncle Nathan. Maybe they're following us?"

"Maybe they are, Jamal. Let's hope so, and if they did by some miracle make it out, then they'll catch up with us. Your daddy, my brother Jerry, knows the plans if we ever had to flee. He'll know where we're going and how we intended to go. They'll catch up."

Jamal jerked away from him. "You don't think they made it out like Selma and me, do you?"

"Jamal, I can't expect someone your age to understand, but the government has fallen. President Jefferson is dead and African rebels led by Arab fanatics are overrunning the city, killing Americans wherever they find them. We're heading to Kingsville. If Jerry, Ullma, and Abdul are alive, they'll meet us in Kingsville."

Jamal looked at the jungle edge. Kingsville! Last year he had gone with his parents to visit this African-American town.

A small piece of the United States hacked out of the jungle by retired U.S. Army Lieutenant General Daniel Thomaston. Even his father had called the man "General." Everyone did, and he remembered his father lightly slapping the back of Jamal's head, after shaking the man's hand when this Thomaston walked by, and whispering for Jamal to stand. Everyone in the community center had stood and waited as the "general," who had led so many African-Americans back to their roots in Liberia, entered. Jamal had even shaken the general's hand, and the general had asked him his name, what grade he was in, and what he wanted to be when he grew up, before moving off to talk with others. He wondered if the general would remember him. Uncle Nathan was right. General Thomaston would kick these rebels' asses from here to kingdom come.

A group of men, shouting, came running down the road toward them.

"Nathan! Can't hold them. More showing up by the minute."

A whistling sound, increasing in intensity, drew everyone's attention. Heads spun upward, searching the night sky, and then the sound headed downward. A nearby house exploded as the mortar shell hit. The concussion knocked Jamal off his feet. It wasn't as bad as when Kafla tackled him minutes ago. Flames shot out of the roof of the house as pieces of it spun crazily in all directions.

"We've got to go," Nathan said.

Jamal stopped and watched his uncle march a few more steps before turning to face him. "I've got to go back and see if I can find Daddy and Momma," Jamal said.

Nathan walked back and took Jamal by both shoulders. "Son, if you do, then you'll just get lost. If your parents are alive, they'll find you at Kingsville. If they don't, then I'll come back with you and we'll find them. But right now, we've got to get out if we want to live."

Jamal stared up at Uncle Nathan, their eyes meeting. A couple of seconds passed before Jamal nodded. Nathan let him go.

Nathan motioned the men running toward them toward the houses at the rear, shouting, "Get everyone in the cars!" Jamal ran behind him. Uncle Nathan moved at a half trot, touching people on the shoulders as they ran past, urging others to pick up the pace. The two of them headed toward the back of the farthermost house. Kafla, carrying Selma, ran to their left.

"I want my SUV in front and the pickup truck bringing up the rear with the men on it. We've got to get the hell out of here, now!"

Nathan glanced down at his nephew. "Go! Go with Kafla here," he said, pointing toward the house at the end of the cul de sac.

Kafla put Selma down. "Follow me!" Kafla ordered, and took off running.

Jamal grabbed her hand and the two ran, trying to keep up with the young man who seemed intent on leaving them behind. Around the side of the house they sped. Kafla turned along a dirt road that disappeared into the bush behind the house. Another sharp curve and he stopped. Jamal counted four SUVs. People waited patiently for their turn to crawl into the large vehicles. The straining sound of an engine behind him caused Jamal to turn his head. A dark pickup truck appeared. Three men slid into each front seat of the five vehicles, each carrying a weapon.

Other men began to appear from the dark shadows between the houses. Several pulled themselves into the pickup. Jamal looked around. Where was Kafla? He squeezed Selma's hand tighter. A woman stuck her head out of the third SUV. "You two children. You get yourselves over here with us." Her hand waved them toward her.

Jamal pulled Selma with him as they hurried toward the outstretched hand. When they reached the SUV, the door opened and hands pulled Selma inside. Kafla appeared suddenly beside Jamal. "Here," he said gruffly, handing Jamal a rifle. "Your uncle said give you one. It's loaded, so don't shoot your fool self." The young man reached forward, shoved the door shut on the SUV, and leaned down beside the passenger-side window. "Keep up with the car in front of you," he said to the driver. "Keep your lights off and don't use your horn unless it's an emergency."

Jamal stood there listening until Kafla turned to him. "You come with me. We're going to put you in the next SUV," he said, nodding toward the one in front of the Selma's.

Kafla walked quickly toward the front of the column with Jamal hurrying to keep up. A sudden explosion followed by the sound of automatic gunfire drowned out the noise of the convoy. Through the canopy of trees, a blast of bright light followed for a few seconds and then disappeared. Jamal glanced behind him. Selma was in a British Land Rover. He couldn't read the front license plate, but noticed it was bent slightly at the top where something must at one time have caught it and pulled it down.

Kafla's foot hit the step of the second SUV. He opened the back door, and in one smooth motion motioned Jamal to climb inside it. Jamal watched as Kafla sprinted forward to the lead SUV and scrambled inside it. Why couldn't he ride with Uncle Nathan?

"Here, let me shut the door," the woman sitting beside Jamal said, reaching over and pulling the door shut. The driver and an armed man sat in the front seat.

Another armed man ran up to the far side of Uncle Nathan's SUV, and stood alongside the idling SUV for a couple of seconds before jumping inside and slamming the door. Everyone was riding with Uncle Nathan but him.

"Let's go!" someone leaning out of the back window of the lead SUV shouted. That sounded like Uncle Nathan.

The right door opened on Jamal's SUV and a third man leaped into the front seat.

The motor revved for a moment before the SUV lurched forward. Jamal nearly fell forward off his seat. The lady beside him leaned over.

"Might be a good time to wear our seat belts," she said nicely.

Jamal mumbled a thank-you. So much had happened that he was confused. What was going on? Where were Mom and Dad? Uncle Nathan had said they were gone, but did he mean "gone as in gone" or "gone as in dead"? He shut his eyes. He refused to believe his mother and daddy were dead. Abdul, the bully, would never allow anyone to kill him. Of that, Jamal had no doubt.

Behind him, a cacophony of screams and shouts were followed by the sharp sounds of gunfire, bangs, and explosions. His eyes flew open and his head whipped around toward the sounds. Tongues of orange flames reached upward illuminating the area. As far as he could see, the houses just on the other side of the row separating them from the attackers were burning.

Another round of explosions followed, with the orange glow of the fires highlighting the fading horizon behind the darkened convoy of refugees as the vehicles penetrated farther into the darker jungle ahead. Jamal wasn't sure where the road led, but he recalled hearing his father and Uncle Nathan talk about an old road behind Uncle Nathan's house. They said the original diamond miners in this West African country of Liberia had used it. Probably built by some of the original American freed slaves who returned in the early nineteenth century.

Jamal leaned back against the seat, cradling the rifle between his knees, his hands gripping it tightly, his thoughts playing havoc within his mind. He turned. The silhouette of the Land Rover where his sister rode was about twenty feet behind them. He reached up and ran his hand over the top of his short-cropped head.

"Here, son," the lady said, handing him a small washcloth. "Use this to keep the sweat out of your eyes."

He nodded and took the terry cloth, running it across the top of his head and his brow. When he wiped his eyes, for some reason he failed to fathom, he discovered he was crying.

"It'll be all right," the lady said, patting him on the knee.

Tears rolled down his cheeks. No, it wouldn't be all right. It would never be all right again. He reached up and brushed the tears from his cheeks, turning his head toward the window, and hoping the lady was the only one who had noticed. It was okay for women to see you cry, but he didn't want the other men to notice.

Behind, a whistling sound of mortar rounds hitting the houses and the areas where the convoy had just left stilled the night sounds of the African rain forest. The small convoy drove deeper into the wilderness, leaving the chaos and mayhem of Monrovia behind them.

Jamal shut his eyes and silently said a prayer for his mom and dad. His brother could take care of himself. Uncle Nathan was wrong. Maybe he didn't say they were dead, but Jamal knew his uncle thought they were. But if they hadn't made it out, then where were they? Sometime within the next hour, despite the rocking and jerking of the vehicle, Jamal fell asleep. Exhaustion overcame his worries and concerns.

CHAPTER 2

REAR ADMIRAL DICK HOLMAN, THE COMMANDER OF AM-
phibious group two, paced the bridge wing of the USS *Boxer*.
The complaints emanating from the other bridge wing by his
Chief of Staff about the exercise brought a wry smile to his
lips. Holman, former fighter pilot and holder of the Silver Star
after taking a carrier battle group through the mined Strait of
Gibraltar, patted his shirt pocket for the third time. Damn, he
thought, it's like a security blanket. He had to quit checking
every few minutes to see if he had a cigar.

From his viewpoint, the amphibious exercise was going
well. You would never know it from the anguished comments
from his Chief of Staff—Captain Leonard Upmann—Navy
surface-warfare officer. But what could you expect from black
shoes whose idea of fun was to work longer hours?

Shoes had divided the warfare specialties of the Navy until
the early 1990's, when it was decreed that officers, regardless
of whether they were aviators or surface-warfare officers or
submariners, could wear brown shoes. While they had previously complained and griped about aviators being singled out
for special uniform considerations such as the brown shoes,
when given the opportunity, no self-respecting SWO or submariner would dare be caught wearing them.

Holman patted his shirt pocket for the umpteenth time. He was going to smoke this Havana cigar sometime this morning. He hated the idea of starting it and then have something happen that forced him to toss it overboard—*God forbid*. They cost too much. So the big question was, while Leo complained and held the floor, did he have the time, or should he even take the time, to enjoy it? After all, it was one of the many reasons he preferred the bridge to the crowded Combat Information Center belowdecks. From the other side of the bridge, another burst by Leo brought a quiet chuckle from the officers and sailors manning the bridge. Must be something with the deep bass voice that reminded him of frogs croaking that made Upmann's comments comical. Holman glanced at his watch. In about three to five more minutes, Leo would march through the bridge between the adjoining bridge wings to tell him how bad everything was going.

"What are they doing?" Captain Leonard Upmann shouted to no one in particular. "Oh, my God, oh, my God," the tall, lean Navy officer from Frederick, Maryland, moaned.

Holman turned, squinting from the summer sun, and looked through the opened bridge at his Chief of Staff on the other side. Leo was leaning against the bridge wing stanchion, slapping his palm against his forehead. Over the shoulder of his Chief of Staff, Holman saw landing craft circling in the lee of the huge amphibious carrier, USS *Boxer*. Two of the landing craft collided, bouncing away undamaged from the slight impact, wheeling their helms in opposite directions to open space between them.

"Oh, Christ! Boatswain Mate!" shouted the Chief of Staff. "Bring your knife out here and slit my wrists! What are they doing? Who trained them coxswains on helmsmanship while in a holding pattern? The Three Stooges?" The statement and questions rolled in a staccato of raspy bursts.

Dick grinned and shook his head. Winks and smiles passed between the bridge team members. Upmann was good for morale. The words and actions were for show. The junior officers and crew both liked and respected the tall Naval Academy officer. It was unusual to be both liked and respected. Usually, you get one or the other.

Dick wished he had the ability to remember names the way

his Chief of Staff did. One thing he appreciated, but never told Leo, was that whenever they met people, Leo always spoke their names so Dick could hear them. He shook his head. *Maybe Leo does that on purpose, so I don't embarrass anyone by calling them someone else.* Yes, Leo was a character, and just as he and his SEAL friend Rear Admiral Duncan James were discussing in Washington a few months ago, the Navy could use a few characters. Some of the Navy's most famous leaders were characters. They were characters who knew what they were doing and drew people to them with heroic antics, actions, and tenacity.

Dick turned away, lifted his binoculars, and focused them on the North Carolina beach several miles away. This rehearsal exercise was going better than most, but you would never believe it listening to Leo.

"Boatswain Mate! To hell with just one knife! Bring two! I've got to end this shame!"

The quartermasters surrounding the navigation table near Dick's hatch laughed until the chief petty officer told them to shut up, quit listening, and focus on their jobs. Where would the Navy be without those three enlisted pay grades of chief petty officers?

Along the beach, the first wave of landing craft pulled away, except for three that remained ashore, their landing doors dropped onto the sand. Small dots marked individual Marines scurrying up the high sand dunes about a hundred yards inland. Here and there, smoke rose to mark simulated enemy artillery shells hitting the beach. Though he couldn't tell which ones were the referees, Dick knew they were running among the arriving assault force marking some as dead, others as wounded, and even others wounded but capable of combat. Marines who earned the stamp of "Dead" always argued with the referees. "Dead meat," they called it. Being dead meat meant sitting out the war games in a roped-off area of the beach. At least being wounded, they could argue that they weren't wounded enough to evacuate and should be allowed to continue forward with their buddies into combat. He smiled as he recalled the story they told during the early months of the war on terrorism in Afghanistan.

A Marine walks to the top of a hill and shouts down at a

bunch of Talibans that one Marine is worth ten Talibans. The Taliban leader sends ten fighters over the hill. There is a lot of shooting and screaming and after several minutes, only silence. As the Taliban leader watches the top of the hill, the lone Marine appears again and shouts down that one Marine is worth more than a hundred Talibans. This time, the Taliban leader sends one hundred fighters over the hill. Same thing, lots of screams, shouts, bullets, and explosions, followed by silence. The Marine appears again. This time the Taliban leader is angry. He orders a thousand fighters over the hill after the Marine. Screams, shouts, bullets, explosions follow, and then over the hill comes a lone Taliban fighter, wounded and crawling toward the leader. As he reaches the leader, he tugs on the long Taliban robe and whispers, "It's a trap; there's two of them."

Dick laughed. Behind him, the quartermasters winked at each other. They nodded at each other. Even the admiral found Captain Upmann's antics amusing.

On the beach, corpsmen, dressed in Marine Corps combat utilities, carried simulated wounded on stretchers toward the three landing craft. Belowdecks in the main medical compartments of the USS *Boxer*, doctors and nurses would be waiting for the simulated injuries to arrive. Developing triage experience was very important in military operations. Many believed triage was the medical management procedure for identifying the most critical who needed immediate attention. Most failed to realize that triage also meant identifying those who were so critically wounded that others might die if necessary medical personnel and equipment were diverted in an attempt to prolong the lives of the dying. War was cruel, and cruelest of all was knowing that your survival could depend on how badly wounded you were, balanced against available medical personnel and supplies.

Leo appeared unexpectedly by his side. "Admiral, the third wave is ready to go, sir. Though the way they are handling those landing craft, I expect them all to capsize before they're a hundred yards to the beach."

Dick lowered his binoculars and looked up. "Leo, they'll do fine. The exercise is going as well as can be expected. This is the third wave, right?"

"Right, sir, but the helmsmen of this wave must still have their learners' permits."

A steward stepped onto the bridge wing with fresh cups of coffee and a plate of fresh pastries. The young petty officer handed the first cup to Dick, who thanked him, and offered the second to Captain Upmann. The plate with the pastries he placed on the shelf that ran below the lip of the bridge wing.

Captain Upmann reached over and took two of them.

Dick shook his head and grinned. "Leo, how do you do it? Every time I see you, you've got a mouthful of something— *about the only time I don't hear your words of doom*—and you're probably the only officer on my staff who has a negative body-fat ratio."

"Six percent," Leo mumbled through the raisin bread.

"And for me," Dick continued, patting a stomach that hung slightly over the belt line, "I can look at that stuff and put on weight."

Leonard Upmann swallowed. "You've lost weight, Admiral," he replied, taking another big bite.

"A little maybe, but only because an old friend of mine, Rear Admiral Duncan James—a Navy SEAL—made me work out with him when he and I spent our four weeks at CAPSTONE." CAPSTONE was the military executive training for new flag officers held at the National Defense University at Fort McNair in Washington, D.C. Everyone who made the stars eventually sat through the series of lectures on what it meant to be a flag officer or general officer. Lectures given most times by those who had never made the rank.

"I've met him," Leo said, reaching out and taking another cake. "Nice man."

"Nice man? If you had read the reports of his rescue of the Algerian President, you would say 'trained killer' more likely. Which is why I made sure I kept running when he so ordered. I didn't want to find out if the SEAL rules for putting hurt animals out of their misery also applied to overweight *'gasping for breath'* aviators."

"Didn't he have the first woman SEAL on that mission?"

Holman nodded. "Yeah, Heather J. McDaniels, *but all my friends call me HJ.* Lots of gossip that she was the reason a certain two-star SEAL admiral retired early."

"I recall he tried to rig it so she would be thrown out of the SEALS?"

"We'll never know," Holman said, shaking his head. "Lots of things go on in the Pentagon that never come out of that five-sided building. Some of the greatest intellectuals you've ever met are in there. Just ask them; they'll tell you so."

The familiar sound of jet engines drowned out Holman's last words. The two officers peered below at the flight deck. The four fighter aircraft maneuvered by pairs to the center of the flight deck on the USS *Boxer*. The jet engines wound down from the test, and on the nose of each of the small fighter aircraft propellers turned.

"Just isn't right," Holman said, reaching in his pocket, pulling out the cigar, and pointing at the aircraft.

"Oh, I don't know," Upmann replied, with an amused twinkle in his eyes. "I kind of like the new fighter aircraft. Sleek," he drawled. "Use less gas—"

"It's called aviation fuel, butt-hole."

"And the pilots are so different. Wouldn't you agree, Admiral?"

"Oh, screw you, Leo, and the rest of the surface-warfare community. You are enjoying this way too much. And since I am the one in charge, I do not want them called fighter aircraft."

The engines revved up on the first pair, drowning out Leo's reply. They watched in silence. A moment later, the four aircraft were airborne. Holman lifted his binoculars and watched the transformation. A short burst of black exhaust from the jet engines showed the flyers shifting from propeller to jet power. He couldn't see the front of them, but knew small hydraulics had withdrawn the propeller blades into the nose of the prototypes to reduce drag and to protect them. Without the propellers, the aircraft wouldn't be able to land on the USS *Boxer* when they finished their mission.

As the aircraft circled higher and the noise faded, a cough caught his attention. He lowered his binoculars. Standing halfway inside the bridge was the ship's Communications Officer, Lieutenant Commander Rachel Grande. Her rich brown hair was pulled tight and upward into a bun before disappearing beneath the khaki garrison cap. It pulled her eyes into a permanent expression of surprise and at the same time highlighted those light blue eyes.

"Morning, Rachel," Admiral Holman said. "And, what do we owe the pleasure of your visit this bright, summer afternoon off the fine beaches of North Carolina?"

"Morning Admiral; Captain Upmann. Sir, I have an urgent PERSONAL FOR message for you from the Director of Operations, Joint Forces Command, Norfolk, Virginia," she replied.

Dick noticed the usual smile missing. Their eyes locked briefly, long enough for him to see the concern that had replaced the normal mischievous look that resonated within those blue eyes. The fact that she was the only blue-eyed Mexican-American he had ever met passed through his thoughts also.

Dick took the envelope, ripped it open, and read the message. Finished, he handed it to Leo. He lifted his binoculars, twisted the focus slightly, and scanned the beach while Upmann read the message. From the south, four V-22A Osprey tilt-rotor aircraft approached the far end of the beachhead. They ascended several hundred feet as they passed the shoreline, and Dick watched as they split off into two pairs and continued inland. The exercise scenario called for the beach landing to lure the opposing forces forward. Then, once they were "bunched," the airborne part of the operation would circle and land Marines behind them, cutting off the enemy from his supply lines, splitting enemy forces apart, and then defeating each opposing force element one by one.

The USS *Boxer* amphibious task force had six of the prototype aircraft on board, along with a mix of CH-53 Sea Stallion helicopters, Cobra Attack helicopters, and a couple of Harrier fighter jets. Belowdecks, this great amphibious ship carried two LCACs—Landing Craft Air Cushion vehicles—along with a few conventional landing craft.

Those conventional landing craft from the USS *Boxer,* USS *Nassau,* and the USS *Belleau Wood* made up the bulk of Holman's attacking force. The *Boxer*'s two LCACs, traveling with the two from the *Belleau Wood,* passed across Holman's line of vision, heading north along the coast. The four air-cushioned vehicles flew across the water like aircraft without wings. Holman lowered his binoculars. Heavy rubber skirts surrounded the hulls of the LCACs, directing high-pressure air downward to bounce off the surface of the water and ricochet up against the craft, keeping them floating a few feet above the surface of the Atlantic Ocean. Without the drag of having to bore holes through the water, the LCACs were capable of speeds in excess of forty knots. Armor plating surrounded the exposed hulls and decks of the LCACs. Heavy machine guns provided additional protection and limited firepower to support an assault. This was essential because a capability the LCAC had over conventional landing craft was that it could hit the beach without slowing and ride that air cushion farther inland to disembark Marines. With the LCACs, the conventional landing craft, and the versatile Osprey, the United States Marine Corps could disrupt any hostile defense in a matter of minutes.

Unlike conventional landing craft, rough shores and shallow water had little effect on the LCACs' advantage of being able to slip ashore nearly anywhere along a coastline. They could transition from an at-sea environment, continue over the sand, up the dunes, and through the grasses until terrain, logistics, or operations forced them to stop. LCACs were another transport arm that added to the Marine Corps capacity to attack from more directions than just a sandy, sloping beach.

The four LCACs passed between a second wave of conventional landing craft that were dropping their ramps onto the main beachhead and the third wave approaching from the shelter of the amphibious task force.

"If they knew how much danger those helmsmen in the third wave presented, they'd be at maximum speed and running for cover," said Upmann.

Holman watched the crossing, his tactical mind churning through the possibilities of how LCACs could disrupt an opposing amphibious landing. Using the same situation he was watching, it would be similar to the old warships of sail whose tactics involved crossing the bow of an enemy ship so all their cannons could be fires simultaneously. Right now, he thought, if those LCACs were enemy, the heavy machine guns on their decks would be sufficient to tear through both waves of unarmed conventional amphibious craft. Not only would it defeat a beach assault, stranding those already on shore, but also it would destroy the very craft needed to mount a second attack or effect a rescue. He bit his lower lip. It would also send hundreds of Marines to the bottom.

Holman shrugged his shoulders. While he could envision the tactic, he couldn't see where he would ever have an opportunity to employ it. There were no Naval forces in the world with the capability to mount such a projection of force from the sea. Then he thought of People's Republic of China. He was one of those die-hard warriors who knew in his heart that someday America was going to have to fight that Asiatic giant. China had been hard at work building its armed forces and increasing its amphibious-assault capability. Its national strategy indicated a belief that the only way to bring *"the rebel province"* of Taiwan under control was through military conquest. He put both hands on the railing and leaned forward, watching the air-cushioned landing craft finish passing. He would write the tactic up and submit it through the chain of command. Holman would incorporate the tactic in his next exercise, and share the lessons learned with his counterpart on the West Coast, Rear Admiral Prentice, Commander, Amphibious Group One. He experienced that little thrill of pleasure that came from identifying an innovative use of a weapon system that only a warrior could appreciate.

Leo finished reading the message. "Sir, should we stop the exercise and reembark the Marines?"

Dick lowered his binoculars and shook his head. That little spark of pleasure evaporated as his mind returned to current events. "Won't work," he said, shaking the ashes off the end of his Cuban cigar. "We're too far along with the exercise to do it properly. All that would happen is we would have a lot of confused Marines milling about smartly ashore, wondering where in the hell the rest of their comrades had disappeared to." He took a deep puff. "When we reembark, I want them embarked in such a fashion that they are ready to conduct another amphibious operation without us having to pull into port, offload, and reload. Besides, I want to see how this new wave of the future for Naval aviation pairs off against those F-14 Top Gunners from Oceana."

"Understand, sir; but if we stop now, we should be able. . . ."

Dick looked toward the shore. The second wave had landed their Marines, hoisted their ramps, and were turning back out to sea. He glanced at his watch. Five minutes, he figured, before the second wave would pass through the third wave of conventional landing craft. "No, Leo. The good thing is this exercise will serve as a rehearsal in the event we have to do one once we reach Liberia. Normal steps of an amphibious operation—embark, plan, rehearse, reembark, execute." He grinned. "Shoot, Leo! We're already sixty percent ready unless we stop the exercise. If we stop it, then sortie across the Atlantic to arrive without the Marines having had an opportunity to flesh out any operational cliches . . ." He stopped, leaving the rest of the sentence unsaid. With the slow-burning cigar held loosely between the first two fingers of the right hand, Holman pointed at the message his Chief of Staff held. "Rachel, keep this to yourself for the time being. You may share it with Captain Hudson, but pass along my orders to keep the contents close-hold until I say differently."

"Aye, aye, sir," she said. She saluted and left the bridge wing.

Dick knew she would return to the radio shack, print another copy of the PERSONAL FOR message, and take it to Captain Jeremiah Hudson, commanding officer of the USS *Boxer*. Only flag officers had the privilege of sending informal PERSONAL FOR messages via official channels. The tradition of sending formal PERSONAL FOR messages had been replaced by e-mails sent via classified channels, but most of his peers knew Dick's propensity for staying well clear of computers. Computers meant being indoors. Dick preferred the fresh smell of salt water and sea breezes passing over the deck of whatever ship permitted him to embark. Until he was appointed as Commander, Amphibious Group Two—the premier Navy organization for the Atlantic amphibious fleet—PHIBGRU Two seldom went to sea. In the one year since he had taken over, the administration functions of the group had been passed to a subordinate amphibious squadron and he had packed PHIBGRU Two's seabags and headed out to sea.

So many times at sea that many of the senior captains and

commanders who had fought for orders to the group as their last tour before retiring looked for easier billets elsewhere, which was all right with Dick. If you didn't want to go to sea, in his book, then why in the hell were you in the Navy? It was like being in the Air Force and refusing to fly, or in the Army and despising camping. He flicked ash off his cigar over the side of the ship.

"Always knew we would have to rescue those Americans in Liberia one day," Leo said.

"The global war on terrorism continues, Captain Upmann, and Liberia appears to be just another front that has jumped up."

"Says here," Leo said, lifting the message in his hand slightly for emphasis, "that the Liberian President, Harold Jefferson, is believed to have been killed when rebels hit Monrovia."

"Could be. I know there are supposed to be several hundred American expatriates living in the city."

"Why they ever wanted to move there, I will never know."

Dick shrugged. "Guess those Liberian passports meant more than the Liberian President thought they would."

"I read once, about two years after he offered dual-citizenship passports to all us Americans of African descent— *as he phrased it*—that he never expected any of us to emigrate to Liberia. Supposedly, he only made the offer figuring that at thirty-five dollars for a passport and fifteen dollars administrative fee, it would bring in some much-needed dollars to the economy."

Both men stopped talking as two pairs of F-14 Tomcats from Oceana Naval Air Station in Virginia Beach blasted by overhead, drowning out the noise of the ship and their conversation. The Tomcats did a 360-degree roll before leveling out. The decibel level crept lower as the four fighter aircraft reached the coastline, split apart, and made simulated ground-attack runs against the opposing Marine landing force.

"Well, he was right. It did. And with that money, he improved the infrastructure of the country—building roads, electric plants, water-purification facilities. Shoot, Leo. Harold Jefferson was even *Time*'s Man of the Year two years ago. A beacon for what Africa can be and can become. Until this"—

he pointed at the message—"Liberia had been a peaceful democracy for over eight years. Ever since the United Nations peacekeeping force helped orchestrate its return to a freely elected government. Although I don't believe we played a major role in that political development, Liberia has refused to let the United States forget its historical ties. Even the Liberian democracy parallels our own with a Congress, a Supreme Court, and an Executive Branch. Just like ours. The only thing they were still working at was finishing that Constitution."

"Well, he got more than he planned," Leo complained. "What he got was a lot of Americans who not only bought the dual-citizenship privileges of a Liberian passport, but who decided 'what the hell' and moved to Africa." He paused for a couple of seconds. "Some of my friends and friends of my wife's parents took up that offer. A couple of them even moved to Liberia."

The Tomcats turned nose-up and ascended.

"Have you ever seen anything so beautiful?" Holman asked, staring at the Tomcats as they ascended.

"Yes, sir. On liberty once in a bar in Singapore."

Holman caught a reflection of the sun off an aircraft to the south of the beach. He raised his binoculars. It was the four prototypes. Movement to his right over the beach caught his attention at the same time. It was the four Osprey tilt-rotor aircraft, heading back to the amphibious ship formation. It would take a few minutes for them to land, load up again, and take back off. If Dick recalled the operation order for this exercise correctly, the Ospreys had two more sorties to do. The first group of Marines behind enemy lines had just been delivered.

"OKAY, AVATAR FORMATION, THIS IS AVATAR LEADER," Lieutenant Nash Shoemaker said into his mouthpiece. "Avatar Three and Four, you take the two Tomcats to your right and Avatar Two and I will take the pair on the left." He reached over and tugged the flight glove on his left hand, flexing the fingers without moving them off the stick.

Acknowledgments echoed through the earpieces from the three other prototype pilots.

Shoemaker pushed the stick to the left as far as it would go. He glanced left. His wingman was fifty feet away according to the heads-up display and about twenty yards back. A quick look at the display screen in front showed him the location of the two other prototypes. This was a real test. Not some laboratory bullshit where they had every white-robed Naval Research scientist leaning over their shoulders mumbling "uh-uh" and "uh-oh" and not once did he hear the "eureka" he expected from a bunch of scientists. What the hell kind of job is it that you don't have an occasional "eureka"?

This exercise would determine the future of this black program. Black programs were secret weapons developments designed to boost the United States military far ahead of any enemy if and when war struck. Until then, they remained behind the proverbial green door. This project, for some unknown reason to him, was hidden deep within the secretive and controversial Naval Security Group Command *with their black silent helicopters and trained killers.* Of course, you'd never get his number-two man, Alan Valverde, to admit they had them.

Shoemaker reached forward, pressed a button, and nodded at the results. Small green lights on the console blinked rapidly several times before glowing steadily for four seconds. Then, the system turned the diagnostic lights off. The cameras were ready, armed, and functioning. His F-14 opponents from Oceana Naval Air Station, Virginia Beach, had argued they should have been permitted live ammunition. Leave it to pilots to act like kids who think someone else is eating their ice cream. He grinned. In this case, they were.

"I have bandits at eleven o'clock."

Shoemaker recognized the voice as fellow Lieutenant Pauline Kitchner flying Avatar Three. She had the lead in the second pair of prototype fighters.

"Avatar Two, Avatar Leader," Shoemaker said to Lieutenant Valverde. "Full throttle. Let's go surprise some Navy aviators. Follow me."

A laugh came across the radio. Pauline's enjoying this too much, he thought.

"Yes, sir," his wingman, Lieutenant Alan Valverde, Naval Security Group Command, replied.

"Ma'am, I am in position on your left," Ensign Jurgen Ichmens said.

"Spoken like a true Naval Academy graduate," Lieutenant Alan Valverde broadcast.

"Alan, Pauline. Focus on the exercise, please," Professor Dunning said. Shoemaker grinned. The man's voice sounded calm, but everyone knew that down deep, beneath that voice of calmness, beat the heart of an arrogant scientist who would gladly sacrifice everyone, including his mother, for the good of *"his"* program. If you ever needed a verb conjugated with the first-person pronoun, then Professor Dunning could do it for you in a heartbeat.

The land disappeared as Shoemaker pulled back on the stick. Clouds raced across the front of his vision. The prototype's radar reflected Tomcats crossing right to left ahead of him. He watched as the radar returns split apart. The electronic-countermeasure suites on the F-14's weren't supposed to be able to pick up this new radar, but you couldn't trust those Navy aviators to play by the rules. You tell them about your systems because of the new technology involved, and the next thing you know they go out and jerry-rig their aircraft to defeat it. He shut his eyes for a couple of seconds. What would happen if they failed this operational evaluation? This guy Holman, commanding the amphibious exercise, was an aviator. Shoemaker felt he was good at reading body language, but when they briefed the admiral in the hangar bay, he couldn't determine whether Holman believed the program was heresy or a technological breakthrough. But of course, the pilots of yesteryear probably thought it was horrible to go from biplane to a single-wing contraption. *Wonder what he really thinks.*

"Avatar Two, this is Avatar Leader; break left and commence a rear hemispheric approach against the bogie to your left. I'll take the one to the right."

A Tomcat blacked out his vision ahead as it passed in front of Shoemaker, its afterburners blazing. Startled, Shoemaker jerked back against the seat. His view vibrated as the jet wash caused the smaller fighter to be tossed about in the air. *Dunning won't be happy if I lose this jet. Of course, then you have to ask yourself the question as to when has the man ever been happy?*

Shoemaker glanced down at the display. Avatar Two was doing okay. He couldn't see anything to indicate the F-14 was even aware of Valverde's approach. How in the hell did this Tomcat get this close? The red electronic-warfare light flashed in his cockpit. *Damn!* The F-14 pilot had radar contact and *he* didn't have a damn thing. He pushed down and to the left on the stick while simultaneously pushing his left foot down, allowing the right one to ease up slightly. The maneuver brought the fighter around. The F-14 shot by him, the afterburner rocking the prototype slightly as the faster Navy fighter twisted into a hard left turn. Shit! The F-14 was bouncing him all over the sky and he couldn't find a moment of advantage. This was not looking good.

"Tallyho! I've got him! I've got him!" shouted Ensign Jurgen Ichmens. "Take that you human no-load!"

"Such language for a young man," Valverde broadcast.

"I find it sexy when he talks like that," Pauline added. "Switching radar signature to simulate F-14 Tomcat. That should confuse them."

"If you two would focus on the job at hand, you might be able to find your targets," Professor Dunning said. "Pauline, if you are going to fool with the electronic-warfare system—"

"Doc, it's just a matter of punching in the right code. Right?"

"Well, yes, but—"

"So, there you are."

"—we were going to do this exercise with our high radar. The stealth mode."

"Hate to tell you, Doc," Shoemaker said. "But the stealth mode—*she no can to be working.* Either these jocks know the electronic signature, or it just doesn't work."

"They may know," Ensign Jurgen Ichmens said. "But the exercise doesn't call for them to use it. It calls for us to use our stealth mode and them to use—"

"There you are, Doc," Pauline added. "The thing doesn't work because we know Navy officers would never cheat during an exercise. Especially pilots. Of course, I could simulate an F/A-18 Hornet?"

Shoemaker grinned. What would they do without their ensign? Every officer ought to have one. Every chief petty officer had one, why shouldn't they?

A glint of sunlight caught his attention. There he was. The F-14 was in a left-hand bank. Shoemaker waited until the F-14 was two thirds of the way into the turn before pulling the stick hard left. With his right hand, he gave it full throttle. The gauge indicated he was pulling just under an eight-G turn. In a normal fighter, his body would have been wedged against the seat, blood draining from his upper extremities to pool in his buttocks and legs. He stretched his neck and rotated his jaw. Amazing how he felt nothing, but then he wouldn't. No one would ever feel a G turn flying these aircraft. "Ain't technology great," he whispered softly to himself. He looked up. The F-14 was gone. "Damn!"

"Avatar Leader, Avatar Four; you call me?"

"No, Jurgen. Just talking to myself."

"Then you need to talk silently, Lieutenant Shoemaker, and not risk the exercise."

"Roger, Professor."

The electronic-support-measures system on his console started blinking again. Instinctively, Shoemaker turned his head to look behind him before realizing it was impossible to see that angle from his cockpit. He jerked the stick right. Nothing in front. He caught a faint blip on his radar, and then the F-14 disappeared from the scope. How far away was his target when he lost him? He flipped back to the left. Still nothing. He banked farther left, watching the clouds race across his vision as he twisted his head back and forth trying to gain a visual on his target. He glanced several times at the air-search radar, but other than Lieutenant Alan Valverde's aircraft, it showed nothing. Out there, somewhere, was his F-14 and by God, he was going to find it. The electronic-countermeasures system was still blinking, so the opposing fighter did have him on his radar screen. Shoemaker just couldn't reciprocate.

He pushed down, sending the fighter into a left-hand spiral descent. The blinking stopped. *"There, at least I've lost his radar,"* Shoemaker said to himself. A shadow passed down his right side. Shoemaker jerked back on the stick. A series of warning beeps sounded and red lights flickered across his console lighting up like a Christmas tree. *Too many Gs*, he said to himself, fighting to ease up on the turn. *Over 14 Gs! Christ, Dunning was going to kill him.* The warning tones stopped. He might not feel the G's, but the aircraft would, and if it fell apart through his hotdogging, Doc would kill him, if the experience didn't.

"He's not moving!" Pauline shouted. "Dumb shit must think I'm another F-14 coming up beside him. *Must be a male pilot.*"

Across the radio came a series of exclamations as Pauline, Alan Valverde, and their ensign reported successful camera shots. Those camera shots recorded successful kills during an exercise. Moreover, here he was the formation leader and he couldn't get his target to stay still long enough. Movement to his left caught his attention. He glanced at the radar. There he was! The Tomcat was back on his scope.

"Should have seen the look on his face when I flew down his side," Pauline said. "It's times like that when I can understand the overwhelming male desire to moon someone."

"Got you, buddy," Shoemaker mumbled through clenched teeth as he eased his fighter to the left, aligning his nose with the radar return of the Tomcat dead ahead of him. He flipped the radar mode from search to fire control.

The pilot of the Tomcat must have either seen him or caught him on radar, or his electronic-countermeasures unit caught Shoemaker's radar shifting modes, for the Tomcat pulled away, running, flames of afterburner shooting from its exhaust. The heavy Navy fighter pulled up, climbing rapidly. No way the prototype could catch a heavy. Big fighters such as the F-14, F-18, F15, F-16, and F22 were called heavies because of their weight, size, and performance characteristics. The Tomcat climbed, quickly going nearly vertical in its haste to escape the telltale radar reflection. Of course, the light weight and flight endurance of the prototype meant they could stay airborne nearly twice as long as a heavy. He watched the F-14 disappear into a small cloudbank as it passed the ten-to-twelve-thousand-foot altitude. Nothing makes a pilot more nervous than to know he or she is on a foe's radar screen. He pulled up in pursuit. He knew he couldn't catch the F-14 if the heavy decided to separate, but he had to try. As long as he had him on radar, then he had a fighting chance. If the Tomcat broke off, Shoemaker could always argue that he accomplished the mission because he had cleared the skies of enemy fighters.

Shoemaker glanced down. The radar painted the Tomcat a couple of more sweeps, then the video return was gone. Shoemaker leaned forward, twisting his head in all directions, searching for the aircraft. Above him, he caught a reflection of sunlight off the fuselage of the Tomcat. A dark contrail from the Tomcat afterburner broke the summer blue of the sky in front of him, revealing the direction the opposing fighter was flying. Shoemaker pulled back on the stick, switched his radar to standby, and smiled when the Tomcat shut down its afterburner and leveled off. The Tomcat must be running low on fuel by now, he thought. Dogfights sucked up fuel. Shoemaker made a visual approach toward the right rear side of the F-14. The pilot would have to have good eyesight and a lot of luck to see him. Spotting aircraft with the naked eye was tricky when you were engaged in aerial combat maneuvering. He focused on the target, ignoring his console, and hoping he could fly this thing by feel for just a little longer.

Without warning, the Tomcat rolled right. Shoemaker licked his upper lip. *Oh, you've done it now, my fine fellow of an aviator.* The F-14 engines were pointed toward the nose of his aircraft. Shoemaker reached down and flipped on the fire-control radar, which was connected to the camera. He took several digital photographs as the Oceana aircraft headed back down, rocking and rolling side to side, trying to break fire-control lock-on. Shoemaker glanced at the altimeter: 32,000 feet. Nearly the maximum altitude for this small boy he was flying.

"Avatar Leader, Avatar Three; mission complete. Request permission to return to Mother."

"Avatar Three, what is your fuel?"

Shoemaker leveled off. He had his photographs.

"Fuel one-two. Got enough for another couple of hours, Boss. Why? You got another mission for this hotshot FEMOP?" Pauline asked, using the term for "female operator."

Shoemaker thought for a moment. "Sure, why not on the way back out to the *Boxer,* you and Jurgen," he said, "make a run along the beach and take some combat footage of the Marines. It'd be nice to show the versatility of the prototype program."

"My pleasure, sir," Pauline replied in a singsong cadence.

He pulled back on the throttle, allowing the decreasing speed to send the prototype fighter into a steeper descent.

"You are enjoying this too much, Pauline."

"If I was enjoying this much more, it would be obscene."

"Things that make you go ummmmm," muttered Valverde.

A warning light flashed on the engine gauge. Shoemaker reached forward and tapped the display. No change.

"Professor, I have an engine warning light," Shoemaker broadcast.

"I see it," Dr. Jesse Dunning replied. "Try pulling back on the throttle . . . *not so far back you shut off the engine!* That's it, ease it back."

The nose of the aircraft increased its downward angle. The stick began to vibrate, increasing in intensity as the rate of fall grew. Shoemaker gripped the stick with both hands, trying to bring the prototype fighter level. He fought the stick farther back. A violent shake knocked his hands off the stick. He reached forward and grabbed it. The aircraft slid into a right-handed spin. He pushed the left pedal down as far as it would go. The spin slowed, but there were no gauges to measure its rotational speed, only the visuals in front of him and to his sides.

"Lieutenant Shoemaker, you must stop that spin. If you don't—" Dr. Dunning said.

"You're going to splatter all over the North Caroline hills," Lieutenant Pauline Kitchner finished.

"Lieutenant Kitchner, please get your aircraft back to this floating *whatever* and stay off the circuit," Dunning ordered, his voice tense. "I have this now and I know what I am doing."

"No problem, Doc. I'll just open the cockpit and shout to my wingman."

"Don't piss off the Doc, Pauline," Shoemaker said silently to himself. *"Don't want to have to pack up and move again."*

Shoemaker eased the throttle forward, looking at the heads-up display across his front screen. The engine RPMs weren't increasing as he pushed the throttle forward. *What the hell!*

The digital altimeter showed him crossing fifteen thousand

feet. Those descending numbers were picking up speed. Scattered clouds ahead and below showed the ten-to-twelve-thousand-foot altitude. Below that altitude, pilots could breathe without an oxygen mask. That's bloody nice to know, he thought, pushing the stick left. Maybe if he increased the spin, hit the rudders, and pulled back on the stick, he could shoot the aircraft out of this one-way trip earthward. With luck, the effort should catapult the aircraft up, long enough for it to slow sufficiently so maybe he could switch to propeller power. He leaned back, wiggled once for comfort, and executed the plan. The aircraft increased in speed of descent for a few seconds. He pulled back on the stick. The prototype fighter shot out of the descent, heading up. The spin slowed, and then stopped. His vision steadied.

"Mother—"

"I'm coming, Nash!" shouted Alan.

"Alan, this is Dr. Dunning. What in the hell are you going to do once you get there? Bring your aircraft back to the ship and let Lieutenant Shoemaker and me save my fighter. You know how much they cost?"

"But—"

"Lieutenant Valverde, think about it. Think what you're flying. We all know nothing is going to happen to Lieutenant Shoemaker. Prototype fighters are the ultimate in pilot safety. I personally identified to Congress that factor. Unless he goes squirrelly and his mind convinces his body that—"

"Doc, I know that, but in a real fight—"

"Lieutenant Kitchner, stay off my circuit."

"Alan, do what the Doc says," said Shoemaker, "Let me try to work this out. Doc, I'm going to shut down the engines when I reach apex and try to switch to propeller power."

"You can try that, Lieutenant, but if you aren't careful, the wind speed will tear the propeller to bits before it can deploy."

"I should have about a minute to transform to propeller power before I begin to descend again."

A pair of F-14's appeared on both sides of him. One of the pilots shot him the bird while the other saluted. Wasn't hard to figure out what camps these two pilots supported.

As if reading his mind, the two heavy fighters hit their afterburners, turned their noses up, and crossed directly in

front before disappearing above him. Jet wash shook the
stricken aircraft.

"Hey, Doc. Anyone told those f'ing Tom Cruise wanna-
bes to stand off? That I have an in-flight emergency?" asked
Shoemaker through clenched teeth. *"Oh, shit!"*

The aircraft fell to the right, going into a right-handed spin,
heading back toward the earth. The spin increased in tempo.
Clouds blocked Shoemaker's vision for a couple of seconds
until he fell through them. Altimeter showed ten thousand feet.
The spin continued to increase. The cockpit screens blurred
into a kaleidoscope of browns, greens, whites, and blues as
North Carolina land, beach, ocean, and sky merged.

He reached up and shut off the engine, simultaneously pulling the throttle back to zero. No effect. The aircraft was nearly
vertical on its one-way trip. Sweat poured from his face, but
he was too busy with the controls, trying to right the aircraft.
His heart raced. He could hear the damn thing it was beating
so fast. Shouldn't be this way.

Airspeed gauge showed 350 knots and heading upward. He
flipped the engine back on. What were the stress factors on
the damn wings? *Shit, shit shit!* He had maybe two minutes to
get power or it would be his last flight in this aircraft.

"Your heart rate is increasing, Lieutenant Shoemaker," said
Dr. Dunning. "I would suggest—"

"Suggest, hell! I'm the one riding this thing down!"

"But you must understand—"

"Leave him alone, Doc. This is our first in-flight emergency. If anyone can pull it out, Nash can. Show him, Nash!
Be one with the plane," Pauline said, saying the last few words
like a mantra.

Shoemaker ignored the banter. He grabbed the throttle,
flipped the ignition switch, and scrunched his eyes. The blur
was causing him to lose concentration. He pushed the stick
and throttle forward. His head pressed against the headrest.
The stick didn't move. *Damn!* The outside air pressure and
spin had pinned the flaps. Even with hydraulics working with
him, the flaps refused to budge. He pulled the throttle back,
reducing power, hoping it would reduce the pressure just
enough for him to manipulate the flaps. He leaned over,
grabbed the stick with both hands, and pushed forward. Noth-

ing. He put his entire weight behind it, but nothing moved. Holding the stick, he took his right hand and unbuckled his seat belt. Then, putting all of his body weight against the stick, he felt it move forward. His eyes widened. *All right, baby, come on!* He leaned his chest against the stick and reached over, pushing the throttle forward. Power increased. The nose of the aircraft shifted slightly from a head-on rush toward the earth to a twenty-degree descent. Shoemaker was still heading toward a fast-approaching ground. *"It's not the fall that kills you,"* his flight instructor had told him when he first entered the Navy. *"It's that sudden stop when you hit the ground."*

He was vaguely aware of listening to the other aircraft entering the landing pattern of USS *Boxer. Christ!* He was formation leader. It just wasn't right that this was happening to him. However, he might pull this out by the seat of his pants. He would try it again.

Shoemaker pulled back on the stick, flipped the pressures on the pedals, trying to bubble the aircraft out of the tornado-like spin taking him to the ground.

"You've got power, Lieutenant Shoemaker," Dr. Dunning said.

Dunning was not happy. It was never his technology at fault. It was never his ideas. It was never his concepts. It was always the pilots, or the junior engineers, or the contractors, but never him or Naval Air Systems Command—better known as NAVAIRSYSCOM—or Naval Research Labs that was at fault.

"Spin is slowing," Shoemaker reported over the radio. He took a deep breath. He had not realized he had been holding it.

"I can see what's happening, Lieutenant," Dunning said with a hint of petulance. "I have the master control panel here with all the gauges, so you just bring my prototype home and don't lose her."

"What about me?" he asked sarcastically.

"What about you? It isn't as if we can't replace you."

Asshole. Shoemaker reversed the pedals again. Wrong move! The spin was back. It shoved the aircraft forward. Once again he was headed toward the ground. Five thousand feet! Warning lights and beepers broke the cockpit isolation.

"Lieutenant! What are you doing?" Professor Dunning shrilled, his voice high-pitched in anger.

Five thousand feet, too sharp a descent angle—he was losing what little control he had had. All he needed now was for one of those F-14 glory hounds to light him with their fire-control radar and set off the warning blare from the electronic-countermeasures suite.

Engine power died. Shoemaker watched helplessly as the RPMs rapidly dropped until only the speed of descent was being measured.

"Shoemaker! What in the hell did you do?"

Nash bit his lip. He flipped off the power, pulled the throttle back. Almost immediately, he flicked the power switch back on and shoved the throttle forward all the way, mentally making the sign of the cross across his chest and forehead. So, this is how a pilot felt when he knew death was rushing to meet him. His breath was short, rapid. He felt this urge to urinate.

Shoemaker pulled back on the stick. Surprised how easy it came back. The spin slowed. He had power again, but it was increasing too slowly. *It wasn't going to be enough!*

"Come on, baby, come on," he whispered.

He reached forward and slapped the gauge. Power hung at fifty percent. He pushed the throttle again, but it was already fully forward. The speed gauge showed three hundred knots. No way he could switch to propeller. The wind would tear the thing apart and the pieces would rip through the fuselage—the small cockpit on board it being one of the things torn apart.

"It don't look good!"

"DON'T YOU CRASH MY AIRCRAFT!"

"Damn, Doc! What the hell do you want me to do?"

Five hundred feet.

"Get her up! Get her up!"

"I have tried everything—"

The ground! Shoemaker instinctively covered his face with his hands. The screens went black. The sounds of the displays, gauges, and electronics controlling everything around him in his cocoon wound down.

He sat there, breathing rapidly, his hands crossed in his lap. The hydraulic noise of the top of the cockpit rising caused him to look up. Looking down at him was Dr. Dunning, his face a work of thunder, and the other three pilots.

"What in the hell were you doing, Shoemaker?"

Nash unstrapped and pushed himself up. His head was even with Dr. Dunning's. "How in the hell do I know, Doc? One moment she was flying fine. You saw the photographs. We splashed those Tomcats, and the next moment, power to the engine failed."

Shoemaker stepped over the side of the cockpit onto the hangar deck of the USS *Boxer*. He turned to the other three pilots. "Were you able to land your UFAVs?" he asked pronouncing the acronym for "Unmanned Fighter Aerial Vehicles" as a word.

"Piece of cake, Top Gun!" Pauline said.

Nash Shoemaker would have grinned if he weren't so angry with Dunning and the mishap. Pauline was almost dancing with joy over her victory. And that's what it was.

"This is really going to hurt the program," said Dunning.

Lieutenant Valverde reached forward and touched Nash Shoemaker on the shoulder. "You all right, shipmate?" he asked, concerned. His dark brown eyes looked Nash over as if searching for a wound.

Nash nodded. "Another lesson learned," he mumbled.

Shoemaker tossed his helmet onto the seat of the cockpit. "Doc, aircraft crash. It's a fact of life that things not meant to be in the air tend to return to the ground when the things keeping them up stop. You have a victory here."

"Yeah, Doc. When a non-flying object discovers itself at ten thousand feet and returns to Mother Earth by the most direct route, there tends to be a great reunion much to the detriment of the object," Pauline added. "Ensign!" she shouted at Jurgen Ichmens, who was walking over to the group, his helmet tucked under his left arm. "Write that quote down. You'll be able to use it someday at the Academy teaching new Navy officers about the laws of physics."

Dunning's eyes shifted back and forth. Shoemaker knew the man was weighing the pros and cons of the exercise. "Sure, Lieutenant Shoemaker. You are right. We have had a victory against manned fighters. But do you think they're going to latch on to that? You can bet your sweet cheeks that every pilot—especially the flag-officer ones—are going to point to your crash."

"You may be right, Doc."

Lieutenant Valverde reached into the nearby ice chest, pulled a water bottle out, and handed it to Nash. "You sure you all right? You don't look it."

"Doc, on the other hand, you can also point out that while the prototype crashed, it was less expensive than having a heavy crash, and you didn't lose a pilot in it."

Nash nodded at Alan. "Thanks." Then he looked at Dunning. "Doc, you sent four unmanned fighter aerial vehicles—UFAVs—piloted remotely by the four of us sitting in the hangar bay of an American warship fifteen miles off the coast. Those UFAVs engaged four of our top fighter aircraft flown by some top fighter jocks, and we won. In a live war, we would have shot them down."

"And don't forget, Doc," Pauline added. "On our way back we have photographs that show us strafing the Marines on the beach. Man, oh, man, Doc, you are going to be one very important person when you get back to Washington. When do you think you'll leave?"

Dunning glared at the taller female officer.

"Yeah, and you could be right about the crash," Valverde added. "Those fighter jocks are probably scrambling all over themselves to get to the telephones to call Washington to tell them about it. And here we are stuck out at sea without a way to tell our story."

Pauline reached over and tapped Dr. Dunning on his right shoulder. "This will be one time the Navy and Air Force join forces against a common enemy," she said, chuckling.

"What'd you mean?" Dunning asked.

"You don't think the aviation community is going to sit by and watch their piloted aircraft be replaced—*even a little*—by a bunch of amateurs who never leave a ship or a building and who can eat a sandwich while they engage in a dogfight?" Valverde added. "Man, oh, man, Doc. I am glad I'm not going to be at the Pentagon when the results of this reaches the inner ring, top floor, third door, second office."

"Doc, don't listen to Alan," Pauline said, pulling the scientist around by his shoulder to face her. "He's just trying to upset you. Here's what I'd do if I was you. I would get the hell off this ship ASAP. I would fly directly to Washington. I would show all the positive sides of what we've done today. Even point out the crash as an example of how this UFAV program will save lives."

"Pauline's right, Doc. Why, at one point I was pulling over ten Gs. Tell me what pilot can do that and not lose consciousness? I'll tell you. None," Shoemaker said, jumping on the bandwagon. "You've got a great success story to tell. Of course, we're all stuck out here and they'll have first chance at telling that story at second door . . ." His voice trailed off and he looked at Valverde.

". . . second office, inner ring, top floor, third door," Valverde finished.

Shoemaker leaned back against the cockpit. A wave of fatigue rushed over him. He had to go to the head before he peed his pants.

"You may be right," Dr. Dunning said, reaching up and stroking his chin before walking back to the master console. Shoemaker shook his head. To some, it would seem shameful the way they played his vanity. Pauline winked at Shoemaker, her blue eyes sparkling. He had never met a woman quite like this redhead. Beneath her cajoling, humorous, snide comments, and bravado was a temper that could rip your lips off and stuff them up your butt.

Pauline cocked her head at him. He must have been staring. She took a step forward, briefly wrapped her arms around Shoemaker's shoulders, and grinned. "I'm not even going to ask what you were thinking." She stepped back, blew on her fingers, and brushed them against her chest. "Most men have those thoughts every six seconds. With me around, I am sure the time is reduced."

He would have said something back, but he was just too tired. He grinned and hoped he didn't stumble when he started away from the cockpit.

"Yes, I agree," Alan said to Pauline. "But that reduced time is from fear."

"Someday *JAG* will make an episode about this," Kitchner said, chuckling.

"I've got to get my data together," Dunning said as he started to pull himself up the short ladder to the mother console. "You are right. The sooner I get the data read, consolidated, and analyzed, the sooner I can present my findings."

Pauline shook her head and shouted, "Going to be hard to do, Doc! Right now, I bet those fighter jocks at Oceana are already on the ground, running toward the ready room, knocking each other out of the way to be the first to call the Pentagon." She put her hands on her hips, leaned her head down, and shook it several more times. "No, I think wc may be dead on arrival on this one, Doc. You'll never get us off in time. We're stuck out here while they're with reporters from all the major news agencies. We're going to be fighting an uphill battle unless you get us off this floating bathtub and back to Washington."

Dunning stared at her for a moment, and then started nodding. "You're right. You're goddamn right! I have to get off here and get back there now. Right now! I can do the data reduction at Pax River Naval Air Station tonight and by tomorrow be at the Pentagon."

"Right, Doc! Now you're thinking. This is a good news story. Your face is going to be plastered all over the newspapers. So, how long do you think we have before we can fly off here?" Pauline asked, her smile disappearing as she waited for the answer.

Dunning's eyebrows scrunched into a V shape and he briefly bit his lower lip, causing his gray mustache to fall over and hide his mouth. He shook his head. "No, you four will have to stay here with the equipment," he mused. "The remaining five UFAVs have to be crated and the cockpits packed. Not to mention you'll have to oversee dismantling of the antennas and data-link-control packages between here, the ship's radio shack, and the masts. No, no, no. Can't have all of us flying off today," he said, his voice picking up in tempo. "I will go first. You're right. I'm the one that must argue our case before the Department of Defense. I know the plan was for us to stay on board until the ships returned to Little Creek Naval Base in Norfolk, but we must be proactive. Lieutenant Kitchner, for once you have made an accurate assessment of what we must do. You four will ride the ship back, see to the transportation of everything, and by then I will be in Washington and have successfully presented our case." Without waiting for a reply, Dunning pushed his way between Kitchner and Valverde and hurried toward the master console.

"Well done, shipmate," Shoemaker said.

Pauline sighed. "Look at the good side of it, our brown-hair, blue-eyed, super-jock. We've at least gotten rid of Dunning."

"Does this mean we won't be flying any more missions?" Ensign Jurgen Ichmens asked.

"Ensign, write this down," Pauline said. "It is always better to be asking questions than answering them. Now quit asking questions. Alan, we better get the boss into the rack before he falls down."

"Sounds good," Nash said. "A quick stop by the head on the way to the stateroom."

He looked at Valverde. "Inner ring, top floor, third door, second office? What was that?"

Alan Valverde shrugged his shoulders. "Don't know. But it sounded good."

Pauline slapped him on his back. "That it did, my fine spook friend," she said.

"What was it like?" Alan asked as they started toward the hatch leading off the hangar deck.

Kitchner and Ichmens moved closer to hear the answer.

Shoemaker stopped, shut his eyes, and took a deep breath before opening them. "I had to fight to convince myself I was back here in the hangar deck inside a mock-up of a fighter aircraft cockpit and not actually inside the aircraft." No one said anything. "I . . ." He stopped, his throat constricting slightly. He shook his head and continued toward officers' country. He didn't want them to see the moisture in his eyes. He couldn't explain it, but it wasn't something he wanted to do again.

DICK BLEW OUT A SMOKE RING. "I THINK WHAT JEFFERSON expected, according to what I have read and heard, is for some African-Americans to come to Liberia, buy holiday homes, develop the country, and maybe—just maybe—a few would take it seriously enough to exercise their Liberian citizenship. Even in the passports sold to African-Americans, there were limiting clauses that took away their right to vote or hold office in Liberia unless they actually lived as full-fledged residents of the country."

Leo nodded. "Yeah, I can agree with you. I thought about getting one of those passports. Probably would have if there hadn't been a problem with security clearance. But ergo, lots of money. Great public relations coup. And no disruption of the normal progression of Liberian politics."

Dick chuckled. "He just never expected to run into someone like retired Army Ranger Lieutenant General Daniel Thomaston. One of the runner-ups for *Time*'s Man of the Year last year."

Leo grinned. "Not many have ever run into someone like Thomaston. He sold everything he owned in America two years ago and moved lock, stock, and barrel to Liberia."

"I read where his wife dying had a lot to do with that."

"May be one of the reasons he decided to lead nearly a thousand families to Liberia."

"One thousand families that may be dead or dying. We won't know until we hear from them. Most of those families followed him into the wilds of central Liberia to build their own city."

"No, I believe a few hundred families is nearer the true number of those that came with him to Liberia, and of those, only about a hundred followed him to establish Kingsville."

The third wave of amphibious landing craft reached the beach. Like angry ants scurrying out of a disturbed nest, Marines fled the cramped confines, spreading across the white sands, crawling across the top of the dunes where the second wave held the ground. Dick and Leo watched as the newest wave of Marines reached the defensive line of the second, passed them, and continued inland.

Dick pointed at the message. "Take it with you, Leo, and find Colonel Battersby and make sure he knows about the impending OPORDER."

Leo saluted and left the bridge wing. Dick lifted the binoculars to continue monitoring the exercise on the beach. Most commanders of an amphibious task force would be inside the ship, down in its bowels, hunkered over a holograph display of the action. He preferred to see the real thing. There were enough smart operational types on his staff to handle the complexities of an amphibious operation without him—an old aviator—leaning over their shoulders giving advice and disrupting a smooth exercise with a lot of flag-level testosterone.

The three landing craft at the far end of the beach pulled away. They would be bringing those Marines identified by the referees as dead, dying, or too wounded to keep fighting. Those inside the three landing craft would also be the angriest of the bunch. Marines could really get pissed off when they discovered they were dead, dying, or wounded. Even in real life.

"LADIES AND GENTLEMEN, THE ADMIRAL," CAPTAIN UP-mann said, holding the door to the Operations briefing room open.

Everyone stood as Rear Admiral Dick Holman entered. "Sit down, relax," he said as he walked to the head of the table and took his own seat.

Dick Holman stirred his coffee slowly, thinking about the contents of the tasking message. "Don't stop because of me, Mary. Carry on with your briefing."

"Would the admiral like me to start over, sir?"

He shook his head. *Christ, no.* He hated briefings in the first place, and any briefing longer than thirty minutes was a waste of time as far as Dick Holman was concerned. "That won't be necessary, Mary. Just pick up where my entry interrupted."

She nodded. "Yes, sir, Admiral. I was providing a brief history of Liberia."

"Brief!" exclaimed Commander Churchill Walden, causing most of the officers in the small operations briefing room to laugh. "More like an epic, Admiral."

Mary ignored the supply officer and continued. "The first colonization of Liberia by freed American slaves and freemen was supported by the U.S. government at the time along with various antislavery groups. . . ."

Dick looked at the screen mounted against the far bulkhead. The intelligence officer, Captain Mary Davidson, stood to one side. A red dot danced across the words on the screen as she moved her laser pointer across the bullets on the briefing slide. Khaki uniforms did little for women, thought Dick, but maybe it was just the way the Navy work uniform looked on Mary. The tight khaki pants did little to complement the huge hips, though they did highlight the narrow waist of the Assistant Chief of Staff for Intelligence. It wasn't her body that got Mary where she was today. No argument about that. She was one of his intellectual warriors. A graduate of a small private college—Villa Julie near Baltimore—the Navy officer had gone on to obtain a master's degree in computer science from Johns Hopkins. Her choice of a Navy career was something that sometimes even amazed herself, considering that by now she could have been a CEO of some major corporation if she had chosen a civilian career. As far as he was concerned, she was easily a contender for admiral. A rank still a couple of years off before she would be eligible. She had only put the eagles of a captain on her lapel six months ago, and was still going through that transition period of learning to call her fellow captains by their first names.

How does she do it? he wondered. Some were natural briefers, and she was one of them. No *uhs,* pauses, or rambling for explanations. He had seen her throw together a flag-level briefing in minutes without any preparation. On the negative side, she was known for inflicting death by Power Point on those in her audience. Nothing was too down in the weeds for Mary Davidson.

If he still believed she was a contender for admiral in her small community, then next year would be the real challenge. In the ever-shrinking Navy intelligence community, her next set of orders would determine the strength of that opportunity. She needed a joint billet. A billet such as on the Joint Staff or at one of the warfighting CINCs like Commander in Chief Pacific or Commander in Chief Central Command to improve her chances for admiral. Even Commander in Chief European Command could be a stepping-stone, though he couldn't recall any intelligence officer who had made flag after serving a tour as a director at EUCOM. How much weight, he wondered, could he carry in getting her one of those jobs? Or would her community decide she had reached her pinnacle and send her to a dead-end job like that parochial Federal Information Systems Agency? Now, there was a money sump if he had ever seen one. Could save the nation and the Department of Defense millions by dissolving it . . .

He stopped his train of thought. FISA was his pet Washington peeve, and it never failed to get his blood boiling every time he thought of it. Dick turned his attention to Mary, although he had reviewed the slides before the brief and knew the material she was passing on to his staff. He caught Colonel Battersby looking at him. The Marine Corps Commander of the Amphibious Landing Force—CALF—nodded. Dick returned the silent salute and moved his attention to Captain Davidson.

". . . from being a colony of the United States to a republic in 1820. You!" she shouted in a mocking voice, pointing her finger at the Assistant Chief of Staff for Supply. "Keep those eyes open!"

Commander Churchill Walden—*Ready Freddie to his friends*—grinned, winked at Mary Davidson, and grabbed his throat. "Doc! Doc! Where are you? I can't see. I've been wounded by a hostile Power Point attack." Churchill was Holman's mustang. Navy referred to them as Limited Duty Officers—LDOs. Behind their backs, LDO was said to stand for Loud, Dumb, and Obnoxious. Churchill was not dumb, seldom obnoxious, and always loud.

A former master chief disbursing officer, the tenacious sailor had been selected for warrant officer, and then within two years promoted past the junior rank of ensign directly to lieutenant junior grade. Ten years later, this old-timer at forty-eight was a full commander. A rank most officers obtained by the time they reached forty. Although it was early afternoon, already Walden's salt-weathered face was showing the gray tips of heavy face hair.

"I just wanted to be sure you were still awake," Davidson said. "I know it's afternoon and men your age need their sleep."

"Well, my fine intelligence captain, I'll have you know that I sneaked my geriatric nap just prior to lunch."

The banter broke just what Dick knew was becoming a monotonous briefing. He also knew they needed to act serious about this. In the past year and a half, Amphibious Group Two had had over six of these 911 calls to evacuate American citizens. Each time the crisis had been resolved before they were halfway there, or they'd arrived to discover the situation had calmed. This was probably another one, though it was the first in Africa since European Command took control of most of the Atlantic away from Joint Forces Command in Norfolk.

Holman had asked Mary to provide some background on this small African country that was integrally linked to the United States. A country that in the last five years had become America's African version of Israel.

"Thanks, Mary," Dick said, interrupting conversation that had started to break out around the table. "Guess I was wrong to ask for a short review of the history of Liberia. I think everyone here knows the background. Liberia has been around almost as long as America. Originally a republic; more or less abandoned by its mother country in the nineteenth century. Left to stumble along on its own merits through the twentieth century, only to rise like a phoenix to become a model of African democracy. Let's skip to the current events." Dick glanced at Walden. "That suit you, Churchill?" He looked across the table at the PhibGroup Two Surgeon. "Doc, think he'll survive?"

"Only, if we're unlucky," Captain Paul Montage replied mockingly.

Everyone laughed at the elderly fleet surgeon who had retired as a doctor and two years ago accepted a permanent appointment as a captain in the Medical Corps of the Navy.

"That's not what you said at our last meeting of AARP," Churchill replied.

"That's only because your snores drowned out the proposals of the others."

"What others?"

"Doc, Commander Walden," Mary interrupted. "There are only you two in the ship's American Association of Retired People's chapter, so if you would reconvene later, I'll try to finish up this briefing."

"Mary, go ahead," Dick added good-naturedly. "Churchill, stay awake and keep the comments down."

"Of course, Admiral," Commander Churchill Walton replied, nodding respectfully.

The intelligence officer moved the presentation forward several slides. The photograph of the middle-aged African wearing his familiar dark Western suit appeared. "I think we all recognize this gentleman," Mary said. "President Harold Jefferson of Liberia." She paused. "Or he *was* President Harold Jefferson." She reached down, picked a Navy message off the table, and held it up. "Approximately twelve hours ago, African rebels, led by Islamic extremists, attacked and overran the Presidential Palace in Monrovia, killing President Jefferson. Since the terrorist action, additional rebels have been arriving, spreading through the capital arresting members of the Liberian Congress. They overran the American Embassy about four hours ago, but not before the Chief of Station released a situation report telling the State Department that Americans rounded up were being executed."

The humor of several seconds ago vanished as the severity of the crisis unfolded. They listed silently as Mary Davidson reported some of the atrocities that were occurring. This did not sound like the other crises that Amphibious Group Two had been called on to respond to. Nothing could ever equal the horror of September 11, 2001, but as the War on Terrorism continued, more and more barbaric acts surfaced as radical Islamic elements sought to destroy the modern Western world.

She laid the Navy message on the table, pointed the controls at the projector, and advanced the presentation to the next slide. A series of bullets appeared. Captain Mary Davidson glanced at the text and faced the group of officers seated at the table.

For the next ten minutes, she reviewed the flow of information that had arrived off the global information grid to the intelligence spaces of USS *Boxer*, LHD-4. The number of Americans killed could only be estimated. Most of the information being received came from the few ham operators that were still up and transmitting on their radios. Even those were going out one at a time, and none had been heard for the past four hours.

"Admiral," Mary said, holding another message in her hand. "This arrived just before the briefing started, sir, and I haven't had a chance to discuss it with . . ."

Dick put his coffee cup down. "Go ahead, Mary."

"A ham operator with Lieutenant General Daniel Thomaston told the American Embassy in Monrovia before the embassy was overrun that the Liberian-American city of Kingsville was still safe and had not seen any action. American refugees from elsewhere in Liberia have started arriving in Kingsville. It seems to be the central congregating point for American refugees. Another thing the embassy passed on was that they had lost contact with the American expatriate enclaves in the northern suburbs of Monrovia. They expect the worst for those in and around the capital."

"That's something," Leo added. "As long as we have contact with General Thomaston, we can keep track of how they are doing."

"It's not too good. The signal has not been regained from Kingsville. We suspect this is due to sunspots. We should regain contact as we close the coast. In the meantime, the good news is that Kingsville is safe and the surviving Americans are heading there. The bad news is Thomaston expects the rebels to advance on Kingsville. We will be unable to follow those events closely because our communications are suffering severely. Our weather-guessers report the sunspot storms, not expected to reach maximum intensity until later this month, have instead already commenced."

"Satellites?" Holman asked.

Davidson shook her head. "Sorry, Admiral, they are all committed to the war in Indonesia. In addition, I haven't seen any press stories to indicate the news agencies have anyone in Liberia in position to report events. This is one time in this information age we may be going into a crisis with little or no knowledge."

CHAPTER 3

LIEUTENANT GENERAL DANIEL THOMASTON, U.S. ARMY RE-
tired, stood with his legs spread on the wraparound porch of
the town's community center, his hands grasped behind his
back. He looked over the American town that he had helped
build. It wasn't big, but it was their little piece of home on
the continent where his and the others' ancestors had originated. Daniel walked to the edge of the porch and braced a
foot on the banister. From there, he could see the entire town.
The jungle to the south marked the end of this slice of civilization. He glanced behind him. The screened door gave him
a direct view through the center of the community center out
the rear door. About a hundred yards of grassy terrain separated this building from the edge of the ancient Liberian rain
forest that rose like a gigantic dark wall. He crossed his arms
across the top of his raised knee. Everything they had worked
for and built could be swept away by the rebels heading this
way.

He brushed an insect off his right arm. He personally had
selected the site for this town. It was a good location. One
where sweeping waves of towering bushes and grasses ran up
against jungle and rain forest bordering to the south and west.
The main road, running through the center of the town, was

paved. Unfortunately, a half mile out it turned to dirt. They had bulldozed the road, scraping away lush topsoil to expose sandy loam beneath that turned into sinking, sucking mud during their first rainy season. Since then, gravel and drainage plans had improved the utility of the road, but when the early summer rains arrived, the small American enclave became an isolated outpost.

Unfortunately, the rainy season had been over for nearly two months. They had the afternoon rains, but that didn't count on a continent where daily temperatures most times exceeded one hundred degrees. Thomaston knew from experience with the African rains that one moment you were soaked with sweat, then the rain hit, flushing the body salt away, soaking you to the skin. Five minutes after it stopped, you would be as dry as if you had put on fresh clothes. Five minutes later, sweat-soaked again. He picked up the plastic bottle of spring water from the nearby coffee table and took a deep drink. The heat could kill you. Fooled by high humidity, several had died of heat exhaustion in the first two weeks after they arrived to carve this town from the wilderness.

The main street ended at the southern end of the town. The paved portion ran north, curving around a couple of shallow depressions, cutting through the center of the four-year-old town, turning to dirt and gravel before disappearing over the bush-ridden hills to the north. Thomaston took a deep breath. Was this four-year attempt to build a Liberia-American showpiece in this African country going to fail? Was it going to become another example of African failure? Could be. The Liberians who frequented Kingsville and those who worked for the American expatriates were gone. They had disappeared sometime during the night and failed to return this morning. He took a sip from his second cup of coffee. His one vice to start the mornings.

This town was a showpiece. A showpiece to entice other African-Americans to purchase vacation homes in the country. Several had. Thomaston looked at the houses bordering the lake near the southern end. Most of those houses were vacant, their owners back in the States, and they would stay vacant until around spring, when their owners would return to spend several weeks in Liberia.

"Look, General," Sergeant Major Craig Gentle said, pointing north.

Thomaston raised his hands to shield his eyes from the bright sunlight of noon. A cloud of red dust rose into the air. Something was coming toward Kingsville. A few seconds later, a large white pickup truck crested the hill.

"It's the patrol returning," he said.

"Moving kind of fast."

"Let's go see."

Retired Sergeant Major Craig Gentle followed the retired lieutenant general down the wood steps toward the main street of their small town. The pickup truck beat them to the front of the general store by a few minutes.

Wailing and screams of anguish drowned out the noise of the truck engine. A group formed around the pickup. The doors to the cab opened. The engine ground to a stop. Four militiamen poured out, leaving the doors open, and trying to force the people away from the bed of the truck.

As Thomaston and Gentle approached, one of the militiamen pointed to them. The group pulled back, opening a gap for the two men. Thomaston looked at the partially covered bodies in the back. The entwined legs and arms told him the patrol had fled in haste from whoever had attacked them. He recognized bullet damage when he saw it. The wailing changed into sobs. Behind him, he felt the anxiety of the civilians—he could never feel they were anything else but civilians. Somehow, a career in the military divided humanity into various compartments of good and evil; right or left; and, eventually, civilians and military. Military retirement didn't bring the title of civilian with it.

He knew what they wanted. What they wanted was for him to tell them it was going to be all right. These deaths shattered what hope they held that what had happened in Monrovia wouldn't happen here. He glanced at Gentle, and watched the soldier who had been his right arm for the last ten years of his active duty visibly straighten. Words were unnecessary between them. Going into combat together and working side by side for those years had sealed a bond between the two men that no civilian could ever understand. He reached in and pulled the rest of the canvas cover off the bodies.

The last word received from the American Embassy in Monrovia was that it was being overrun and they were evacuating. The last radio contact with other American expatriates in Monrovia had been around midnight. President Jefferson had been killed, and rebels—*no, terrorists, let's call them what they are*—were killing anyone who was American or had helped the Americans.

A slight breeze stirred the hot, humid air, bringing a moment of relative coolness to the open area. Electricity from the Liberian Electric Company had ceased earlier in the morning. Thomaston had ordered the generator be run only for the radio shack where Beaucoup Charlie had his ham radio. Beaucoup was trying to reestablish contact with the American Embassy in the Ivory Coast. The rotund former Navy cryptologic technician also had a Bearcat scanner to monitor Liberian military and police communications. The intelligence Beaucoup brought was small, but it was better than nothing.

The four militiamen stared. Thomaston took a deep breath and consciously stood straighter. He had to give these people hope, of which he had little, and confidence, of which he had plenty. The fear of what happened in Monrovia and the knowledge that the rebels were moving toward Kingsville brought back memories of the days immediately after September 11, 2001. Memories of the feeling of being unsafe. Where knives and guns were placed near the bed to fight an enemy whose sole purpose was to kill Americans.

The security of a Liberia built on democratic ideals and a growing economy had died in less than twenty-four hours.

Thomaston shifted the Navy Colt .45 on his hip slightly to take it off his hipbone so it wouldn't rub. Exposed sores became infected quickly in the moist African environment.

The fact that they had brought their fellow townsmen back gave him satisfaction about their ability to overcome fear and do what they had to do. In the days to come, these young men and women would discover something he had known his entire life. He truly believed that deep within every American was a heroic spirit that, when faced with adversity, rose to the occasion.

"What happened?" he asked the young man standing in front of the other three. He hadn't been the one in charge. Thomaston glanced at the bodies. His eyes roved over the four dead faces. The last face was that of the man he had put in charge of the patrol, Dan Arts.

He had forty trained militiamen—well, thirty-six now. Members of the Kingsville vigilantes, as the Liberians referred to militia. These young men and women—most in their twenties—working only with the training he and Gentle had provided, now found themselves fighting for survival against a fanatical enemy—a deviate, evil Islamic cult. This ten-year War on Terrorism was more than a war on Islamic extremism. It was a clash of cultures that one day would force the Western world to crush the ancient, tyrannical beliefs of millions of Muslims. He was the only one who believed this, and he recalled the chewing-out he got from the Army Chief of Staff when he voiced it to a journalist.

"They killed them," a female voice cried, her voice muffled by the chest of her husband. He glanced. John and Mary Johnson from Ogden, Utah. Another African-American family who'd wanted to return to their roots and seen Africa as their Israel. Two weeks ago, they had decided to return to Utah, taking their teenage son with them. He looked at the bodies in the bed of the truck. Now, it was too late. There he was: John, Junior. Eighteen, good-looking, and Thomaston recalled an incident a month ago when two young American girls had to be pulled apart because of him. There would be no more fights over this young man.

Behind the crying Mary, another woman had collapsed, and other ladies of the church, with the help of the nearby men, lifted her, carrying her toward the community center. Near the front of the truck stood Harold Pearson, his broad shoulders shaking, tears streaming down an expressionless face. Pearson was a huge man who towered several inches above Thomaston's six feet two. Thomaston had seen Mahmoud Pearson in the back of the pickup. Harold would recover. He and Harold had joked about being two of the more eligible widowers in the town. Now, Harold was more like him. Thomaston had no children, and Harold had just lost the only child he had. The man would bear watching in the days to come. When the reason for leaving died, either men killed themselves physically or mentally, or they became avenging angels of death, destroying everything and anyone who'd brought them to that point. In the days to come, avenging angels would be what Thomaston needed.

Retired Lieutenant General Daniel Thomaston pulled the tarp back over the faces of the dead men. He stared a few seconds at the bumps under the waterproofed green tarp.

"Tell me what happened," he said, lifting his beret and using the back of his arm to wipe the sweat from his broad forehead.

"We left Dan and them about twenty kilometers up the road, General. He told us to take our truck, drive back toward Kingsville, and patrol the roads for any more refugees or rebels sneaking along the sides of it. When we turned around and headed back, about ten kilometers later we saw smoke. When we got closer, we heard gunfire. I hit the gas and we drove like mad to get there. The gunfire stopped before we reached them. When we turned the corner, they saw us. There were a bunch of Africans running from the bush toward Dan and them. Bill and Jesse turned their M-16's on them from the top of our cab, and the Africans took off into the bush. Dan's truck was on fire. We found the bodies near it."

Thomaston nodded. He licked his lips. What would be the rebels' next move? They had been broadcasting incessantly all morning from a captured radio station in Monrovia about their victory—urging loyal Liberian citizens and Moslems to rise up and slay the infidel Americans violating their land. He had little hope it was rhetoric. Since September 11, 2001, no one doubted the violent desire of Islamic fanatics to kill Americans. Threats were no longer taken as rhetoric, even when an inclination to accept it as such was strong.

He would have enjoyed having Beaucoup turn off the radio. He wanted so much to turn around and tell everyone to forget the bodies in the pickup truck. Bandits did it. Go back to what you were doing and forget it. He wanted to return to the small genealogy-DNA business he ran for African-Americans searching for their roots.

But he couldn't. The circle of frightened faces surrounding him was waiting for him to say something. He sighed quietly, then hoped no one noticed. He knew the look. The scared faces of people who had followed him two years ago when he raised funds to set up this small bit of America in the African countryside in the center of Liberia. He glanced over the heads of the growing crowd for a moment.

Then, his eyes traveled the crowd, pausing infrequently on faces of men and women whom he recognized as former U.S. military—there was retired Master Chief David Seams, one of the few whites in the town. What Thomaston wouldn't give to be able to sit around this evening at the community center swapping stories with other veterans. But that was gone. He had learned on September 11th that you can never go back to what was normal after such an event. Normality itself is always changing, and while Americans unconsciously experience the small changes of normality, something like what happened in Monrovia and the approach of the rebels means never being able to go back. He bit lightly on his lower lip. All those thoughts passed through his mind in seconds.

"General?" the young man in front said, his eyes raising in a question mark.

"Yes," Thomaston replied, then realized the young militiaman had asked him what they were to do. "First, let's bury our comrades."

He turned to the older man—retired Sergeant Major Craig Gentle, a thin reed of a man with long arms out of proportion with his body. The craggy face had been a near-permanent fixture with Thomaston through much of his Army career. He had been happy when his Command Sergeant Major from the 82nd Airborne had elected to follow him to Liberia. Gentle was just another military careerist who finished his thirty years with no wife and no family. Gentle had two kids from his short marriage, but they had been raised half a continent away and he was just a stranger they called Dad.

Sergeant Major Craig Gentle saluted. Like General Thomaston, Gentle had dragged out jungle fatigues from the storage trunk when the news from Monrovia had reached the town. Others had followed suit, and speckled throughout the anxious crowd like a patchwork quilt, former members of the Army and Marines wore their old battle fatigues.

Thomaston wondered briefly what the average age was for these veterans. He was fifty-eight. Gentle had to be about the same age. These militiamen standing in front of him were in their early twenties. It had been a smart thing after arriving here with those ninety-six families to organize a militia to function as both a police and security force.

"General," Gentle interjected. "With your permission, I will muster the militia."

"Good idea, Sergeant Major, plus put out two more forward posts on the road at ten kilometers, with backup force at six kilometers—out of sight. In the event of contact, I want those forward posts to fall back to the six-kilometer mark. When you finish the quick muster, I want a ready-response unit in the armory ready to respond to wherever they may be needed." Thomaston paused. He lifted his Army beret, ran the back of his right arm across his forehead and up over the high brow created by a receding hairline. Gray hair accented the small gray mustache Thomaston had allowed himself since retiring from Army Special Forces. Not many three-star Rangers were on active duty, and after he retired there were no African-American three- or four-star Rangers in the Army. Only two two-stars that he recalled, and he regretted failing to keep up with their success.

Vigilante—there was a word that conjured up all kinds of ghosts among his fellow African-Americans who made up this community. In Africa, however, a vigilante was a government-approved law enforcer authorized to use deadly force to protect properties and lives. Even *he* carried a Liberian vigilante card in his wallet. A few had had problems with becoming vigilantes, but eventually he'd overcome their objections, and had personally helped each militiaman fill out the one-page paper required to register as a state-sanctioned vigilante.

A young woman ran toward the group of men. The M-16, strapped across her back, bounced as she moved. The slight cotton dress normally on the attractive twenty-year-old Tawela Johnson had been replaced by blue jeans and a long-sleeve blue cotton shirt that clung suggestively to small, firm breasts. It would be better for all concerned if the young lady would wear a bra.

"General!" she shouted as she approached, drawing the attention of the crowd.

Cries from behind startled him. A couple of women stood beside the pickup truck. It was Dan Arts's wife and mother,

Must have came from the other side. Others helped them away, hushing their pleas to take Dan's body. In this equatorial heat, the bodies had to be buried quickly. Reverend Hew could do it.

Tawela stopped in front of Thomaston and Gentle, her breathing deep. "Just a moment," she gasped. "Let me get my breath."

Thomaston turned to the men. "Go ahead and take care of burying them."

"General, Mr. Beaucoup has gotten some news from Monrovia," Tawela said quickly, still breathing heavy. "Sorry, General. I ran all the way over here from the radio shack. I was as surprised as—"

"What did you hear, Tawela?" Thomaston interrupted.

"Yes, sir. Nathan Hammonds is on the road headed this way with five vehicles full of Americans. He is taking the back roads, he said, and expects to be here late tomorrow if everything goes well and they avoid the rebels."

"How did he get through to us?" Thomaston asked. "We haven't been able to establish contact with anyone since last night. Beaucoup said those sunspots are playing havoc with communications." Nathan Hammonds was a friend. The man was a retired Army infantry officer, though for the moment, Thomaston couldn't recall which unit. His thick eyebrows bunched as he bit his lower lip in thought.

"Hammonds has a radio in his car, General. It wasn't loud and it was hard to hear, but Mr. Beaucoup Charlie talked with him for a few minutes before he faded away. Yes, sir, he sure did."

Thomaston nodded. "Okay, Tawela, you run back up there to Radio and you tell Mr. Beaucoup Charlie that I said to keep in contact with Hammonds. If you get Hammonds on the radio again, get a location so we can keep track of him."

She threw up her hand in an awkward salute, nearly sticking her thumb in her eye. Thomaston caught the raised eyebrows of retired Sergeant Major Gentle. If the situation hadn't been so dire, he would have laughed. Instead, he winked at Gentle as they watched the athletically challenged Tawela run off.

Though Gentle had been retired for five years, Thomaston

knew he still found civilians exasperating. "How in the hell do they manage to live to ripe old ages and still be so disorganized and dysfunctional?" Gentle always said. "How can anything survive with everyone trying to be in charge?"

He and Thomaston spent a lot of time over beer and pretzels discussing the genetic makeup of civilians and pondering the great mysteries of their survival. Conversations that became more jovial as they sat on the veranda of the community center, watching the sunset while opening their third—or maybe fourth—cold beer. He had to admit beer tastes better after a day in the steaming-hot humidity of the African countryside. Almost as good as those first beers after a ten-mile summer run around Fort Bragg.

"Command Sergeant Major," Thomaston said firmly. "I thought you were going to muster the troops?"

"Yes, sir. Should . . ."

Everyone looked to the sky. The faint sound of an aircraft broke through the noise of the crowd. "Jet," Thomaston said softly.

Heads turned right and left as people moved apart, searching for the source of the approaching aircraft.

Then, suddenly, there it was. The aircraft popped up over the top of the community center. In that split second, Thomaston recognized it as one of the four Liberian Air Force Cessna A-37 Dragonfly attack aircraft.

"RUN!" shouted Thomaston, waving his arms frantically. It could be friendly, but this was the first time the Liberian Air Force had ever flown over Kingsville—

The earsplitting sound of the six-barrel machine gun peppered the jet noise. Thomaston ran toward the concrete wall of the community's warehouse. He looked east and saw Gentle disappear into the armory. Harold Pearson stood at the front bumper of the pickup. The cannon burst went harmlessly over the top of the pickup truck. Rivulets of dirt ricocheted into the air marking where the shells hit. The sound of the aircraft engine increased as the unidentified pilot applied power, sending the aircraft into a turning climb.

Thomaston drew his pistol. Not much use against an aircraft, but you fought with what you had when the fight came to you. He glanced again toward the pickup truck. Harold

Pearson stood there, turning his body slowly, tracking the attacking aircraft as the Cessna made its turn.

Sergeant Major Gentle burst back through the gates of the armory. He carried one of the four Stinger antiair weapons, Thomaston had talked the Central Intelligence Agency Chief of Station at the embassy in Monrovia into storing them at Kingsville. The man thought they were locked in the armory.

Thomaston holstered his pistol and ran toward Gentle.

The sergeant major knelt in front of the armory, braced the canister between his legs, and whipped the cover off the front of the weapon.

"I've got it!" Thomaston shouted, falling to his knees behind Gentle. He opened the back, pulled the activation switch, and then slapped his former Command Sergeant Major on the back.

Gentle squinted his left eye as he aimed the weapon. The aircraft's 7.62MM machine gun opened up again as the small fighter jet finished its circuit. Dirt erupted from the ground in a single line as the pilot corrected his aim toward the pickup truck and Harold Pearson. The tall man raised his right hand and extended his middle finger. About a hundred feet behind the defiant Pearson knelt Thomaston and Gentle.

The blast from the Stinger shot out the back of the tube. The heat singed slightly the left side of Thomaston's face as the missile left the tube. The missile curled upward toward the approaching aircraft. It was going to be a hard shot. The Stinger was an old handheld antiair missile, designed for infrared detection. The jet engines pointed away. He held his breath as the white contrail of the missile looped and swirled, seeking a target. If the heat signature of the jet engines was masked sufficiently, the missile would be past the aircraft before it could lock on.

The Dragonfly stopped firing, flipped to the left, bringing the aircraft almost vertical to the ground. The missile passed along the bottom of the jet fighter. The A-37 shook from the near miss. The aircraft continued its turn. The wings whipped down suddenly, bringing the aircraft level. The sound of engine power increasing reached their ears. The light-attack and reconnaissance aircraft disappeared behind the community center and out over the rain forest. The pilot was leaving. An explosion from behind the community center announced the impact of the Stinger missile.

"Good work, Sergeant Major," Thomaston said, patting Gentle twice on the shoulder.

"Shit, it was," Gentle said angrily. "If it had been a good shot, it would have splashed that son of a bitch across kingdom come."

People emerged from where they had taken cover.

"The good news is no one got hurt," Thomaston said. "They have you to thank for that."

Sergeant Major Gentle stood. He tossed the useless antiaircraft-missile canister to the ground. "The bad news is, it can come back anytime it wants."

"That's true. But now that they know we're armed, they won't be as willing to come," Thomaston said. He also knew if he were on the other side, he would increase the number of aircraft, change the tactics slightly, and mount a combined infantry and air assault.

The option of heading toward the Ivory Coast was available. But when was the question. The Ivory Coast was a smaller African country east of Liberia. The French Foreign Legion provided the security for the Ivory Coast. If the people in Kingsville reached the border, they would be safe.

JAMAL REACHED UP AND WITH THE BACK OF HIS HAND wiped the dust from his eyes. Sunlight filtered through the canopy of the jungle casting rapidly changing shadows of deep brush and trees into shades of greens, black, and brown. Along with the coming dawn came a better view of what Jamal and the others called "the road." The leafy limbs of a bush splashed through the open window as the SUV passed it. Morning dew splattered the three in the backseat. The few feet of separation between the lead SUV, where Uncle Nathan rode, and Jamal's revealed two deep ruts leading farther into the jungle ahead of them. Jamal looked at the driver, who yawned and cupped his fist against his mouth. In the center of the front seat was a young man who Jamal didn't know. The man was sleeping, his head tilted back against the seat, lightly bouncing with the bumps, dead to the world in his exhaustion. Riding shotgun

was a man Jamal had met during one of the American pic-
nics—he couldn't remember his name, but it didn't manner.
His mom and dad always told him to call grown-ups Mister
and Missus. The older man blinked his eyes several times,
reached forward, opened a bottle of water, and splashed some
of it on his hand to wash around his eyes.

Behind Jamal, in the compartment area, were rows of plastic containers full of gasoline and water.

The engine sounds of the four SUVs and one pickup mixed
with the loud cacophony of waking Africa. They weren't going
fast. He leaned forward and saw the speedometer wasn't even
registering a speed. The car hit a hole, throwing everyone up
off their seats. If he hadn't been belted, his head would have
hit the ceiling. As it was, the edge of the rifle barrel clipped
his chin, bringing water to his eyes from the brief burst of
pain. He touched it, discovered no blood, and moved his jaw
back and forth. It was sore. Mom told him he bruised easily.

The wheels tore up the slight vegetation, sending gray dust
whirling around the vehicles to settle on the ones following.
Jamal rolled the window up another half inch, shut his eyes
again, and waited for sleep to come again. At least with his
eyes shut, nobody bothered him with cute questions grown-
ups enjoy asking kids his age. He didn't feel like a kid his age
anymore. And, he sure didn't want to feel forced into a series
of Yes'ems and No'ems with a bunch of grown-ups. He concentrated on slowing his breathing as his cousin taught him.
She told Jamal that you could go to sleep if you lay on your
back, relax your muscles until they feel like jelly, and slow
your breathing. He never figured out if it worked because he
always fell asleep. With his eyes shut, and morning wakeful-
ness fighting off further sleep, thoughts and travails of last
night whirled around his twelve-year-old mind. After several
minutes, Jamal decided having his eyes open was more com-
forting.

He turned in the seat to look behind them. Selma should
be in that Land Rover. The dust was thick across its windshield. Jamal could only make out the outline of the driver's
face. It wasn't only dust that made it hard to see. The jerking
of the vehicle made his head bounce, and the light haze of the
African rain forest morning wavered a few feet above the

ground, almost at eye level. Probably wouldn't have been able to see the driver if the man hadn't been leaning with his face nearly against the windshield. Jamal faced forward again, resting his hands on his knees.

The driver had the window down with an elbow propped through the window. He had turned off the air conditioner hours ago to save gasoline. They had two choices: roll down the windows and suffocate on the dust, or leave them up and suffocate from the heat. Jamal was hot and dirty. He held his hands up, amazed at the dirt caked on them. He'd never thought he would wish for a bath.

The SUV slowed, and then stopped to the sound of emergency brakes being set. Uncle Nathan got out and walked back along the convoy.

His uncle leaned down at the driver's window. "Richard," he said to the driver, patting him a couple of times on the arm as he looked around at the others inside the SUV. "Rest of you, just talked with the radioman at Kingsville. They know our situation and will try to keep in contact with us. It's going to be hard during the daylight according to Beaucoup Charlie. Sunspot activity and all that. We should be able to regain contact tonight. Meanwhile, we keep moving. Richard, how is your gas situation?"

"They going to come out and meet us when we get closer?" the man sitting on the other side of the nice lady asked. He was heavyset; a slight paunch hid his belt. The short-sleeve shirt revealed a dark tattoo on the deep black skin. "Don't he know how few we are and how we need some help?"

Uncle Nathan looked at the man, but didn't say anything.

"You're leading this bunch, aren't ya, Nate."

Uncle Nathan nodded. "Yeah, George, I guess I am leading this bunch. But this back road—*this trail, or whatever we are on*—none of us know. You know where it goes?"

"Nope, guess not," George replied, leaning back.

"George, if you haven't traveled it, you know none of the rest of us have." Uncle Nathan sighed. "We're all in the same boat. All I can do is keep following this trail we call a road and keep an eye on the compass. If we're lucky, this track will keep heading east and cross the main road. If it does, then we can jack up the speed to a blinding ten miles per hour and maybe get to Kingsville by tomorrow night."

"And what if we reach the main road and find rebels have it?" Richard asked as he reached up with a cloth and wiped the dust and sweat from his face.

The young man in the center woke up, stretched, and leaned forward to listen to the conversation.

"Then I think we'll have to go faster," Nathan answered, smiling. "Gas, Richard?"

The driver looked at the gauge. "Just under half a tank, Nate."

"Man, we ain't gonna make it," George said, his voice high.

"We're going to make it, George." Nathan patted the driver on the arm a couple of times and walked away, heading toward the third vehicle. The men in the pickup had laid their weapons in the bed of the truck and were stretching.

Jamal looked at the man Uncle Nathan called George. *What if they didn't make it? What if he never returned to Monrovia? How would he know for sure if Mom and Dad escaped?* Jamal leaned back against the seat, his head turned upward, feeling the heat working its way down from the roof. Though the movement of the vehicle had been slow, it had at least provided some circulation of the air and kept the heat manageable.

The lady reached over and put her arm around Jamal, startling him. He jerked away, opening his eyes. Staring at him, the woman said over her shoulder to the man called George, "You quit that type of talking, sir. Even if you're not scaring the young man here, you're scaring me."

Jamal saw the man open his mouth to speak, apparently think better of it, and close it. Instead, George shook his head as if the whole thing exasperated him.

Jamal looked at the attractive woman, admiring the thin lips, light complexion, and Roman nose. The caked dust did little to hide the natural beauty.

Richard spoke from the driver's seat. "You're right, Victoria. George, don't be an ass—"

The huge man's eyes narrowed. Victoria turned in her seat and touched the giant once on the arm. "We're still alive and we're moving toward General Thomaston and his group.

That's all any of us can do. There's no safety behind us and there may be no safety around us."

"Yeah, George," Richard added. "None of us even know when we reach Kingsville if we'll be safe. All we know is that there are fellow Americans ahead. Brothers and sisters who we can join and offer mutual protection. To do that, we've got to get there. We're all right."

Jamal leaned back again as the woman removed her arm from the top of the seat.

"We're all right?" George shouted. "You trying to tell me we're all right! If we're all right, then why in the hell did only five carloads of us make it out of town? I'll tell you why," the heavy man said, leaning forward, bringing his face close to the back of the driver's neck. "Let's be truthful," George went on, his voice low, powerful. "The fact is, it's going to be awful hard to make Kingsville. I think we know that by the time we near Thomaston and his band of merry men, the rebels will be between us and him."

Jamal turned his head and watched the man. He jumped when George jerked his thumb at him. "And you, boy, might as well get used to the fact that none of us may make it out of this hellhole." George's head twisted from person to person as he continued. "If we'd been smart, we'd've listened to Thomaston when he asked us to move to Kingsville and help them build his dream out of the jungle. But no, we hadda believe that bullshit about living in the capital. We had to listen to our State Department geniuses who told us how much influence we could have if we just lived in Monrovia." The man pulled his M 16 up from between his legs and pointed it out the window. "Don't worry. I'm just shifting the weight a little." The man paused for a moment.

"There may be others," the woman said.

"Woman, they're all dead but us. They are dead, dead, dead, and the only reason we ain't dead is those assholes were having so much fun killing the others that it gave the rest of us a chance to escape."

The woman reached over and touched George's arm. "That may be true. Is it Mr. George?" she asked.

"Just George. I don't use my last name."

"Well, George, that may be true, but sometimes we must

face our fears and put our concerns aside until we have time
to worry about them. If we make it, then it'll be because of
people like you who help us through this jungle."

George opened his mouth as if he was going to say something, but instead he looked down at her arm and stared at it
until she moved her hand. "And who in the hell are you?" he
asked. "I ain't seen you around before. And don't patronize
me, woman. Just because I say it like it is, doesn't mean I'm
gonna run off into this jungle and leave you, the brat, or anyone else to those fanatics. I may bitch, but don't confuse my
bitching with being afraid."

The man leaned back against the seat, his face turned toward the open window. Branches from a nearby bush trapped
against the side of the SUV freed themselves, swinging
through the window across George's face. Big George reached
up and pushed the broad leaves outside and away from the
vehicle. "This ain't gonna be a good day," George muttered,
just loud enough for those inside the SUV to hear. He spit out
the window a couple of times, clearing plant trash from his
lips.

Silent minutes passed before Nathan worked his way back
up the convoy, past their SUV.

"We have to keep going, Richard," Nathan said as he
walked by, leaning inside the window. "Just keep going. We'll
refuel later when we reach a more open area."

"Nathan, this is farther than we came three months ago."

Jamal's uncle straightened, his chest even with the open
driver's window. Jamal couldn't see Uncle Nathan's head
above the window, but he heard his reply. "I know. Back then,
Richard, we were just seeing where the road led."

"I think we both knew we would need a way out if something happened in Monrovia."

Nathan patted the arm again. "Yes, I think we did. We just
never said it. Now, we're committed to what is becoming more
of a foot trail than a road."

"It's an old logging road," George said sharply, his head
stuck partially out the window. "I've also heard it's an old
diamond mining road. It could be either, but I know that we've
been using it to identify woods with export value. Just never

used it to haul them out because it wasn't wide enough. Wish I had come farther down it."

"So do I," Uncle Nathan said. "So do I. Either way, we know we're heading in the right direction and those ahead of us know we're coming. It is the best we can do."

Jamal watched as Uncle Nathan faced the huge man. What if this man reached out and grabbed his uncle Nathan? Jamal looked at his gun. He wondered if he would be able to shoot—

A scream pierced the jungle noise, startling everyone. Even Uncle Nathan whirled with his M-16 pointed toward the jungle.

"Relax," Victoria said. "That's just the red colobus—a long-tailed monkey. Lots of animals out here, and that won't be the first we hear or see. This rain forest is also the home of the bongo antelope, and when we cross the Cestos River, which should be ahead of us, we may be lucky enough to see a pigmy hippopotamus."

"I can hardly wait," George said, shaking his head.

Uncle Nathan's face appeared in the back window. His eyebrows bunched. "Hi, you're new, aren't you?"

"Victoria Pearl," the woman replied, reaching forward to shake Nathan's hand.

"Pleased to meet you, Mrs. Pearl. Didn't realize we had a conservationist along with us."

"Probably explains why we've hit it off so well," George said roughly.

"Jamal, how you doing, my favorite nephew?" Uncle Nathan asked, diverting the conversation.

"I'm fine, Uncle Nathan."

Nathan smiled and winked at him. "Your sister Selma is doing great. She's in the Land Rover with Miss Jenny. You and everyone here are going to be okay."

"Right," mumbled George sarcastically.

Nathan's face disappeared. "Richard, we'll go another hour. Should reach the Cestos River by then, if the obstacles in front of us don't grow any worse. We'll stop out of sight of the river; take a short break. Top off the gas tanks and give everyone a chance to hit the bushes before the sun sets. Then we'll decide whether to ford it tonight or wait until morning. Either way, we're going to be in Kingsville in the next twenty-four hours."

"Sounds like a plan, but I think most of us would like to take a quick pee break now," Richard said. "Me, for one."

Uncle Nathan looked both ways. "No place to go, Richard. Let's move up until we find a place where people can step away from the vehicles."

Nathan inched his way toward the lead vehicle.

"We'll do fine," Victoria said. "We haven't seen a soul on this road. Most likely, those rebels don't even know we're here."

"What you smoking, woman? And they ain't rebels. They're fucking terrorists. And of course we ain't seen anything on this road. That's because you can't see anything on this road. What are those things sticking through the windows? They're bushes. Hello!" George slapped his palm against his forehead. "That's why we haven't seen anything, woman."

"You know, Mr. George, if you really try hard, you may turn out to be quite the conversationalist."

"I ain't no conservationist. I already told ya that."

"Take it easy, George," Richard said. "She said conversationalist," he drawled out.

The young man in the center turned in his seat. "I've seen you fight, Mr. George. It was in the—"

"Yeah, we've seen him fight," Richard interrupted. "But I don't think we've seen him do it sober."

"Man, I'm gonna rip your lips right off—"

"You two leave Mr. George alone," Victoria said. "He's as concerned for his safety as we are for ours."

George stared at Victoria for a few seconds, his face twisted in anger, before turning away to stare into the wall of vegetation that blocked his vision. Jamal shivered involuntarily. The man was scary. Jamal looked forward. Uncle Nathan slid into the backseat behind the driver of the lead SUV. The high screams of monkeys skittering overhead among the limbs and vines of the rain forest drowned out the idling engine sounds.

Jamal lifted his buttocks one at a time, freeing his sweat-soaked pants from the seat. He glanced behind, hoping to see Selma in the Land Rover. Mom told him he was responsible for his sister, and he wasn't going to lose her. He reminded himself to keep Selma near until they found Mom and Dad. He faced forward. The woman named Victoria was staring at him. Jamal forced himself to smile. There was tiredness around her eyes that failed to match her smile.

She reached forward and awkwardly shook Jamal's hand. "I'm Victoria Pearl. I work for the World Wildlife Fund," she said. Jamal realized she was speaking to everyone in the vehicle, not just him. "I've been here about two weeks, visiting friends in Monrovia. And what's your name?"

"Jamal," he replied softly as she released his hand. His voice sounded raspy, dry. He cleared it several times. The older man riding shotgun and who had yet to say a word reached over the back of the front seat and handed him a bottle of water.

"Here, boy."

Jamal drank deeply. The soothing feel of the warm water flowed down his throat. He hadn't realized how thirsty he was. With the water came the tinge of hunger. His last meal had been lunch yesterday.

"Friends ahead?" George asked, talking to himself. "I just hope he's right."

Jamal fell back against the seat as the SUV jerked forward. Without turning his head, he glanced at the woman called Victoria. She had turned her attention to George. Jamal looked out the window. Tumbled thoughts of Mom and Dad, mixed with what Uncle Nathan had said, sailed around his mind like a disjointed Ferris wheel.

"Mr. George, we'll make it," Victoria said softly, her voice shaking slightly. "Unfortunately, you're probably right about what happened to our friends in Monrovia and why we were able to escape. Those are things we know are true, but hate to—"

"Woman, of course I know I'm right. They are dead, dead, dead."

"Mr. George. Can we do each other a favor, okay?"

"A favor?"

"Yes, a favor. If you will call me Victoria instead of 'woman,' I will call you George instead of 'asshole,' " she said, her voice level with the same tone.

Jamal grinned for the first time since the attack on his house last night. The look on the man's face was spectacular. His eyebrows rose almost to the top of his head, causing his eyes to appear as large, round white eggs. Jamal bit his lower lip to keep from laughing.

"Well, I guess—" he mumbled.

"Good," she said with a sharp nod of the head. "George and Victoria it is. Now, wasn't that a nice way of resolving our differences? George and Victoria—sounds much better than 'asshole' and 'woman,' don't you think?"

"Sorry. It's just that we are . . ." stammered George, his eyebrows coming down.

She patted the big man's arm. "I know." This time he didn't act offended from her touch.

What did she know? Jamal asked himself. He wanted to know what she knew, then thought better of asking. Sometimes not knowing the answer was better.

Jamal had his window half down, suffering dust rather than the rising humidity and heat. Broad leaves slapped against the SUV as the vehicle bounced over the uneven narrow trail overhung by the bushes of the rain forest.

He caught a glimpse of something sleek and furry as it ran across a small opening to the left. It was gone before he could tell or ask anyone about it. Leaves closed on the travelers again. Somewhere ahead was the great man Daniel Thomaston. His father had told him how the Army general had led a bunch of families to Liberia. How the man had carved from the rain forest jungles of central Liberia an American town. A town where African-Americans could have their DNA profiled and matched against African tribes. Jamal wondered briefly from which tribe his family had originated. His mother told him his tribe was American. His mother never wondered like his father about the tribe or the place in Africa where their lineage originated. For his mother, it was enough to say he was an American. That settled it. No other reason to argue.

Were they even from this side of Africa? Like his father, Jamal wanted to know. He shut his eyes and soon drifted into a light sleep. Later, the sun dropped behind the SUV, casting a shade over him as the convoy continued its monotonous trek through the jungle and rain forest of central Liberia.

Victoria reached over and rolled the window farther down,

increasing the airflow across the oven of the SUV. A few minutes later, she shut her eyes and slipped into a half sleep, no longer billowing her blouse to cool herself. George looked over at his two riding companions, grunted a couple of times, and then continued his wary search of the surrounding land as they passed.

THE SHOTS BROUGHT JAMAL UPRIGHT, WIDE AWAKE AND alert. All along a ridge paralleling the road, gunfire erupted. Heads popped up and down as the attackers fired on the SUVs. He pulled his rifle from between his legs, the barrel hitting the roof, causing him to drop it. It fell against the front seat. The engine of the SUV revved up as the convoy attempted to speed away.

The sounds of a crash broke over the noise of small-arms fire. Ahead, Uncle Nathan's vehicle swerved to avoid several trees across the path. The SUV turned over, wheels still spinning as it came to rest on its right side. The doors popped open as Uncle Nathan and the others inside clambered out.

Jamal's SUV swerved left. The hard turn slammed Jamal into the side of the door, his head banging off the window as the front end tore into the bushes. The engine sputtered to a stop, its rear sticking halfway out of the bushes.

"Damn, this door!" George shouted, putting all of his weight against it and forcing it open enough against the bushes so he could get out. "Hurry up, y'all. Get out while I hold the door."

"Beaucoup Charlie! Come in! We've been ambushed about three miles east of the Centos River!" It was someone shouting into the radio in Uncle Nathan's SUV. Jamal heard Uncle Nathan shout something, and then others began firing at the attackers.

Jamal stopped at more shouts by his uncle. His head twisted from side to side as he tried to see Uncle Nathan through the smoke and dust obscuring the scene. The other voice kept repeating the call over and over to this Beaucoup Charlie. Then Victoria's hand touched his shoulder, beckoning him to come with her.

With the voice ringing in his ears, Jamal followed. She

knelt on all fours and crawled under the bush where the car was wedged. Behind them, the three men in the front seat forced their way out of the vehicle and fought their way through the bushes toward the sound of battle. George bent over and, hugging the side of the vehicle, crawled in a half crouch to the rear bumper. The huge man looked down at Victoria and Thomas.

"You two, don't stay there," George growled. "That ain't no hiding place. Even I see ya and I ain't even looking. Get yoreselves into the jungle. Get far enough so you can get away if you have to. Boy, you got the gun. Don't use it unless you have to. It's better they pass you by than know you're there." Then the big man disappeared around the SUV to join the gun battle.

"Come on," Victoria said, taking him by the arm.

"No, ma'am," he said, jerking away. "My sister. My sister Selma. Got to get her first. She's in the next car."

He pushed out of the bushes before the woman could grab him, falling against George for a moment as he ran around the edge of the car. He felt the brush of the big man's hand. He instinctively dropped his shoulder, causing the loose grip to fall away.

"Wait a minute!" Victoria shouted. "I'm coming with you."

"Boy! You stupid or something! Oh, wait a minute! Don't you be stupid too."

Jamal glanced over his shoulder. George had Victoria, his free hand wrapped around her thin waist, fighting her struggles. The M-16 in his other hand vibrated as George raked the top of the rise across the road, forcing the attackers to drop behind the hill.

"I'll be back," Jamal shouted.

"What in the hell are you two trying to do?" George shouted, shoving Victoria backward.

An explosion knocked Jamal off his feet. Screams rose from the last vehicle in the convoy. Flames roiled above it, darting through dark clouds. A smell like burning bacon assaulted his nostrils. He touched the side of the Land Rover and knelt. The British vehicle was nose-first in the bushes like theirs.

Jamal looked around. Several men were on the other side

shooting, but he didn't see Selma. He shoved himself up, holding the rifle tight in his left hand. As he rose, he caught a glimpse of color beneath the back wheels of the vehicle. It was Selma. She was on the ground, her head pressed into the grasses with her hands moving back and forth over her head.

He crawled toward her, shouting her name and receiving no response. When he reached beneath the Land Rover and touched her, she jumped and screamed, her eyes clamped shut.

"Selma, shut up. It's me."

"Jamal, Jamal," she cried, her eyes opening. She crawled frantically from beneath the Land Rover, throwing her arms around his neck and hugging him so tight she choked him.

Jamal dropped the rifle and pulled her arms from around his neck. She grabbed his free hand and gripped it tightly to her chest.

"Come on, Selma. We gotta get out of here," he said, squeezing her hand a couple of times. He stood, grabbed his rifle, and with him holding her hand tightly, they ran around the front of the Land Rover, dashed to the right, and worked their way around the bush toward where he last saw Victoria and George. What if they weren't there?

Another whooshing sound drowned out the gunfire, and the SUV Uncle Nathan was using for cover exploded into metal and glass. The concussion threw Jamal and Selma into the air. They landed in the bush, branches scratching and whipping them as they tumbled onto Victoria, knocking the breath out of her. Jamal moaned and sat up. His head moved back and forth a couple of times until he saw what he was looking for. He reached out and pulled the rifle to him. A couple of feet away inside the natural clearing within the huge bush, Victoria had pulled the unconscious Selma into her lap, whispering to the young girl as the woman ran her hands over Selma's arms and legs. "You okay, honey. I don't feel anything broken."

Selma's eyes opened. "I'm hurt!" And then she began to wail.

"Hush, Selma. You want them to hear us?" Jamal pleaded. His head hurt something fierce.

Victoria put her finger to Selma's mouth. "Shssss," she said.

"Selma, do what Miss Victoria tells you. You don't want those bad men out there to find us."

"Jamal," Victoria said quietly. "You two come on. George said move away from here. We need to move farther into the jungle. Far enough away that they won't find us."

He shook his head. "I can't leave Uncle Nathan."

"And you can't help him by getting yourself shot or killed. We'll come back when it's over," Victoria said. Taking Selma by the hand, the lady crawled to the far edge of the bush, and pushed herself through its branches.

Jamal watched for a few seconds. He wanted to go with them, but his uncle needed him. He pulled his rifle across his chest and looked toward the sound of gunfire. When he glanced back, Victoria and his sister were gone. The bush rattled where they had entered, the branches parted, and Miss Victoria looked at him.

"Come on, Jamal. We need you to protect us," Victoria said, motioning to him.

He looked one more time toward the fighting, and then crawled across the space toward her.

Behind them, shouts of *"Allah Alakbar!"* followed another explosion. The explosion blew open the part of the bush where Jamal only a moment ago had been sitting. He glanced back, and what looked like hundreds of rebels flowed over the ridge. His knees felt watery. He wanted to curl into a ball and cry, but he also wanted to run. Never in his life had he wanted to run and run and run like he did now. How do you run when the bones in your legs have evaporated? From somewhere, a scream followed by crying drew him away from his own fears. Selma, no longer able to contain her own fear, was fighting Victoria's grip. The young girl practically dragged the older woman with her as she fought to get away from the fighting, trying to escape into the rain forest jungles of Liberia.

Finally, Victoria scooped up the small girl and took off running. Jamal followed. They ran for a long time, crashing through thick bushes, long grasses. Briars the size of shark teeth scratched their bodies and ripped clothing. It was only when the woman tripped and fell, dropping Selma, that they stopped. He turned and looked back the way they'd come. Their path was easily visible through the tall jungle grass. The jungle was quiet around them. He realized there were no sounds of gunfire. He turned back and helped Victoria and Selma up, wondering how far they had run.

Victoria brushed herself off, squatted, and brushed the debris away from Selma's face. "You okay, honey?"

Selma nodded. His sister's eyes seemed focused past Victoria on something only she could see. They seemed to be looking off into the distance somewhere else. Jamal knew his sister. At home, she would be crying and complaining. Instead, she stood silently without wiggling as Victoria brushed her face.

"You're bleeding," she said to Jamal, reaching up and running her hand down the side of his cheek. A streak of dark red blood smeared the light skin of her palm.

"We've got to stop that," she said, looking around as if expecting to find something out here in the middle of the Liberian jungle.

Jamal ran his hand across his left cheek. Blood. He looked down and saw blood dripping from his chin onto his shirt. A dollar-sized stain grew as he watched. His mother would kill him if he ruined his shirt. Good clothes were hard to come by in Liberia. Looking down, he saw a tear on the knee of his blue jeans. His pants were now covered with dirt and grime.

Victoria took his hand and put it against the open wound on his cheek. "Hold your hand here. Press hard and that may stop the bleeding."

Selma never moved. She just stood there, her arms lifeless by her sides. Almost as if she felt Jamal's eyes on her, she turned slightly toward him, staring past him at something visible only to her. He glanced over his shoulder to see if he could see what she was staring at, but only saw the other side of the bush.

Victoria ripped a long strip of cloth from her dress. She withdrew her arms through the sleeves of the blouse, and with a few deft movements removed her bra, allowing it to drop to the ground.

"Now, we're going to bandage that," she said while putting her arms back through the sleeves of her blouse.

She picked up the bra and tore off the two shoulder straps. She pressed the cloth patch against his cheek and then tied the ends of the bra straps together. She wrapped the makeshift binding around his head and across his chin, tying the ends, to hold the bandage in place. He was glad he couldn't see what he looked like.

"There," she said, stepping back. "Don't look so good, but should do it for a while."

"Should we go back?" Jamal asked. He wiggled his chin, casting his eyes down to see if he could see the black strap. He couldn't.

She shook her head. "Let's wait until dark." She reached over and took Selma's hand.

Selma looked up and nodded. *Whatever she was looking at must have gone away,* thought Jamal.

"Come on, honey. Let's find a place. We need a short rest and best we hide while we do it."

Ten minutes later, the woman led them under another bush. "We'll stay here for a bit."

"I'm scared," Selma whimpered.

"We're all scared, honey."

Jamal faced the way they had come, aiming his rifle and praying no one followed. He wondered if they were going to go back to the convoy. The shooting must have stopped by now.

The woman squeezed Selma's hand. "You stay with your aunt Victoria. You're going to be all right. You hear me?"

Jamal thought he heard a slight tremble in her voice.

Selma had opened her mouth to answer when crashing sounds of someone running through the jungle turned her response to a whimper. Jamal's eyes widened. Selma was biting her lower lip. Her eyes squeezed shut so tight that it caused her face to scrunch into a mask of dirt and wrinkles. Jamal raised his gun. It felt so heavy. The bush blocked his vision. All he could do was listen to the noise of someone approaching.

The three of them pulled as quietly as possible toward the center of the bush. The noise increased as the runner approached, and then stopped for a moment. George broke through the underbrush headfirst, knocking the barrel of Jamal's rifle up.

"George!" Victoria shouted, leaning forward.

The huge man pulled his back half into the bushes and put his finger to his lips. "Shhhh," he said, pointing his gun back the way he had entered. A sudden crack of thunder rolled through the jungle. The afternoon torrent of tropical rain followed. Within seconds, they were soaked.

"GENERAL," SERGEANT MAJOR GENTLE SAID, REACHING down and shaking him slightly to wake him.

Daniel Thomaston opened his eyes, gripping the arms of the rocking chair. The sun was a bright orange as it touched the edge of the horizon. "How long have I been asleep?"

"Not long, sir."

He lifted his arm and looked at his watch. "Sergeant Major, you are a terrible liar. It's five o'clock—seventeen hundred hours for you old retired Army sergeants who have never quite grasped the civilian twelve-hour clocks."

Gentle's grin highlighted the slight scar on the right side of his cheek. Thomaston recalled how his friend had received that wound. Nearly fifteen years ago, when Thomaston led a brigade of the 82nd Airborne into Liberia in what was called the start of the African Wars. A natural outcrop of the War on Terrorism that led the United States from Afghanistan to Iraq, then Somalia, through Yemen, and across North Africa to defeat that madman Alqahiray. Only to discover afterward that the radical Islamic horde dedicated to world anarchy had found a natural breeding place in Africa—a place where nearly an entire generation had been wiped out by AIDS.

"General?"

"Sorry, Sergeant Major. Just thinking of our first trip to Liberia."

"Seems as if the more things change, the more they remain the same." Gentle reached up and touched the scar.

During that Liberian campaign, Thomaston and Gentle had led an ambush against a convoy of terrorists who were using the main highway north of Liberia. An ambush that had turned out to be a trap to encircle and kill American soldiers. They had fought their way out of the ambush against an overwhelming force of fighters who wanted to die. Most think that when a force is encircled, it goes to ground and fights hoping that rescue will arrive in time. That might be true in most instances, but the 82nd was not just any force. He recalled Sergeant Major Gentle displaying that same grin as they wallowed in a depression, bullets passing overhead, and the occasional hand grenade whirling through the rain at them, exploding sometimes only a few feet away.

The words still rang in his ears. "Ain't this great, General?" Gentle had said. "No matter which way we attack, we can kill us some terrorists. Now, which way would you prefer us to launch an offensive?"

Thomaston had led his beleaguered force south, through enemy lines stretched thin by their strategy of encirclement. Much like the Battle of Gettysburg, he recalled thinking, where the South had stretched their smaller force so thin that General Lee was unable to maintain any command and control over his troops.

Sometime during the next few hours, an irate grenade hurled by a fleeing terrorist, who had decided that that was not the time to give his life for Allah, had exploded. A piece of shrapnel had ripped along Gentle's cheek. The scar was still there: a reminder of their first visit to a country that would one day offer African-Americans ethnic citizenship.

Thomaston pushed himself up from the rocker. "Here." Gentle handed him a plastic bottle of water.

"What have we got, Sergeant Major?"

"Two patrols out along the road. One to the west and one to the east. We have a backup force two miles, each way, in the event the forward observers request help. So far, sir, everything's quiet. As you requested, I dispatched a couple of squads toward the Ivory Coast border to see how the situation is between here and there in the event we have to make a run for it. Told them to contact the embassy once they crossed the border."

Thomaston nodded. "What about Nathan Hammonds and his group? Don't want to leave here until he and his refugees from Monrovia arrive."

"One of the reasons I woke you, sir. Beaucoup Charlie got a broke-up radio call from Nathan about thirty minutes ago. He couldn't make out everything being said, but heard gunfire and what he thought were mortar rounds—could have been rocket-propelled grenades—over the radio." Gentle shook his head. "We haven't been able to reestablish contact, General."

Thomaston pulled his feet up under him and stood. "How far out are they, Sergeant Major?"

Gentle shook his head. "All I know, sir, is that they had expected to arrive near the Cestos River about this time. According to Nathan, he was going to decide whether to cross it or not once they arrived. I was thinking that maybe I could take a squad and see if we can connect with them."

General Thomaston shook his head. "Why doesn't that surprise me, Craig? I know you'd do it. I want you to do it, but we can't separate our forces. They're going to have to work their way to us."

"Sir, if we don't send someone, we could lose them all."

"And if we do, then more than just them will die."

"But General—"

Thomaston held up his hand. "Craig, you and I both know the rules of combat. They're either alive and managed to escape or they're dead. Sending someone out will only result in the loss of more lives, and the one person I—we can't afford to lose is you."

"Sir, there're others who can fill in until I return. Just as capable. I think you know that once I'm there, if I find there's no chance to rescue them, then I'll hightail it back here."

"I know you well enough that if this old sergeant major gets out there and finds survivors and he has to take on a superior force to rescue them, he'd do it. Even if it meant him dying in the fight."

Gentle turned and walked to the edge of the porch. Thomaston took two steps to stand beside him. "I don't like making this decision, Sergeant Major." He put his hand on the man's shoulder.

"I know, sir. I know it's the right decision for the greater good, but leaving someone to the enemy is not an ingrained Army tradition."

"We aren't in the Army anymore, Craig. We don't have the resources, the logistics, the communications to effect a rescue that would have been second nature when we were on active duty." He sighed and dropped his hand. "We've no choice. It's not a decision I make likely."

"I know, General. But it's a decision that I don't enjoy hearing." He turned and faced Thomaston. "General, different subject. We've a couple of families who've arrived while you were regaining your strength."

"Let's go check on them and the others." Thomaston started down the steps, his combat boots echoing off the hard wood. Gentle hurried after the officer, falling into step to the left of the taller man. "When do we expect the group heading toward the Ivory Coast to return?"

"You were awake when they left. They've been gone about eight hours, I'd say. I suspect we won't see them until tomorrow morning, earliest. They said they'd try to return tonight, but rather than wake you, I took the liberty of telling them to wait and travel during the daylight."

Thomaston nodded as they reached the walkway. Steps bothered him. You would think after thirty-six years of Army service, jumping out of perfectly good aircraft and fighting around the globe, his knees would be hardened to physical discomfort by now. The doctor said that was exactly the reason his knees were bad. Said to think of them like shock absorbers. In Thomaston's case, the warranty had expired.

"Good job," Thomaston replied. "What we need to do, Sergeant Major, is get the cars and trucks organized. I think we may have to make a break for the Ivory Coast."

"Done, sir."

"Then, I would like to outfit a couple of those pickup trucks. Put some weapons on the top of the cabs."

"Two have been outfitted with the only M-50 heavy machine guns we have."

Without stopping, Thomaston, his eyebrows arched upward, turned and glanced down at Gentle. "And we also need to make sure that everyone knows which vehicle they are assigned to, and also we need to identify a couple of vehicles for nothing other than fuel, food, and water."

"Yes, sir. We're already filling a couple of the bigger trucks—the ones we've been using to haul vegetables to the Pyne Town market—with the fuel, food, and water. A couple of younger militiamen are distributing lists telling everyone which vehicle they're to ride in."

"Sergeant Major, seems to me I could have continued on

with my nap," General Thomaston said, his head turning toward the sound of bells ringing. "Who's at the church?"

"Reverend Hew is having a memorial service for those killed today. I thought you might want to attend."

"Church is not somewhere I prefer to see myself," Thomaston replied.

"As always, the general has thought of everything ahead of time."

"Sergeant Major, if I didn't know better, I would swear you only hang around to see how far ahead of me you can stay. And with the United States? Have we reestablished contact with the Navy force headed our way?"

"No, sir. Beaucoup Charlie is still at his radio and we still have the generator churning and burning so he can keep broadcasting. Said he'd send Tawela if he hears anything."

"I would like to know what Washington plans. Whatever they are planning, they need to know our situation. Otherwise, we could be like lovers passing in the night."

"The mind boggles at the thought, General." The radio on Gentle's belt crackled. "Homeplate, Rover One calling. Do you copy?"

Gentle pulled the radio out, clicked the switch, and replied, "Rover One, this is Homeplate. Go ahead."

"Homeplate, Rover One is about twenty kilometers along Route One. We're taking gunfire and are pulling back."

Thomaston asked for the radio. "Rover One, Mother; what is your situation? What is the size of the enemy force?"

There was a pause on the radio. "Sir, we've one dead and two wounded. I counted more than ten vehicles; some of them huge open-back trucks filled with rebel troops."

"Are you sure they aren't more refugees fleeing west and thought you to be rebel fighters?"

"Sir! They opened fire first, and above the firing were the shouts of '*Allah Alakbar!*' They're rebels all right, and they're coming our way. The good news is we disabled the first two vehicles with small-arms fire. I don't think they'll be using them."

"Okay, fall back to where the backup elements are waiting."

"This is Backup One," a new voice said on the radio.

"We're already en route forward to help Rover One."

"We're heading toward you, Backup One."

"Backup One, this is Thomaston. How far away from your assigned position are you?"

"Sir, we are about four kilometers west and—"

"STOP! Wait right there for Rover One. Find a good position along the road—I seem to recall around the 233-kilometer marker the jungle forces the road to narrow."

"Yes, sir. We passed that marker a few minutes ago."

"Get back to it. Take a defensive position. Rover One, join them. If hostiles appear, let them know you are there. It should slow them down. If you can hold until after dark, then you should be able to slip away and make your way back to Kingsville."

Both elements roger'd out. Thomaston handed the radio back to Gentle. "What do you think, Sergeant Major?"

"I think we should be heading toward Ivory Coast."

"I think you should be right."

Thomaston marched up the steps of the church, Gentle alongside him. "Guess I've got no choice but to go to church," Thomaston said. "We might as well use this opportunity to let the rest of the town know what our options are."

Gentle looked back at the small American town. Several main buildings such as the town market, the general store, and even a small bank lined the street. "Hate to leave it."

"I know."

"They'll burn it."

"We'll rebuild it."

"They may burn it again."

"Then we'll have to rebuild it again."

The two men slapped hands. "Won't be the first time," Thomaston said.

"No, sir, but someday it'll be the last time."

"Let's just hope these civilians are up to the fight. Are you ready?" Thomaston asked softly.

"Yes, sir," Sergeant Major Craig Gentle, formerly of the 82nd Airborne, replied. He moved to the left of the former general and took one step back.

Thomaston nodded. "Let's do it." He opened the door to the church and the two entered. Voices stopped as they stepped inside. He saw the hope in their eyes as faces turned toward him. He alone knew the precariousness of their situation. Even Craig Gentle would not appreciate it because Sergeant Major Gentle never accepted anything that smacked of the possibility of defeat. Pessimism was not a word in the sergeant major's vocabulary. The two of them—the yin and the yang. And never more did he need that optimism than now. The only other thing he needed was a good intelligence picture, but the worst part of civilian life was never knowing something that everyone else already knew. Even CNN would be welcome right now. The benches of the church were packed.

One thing would either forge their resolve in the coming fight, or cause them to flee with fear into the jungles and rain forest that made up the southern border of this enclave. That was knowing only one option exists to save your life. Such knowledge really limits the bullshit arguments in trying to decide what to do. The report by Rover One was enough. They had two options at this point of time and knowing what they knew—flee to Ivory Coast, or stay, fight, and defeat the rebels. The first option was the best. He didn't know how many rebels were heading this way, but he knew they would know how many Americans were at Kingsville. His years of combat experience against Islamic radicals had taught him they only attacked in force when they knew they had the numerical advantage. Otherwise, it was suicidal bombers and asymmetric warfare. Most terrorists didn't want to die. Look at Afghanistan. When the choice was die or change sides, the rush to the winning team left a dust cloud around the opposing bench on the other side.

Hands reached out and touched his as he walked up the aisle. Sergeant Major Gentle stopped at the door. As Thomaston neared the pulpit in front of the church, more hands touched him and whispers of *"God Bless you"* accompanied him all the way to the front. By the time he shook hands with Pastor Jonathan Hew, he knew what he needed to say.

CHAPTER 4

DICK HOLMAN EASED THE HAVANA CIGAR OUT OF HIS mouth, turned his head toward Captain Upmann, and inadvertently blew the smoke into the wind. The wind immediately wrapped the smoke around his face. *Damn, that burns.* He shut his eyes for a second until the wind blew it away, before taking his handkerchief and wiping the moisture away.

He ignored the chuckles from Captain Leo Upmann. The man just didn't appreciate a good cigar, but what could you expect from a surface-warfare officer—a person who lived to be at sea, sailing in harm's way, looking for a battle against another Navy on the high seas. Something that, as far as Holman was concerned, would never happen in the twenty-first century. After all, America ruled the seas, but it still had those Navy officers who would love nothing better than to stand on the bow with their swords drawn, waiting to hop aboard an enemy warship and engage them *mano-a-mano. Now, us aviators we've got it right. Mount those swords in a framed display, hang 'em over a fireplace, and invite the girls back.* It was a whole lot less dangerous and a hell of a lot more fun. A person could get hurt playing with swords.

Off the starboard side of the USS *Boxer,* about five nautical miles—ten thousand yards—sailed the USS *Belleau Wood,*

LHA-3. Dick squinted as he peered through the open bridge at the USS *Nassau*, LHA-4, sailing off the port side. He hoped those helicopters jumping between the ships took a few photographs of this battle group. It had to be impressive. When was the last time the Navy had a three-amphibious-carrier battle group or a three-amphibious-carrier amphibious task force? Talk about versatility! Talk about tongue twisters!

The last time he'd asked the navigator for formation details, she'd held the *Nassau* fourteen thousand yards—that was seven miles—off port side. The two *Tarawa*-class amphibious helicopter assault ships were old, but within their 820-foot-long hulls, Dick had the resources of 3,500 Marines if he needed them. Kind of like having a hornet's nest waiting for someone to hit it.

The USS *Boxer*, LHD-4, on the other hand, was a newer-class amphibious warship at 888 feet, with 1,200 Marines embarked. *Shit! When whatever aircraft carrier showed up, I could own Liberia in a week.* Dick grinned and took another puff on his hand-rolled Havana. *Best thing we ever did was lifting the Cuban embargo when old Fidel had his stroke.* If that bearded terrorist had been able to speak, he would have had another one when the new Cuban government opened the country to democratic reforms and pegged the peso to the dollar. As long as they didn't change how they make cigars, he could give a damn about their government. *Shit! Ain't life grand!*

On the flight deck of the USS *Belleau Wood,* a Harrier taxied toward the bow of the ship. A second Harrier, its cockpit down and locked, waited behind the first. He glanced at the Ops Schedule—daylight landing qualifications. That would be the Marine *"newbies"* getting their sea legs or some of the veterans requalifying. Landing on a bouncing deck that never stopped moving horizontally and vertically was hard enough. When you added seas that caused these huge ships to roll, it really made the landings exciting—*butt-cheek-gripping.* He recalled some of his own aircraft-carrier qualification flights, and aircraft carriers were a lot larger than the amphibious ships he commanded. He recalled a couple of landings when he was a junior officer where, if he'd had teeth in his butt, he'd have chewed a hole through the seat.

He tossed the clipboard back on the shelf beneath the ledge and glanced at his watch. Just about time for dinner.

"Navigator!" Dick shouted into the bridge.

"Yes, sir, Admiral," the young female lieutenant replied.

"Course and speed?"

"One-two-zero at fourteen knots, sir."

"Thanks."

They had passed the hundred-mile marker off the North Carolina coast an hour ago. He would keep the designation for his group of warships as an amphibious task force until the carrier arrived; then he would transition to a carrier battle group. Already, his mind was planning the strategy for their evacuation of Americans.

They had been at sea for over twenty-four hours. Off the coastal shelf, Dick had ordered the amphibious task force to a great circle route that would bring them off the coast of Monrovia in another four or five days. He leaned against the port bridge wing, the ships in the formation easily visible in the clear summer skies of the Atlantic. And not another ship nor land in sight all the way to the horizon. No one but a sailor could appreciate the view. He took a deep breath and tightened his lips, watching this broad spectrum of Navy power. No one who had never served at sea, *and he meant no one*, could ever understand the honor of commanding such power, and the pride of serving alongside America's best.

He stuck his head inside the bridge. "Officer of the Deck, what other traffic do we have in the area?"

The lieutenant commander commanding the bridge leaned over the radar repeater and looked through the rubber eyepiece that shielded the surface radarscope from the glare of daylight. Almost immediately, the gangly officer turned his head toward Admiral Holman. "Surface radar shows nothing within detection range but United States Navy warships, Admiral." When Admiral Holman turned away, the lieutenant commander reached up and wiped around his eyes, looked at his fingers, saw nothing, and returned to his duties. He was damn well going to catch that son of a bitch who'd put black shoe polish on the rubber eyepiece that covered the radar repeater.

Dick grinned. "Damn! Couldn't ask for a better report, Commander." *What a great Navy Day!* If he could go faster than fourteen knots, it would make it even better.

The speed of convoys and battle groups were limited to that of the slowest ship. Kind of like walking with an older relative. He had two ships slowing them down. He could sprint toward Liberia and leave them behind. He might have to do that, depending on circumstances. The oiler USNS *Mispellion* and the auxiliary ship USNS *Concord* were older vessels. Shoot! The *Mispellion* was post-Korean War era. She should be someone's razor blade already; instead, she kept plugging along with the Navy. *Concord* wasn't much younger. It had been commissioned in the late sixties of the previous century. Probably sea rust was the only thing holding both of them together. Decades ago, both ships had been active-duty U.S. Navy warships. Now, they were members of Military Sealift Command, hence their nomenclature as USNS—United States Naval Ship—instead of USS—United States Ship. USNS meant merchant navy manned it, while USS meant it was a warship.

While Congress had been gracious in supporting the Navy in keeping its maritime teeth, it had done little to replace the logistics teeth needed to keep the maritime force forward-deployed for longer than a few days. With the growing involvement of America in Indonesia, fighting radical Islamic terrorists who had overthrown a slightly less radical government, the more modern auxiliary fleet ships had been allocated to Commander in Chief, U.S. Pacific Fleet. They were supporting a four-carrier battle group half a world away. Dick wondered briefly which of the carriers the Joint Chiefs of Staff would divert from current operations to support this emergent evacuation mission in West Africa.

He recalled that in the 1990's, when the Mediterranean Amphibious Task Force had been sent from the United States Sixth Fleet to do a similar operation when the Congo went to *shit in a handbasket*.

Holman took a sip from his cup of strong lukewarm coffee sitting on the shelf of the bridge wing. Then he lifted his binoculars. He could probably do the job with the forces he had, but having a true, large deck carrier like his old ship, the USS

Stennis, was something that sealed superiority in battle. *Stennis*—a great warship—was in the eastern Mediterranean supporting the U.S. Sixth Fleet. The Palestinian-Israeli crisis, *more a continuum moving from one crisis into another,* had heated again with Hamas throwing suicide bombers almost daily into Israeli life. One day, America would step back, nod quietly, and Israel would *stomp ass* across this new nation of Palestine and wipe it from the face of the earth.

They'd shoot him if he voiced his opinion about giving war a chance. Sometimes, he truly believed war was the best path to peace. Shoot! It might be the only option. War resolved political gambits. If conducted quickly and properly, a quick war might actually save lives in the end. Might even restore a good quality of life to the people who survived. He took another puff on the Cuban cigar. As much as he thought about how to solve the crises of the world, Holman didn't believe war should be the first option out of the diplomatic bag. It should be the last option. It should be the last card played. Not just throwing that ace on the table when you need it. Once played, though, war should be left alone until the game is done. Leave it to the professionals. They might screw up, but it was their lives they were playing with.

"A great sight, isn't it?" Upmann asked, interrupting Dick's thoughts.

Lowering the binoculars, Rear Admiral Dick Holman replied, "You don't truly realize the might of the United States Navy until you are standing in the center of a battle group surrounded by firepower that no other force on earth can match. Remember the immediate months after September 11th. It was American aircraft carriers who carried the war initially to the enemy."

"It does let me sleep at night; especially when I'm at sea in the center of one of these battle groups." Upmann took a deep breath. "Smell that salt air."

A cloud of exhaust fumes swirled up from the flight deck over the bridge wing before dissipating into the atmosphere. Upmann coughed. "Of course, aircraft really mess it up."

Dick lowered his binoculars as they wiped the sting from their eyes. He waved the cigar at Leo good-naturedly. "Don't give me that, Leo. I already know surface-warfare officers never sleep. Naval Research Laboratories did a survey once. They sealed a surface-warfare officer in a room with nothing but a bunk, a desk, a sheet of paper, and a pen. Within twenty-four hours, he had developed a watch bill and assigned a work schedule for himself."

"What a horrible thing to say, Admiral," Leo mocked, placing his palm against his chest. "Almost makes me wish I wasn't handing this to you to approve."

Dick reached forward and took the folder from Leo. "What is it? A leave chit?"

"It's the underway duty-watch-officer bill for your staff. I had a few moments after breakfast this morning, sat down with our Operations Officer, and between the two of us we ginned this up."

"Buford Green? Our dyed-in-the-wool Rebel from the City of Homes, as he likes to call Newnan, Georgia? Let me see if I got this straight, Leo. Two surface-warfare officers, one sheet of paper—"

"Two pens."

"—drinking coffee and developing work schedules. Now, why doesn't that surprise me?" Dick grinned as he handed it back without opening it. "Leo, that's your job. You and Buford decide the duty roster." He took a puff, and winked when Leo moved to one side so the smoke blew past him. "Besides, Leo, if you do the roster and do everything else I expect of a Chief of Staff, then when things go wrong, *which they will*, then I can turn somberly toward you and say, *'Chief of Staff, what in the hell were you thinking?'* Or, *'I would never have approved that if I had known!'* " Holman paused and waved the cigar a couple of times. "Plus, it's good for morale."

"Whose? Yours or mine?"

"Why, mine, of course."

Leo tucked the folder under his arm and grinned, "Admiral, with all due respect, sir, I only offered this to you to prove a point what all good 'black shoes' know."

Dick's eyebrows bunched. "What point is that?"

"That airedales—*brown shoes*—can't read."

Dick's mouth dropped in mocked indignation. "Chief of Staff, I'm appalled that a black shoe—*a surface-warfare offi-cer*—would even think we aviators need to read. As long as there are pictures, charts, maps, and bombs, who needs words?"

Leo saluted the shorter officer. "Yes, sir. That is exactly what I meant to say. With the admiral's permission, I will drop this off at operations and have them disseminate it and then meet you at dinner, sir."

The sound of AV-8 engines revving up for the hardest launch of any fighter aircraft drowned out Holman's reply. The Marine Corps ground-support fighter aircraft on the USS *Belleau Wood* crawled forward along the flight deck, picking up speed, until it sped up the small jump ramp at the bow of the amphibious carrier. Then it seemed to leap into the air, quickly aloft, its engines screaming as they rotated from vertical to horizontal, and the Harrier started a rapid ascent, zooming upward toward its assigned altitude.

"Those aircraft must really make the pucker factor go up," Leo shouted over the noise.

"Wouldn't catch me flying them. Give me the thrust of a strong aircraft carrier catapult trying to rip the skin off my face as it throws a well-armed F-14 Tomcat wrapped around me from zero to two hundred miles an hour in six seconds. I want to feel the power between my legs when I hit the end of the flight deck, just after that brief period of weightlessness when the jet engines take over and whip you into the skies. Now, that's reliability and confidence."

"On the other hand, Admiral. If that Harrier pilot has a problem, he or she can sit the aircraft down anywhere and most likely walk away from it."

Dick Holman nodded. "I would say, Leo, the main difference between a Harrier having a problem on launch and an F-14 Tomcat experiencing difficulties is that the Harrier pilot has a slightly longer time to pray.

"Different subject, Leo," Dick said before his Chief of Staff could reply. "The carrier. Have we heard anything from CIN-CLANT Fleet as to when the carrier is going to show up?" Dick asked, referring to the four-star admiral in Norfolk, Virginia, who was Commander in Chief, U.S. Atlantic Fleet.

The smell of burned jet-fuel exhaust drifted over the bridge wing, stinging their eyes slightly before the wind swept it across the signal bridge overhead and out to sea on the starboard side.

"Nothing yet, sir. Commander, U.S. Second Fleet, in Norfolk has been ordered by CINCLANT Fleet to work the issue, but between us, sir, I don't have a *'warm-fuzzy'* we'll have a carrier by the time we reach Liberia. So far, Joint Chiefs of Staff haven't directed them to release a carrier, so everything that CINCLANT Fleet and Second Fleet are doing may be for naught."

"That's not good news, but if we don't, then we'd better hope all we have to do is evacuate American and allied citizens."

"Means we'll remain a battle group rather than transitioning to an amphibious task force. We can expect European Command to designate us as a joint task force once we inchop their area of operations."

"Ah, what a shame!" replied Dick, smiling as he drew out the exclamation. "Means I will have to stand tall and accept that mantle of leadership they are going to toss my way." The appearance of an aircraft carrier usually meant the embarkation of a senior flag officer, and nearly every flag officer in the Navy was senior to Dick Holman. Christ! He was still a lonely one-star admiral, and it had been two years since the Navy had bitten its lip and bestowed the coveted silver five-pointed star on his collars. Holman still had enough friends in the Pentagon to know the physical-fitness mafia had shoved their hands into their chests and wrenched their hearts out when he had been selected. Personally, he had never thought that being able to run fast was a good leadership trait.

Without a carrier, the amphibious formation would remain a battle group. He would remain Senior Officer Present—SOP. When warships massed together for a specific mission, they were assigned certain nominative titles; a carrier battle group being the most powerful. The amphibious task force he commanded was the one that projected power ashore. It did it in the form of United States Marines.

From the other side of the USS *Belleau Wood,* the DD-21-class destroyer USS *Stribling* appeared, taking station about five hundred yards behind the amphibious carrier. It would be the plane guard for air operations. Its primary mission would be to pick up pilots if they ejected during the launch phase. They also pulled from the drink the odd sailor who every now and again was blown overboard. Helicopters hovered off the port side of the *Belleau Wood,* nearer the USS *Boxer* than its parent ship, to assist if an aircraft went into the drink. Nothing stopped aircraft carrier operations except a massive catastrophe, of which Dick Holman preferred not to think. He recalled the film of the USS *Forrestal* fire off Vietnam in the sixties, and the collision of the cruiser USS *Belknap* with the aircraft carrier USS *John F. Kennedy* in the seventies. Carriers were built for survival. That survival depended on the damage-control skills of their crew, and many times their lives.

He leaned against the railing of the bridge wing, bracing himself with his elbows. Through the bridge across the far starboard side, he watched the USS *Spruance*—the first of the DD-963-class destroyers and the oldest destroyer still on active duty—move into position off the port side of the USS *Nassau.* The *Spruance* had a reputation for making every commitment and putting itself in harm's way so many times that this caused it to be regarded as an old warship fighting to mark its end of Naval service with combat action rather than scattered across America as razor blades. Up ahead, near the horizon, the Aegis Ticonderoga-class cruiser USS *Hue City* sailed. Its air-to-air-warfare capability was able to project destruction hundreds of miles ahead to protect the battle group from air attack. Not that in this era of the twenty-first century he expected any air attacks. The last great superpower that had that capability was the now-dead Soviet Union. Only America and its allies had aircraft carriers today, though the People's Republic of China was building a couple.

He shook his head. Things had changed so much for a young man such as himself who'd joined the Navy when the Russian Bear was the only enemy and America the only superpower capable of facing it.

"Leo, before you go, what is the latest on the situation in Liberia? Have we heard from Lieutenant General Thomaston this afternoon?"

Leo stopped halfway through the hatch, turned, and shook his head. "No, sir. If we had, you would have known. But I can have our intelligence officer, Captain Mary Davidson, come up and brief you if you would like. . . ."

Holman pushed away from the railing, paused, and then shook his head. "No, Mary has her hands full trying to develop a disposition of forces in Liberia and identifying target priorities for us. I just wondered if you had heard anything since we saw her at lunch."

Leo shook his head. "Not too much. Did see a special-category message that came in through intel channels that said the Liberian Army had disappeared." He shrugged his shoulders. "Doesn't surprise me. Those that didn't change allegiance from Liberia to the Islamic radicals have melted into the rain forests, jungles, and mountains of Liberia. They'll miraculously reappear when the danger has passed."

"Just what we need. An army afraid to fight."

"Wouldn't know if they're afraid. I would think in a country where changes of government are violent, weak military institutions, such as the one in Liberia, keep down out of sight until the fog has lifted and the new terrain is visible."

"How about the situation at Kingsville?"

"Nothing new since this morning. Last word we had was Thomaston was waiting for us. As Mary said, barricades have been erected across the roads leading into and out of the town. Imagery analysis shows several groups, believed to be roving patrols, sent out by Thomaston. Seems to me that Thomaston is doing everything he can to give himself early warning if the rebels move toward them."

Holman grunted. "It is not a case of 'if,' but 'when.' Abu Alhaul, this unknown leader of this resurrected ring of global terrorism, is not going to let an opportunity to overrun an American expatriate community pass him by. Wherever this asshole is, he knows he has a few days before we can be in the area. Four, maybe five, days in which to wreak havoc with his warped doctrines against America wherever and whenever he can." Holman took another puff on the stub of the cigar and then tossed it overboard.

"We could always do what we did in Afghanistan and in Egypt," offered Leo.

Holman shook his head. "Both places were wide-open spaces. We drove the Taliban out of Afghanistan because of

Naval airpower, Army spec-ops, Air Force bombers and tankers, and the presence of an organic opposition military force. Reopening the Suez Canal when the Islamic Republic of Egypt closed it to Western shipping was a little harder because Egypt had a functioning armed forces that stood their ground and fought. The difference with Egypt was we had to land heavy armor to defeat its ground force. The good news is the new government of moderate Muslims seem to be making headway in forging an Islamic nation that wants to join the twenty-first century. Just like Iraq."

"Ironic in a way, isn't it?"

"How's that?"

"No matter how patriotic and how benevolent religious fanatics are, once they take over a government, if the people don't worship God the way they want, then they tend to kill them. It doesn't take long before you realize that zealotry in any religion is worse than zealotry in government."

Holman chuckled. "Leo, don't hold back. Tell me what you really think," he said, his laugh stopping. "Don't let others hear you say that. You'd be the number one devil on religious programs throughout America." He reached over and slapped Leo on the shoulder. "You go drop off that watch bill that you surface warriors worked so diligently to produce. I'll meet you in my in-port cabin when you're done."

The noise of a Harrier fighter passing overhead drowned out Leo's reply as the Chief of Staff departed the bridge wing.

Admiral Holman looked up, shielding his eyes from the setting sun as the Marine Corps fighter aircraft came into view, turned east, and took off ahead of the battle group. At least, the surface commander was getting some maritime reconnaissance accomplished. He had six of the Marine Corps fighters. Should be more than enough for handling Liberia.

Holman pulled out the metal stool stored against the bulkhead of the bridge wing railing, and sat down. Leaning against the railing he raised his binoculars and began the routine he so enjoyed, watching the other ships and seeing what they were doing. You could tell an awful lot by watching the sailors topside on a ship.

*   *   *

THE SIX OFFICERS AND SAILORS MANNING THE BRIDGE EX-changed looks, raised their eyebrows, and shrugged at each other. This Admiral Holman was a different breed from most admirals they had embarked with on other deployments. They liked him, but they would like him even more if he would stay off the bridge. Senior officers made bridge watches nervous.

"Okay, troops, let's get our attention back on sailing this ship of the line," the Officer of the Deck said as he raised his binoculars and scanned the horizon ahead of them. He wondered what the admiral saw in those binoculars that always seemed glued to his eyes.

BEHIND THE AMPHIBIOUS CARRIER BATTLE GROUP, THE periscope slid beneath the waves. The submarine skipper was nervous. He would have preferred maintaining eight knots, but this American fleet was keeping a steady fourteen knots. Four teen knots made passive sonar inoperable. Of course, on the opposite side of the coin, the two antisubmarine warships with the Americans would be experiencing the same problem with their passive sonars. So, here he trailed the Americans, reporting to his Navy's headquarters, while he had little capability to discover if American submarines had joined this task force heading toward Liberia. The idea of an American submarine caused a mental itch up his spine.

He doubted the two American destroyers would discover his presence as long as he kept the propellers shielded by the long black hull of this modern nuclear submarine. He had purposely slowed twice today to obtain passive signatures against the task force, and after both slowdowns he had had to increase speed past fourteen knots to regain position. Each time, he ran the risk of cavitation from the propellers and increasing opportunities for some sharp sonar operator aboard an American destroyer to pick up his signature. His orders were to maintain covert presence and avoid detection. He had no illusions about his orders in the event he was detected. He would do what the sealed orders said, regardless of how much it grated on his submariner sense of survival to do it.

He turned to the Chief of the Boat and ordered the submarine to one-hundred-meters depth. The warm seas kept the

sound layer of cooler water lower, giving him safety of depth
without losing the sound signatures of the American warships'
propellers. Behind him, crammed across a small lighted table,
a holograph projection of the contacts showed the location of
the American warships along with his own.

His executive officer asked if he wanted to load the forward
torpedoes. *Why would he want to do that?* he asked incredulously. The Americans were, after all, still allies. The reply of
his executive officer was that if the Americans were such close
allies, then why in the hell were they tailing them? He sighed
loud enough to capture the attention of those in the conning
tower, and rather than argue with his hotheaded executive officer, nodded sharply and went to his cabin. He needed some
sleep. This new strategy of his government—*top secret, according to his orders*—to conduct patrols along the American
East Coast bothered him. He had friends in the American
Navy. He had even graduated from the Industrial College of
the Armed Forces at Fort McNair, Washington, D.C., and
when in port he exchanged e-mails with his former classmates.
No, he didn't like this mission at all, but orders were orders
and as long as they weren't illegal, he would execute them.
But what if he was ordered to load the torpedoes? What if—?
No, he wasn't going to think about it. He was going to skip
dinner and take a short nap. Let the others sip the wine tonight.
He knew how the Americans would react if the government
in his country did something dumb under the guise of nation-
alism. Could the socialist government be so shortsighted they
would fail to understand where Americans drew their line in
the sand?

He reached over, lifted the photograph from the small side
table, and looked at his wife and two children. The professional submariner glanced at the clock above the curtain leading to his small stateroom. Right now, Yvonne would be
dropping Michel off at school. Louis, his older son, would
probably still be in bed. The boy must get a job. If he wasn't
going to university, then he could work. He returned the photograph to the table, threw his arm across his eyes, and in
moments was in a light sleep.

CHAPTER 5

"LOOKS AS IF THEY ACCEPT WHAT I TOLD THEM," RETIRED Lieutenant General Daniel Thomaston said.

Retired Sergeant Major Craig Gentle propped his foot on the banister that circled the community center. "General, it ain't as if they've much choice. Some are probably still in a daze from that truckload of bodies."

"Damn, Craig. You make it seem we had a tractor trailer pull up with a couple of hundred dead."

"For them, it might as well been a couple of hundred. Every one of those young men were either kin or known to everyone in this town."

"I know. It's hard to put things in perspective when you're fighting for your families. But we don't have time to mourn. We have to get ready to move out."

"We only have a few militia to protect the convoy as we move toward the border with Ivory Coast."

"That's true, but we have a few veterans. Shove a piece in their hands, and knowledge on how to use it will come flooding back."

Gentle nodded. "They'll also have a better idea of what we're facing than the civilians."

"Yes, but they're facing it with their families."

A vintage station wagon, trailing a cloud of dust, pulled in line behind the other vehicles parked along the side of the main street of Kingsville. The back was crammed with household effects and three—*could be four,* thought Thomaston—young children scrambling around the backseat. Strapped precariously on top were boxes and suitcases.

He pointed at the car. "Won't make it five miles before they fall off. Don't they realize this isn't a picnic we're going on? This is a quick run to the border. Most of their belongings are going to have to be left behind," he said tautly. "It's déjà vu. Like the old settlers heading west on wagon trains and having to dump stuff like pianos and dressers along the way."

"I remember a television show about it." Gentle brought his foot down, walked to where Thomaston stood near the stairs. "Seems to me, when the trail-master told them to get rid of the stuff, they often nearly mutinied." He shrugged. "Can't see any harm in letting them try, General. It isn't as if it's a long way to the border. A couple of days and we'll be in Abidjan," he said, referring to the major coastal city in the Ivory Coast. "If we need the space, we can always break the bad news then."

Thomaston shook his head. "Can't take the chance, Craig. All we need is to find ourselves stopping every few minutes to tighten down or lighten loads. When we leave here, we need to move and we need to move fast. We'll be at our most vulnerable while we're strung out in a long convoy."

Gentle pointed to the armory on the other side of town near the edge of the lake. Almost a mirror-image location to the community center. "At least they're drawing their weapons from the arsenal."

Thomaston looked at the man who had followed him from duty stations to battlefields and into retirement. "Yes, they are, aren't they. Wonder if they realize why we had the good fortune to have those weapons in the first place, or even who provided them and where we got them."

Gentle put his hands on his hips. "It don't matter, General. It isn't as if anyone has had time to sit and ponder the questions this could have raised. Maybe later, when we're sitting around one of those open-air cafes in Abidjan sipping beer and wine. What counts is you got us the money to fund this venture and they even provided weapons. Next time when they offer us arms, ask for mortars and claymores. We have small arms, a couple more SAMs, and a couple of heavy machine guns even if they are Army castoffs. We should have ample firepower to keep us alive until we reach the border." He raised his hand and swept the scene in front of them. "I'm going to miss this. We've done so much in two years, and fallen in love with our little piece of Africa." He sighed. "It's going to be hard to come back and start over."

"That's true, Craig. But we can't start over if we stay here and die. It's not like our fellow townsmen are former 82nd Airborne. Not like they've even had the training your basic grunt soldier gets, which would be welcome right now."

"Wouldn't take it too hard, General. We do have a bunch of veterans with us. Former soldiers, Marines, airmen, and sailors scattered out there. And we are using the soldiers and Marines like trained platoon sergeants and company commanders. The airmen have some weapons training. As for the sailors—"

"Well, if we reach the sea, then we can use the sailors."

Gentle laughed. "Meanwhile, sir"—he bowed slightly and motioned down the stairs with his hand—"would the general like to inspect this army from hell before we move out?"

Thomaston nodded. "Okay, Sergeant Major, let's go build some morale and spirit in our people. Let's give them kick-ass-speech number one, and hope it gives them the attitude they're going to need for the next couple of days."

Thomaston started down the stairs. Retired Sergeant Major Craig Gentle moved left and fell in step, slightly behind the former three-star Army general.

Hands waved as they walked toward the line of vehicles. Thomaston estimated about twenty cars and trucks waiting. The sound of a straining engine caught his attention. From behind the module schoolhouses near the edge of the jungle that bordered the enclave to the south, two yellow buses emerged. They'd come in handy, if their guzzling diesel engines lasted to the Ivory Coast. The buses had been a gift of the NAACP, but since all the students walked to school, the buses had been primarily used to provide shopping trips to Monrovia and the odd school field trip. If they had sufficient room in the cars and trucks, maybe they could put personal belongings in the buses.

The woman from the station wagon saw him. "We heard the United States Navy is coming," the woman said as she walked toward the two men.

He reached out, took her hand in both of his, and squeezed it slightly before dropping it. "I have talked with Admiral Holman"—who he had never met, but general and flag officers always assumed they knew each other, especially in front of subordinates and in crisis situations—"who is leading a three-carrier battle group loaded with Marines."

Others heard the answer and smiled. They nodded approvingly to each other. A few of the men exchanged high fives. "Whoop-ass day is coming," one of them said. "Woo-wee!"

It wasn't new information, but just hearing it again helped ease concern. The information flowed like a wave washing up against a smooth beach as those who heard turned to those behind to pass along this old, but always welcome, tidbit of news. What he didn't tell her was that it would be another two—*maybe three*—days before this Naval force arrived.

"But we have to control our own destiny. Right?" he shouted.

A chorus of cheers broke out around him.

"I know these homes. This land," he said, throwing both arms up as if to embrace Kingsville, "is land we tore from the jungle of our forefathers. Land we've built homes upon. Land to which we have returned with the knowledge and the spirit of America to build a new place in an old world. A place to find our ancestors and a place to raise our children. A place where we have our pride in being Americans and in being children of Africa."

A new chorus of cheers broke out. Men slapped each other on the back, women hugged each other and their husbands while pulling their small children closer.

"Let's kick their ass, General!" someone shouted from the back of the crowd. Another round of cheers erupted.

"Joshua, you hush yore mouth," the man's wife said. She shifted the small child on her hip to a better position and slapped him on the shoulder. "What you gonna do is get us out of here."

Looked as if he didn't have to give too much encouragement. Thomaston pulled his handkerchief from his back pocket and wiped his forehead. In Africa, the heat arrived in waves as the sun rose, by mid-morning burning away the night smells of the jungle. Around one in the afternoon, it peaked and you could cut the humidity with a knife. Moisture filled the air during this early furnace half of a normal African summer day. Heavy afternoon rains arrived with little notice, splattering the soil, soaking the thick vegetation, and dissipating the dust from the air for a couple of hours.

He raised his hands in the air, the handkerchief flowing like a white flag in his right hand. Craig Gentle reached up and took the handkerchief from the hand. Thomaston motioned them all to be quiet, and after several seconds the cheering faded, the conversation tapered off, and movement ceased.

"I agree with what you're saying. If there were just us men and women here who had the training to fight, I would say to hell with those heathens heading this way. I would say, we stay." He balled his fist and shook it. "We fight. We kill. And when we finish, no one else—nothing would ever move us again. We would be the Israelites in the middle of Gideon." He paused for a moment, and wondered briefly if Gideon was the right place or word. Religion was something Thomaston was less than overtly enamored with.

Agreements and *amens* punctuated his sentences.

"But we can't. I don't know how many are out there. Wish I did. What we do know is that there are enough of them that they were able to overthrow the government. They were able to chase the Liberian Army—"

"Bunch of cowards, if you ask me," said a man from the middle of the crowd, drawing a chorus of agreements.

Thomaston nodded. "Could be, but for whatever reason, the Liberian Army is gone. Vanished. They've faded into the jungles and rain forests or joined the terrorists. We can't expect any help from them." He reached over, retrieved the handkerchief from Gentle, and shoved it in his back pocket. He wanted to wipe the fresh sweat from his brow, but every action and word would be interpreted by those watching. Leadership was more than words. It was confidence, action, and decision. It was standing tall in the face of danger.

"What we're doing is just what I said we should in church earlier. We're going to leave Kingsville." Angry mutterings and a few vocal objections erupted; thankfully, not at him, but at the rebels who were approaching. Rebels, terrorists, regardless of what you called them, the approaching force was hellbent on killing Americans. "I know how you feel. I don't want to go any more than you do, but we can always rebuild this brick-and-mortar town. We can't bring back our sons and daughters; our wives and husbands; our friends. So we leave, but we'll return, and when we do, we're going to stay and no one, nobody, no nation, no terrorists or rebels are going to drive us away again."

Cheers burst forth again. He had the crowd. There were a couple toward the back who didn't cheer or clap. The people trusted him more than he trusted his own self. Slightly to the left and behind him, Sergeant Major Craig Gentle rendered the retired lieutenant general a salute. Gentle turned to the crowd and raised his fist. "Three hoorays for the general!"

"Hip-hip hooray!" Gentle shouted three times, and by the third, the entire crowd was screaming at the top of their voices.

Thomaston waved and mumbled thanks, wondering if this little show would provide the confidence needed for the next couple of days.

When the noise of the impromptu rally faded, Thomaston stepped forward and in a loud voice said, "Now, we hurry. Take only the things you truly need." He glanced at the sky. "We'll leave as soon as those sent to our embassy in Abidjan, Ivory Coast, return." He glanced at his watch.

HE AND GENTLE STOOD ALONG THE ROAD, WATCHING THE crowd continue loading the cars. Not one person removed any of the items crammed into them.

"Great speech," Gentle said. "Good to see how you have so moved them they are throwing away personal stuff and lightening the load."

"If I had been any more effective, they'd be putting more on top of those vehicles," Thomaston replied in the same soft voice.

Several men and women walked over and shook Thomaston's hand. So much confidence in him. He hoped it wasn't misplaced. He knew what most of them could never know, and that was regardless of how well you planned, when the first bullet was fired, everything went to shit in a handbasket. Fog of war, they call it, but when you're rolling in the dirt, scrambling through the brush, and returning fire, fog is the last thing on your mind.

"Here comes one of the patrols," Gentle said, pointing north.

Thomaston looked. Dust rose from behind a white SUV speeding down the road leading toward the small town.

Shouts of "General, General" drew his attention. Behind him running down the small incline was Tawela Johnson. The M-16 strapped across her back banged against her legs as she ran. She was waving a sheet of paper in her left hand as she shouted. Another message. The good thing about Tawela was she enjoyed sitting up there in the small shanty on the hilltop with Beaucoup Charlie and running messages for him. The good thing for the men, they enjoyed watching her run. He hoped the safety on her M-16 was on. The way it was bouncing around against her legs and torso, she could accidentally cause it to discharge. He could take it away from her, but if he tried, she would be one upset young lady.

Beaucoup Charlie was their only means of communications with the outside world and their only means until either the United States shifted another satellite to this area or those Navy ships sailed within range.

"General," Tawela said as she stopped in front of him. "Am I glad I found you."

"Didn't know I was lost."

She smiled. *A face that launched a thousand ships,* thought Thomaston.

"Oh, General, you weren't lost. I saw you when I came around the building." She shook her head back and forth, grinning, as she handed him the paper. "Beaucoup said get this to you fast."

Thomaston read the handwritten note.

"He got contact with the Navy," she said, "but sunspot activity broke it up after he told them we were running toward Ivory Coast. I want to—"

"I prefer to think of it as evacuating to the Ivory Coast," said Thomaston

"Running ain't a word in my dictionary either," Craig Gentle added.

"—go if you're sending a patrol to the border," Tawela finished.

Both Thomaston and Gentle looked at her. She was attractive in a boyish way. Just tall enough to keep the M-16's barrel from knocking against her calves, though the gun hit everywhere else on her body. Thomaston shut one eye, touched his chin for moment, and looked at her. If she could just keep quiet . . .

Gentle faced Thomaston. "Sir, what are your orders?"

Behind them, a car horn interrupted their decision. A Land Rover came speeding into the center of the town, its brakes squealing as the driver slammed down on them. The vehicle slid sideways and the doors burst open with four men inside stepping out quickly. The movement of Gentle, unslinging his weapon, was not lost on Thomaston. He had his pistol half out of the holster before he realized it.

It was Edward Jones and the three sent to the Ivory Coast. They were supposed to go to the American Embassy in Abidjan. Though Yamoussoukro was the official capital of Ivory Coast, and had been since the early 1980's, Abidjan, located on the coast, remained the administrative center for the former French colony. The U.S., like other countries, had its embassy in Abidjan.

"Edward, you're back early," Thomaston said moments later when the men made their way to him. He reached forward and shook the man's hand. Edward Jones was as dark as most native Africans. Thomaston had used Edward earlier when they first arrived to go places most African-Americans couldn't because of their lighter skin. Edward was one of the original members of Thomaston's group.

"Sir, we got problems," Jones said as they shook.

"Oh, you are right about that, Edward. We got all kinds of problems, and one of them seems to be that you are back too early to have made it to the American Embassy. Considering everything, you shouldn't be back here until late tomorrow at the earliest. What happened?"

"They wouldn't let us cross the border."

"Who wouldn't and why? I don't understand."

"They have closed the border, General, because of the civil war here, and they aren't going to let anyone cross. The Ivory Coast Army sergeant at the border post said they had orders to shoot anyone who tried to cross."

"Why are they doing this?" Tawela asked. "We're Americans. How can they stop us from going to our own embassy?"

Without looking at her, Thomaston reached out and touched the girl briefly on her shoulder. She stopped talking.

"I don't think it was the Ivornians who're doing it," said Jones. "About a hundred feet behind them, I saw French Foreign Legionnaires. I shouted, but they acted as if they didn't hear me. But they didn't mind strutting around with their weapons for us to see."

"Well, it ain't their country," Tawela said, then quickly covered her mouth when Thomaston frowned at her.

Don't tell them that," Gentile said. "Even when they set Ivory Coast free, the French kept their Foreign Legion there. They continue to rotate career Army units to make sure the Ivory Coast doesn't—"

"Did you tell them you were Americans?"

"Yes, sir, General. They said we were Liberians and Liberians needed to stay on their side of the border."

"Did you show them your passports?"

"Sir, they wouldn't even look at them. The more I tried to explain that we wanted to talk with the American Embassy, the more I got this Ivornian look as if they had forgotten how to speak English."

"Kind of like being in Paris," Gentile mumbled.

Several seconds of silence passed. Tawela broke the spell. "Well, let's just bolt through the border. Look at all the weapons we got." She pointed the M-16 up, holding it with both hands. "We just show up, hold them hostage long enough to—"

Edward shook his head. "Won't work. Not just the French Foreign Legion sitting there with automatic weapons. They've at least one tank and a couple of armored personnel carriers with machine guns." He waved his hand toward the general, his face an expression of exasperation. "General, they even had a command vehicle there bristling with antennas and all kinds of communications shit. If we try to fight our way through, even if they don't mow us down at the border, with the communications they have, backup forces will finish the job."

"Maybe Beaucoup can contact the embassy and tell them what happened?" one of the men with Edward asked.

"Which brings to mind, Edward; why didn't you call and let us know what was going on? You got a radio in your car."

"We do, General, and that radio went 'tits-up'—sorry, Tawela—about ten klicks from the border." He put his hands on his hips and shook his head angrily. "They wouldn't even let me use the telephone in their guard shack. I told them I wanted to call back here inside Liberia. I thought that if they bought that and I was able to use their telephone, I would call the embassy and have them clean up the border-crossing issue."

"Probably wouldn't have worked anyway. Cellular telephones are about the only things that work in Africa."

Gentle looked at Edward. "Did you try your cell phone?"

The man nodded. "Of course I did. They aren't working. Either the antennas are down or someone's jamming the signals."

Thomaston nodded and looked south. Their options had narrowed. He took a pen from his shirt pocket, along with the message Tawela had brought. He turned it over and scribbled something. "Edward, you go with Tawela and help Beaucoup. I want him to contact the embassy in Abidjan." He handed the paper to Edward. "Here is the name of the individual in the embassy who he needs to contact and explain the situation to." Their eyes met. Both understood what the individual represented. "He may be able to influence those State Department outcasts who worked so hard and diligently to be awarded with a twilight tour to Africa," Thomaston said with sarcasm.

Edward took the paper from Thomaston and with Tawela leading the way, the two of them took off running toward the radio shack, Tawela leaving the older, slower man behind.

Gentle turned to the other three men. "Go draw your weapons. Should be enough to go around," he said, pointing to the dwindling queue passing through the armory gates.

Thomaston raised his hand and pointed briefly to the south. "Looks as if we have two choices, Sergeant Major. One, march to the sea through that jungle, swamp, and rain forest, or"— he pointed to the armory—"two, take cover in the armory until the embassy clears this up or the Navy arrives."

Gentle looked south and shook his head. "Oh, sir, you do so have a way with making a soldier's day. South is not going to be fun. It's overgrown, lots of swamps—mosquitoes that you need a shotgun to kill—and no way a car or a truck— much less one of those buses—can make it. If we go south, then we walk."

Thomaston bit his lower lip. "I know," he mumbled. "But it's either escape to the sea and hope the United States Navy and Marines are there waiting, or stay here and fight off *God knows how many rebels or terrorists or Islamic fanatics*— whatever you want to call them."

"What about Nathan, sir? He's a member of our original group."

The "group" consisted of nine men who knew the source of the weapons and where most of the money used to support Kingsville originated. The man was not referring to the African-Americans who had followed him to Liberia.

"It doesn't change anything, Craig. Either Nathan and his group have survived and will get here eventually, or they didn't. We knew when we planned to bolt toward Ivory Coast we were leaving any survivors stranded. If anyone can make it, it'll be Nathan. He's got the smarts, the training, and the tenacity to make it."

Thomaston turned toward the north. "We have patrols out. We already know rebels are heading our way, following the main highway north of us." He looked west, over the community center. The sunglasses cut through the glare of the sun. "We need to have an idea of the size and direction of those enemy forces, Craig. I don't want to send you."

"They'd know real quick if we went south, you know."

"Or they're going to know we have taken refuge in the armory. Either way, we're the ones lacking choice."

"Tawela's idea about busting through the border—"

"Oh, it'd work, Craig. We'd bust through, we'd lose some

to the firefight, and then have to hope that the embassy steps in before the Ivornians massacre the rest of us."

"The rebels have aircraft."

"We haven't seen any aircraft since that first day. To them, we still have surface-to-air missiles. That surface-to-air missile you fired may have convinced the remnants of the Liberian Air Force to stay out of this. Besides, once into the thick of the rain forests and jungles to the south, there is no way aircraft can find us. At least, their aircraft with their technology."

"If we go south, they'll find us, General. And if the Navy arrives and we are in the middle of that mess"—Gentle jerked his thumb toward the wall of jungle that ran along the southern edge of the town—"they'll never find us. Plus, we will lose many just for no other reason than they're unable to keep up."

Thomaston thought for a moment. "Then we fight. Start moving everyone into the armory." He looked at the armory east of the town. A vision of the Alamo came to mind. Beaucoup should have communications with the Navy amphibious task force moving toward them, but he didn't. Why in the hell haven't they heard anything? he wondered. Damn! Blind. Never knew this was what a commander without information felt, and that worried him more than knowing the small group of refugees coming from Monrovia had been ambushed.

The difference between victory and defeat was which commander had the better information or intelligence. It amazed him how blind and helpless he was after being used to the huge information architecture the U.S. military carried into battle. He never realized it was there when they were fighting, but he sure as hell missed it now that he didn't have it.

"I could take a patrol west and see what the situation is like that way," said Gentle.

"And check on Nathan while you're doing it?"

"Well, the thought did cross my mind."

Thomaston nodded with a pained expression. "Sergeant Major, no one's going."

"But—"

Thomaston shook his head. "They're either dead, dying, or working their way here. The rationale earlier today remains the same. Nathan is a smart street fighter. He will either get his people here, or there are no people to make it."

Gentle opened his mouth to object, then shut it. "Yes, sir, I know. But I don't like thinking about it."

Thomaston, smiling weakly, reached out and touched Gentle briefly on the shoulder. "Old friend, I don't think we have much choice. Move everyone into the armory and hope the Navy-Marine Corps team does what they say they do best— project power from the sea. We need you. I need you."

Sounds of running feet and heavy breathing caused them to look over their shoulders. Tawela, wearing a backpack, her M-16 cradled in her arms, ran toward them. Thomaston grimaced at the sight. Where in the hell did that oversized helmet come from? If she tripped, it would take both of them to unravel her from the weapon and everything she was carrying. A few seconds later, Tawela stopped in front of them, rested the butt of the M-16 on the ground, and put her free hand against her chest. "Can't believe I'm out of breath," she gasped. The helmet dropped, coming to rest against her nose. She pushed it back up.

"Can't believe you made it down that hill without killing yourself," Gentle mumbled.

"Good news, I hope?" Thomaston asked.

Picking up her M-16, she nodded. "It sure is. Mr. Jones and Mr. Beaucoup were talking, and they said you're gonna send Major Gentle to rescue the Monrovia bunch."

"It's Sergeant Major, not Major," Gentle corrected.

"Whatever." She held up her hand petulantly at Gentle and continued to stare at Thomaston. "So, when do we leave?"

Thomaston looked at Gentle and slapped him on the back. "You answer the young lady's questions. I am sure this leadership challenge is somewhere in your ample file cabinet of solutions, Sergeant Major."

Gentle's narrowed eyes never left the young woman in front of him. "Yes, sir," he said curtly, saluting retired Lieutenant General Daniel Thomaston.

Thomaston turned and quickly left the two, heading down to where the people of Kingsville prepared to evacuate the town. He bit his lower lip and lowered his head. He had always been told never to play poker for high stakes because he had a face that told everything. If that was so, then right now the word *"worried"* must be embossed across his forehead.

A clap of thunder caused everyone to look up just as the leading wave of afternoon rain splashed across the landscape. Within seconds, Thomaston along with everyone else was soaked. Some ducked into their vehicles, while others ran for the porches of the nearby buildings. He noticed Gentle and Tawela were running up the stairs to the community center. Some remained where they were, stacking supplies into the pickup trucks of the convoy. At least it would be easy to move everyone and everything into the armory.

Thomaston took a deep breath, straightened, and made sure the flap across his pistol was buttoned. Time to tell them of the change of plans. He looked south, trying to see the wall of jungle growth that marked the edge of the town, but the heavy rain blocked his vision. All he could see was a smear of green where the jungle formed an impenetrable barrier trapping them in Kingsville. He hoped he'd made the right choice.

"LET'S GO," SAID GEORGE, JUST LOUD ENOUGH TO BE HEARD over the rain.

"It's raining," Jamal said.

"Boy, that's just the thing we need to cover our tracks. How you think I found y'all? It wasn't luck. You left a trail a blind man could follow."

George pushed himself onto his haunches, his huge frame diverting part of the curtain of rain penetrating the bush where they hid. Tommy wiped water from his eyes. His sister, Selma, cradled against Victoria.

"Come on, Selma," Victoria said to Jamal's sister, who was whimpering softly. Victoria took Selma by the hand.

His sister was scared. So was he.

George pushed his head through the edge of the bush, and after several seconds pulled himself back. "I don't see anything. Stay close and stay together. No talking."

"Where're we going?" Victoria asked.

"Anywhere but here is where we're going, woman."

"Just asking, asshole."

Even the thick flood falling from the skies couldn't hide the smile on George's face. "Victoria," he said softly, nodding.

"George," she replied.

George was gone, his body through the thick leaves and branches hiding the small space beneath the bush. Victoria and Selma followed with Jamal behind them. No way he was going to be left behind.

The jungle looked different in the rain. It was always hard to see far in the tangle of bushes, trees, vines, and vegetation that weaved its carpet across this part of the world, but the afternoon rains isolated him as if he was in his own curtained world. It didn't seem to him they were moving fast. The blurred figures of Selma and Victoria marked the path a few feet in front of him.

"Here!" a voice shouted from the left.

Jamal nearly bumped into Selma as the group stopped. Ahead, he could see George's hand motioning them down. He squatted, raising his rifle.

"Clear, my friend!" called another voice.

"We can't see anything in this rain."

"A trail led this way. Whoever ran this way was part of the infidels we killed. They're here somewhere."

Jamal recognized the accents as Liberian, speaking that familiar clipped, singsong English used as the common language throughout this African nation.

A third voice replied, "Why don't you two just tell them we're out here and be done with it."

The rain smothered a muffled grumble and the voices disappeared. They were looking for them. Jamal glanced ahead at George. Only a few hours ago they had been riding in an SUV heading to safety. Then, he had disliked this man. He was uncouth and whined about everything. The tart exchanges between Victoria and George had done little to convince Jamal the man was to be trusted, but here they were following him, depending on him to lead them to safety. Jamal looked back the way they came, expecting at any moment to see those chasing them jump out of the bushes and through the curtain of rain. It's amazing, he thought, how George's character changed when events shuffled the deck of leadership.

George reached over, gripped Victoria lightly by her shoulder, and turned her to the left. He nodded and gave her a slight push. Victoria pushed through the bramble along the edges of the trail and quickly disappeared from sight. George stared at

Jamal questionably and jerked his thumb toward the point where Victoria and Selma had disappeared.

Jamal scrambled forward to where George squatted. The man leaned down and said softly, "Boy, you stay with them. Keep going the same direction I pointed. The Centos River is out there. I hope that they've sent rescue. If they ain't, then you get across it and make your way to Kingsville." The sound of voices reached their ears. George paused and looked in the direction of the voices. The big man reached out and pushed Jamal, causing him to fall onto a knee. "Go, boy! I'll be along."

Jamal pulled himself up about the same time George gave him another shove, sending Jamal tumbling into the brambles, causing him to trip, and nearly fall. Ahead, he caught sight of Selma's dress. They were only ten to fifteen feet ahead, but vines, interwoven among the larger vegetation and trees, created barriers upon barriers. The heavy rain hid the noise they were making as they scrambled away. He ran to catch them. His foot caught on a tree root across the path, tripping him. He fell, losing his grip on his rifle. It took a couple of seconds to recover the weapon. A couple of minutes later, Jamal caught up with them. His breath came in quick, deep gasps.

Gunfire rode over the noise of the rain. Shouts in one of the guttural African dialects—*Jamal had yet to figure out how to tell one dialect from another when they all sounded so much alike.*

Victoria dropped to her knees, pulling Selma to the ground with her. Jamal squatted on his haunches, his rifle pointed back the way they had come. They had stopped in a small clearing about six feet long and a couple feet wide. Bushes about six feet high surrounded them and from where they had entered the clearing, the leaves had closed, hiding the path.

Shouts, this time in English, but too garbled by the rainfall for him to understand. He could tell it wasn't George shouting. Jamal had no idea if that was good or bad. If he heard George, then it meant the man was alive. If he didn't, did it mean George was dead, hiding, or sneaking up on those bastards?

Then, as suddenly as it had begun, the rain stopped, and like a flash, the jungle reappeared, colors exploding around them. If he was lost before, the enormity of their situation became even more apparent with the stopping of the rain. The late afternoon downpour had saved their lives. Jamal shook, realizing for a moment that if the rain had started later, those men would have found them as easily as George did. They could have stuck their guns into the bush and killed them without ever seeing who they were shooting.

The sound of running footsteps caused him to grip the rifle tighter. His finger was on the trigger. His shaking was causing the rifle to shake. Tears trickled along his cheeks, making him angry that he was so scared. Someone was crashing through the bushes toward them. Running, tripping, jumping up, and running again. Probably George, he hoped, hurrying to catch up with them, but he aimed his rifle where he thought George would appear, and tightened his finger on the trigger, telling himself not to shoot—not to shoot. He mumbled once, "Don't shoot."

Suddenly, an African burst through the curtain of vegetation, seeing Jamal at the same time as he saw him. The man raised his automatic weapon. Jamal pulled the trigger, never shutting his eyes. Behind him, Victoria shouted, drawing the attention of their attacker a fraction of a second before the two fired. Selma's screams joined the sound of the two weapons. As the rifle fired, Jamal heard the sounds of another person running through the jungle toward them. The warm feel of urine ran down his wet pants leg.

CHAPTER 6

THE ENGINE NOISE OF THE FRENCH DAUPHIN HELICOPTER forced Dick Holman, his Chief of Staff—Captain Leo Upmann, and the Amphibious Group Two intelligence officer, Mary Davidson, to put their heads close together, nearly touching, when they talked. Holman had one side of the earmuffs lifted so he could hear Upmann's shouted words. The gray earmuffs reduced the decibel assault from the engines, but obscured conversation unless you read sign or lips. Holman raised his hand between him and his Chief of Staff. He slipped the earmuff back down, shut his eyes, and leaned his head against the heavy tarp that covered the inside of the French helicopter. Fifty miles wasn't that far, but over the ocean it seemed forever. He failed to understand the French insistence on keeping a minimum separation of—*what did they say? Eighty kilometers?* Fifty miles wasn't quite eighty kilometers, but the French were still new at aircraft carrier operations, and he attributed this distance between the battle groups to their fear of colliding with his ships. Must be true for their aircraft carriers as it was for his; *aircraft carriers maneuver, all others avoid.*

Upmann was still bitching and moaning over orders received two days ago detaching the USS *Nassau*, USS *Belleau*

Wood, the auxiliary ship USS *Concord,* and their most modern warship the DD-21-class USS *Stribling.* Watching them turn back and disappear over the horizon had effectively reduced mission options for Holman's amphibious task force. He still had the Marines on board his command ship, the amphibious carrier USS *Boxer.* For escorts, European Command left him the aging destroyer USS *Spruance,* the Aegis-class cruiser USS *Hue City,* and the even more ancient civilian-manned oiler USNS *Mispellion.* The *Mispellion* would probably fall apart if anyone ever sanded the rust off her.

Of course, Upmann wasn't the only one upset over the unexpected reduction in force. Dick had gotten his ass in a sling over it. Twelve hours ago, he went over the head of the Air Force general commanding European Command. He had called the Chief of Naval Operations, who was also a member of the Joint Chiefs of Staff. He had appealed to Admiral Gianti, and asked for his intervention. He should know after all these years that no good deed goes unpunished. But he had to try. If he didn't, and something happened, he would fail in his job by not fighting for more ships, Marines, and firepower.

Dick shook his head slightly. His bosses could have left him with the more modern warships. By God, give him enough forces so he could respond to any mission creep Washington threw at him. What if he was forced to go into Liberia and conduct a combat evacuation? Granted, he still had 1200 Marines, and that was probably enough not only to liberate but conquer Liberia. The challenge wasn't evacuating the Americans in this *gone-to-hell* country, but in finding all of them. The bulk of the American Embassy personnel had fled to Sierra Leone. He would have appreciated someone in authority telling him why they reduced the size of his force. Instead, the explanation they threw at him was that they only wanted to send what was needed for the mission.

The handset he used to talk with the Chief of Naval Operations, Admiral Gianti, was still warm when General Derek Scott, Deputy Commander, European Command, discovered the telephone call. It seemed hotter after he hung up. The Army deputy spoke as plainly as Holman recalled, but of course the Army had little use for small talk. The most im-

portant part of the conversation hid the reason for the small
U.S. force heading toward Liberia.

He wondered if General Scott even knew he had said it. It
was right after the Army general finished chewing him out
about *"phoning home"* instead of going through the proper
chain of command, which was going to the European Command located in Germany. The Army deputy believed he had
to remind Holman one more time. "You are now a Joint Task
Force—Joint Task Force Liberia—under the command of
General Sidney Shane. European Command; not Northern
Command nor the Pentagon. Your orders are to evacuate
Americans and any other friendly citizens from the civil war
in Liberia, and while doing this mission, you are to avoid
entanglement."

"Yes, sir. I understand, General," Dick had replied to the
three-star deputy. "But until two days ago I had a force that
could have taken Africa if I had been ordered. Today—"

"Today, Admiral, you have a force that is tailored to do the
mission at hand, which is bring out our citizens, and at the
same time not threaten American relations with our European
allies."

The last comment caused Dick to raise his eyebrows. "Sir,
I don't understand how rescuing our citizens and our allies'
citizens threaten America's relationship with our European allies."

After several seconds of silence, General Scott said,
"France is especially concerned about our involvement in Africa. That being said, Admiral Holman, you're not expected to
understand the politics about this mission. Yours is but to do—"

"—and die. I know the quote, General, but if I'm to do this
mission effectively, then I need to know everything that affects
it. I don't understand how rescuing American citizens affects
anyone other than us. General, does the fact that a French
Navy force is approaching us from the north have anything to
do with your comments? We expect to rendezvous with them
by noon tomorrow, and my intelligence officer tells me they
have two carriers with them. You know I have none?"

There had been a pause on the other end; a pause so long
that finally Dick had asked, "Are you still there, General."

"Yeah, I'm still here. They've been in contact with you?"

"Of course. They're our ally, aren't they?"

"Well, yes. Most certainly. I was just surprised to hear they were coordinating with you. You know the Administration needs the French influence in the Middle East to ensure our Israeli-Palestine peace initiative works?"

"That's like inviting your mother-in-law to settle an argument between you and your wife."

"Are you coordinating operations with the French?"

"I didn't say we were coordinating, General. When I found out they were heading our way, I contacted them. I assumed they were as concerned as we are about events in Liberia. And knowing the number of French citizens and military they have in the nearby Ivory Coast, I knew that they would be just as concerned about the civil war filtering over into it as we are. Admiral Colbert has invited me to visit the French aircraft carrier *Charles de Gaulle*. So, I intend to, and once we've worked out operation areas, maybe we'll establish some sort of Coalition Wide Area Network—CWAN—so we can share data in a secure mode."

After a few seconds 'pause, Deputy Commander, European Command had continued in an ominous tone. "Admiral, be careful. We don't know why the French are sending such a large battle force down that way. But we are sure that they— the French government—are adamantly opposed to us 'invading'—*their word not mine*—Liberia. They've been major political opponents over us going into Liberia, even raising the issue in Brussels at both NATO headquarters as well as the European Union Court."

Dick had shook his head. "General, I've been invited to visit with Admiral Colbert. My mission is not to invade Liberia; just evacuate our citizens. I am sure Admiral Colbert understands that," Holman said, and then after a short pause when the general didn't jump in with an answer, he added, "Shit, General. Even a fresh lieutenant with a little salt water behind his ears can tell that with only three warships and one auxiliary vessel, we aren't an invasion force. We are barely a rescue force. And if anything goes wrong, we're going to be in deep *kempshi*." *Kempshi* was a spicy Korean dish made from cabbage and similar to sauerkraut, with the exception that it was fermented until nearly rancid.

"Exactly, Dick, and that is one of the reasons the Joint Chiefs have reduced the size of your force. You don't need them for an evacuation. Different subject: Henri Colbert. I've met him, Dick," the Deputy of European Command said. "He's not a friend of the United States."

Dick felt a push against his shoulder, bringing his thoughts back to where they were—on a French helicopter heading toward the French aircraft carrier *Charles de Gaulle*.

"Admiral," Captain Mary Davidson said.

He mouthed the word "yes" over the noise.

She leaned forward, pulled the earpiece of the sound muff away from his right ear, and shouted, "Have you looked out the window?"

He shook his head and turned to share the small double-paned window with her. Below sailed the two aircraft carriers of the French Navy—the FN *Charles de Gaulle* and the FN *Richelieu,* surrounded by four cruisers, several destroyers, and a couple of smaller ships—probably coastal frigates. Damn! Made his own small force of four ships look like a coastal navy. Holman pressed his face closer to the concave-shaped window, trying to spot the oiler or supply ships that a battle group this size would need. After a few seconds, he pulled back. Colbert must have them behind the battle group, or they are on the other side of the helicopter. Logistics ships sailing far to the rear was a protective tactic for a battle group expecting to fight.

"Impressive!" he said as he pulled back.

"Too impressive," Mary replied.

He raised his eyebrows questioningly. The thing about intelligence officers was their propensity for seeing conspiracies in everything and everywhere. Sometimes, they were right. Most times, they just made their bosses paranoid.

"No amphibious ships, sir. If they're here to evacuate their citizens or to go in and restore order, they would have amphibious units with them. Amphibious units loaded with French Marines, Army, or Foreign Legion elements."

He turned back to the window. She was right. This Naval force was designed to fight a war at sea, though the airpower the two French carriers brought could project power ashore. But you didn't win land battles through air and naval power. You won them by putting armies and Marines ashore. Same with evacuations. You needed those grunts with their handheld weapons. He glanced at Upmann, who had listened to the exchange.

"Leo, your thoughts?" he shouted.

Upmann shook his head. "They don't need to bring amphibious units when they have more than enough ground forces in Ivory Coast. All they have to do is motor across the border, drive up the coast or the main highway that runs across the center of Liberia, and *voila,* twenty-four hours later Liberia becomes a member of the francophone fan club."

Holman turned back to Captain Davidson. "Mary, you hear that?"

She nodded. "Not all of it, but enough to get the gist."

"What do you think?"

She shrugged her shoulders.

Upmann's analysis satisfied him. He looked back through the window as the helicopter turned, watching the ships pass slowly across his field of vision. He pulled back when the helicopter steadied up on its approach course. Holman leaned back and shut his eyes. Not one oiler or supply ship or ammunition ship had passed beneath them during the turn. Where were they? Why weren't they with the battle group? He twitched in his seat. Something made him uncomfortable about this French show of strength. Why would the French send so much power south in a crisis that was more of an American interest than theirs? Were they this concerned about their own people in the Ivory Coast?

IN WASHINGTON, WHILE HOLMAN AND HIS TWO DEPUTIES made their approach to the French aircraft carrier *Charles De Gaulle,* the Secretary of Defense, Addison Maltby, had just hung up with the President's National Security Advisor, Mattingly Elkhammer. Addison turned his chair around so he could look out across the north parking lot of the Pentagon toward Boundary Channel. After a few seconds, he nodded, resting his head on clasped hands. Addison hoped Mattingly

passed on to the President his recommendation to tell Admiral
Holman what his rules of engagement were. Without rules of
engagement, the decision to release weapons fell to the senior
officer in command. While this Admiral Holman had a good
reputation for keeping a cool head under fire, Addison had his
doubts about this hidden strategy of keeping the man in the
dark. He turned slightly so he could pick up the TOP SECRET
folder on his desk. Since 9/11, the CIA had been a *"turning
and burning"* organization, developing biographies and back-
grounds on allies and enemies alike. He opened it and stared
at the photograph of Admiral Henri Colbert. This French Navy
officer had been specifically chosen to lead this French Naval
force. Why? Everything in this profile showed a man who was
hotheaded; never asked for nor accepted higher-authority guidance; and most of all, viewed America more as a threat to
French hegemony than Islamic extremists.

That liberal juggernaut at State had managed to convince
the President that turning back the bulk of the U.S. Naval force
would show our European allies that the mission of Joint Task
Force Liberia was strictly defensive. A noncombatant evacuation mission, not designed to widen the global war on terrorism. He shut the folder. True—Washington needed the French
military and political influence to firm up a breakthrough to a
peaceful resolution to the decades-old Israeli-Palestinian issue.
If peace broke out in the volatile Middle East area, then it
would isolate the radical Islamic movements in most of the
Arab countries. It would also move America's thirteenth year
of the global war on terrorism closer to victory—if victory
could ever be achieved. The buzzer broke through his reverie.
Addison tossed the folder back on his desk, where sometime
after he departed late tonight a security officer would *"magi-
cally appear"* and retrieve it. The door opened. His executive
aide stuck her head inside and announced the first of numerous
meetings scheduled for today. Addison looked at his watch—
seven A.M. Everything ran on time in the Pentagon and time
was determined by him.

THE HELICOPTER BANKED RIGHT AND STARTED A STEEP DE-
scent toward the flight deck of the FN *Charles de Gaulle*. Even

through his anxiety at trying to fill in the blanks that European
Command and the disposition of the French battle group had
opened, Holman was looking forward to the visit. He had
never been aboard either of the French carriers, and while they
were slightly smaller than any of the eight American aircraft
carriers, they still wielded a lot of airpower. Enough to eclipse
every nation but America. They carried two long-range surveillance EC-2 Hawkeye aircraft purchased from America.
Both French carriers had two catapults. An American aircraft
carrier had four. Even with two, they could launch two Super
Etendard fighter aircraft every thirty seconds. They carried
forty fighters to an American aircraft carrier's eighty. Without
that American aircraft carrier, the French controlled the seas
around this part of Africa. *Damn good thing they're our allies.*

A couple of minutes later, the wheels touched down on the
deck of the French nuclear-powered carrier. The turbine noise
from the helicopter engines wound down as power to the rotors
decreased. They were on board the command ship of the
French battle group. Both Davidson and Upmann were aware
of his conversation with the Deputy, European Command, and
like him, had more questions than answers as to why the amphibious task force had been downsized. The rationale that
they had been shaped for the mission just didn't hold water.

A tall French Navy officer stood regally a few feet away
from the edge of the slowing rotors as Holman, Upmann, and
Davidson stepped down from the helicopter. Holman moved
forward, hunched over, to avoid the rotors. No one walked
upright beneath revolving helicopter rotors—not unless being
tall was a major concern. The French officer rendered a sharp
salute as he approached. Holman returned it, and immediately
grasped the Navy officer's hand. The shoulder epaulets on the
white uniform identified the Frenchman as a captain. Three
other officers standing slightly behind the French captain
dropped their salutes.

"Admiral Holman, welcome to the *Charles de Gaulle*. I am
Captain Marc St. Cyr," the man said in flawless English and
with only a slight Gallic accent.

"Thank you, Captain."

"Sir, if you and your officers will follow me, we will go to
the wardroom for discussions." Without waiting for a response,

St. Cyr did an about-face and led the way toward the forecastle of the ship.

One thing about warships of our European allies, thought Holman as he followed the lanky Frenchman, they were all a lighter gray than American warships. The other thing was they served wine with their meals and brandy after dinner. No wonder the U.S. Navy always insisted on having at-sea conferences on their ships.

French warships had their numbers painted amidships, while American warships' numbers were painted along each side of the bow. The names of every warship, including American warships, were painted across the stern. *Maybe so you could tell who was running.*

A junior French Navy officer brought up the rear. They crossed the threshold of the hatch into the skin of the ship and out of the bright sunlight of the African sky. The junior officer turned, rotated the locking mechanism of the hatch, and sealed the interior from the smell of aviation fuel and the heat of the day. The air-conditioning quickly dispelled the heat, and the noisy ventilation cleared the air. The *Charles de Gaulle* had come a long way from its first two or three years of service when it kept breaking down and suffering the humiliation of being towed into most of the ports it visited. The French were the first nation other than the United States to build aircraft carriers capable of launching and recovering high-performance aircraft since World War II. Other than the United States, France was the only nation possessing a formidable at-sea airpower capability. China had yet to complete its second aircraft carrier. Its first had never deployed out of its coastal waters and had yet to launch its first aircraft while under way.

The French were ecstatic over the military victories in Somalia back in '07 when the only fighter aircraft capability originated over the horizon from the decks of these two carriers. French morale and prestige had soared. In the shipyards of Marseilles, the keels for two additional French nuclear aircraft carriers had been laid last year. Holman recalled that along with morale and prestige, their arrogance had soared, which shocked everyone since no one believed that it could have gotten any higher.

"This way, Admiral," St. Cyr said, motioning toward the ladder leading upward.

Two decks and several passageways later, they were led into a huge wardroom. Two long tables bolted to the deck and covered with satin tablecloths occupied the center of the compartment. A meter-wide bar ran along the forward bulkhead with a coffee machine—*never visited a Navy ship that didn't have ready coffee for anytime of the day,* thought Holman— and numerous drawers beneath it. He assumed they held the various utensils for feeding the officers. On the starboard side of the wardroom was a television, a couple of leather couches, a few matching armchairs, and a scattering of small tables with lamps on them. The pastel paint seemed at odds with the light gray of Navy life, but he could see where this room would bubble during the evening when the day's work at sea eased. It was easy to see that this was the main wardroom for the officers.

It was where meals were served. It definitely wasn't like any flag wardroom he had visited on allied ships. Even on the USS *Boxer,* he had a smaller wardroom to entertain senior visitors and conduct business. Wonder why they brought them here instead of the flag wardroom befitting a senior officer. "Would the admiral like some coffee?" St. Cyr asked, nodding toward the coffee machine.

"Thanks, Captain," Holman said, and as St. Cyr motioned one of the officers to take care of the request, he continued. "It was nice of Admiral Colbert to invite us to visit. I think between the two of our Naval forces, we will be able to evacuate our citizens with little trouble." Dick looked around the room, expecting the French admiral to appear any moment. He knew from experience that managing a battle group could cause Admiral Colbert to be so wrapped up in circumstances that he would be forced to send a captain to meet a fellow admiral. He watched as Captain St. Cyr directed the officers in preparing the coffee. Personally, he would have either had the visiting admiral brought directly to where he was, or would have appeared as soon as possible professing apologies and such. At a minimum, he would have had the VIP taken to his personal wardroom. Maritime tradition between warriors of the sea was very traditional and circumspect. While Holman didn't hold much credence with rank and its trappings, he did recognize when it was missing.

A lanky French lieutenant placed three cups along one side of the table.

"If the admiral would be so kind and have a seat, we can begin our discussions."

What! Dick's eyebrows raised at the suggestion. He turned and glanced at Upmann, who rolled his eyes slightly, indicating he didn't know what was going on either.

"Shouldn't we wait for Admiral Colbert, Captain?"

The man shook his head, his lower lip pushing the upper up. "The admiral is extremely busy and sends his regrets. He will be unable to attend, Admiral. He has asked that I deliver the restrictions and ensure you understand the limitations on what we will permit the American task force."

It must be a language snafu, he thought. *This Frog couldn't have said what I thought I heard.* Limitations? No one limited the United States Navy. Not in the past, not now, and not in the future.

"Excuse me, Captain. I may have misunderstood what you meant."

Upmann took a step closer to Holman's left.

"I assure you, sir. My English is impeccable. I was an exchange officer at your Industrial College of the Armed Forces years ago, and had a tour at our embassy in Washington as the deputy military attaché. My words have been carefully chosen," St. Cyr replied, his face expressionless. It was as if the French officer had relaxed the muscles in his face with the exception of those needed to speak. His eyes met Dick's without wavering.

"Then, I doubt that we have anything to discuss, Captain," Holman said, his voice calm through his anger.

St. Cyr tilted his head to the left and jerked back slightly. Not much, but enough for Holman to know the refusal to begin discussions was unexpected. If he couldn't deliver—what? What was the man going to say? Deliver some sort of ultimatum?

St. Cyr started to say something. Holman held up his hand. "Go get Admiral Colbert, Captain. Tell him that Admiral Dick

Holman of the American Joint Task Force Liberia is here to see him."

If Holman refused to listen to Captain St. Cyr, then the captain would have to go fetch Colbert. St. Cyr would have to tell him he was unable to execute his orders. Nothing bothered Navy officers and chiefs more than being unable to complete an assigned task. The difference was that chiefs usually found a way around stupid orders. Officers tended to execute them.

When several seconds passed and St. Cyr stood without moving, Dick turned to his Chief of Staff. "Captain Upmann, work with Captain St. Cyr to arrange our immediate return to the USS *Boxer*."

Upmann nodded curtly. "With pleasure, Admiral."

Holman walked past the French captain to the empty lounge area and took a seat in one of the leather chairs. *Screw them.* It wasn't just *him* these French bastards were shoveling shit at, it was the United States Navy and the United States itself. That was what he represented. It was what military officers of every nation represented. They were their nation, and the traditions of respect at the lower ranks permeated upward as signs of solidarity or dissolution. The failure of the French admiral to pay his respects to his allied counterpart, and further, to leave that counterpart in the hands of a subordinate, was a display of diplomatic contempt. A display no self-respecting American military officer could allow, for it was a snub against the United States of America. He wanted off this despicable ship as soon as possible. For a fleeting moment, he wondered what they would do if the French refused to allow them to leave. He mentally shook his head. Even the French wouldn't be that foolish.

He tuned to the conversation between Upmann and St. Cyr. Either one of two things would happen. One, St. Cyr would take the incident to the admiral and Colbert would appear; or two, their transportation back to the USS *Boxer* would be arranged shortly. He refused to consider the third alternative.

The wardroom door slammed. Holman turned slightly and saw that St. Cyr had disappeared. *Probably gone to throw himself over the side or shake his admiral into action.* Upmann and Davidson walked toward him. The French lieutenant who had operated the coffee machine and set the coffee cups started across with them, but Upmann shook his head and motioned the man away. "Thank you, Lieutenant, but we would prefer some privacy."

Holman stayed seated. He wanted to stand, but right now, actions spoke louder than words. Arrogant wasn't in his vocabulary, but the French were good teachers. He had to act the part of the senior American Navy officer. Play and beat the French at their own game of arrogance and pomp, which was hard for an American to do. Come to think of it, not many nationalities had the centuries of experience in those areas as the French. *They did put the r in arrogance,* whatever that means.

"I think he's gone to talk with his admiral," Upmann said softly. He leaned closer. "What's going on?" His eyes shifted toward the three French officers watching from across the compartment, whispering among themselves.

Dick nearly shrugged his shoulders, but stopped himself in time. "I'm not sure, Leo. Mary, what do you think?"

"I believe what we are seeing is the French flexing their muscles because they believe we are intruding into what they feel is their sphere of influence."

"Because we want to evacuate our citizens?" Dick asked incredulously. "How can they confuse a noncombatant evacuation operation—*NEO,* with us expanding influence into a continent that has more failed states than the rest of the world combined?"

She shook her head. "Admiral, they know something we don't and that we should."

For a brief second, Holman mulled over the conversation with General Scott, Deputy, European Command. The man had warned him about the French, but said nothing about why they were sending a two-carrier battle group here or what he should be worried about. He just assumed that like so many times in the past, the French were here to help evacuate civilians from the civil war erupting in Liberia. It wouldn't be the first time the U.S. worked hand-in-glove with the French. In the early 1990's, he recalled, the French and Americans had worked closely in sharing information about North Africa. A relationship that had decayed significantly by the time Islamic fundamentalists had tried to overthrow the Arab countries of North Africa and combine them into one fanatical Islamic state. Then, America and Britain had had to go it alone, with the French coming in afterward. The one country that responded unilaterally without asking anyone's permission had been Spain, which invaded Morocco, kicking ass, and marched across Algeria to protect vital oil pipelines. Two years since that crisis and the third Korean War. Eleven years since the war in Afghanistan when this same French carrier sailed alongside American aircraft carriers to destroy the government and non-government organization that had attacked America on September 11, 2001.

"Leo, Mary; I want us to be able to sidestep this faux pas if that is what it is. If the admiral shows, let me lead, but be prepared for us to ask for transportation back to our battle group."

"Battle group? Thought we were just an amphibious task force going in to conduct a NEO."

"Joint task force," corrected Upmann.

"You're right, Mary. But a battle group sounds meaner, and we need to ensure they understand that we will not accept limitations imposed by anyone other than our own leaders."

"As if that isn't enough."

The wardroom door opened and Captain St. Cyr appeared. He walked purposefully toward Admiral Holman. The other three French officers joined him. He stopped near the chair. "Sir, Admiral Colbert says he is prepared to see you now. If you will follow me—"

"Sorry, Captain," he said, smiling. He gripped his right thigh and squeezed it several times. "Bad leg and all that, you know. Since we are all right here, I am sure Admiral Colbert won't mind coming here for our discussions." Dick bit his lower lip. Now, was that a tinge of fear spinning across St. Cyr's countenance, or shock from being told no by an American admiral? He forced down an urge to chuckle.

"I'm sorry, sir. I did not realize your medical condition, but Admiral Colbert is very busy and it would be most kind if you could accompany me to where he is working. We will take it slow."

Holman leaned forward, rubbing his leg a couple of more times. "And where might that be?"

"Sir?"

"I said, where might the admiral be working?"

"Sir, Admiral Colbert says he will meet you in his wardroom. . . ."

Holman leaned back. "Then, I am sure he can come here much easier than I can go there."

"But—"

"On the other hand, Captain St. Cyr, we were unaware of the high tempo of operations distracting you from our visit, so why don't we arrange for us to leave and next time we will offer Admiral Colbert the comforts of the USS *Boxer*? I'm sure we can afford him similar hospitality."

He shouldn't be but—*damn it,* he was enjoying this, in a perverse sort of way. Nothing knocks a hole in smugness more than innocent-sounding jabs that twist and turn until they find an opening. This St. Cyr had his ass in a sling. If the French captain failed to deliver Holman to Colbert, the French admiral would chew up and spit out St. Cyr when he returned with Holman's ultimatum. They both knew the truth. St. Cyr had no authority over Holman, Upmann, and Davidson. And he had even less authority over Colbert. All the French officer could hope for was to cajole or browbeat them into following his directions. The browbeating approach had already failed.

"But, sir, I assure you, the admiral would be most grateful if you . . ."

Holman grinned at the man's obvious discomfort. He wished he could reach around and pat himself on the back. The cajoling of St. Cyr was music to his ears. Ought to be a song about cajoling.

". . . could find the energy to accompany me. And I would be most grateful, Admiral."

Ouch! That must have hurt. However, Holman didn't start this charade, but he sure as hell was going to play it to the end. The prestige of the United States Navy and the United States itself rested on small diplomatic challenges such as this.

"I sure would like to, Captain, and I know how challenging it is to lead a two-carrier battle group. I have lead smaller battle groups such as this one several times. Luckily, I have been blessed with great captains, such as Captain Upmann and Captain Davidson, who are able to do day-to-day operations and free me for entertaining my allied counterparts." *There! Put that in your pipe and smoke it, asshole!* St. Cyr didn't know that Davidson was an intelligence officer and would be hard put to know the difference between battle group steaming, independent steaming, and tied up to port. Well, maybe the lines over the sides would give her a clue.

"Yes, *L'amiral,*" St. Cyr continued. "Admiral Colbert is also blessed with many capable captains, but he has seen fit to become intimately involved in operations to ensure we execute our assigned mission as ordered."

Holman saw his chance, and from the expression that crossed Davidson's face, he knew she had also.

"And what are those orders, if I may ask?" Davidson asked.

St. Cyr opened his mouth to reply, then thought for a second before answering, "I think Admiral Colbert might be the best person to answer that, Captain Davidson. If you would follow me, you may ask him directly."

"You have me confused, Captain St. Cyr," Mary Davidson continued. "Only a minute ago, you were going to sit us down and tell us what our limitations were—"

"I may have used the wrong word," St. Cyr interrupted.

"—and if you were going to tell us our limitations, then obviously that dovetailed nicely with your mission. Since you felt empowered to lay limitations on an American battle group, then you must have authority to take action if we violate those limitations."

St. Cyr raised his hand at her and looked at Admiral Holman. "Admiral, my apologies, sir. It seems I have inadvertently offended you. It was not my intention."

"I understand, Captain. Tell you what I am prepared to do so we can move forward. We'll wait here for another few minutes while you arrange our transportation back to our battle group. Okay?"

Was that a bead of sweat across the French captain's brow? Damn, what a shame!

St. Cyr started to speak, stopped, and then finally said, "Sir, if you will excuse me, I will go speak to Admiral Colbert and see how long he will be, sir. I know he would not wish you to leave with a false impression."

"I'm sure I don't know what you mean, Captain. If the admiral is too busy, I fully understand. It was hard to rearrange my own duties to come here as a courtesy to Admiral Colbert. We can always arrange another meeting. I would appreciate it if you'd swing by your air boss and have him arrange our return trip. I too have a battle group to lead, and the sooner we return the better."

Captain St. Cyr's eyes seemed to weigh Admiral Holman, the Frenchman's pencil-thin mustache outlining his upper lip appearing to vibrate. Finally, St. Cyr sighed. "*Mais oui*, Admiral. I will go to Admiral Colbert and see if he is able to . . ." The French captain searched for the right words. "—Take time to discuss our terms."

Holman laughed. "Captain, your English accent is flawless, but your choice of words leaves something to be desired."

A questioning look crossed the Frenchman's face.

" 'Terms.' The word 'terms' implies a stronger force telling a weaker force what they can and can't do."

St. Cyr nodded. "Yes, sir, I understand. But . . . we are the stronger force."

Upmann shook his head. "Yeah, you got the ships, but there's more to warfare than having the stronger force."

Holman reached out and lightly toughed Leo's arm. Blood vessels along his Chief of Staff's neck and across his forehead stood out. Holman had seen those marks of anger several times in the two years they had been together. As much as this visit seemed to be heading for the Dumpster, Holman still had a faint hope of salvaging this horrid meeting of two allies. He shook his head slightly at his Chief of Staff. Upmann would have to keep quiet and let him face the situation. A burst of anger would only work against them.

"Captain, we'll be here when you return."

"Admiral, this is Lieutenant Jacques Jean. He will make you comfortable until I return. I apologize for the miscommunications, sir. It was never my intent to upset—how you Americans say—the apple cart. No, sir, not in the least."

The lanky, gray-uniformed officer that St. Cyr pointed out stepped forward, hands clasped behind his back, and nodded.

"Welcome to the *Charles de Gaulle*," Lieutenant Jean said, his accent very heavy. It took Holman a moment to realize what the officer had said.

"With your permission, sir," St. Cyr said, saluting Admiral Holman before turning and leaving the wardroom.

Damn! He must be nervous. He finally saluted.

Holman looked at the French lieutenant standing in front of him. The Frenchman had a grin that stretched across his face, pulling smile lines down from around deep-set eyes that seemed to sparkle. *Here was an officer comfortable with his rank,* thought Holman. But he didn't need the man hovering over them.

"Lieutenant, may we have some coffee?"

A puzzled look crossed the young lieutenant's brow before a smile spread across his face. Jean snapped to attention and said, "Welcome to the *Charles de Gaulle*."

Holman nodded. "Thank you once again. May we have some coffee?"

The man's eyes shifted back and forth. The grin seemed to fade for a moment before it whipped back across the young face. "Welcome to the *Charles de Gaulle*."

"Where the hell did they put the batteries in that guy?" Upmann asked.

Mary Davidson leaned forward and in flawless French asked for coffee. The French lieutenant's eyebrows arched upward, and he responded with a burst of rapid French.

"You speak French, Mary?" he asked.

"I thought I did until he answered my request for coffee."

"Shit," Upmann muttered. He stepped forward, walked around the French officers, and went to the coffee machine installed in the corner of the compartment on top of the shelf.

When he grabbed a cup and stuck it under one of the spigots, the light came on in Lieutenant Jean's head, and he shouted instructions to another junior officer, who quickly took the cup from Leo.

"*Café!*" Lieutenant Jean said. "*Vous voulez figan de café. Une moment.*"

"Somewhere a village is missing an idiot," Upmann mumbled.

Holman motioned Upmann back to his side as the French

officers busied themselves with coffee, arranging the accoutrements on the table. One of them stepped into the back pantry
and emerged with pastries, rearranging the end of the wardroom table. It gave Holman an opportunity to chat briefly with
Upmann and Davidson. For U.S. warships, the unwritten rule
with allies was that Americans visit their ships first—they had
the wine and the beer. The Americans brought the pretzels.

The sea was truly an unforgiving mistress, and at sea all
mariners were brothers; nowadays sisters too. He weighed the
events, anger rising inside him. Not about the slights being
shown, which were sufficient to cause him to be angry, but
realization that his superiors and Washington too, must know
something and were withholding it. Knowing how the military
worked, he decided two things could have caused the Deputy,
European Command to withhold information. One, he had
been ordered not to share it, or two, the deputy had no idea
himself and didn't want to raise concerns where there might
not be any. Either way, someone in his chain of command
knew something that affected Holman's ability to do his mission and they weren't telling him. By God, when he got back
to the *Boxer,* he was going to find out just what in the hell
was going on.

Holman glanced at the three French officers surrounding
the coffee machine. Typical European conference going on
there, he thought, as two of the officers tried to direct the
unwilling third who was operating the machine.

"Mary, tell the lieutenant to forget the coffee. By the time
they figure out how to operate the thing, we'll either be talking
with Admiral Colbert or on our way back to the *Boxer.*"

Coffee was something they didn't need anyway considering
the fifty-mile helicopter flight back to the *Boxer* ahead of them
and no head on the aircraft. The older you got, the less flexible
the bladder.

The door to the wardroom opened and Captain St. Cyr
stood there, holding it open. The three French officers turned
and fell into line for a moment.

Then, Lieutenant Jean leaped forward and took the door
from St. Cyr. Admiral Colbert entered. He was a short man
with a slight paunch, a dark, almost Algerian complexion with
similar-toned eyes shadowed by heavy black eyebrows. The

top of the man's head was completely bald and reflected somewhat the fluorescent light of the compartment. Heavy dark hair ringed the bald spot. Sprinkles of gray near the ears and in long sideburns ran down to the bottom of the earlobes.

Admiral Colbert stopped and stared at Holman, who returned the stare with a nod. Holman looked past Colbert to St. Cyr, who looked directly into Holman's eyes for a moment before breaking eye contact.

For that fraction of a second, Dick saw hostility. Probably lost half his ass having to tell Admiral Colbert to either meet with his American visitors or fly them back to the American force.

Captain St. Cyr pulled out the chair at the head of the wardroom table. Admiral Colbert sat down. He was a stout man. Made Holman think of a football defensive end at first glance. The man the deputy of European Command had warned him about looked nothing like Holman had expected. The French admiral put his hands on the table and pushed away. Holman figured he was about to stand to shake hands, so he stepped forward forcing a smile.

Colbert slid his chair away from the table back sufficiently for him to be able to cross his legs. The man's eyes never left Holman's face. They sparkled briefly, almost as if he knew that the American admiral had misinterpreted his movement.

Several chairs down the table length, Holman pulled a chair out and sat down at the table with Colbert. Everyone else remained standing.

"Admiral Holman," Colbert said. "I had hoped that Captain St. Cyr could answer your questions. I offer my apologies for being unable to spend as much time as you were led to expect, but I am sure you understand from one admiral to another how full our days are." He crossed his arms.

"No, I don't. I don't understand why you invited us to visit if you were too busy to see us. I do understand how the challenges of commanding a battle group formation can be, which is why I have qualified officers under me who are more than capable," Holman said, forcing himself to remain calm. *Who in the hell was this asshole to think he could treat him like this? Moreover, fail to extend even the most common acceptable courtesies to a visiting ally?*

Colbert's lower lip pushed his upper lip upward. His head tilted to the left slightly as he shrugged with his head. "You are right. But of course, you Americans are always right. *N'est pas?*"

"Admiral," Holman said firmly. "I would like me and my officers to be returned to my command ship as soon as possible. I think we have started on the wrong foot. You're very busy and I have many items on my agenda that I need to finish."

Colbert smiled and leaned forward. "Please accept my most humble apologies, Admiral," he said, insincerity dripping from every word. "I do have a message for you, and I am sure it parallels what your government has probably already told you."

Holman hoped his expression didn't reveal his confusion. What in the hell was Colbert talking about? His government? The United States government? No one had told him anything, other than go to Liberia, find the American citizens, and bring them the hell out along with any other foreign citizens who wanted to go. And kill anyone who tried to stop them.

Holman kept quiet. Colbert shrugged and continued. "As you know, Admiral, we are very concerned over America extending its war on terrorism into Africa. We have managed to contain and stabilize North Africa. We, *Europe,* have put the lid on the cauldron your Sixth Fleet stirred up two years ago. Through France's leadership of the European Union, we are working alongside your government to forge a lasting peace in the Middle East between Israel and Palestine. We cannot permit America adventurism into central Africa."

Holman's chin nearly dropped. *What the hell . . .* His eyes narrowed as they met Colbert's stare. "I believe the admiral is mistaken if he thinks we are here to conduct antiterrorist operations in Liberia. We're here to evacuate our citizens and not to become engaged. We will also be evacuating citizens of your country."

To Holman's left, St. Cyr cleared his throat, fleetingly drawing Colbert's attention.

"Admiral, France is considering sending troops from its contingent in Ivory Coast to bring out our citizens. Your offer is noted, but we believe we are able to take care of the few hundred French citizens in Liberia. As for your citizens, we understand there are even less than ours in Liberia."

"We have over two thousand citizens in Liberia, Admiral," Holman replied. "So, from wherever you're getting your numbers, you need to send them back to the calculating table."

Colbert shook his head. "I think, Admiral Holman, of those two thousand, most are Liberian citizens now."

"They still hold American citizenship."

"It is only a sham to give America an excuse to expand your influence into an area that France has served throughout its history!" Colbert shouted.

"Three things, Admiral," Holman replied, his voice low. "One, you're wrong. Two, don't shout at me. I'm not one of your lemon-sucking flunkies. Three, return me to my ship immediately where at least my officers know how to make a proper cup of coffee!"

Holman stood and motioned Upmann and Davidson aside. The French admiral reached forward, grinning, and took a pastry from the table.

CHAPTER 7

AS THE MAN'S HAND CAME DOWN, THE RAISED MACHETE
came with it. The left side of the charging rebel's face had
been replaced by a deep well of bubbling red where Jamal's
bullet had blown it off. The motion of the machete as it came
toward him seemed to slow as the rebel toppled forward.

Jamal jumped, his eyes wide—a startled whimper escaped—
as another figure leaped from the right, slamming into the dying African rebel, knocking the man and the machete into the
brush on the other side of the path.

"You all right, boy?" George asked, pushing himself off
the dead man and brushing debris from his trousers and shirt
as he stood.

Jamal nodded, his throat so tight he couldn't speak. He
started to shake uncontrollably.

George reached over and pulled Jamal to him for a moment
before releasing him. He ran his hand over Jamal's head.
"Don't worry none about it, boy. All men gotta die sometimes.
You just helped him reach his goal. They mostly wanna go to
heaven and talk with Allah. All you did was help arrange the
meeting."

"You're hurt, George," Victoria said.

George looked toward where the rebel had emerged, his

eyes narrowing. "We all gonna be hurt more if we don't move," he said, "They'll be coming. It don't take no rocket scientist to figure out which direction the boy's shot came from. Now, y'all come on." He hefted his gun into the cradle of his left arm.

Jamal noticed the man's right hand wrapped around the base of the M-16, so the finger could slide easily onto the trigger.

"We gotta move and we gotta move fast. We gonna head uphill. There's an old road up there that must have been used decades ago by the lumber people."

"George, how you know all this?" Victoria asked.

Jamal pushed himself up, brushing himself off as he stood. The gun felt heavy. The shaking had stopped, but he wanted to get a move on, like George said. He looked back, expecting rebels to burst through the jungle curtain of vegetation at any moment.

"I thought you're as unfamiliar with this area as we are," Victoria added.

George looked at her and frowned for a moment before a large smile broke across his face.

Jamal reached forward and touched the big man. "I think we should go," he said quietly, his voice shaking.

"Boy, you're right," George answered, then turning to Victoria, he said, "There are some things best left unsaid. Now, come on and let's get the hell out of here."

Victoria grabbed Selma's hand and followed the huge man into the bush, leaving behind the faint animal trail they had been following. They had only gone a few steps when George stopped. "We have to be quiet from here on," he warned, his voice barely audible.

Jamal nodded in agreement, glancing behind him. What if they were out there, waiting to ambush them like they did the cars? He pulled his rifle up, rotating his head to both sides in an attempt to hear anyone sneaking up on them.

"Wait here," George said, "I'll be right back." The man pushed past Victoria and Selma, running his hand over Jamal's head as he passed. "That's it, boy, you keep an eye out and don't shoot me when I come back." Then George disappeared back the way they came.

Several minutes later, the sound of moving brush joined the noise of the rain forest. When the noise stopped, George re-emerged through the brush.

"Okay, they may miss where we got off the trail." He pointed to the hill rising out of the jungle ahead of them. "That hill is more a small mountain. You just can't see the top for the trees," he whispered. "We're going to the top. Up there, the trees thin out and we should find that old road I mentioned. Then, it's just a case of us following it to Kingsville."

"I hope so," Victoria said.

"Me too," Jamal mumbled, licking his lips. His mouth was dry. He licked his lips again. A slight shiver rippled through his body. Vapor rose from his shirt. Looking at the others, he saw the same faint cloud of water moisture rising as the heat baked away the rain from the others' clothing. The heat had returned in force, evaporating the rain as quickly as it had suddenly begun ten minutes ago.

An hour later, Jamal reached down and rubbed his legs. This going uphill was rough. He glanced behind him again. About every four or five steps he did that. He had been watching their rear ever since they left the path. Somewhere out there, rebels or terrorists or whatever were following them. The jungle was too quiet for him and his friends to be the only ones in it. What he didn't understand was why the rebels wanted to kill them. They hadn't done anything. For whatever reason, behind them death followed, and while he had no idea what was ahead, it couldn't be worse than what followed.

At first, trekking uphill had seemed easy. It used other muscles in the legs, but as they moved on—*not stopping to rest*—the muscles in his calves had first tightened, and then begun to hurt. Jamal bit his lower lip slightly. He refused to complain. Selma was doing enough of that for all of them.

A few minutes later, Victoria reached down and picked Selma up. The complaining tapered off after a while.

Jamal put one foot in front of the other. If he kept moving one foot at a time, he could keep up. No hill went up forever. But it sure seemed to him this one did.

*   *   *

"STOP OR I'LL SHOOT!" A VOICE SHOUTED FROM NEARBY.

George and Victoria, with Selma balanced on her side, stopped. They stood perfectly still in the center of the overgrown road. Brown and green grasses bunched around their calves. Jamal waited quietly on the far side of the road from where the warning had originated, near the jungle bramble that marked the edge of the old road. Keeping his head still, he shifted his eyes back and forth, trying to spot the source of the shout. He gripped the barrel of the gun, slowly easing it up.

"Don't be foolish, boy. I could shoot you before you got it up."

"You sound American, so why don't you come out?" George asked.

"Just wanted to make sure you were Americans."

Two overgrown ruts showed where long-ago traffic had once dug holes into the earth. Small three-foot-high trees, thick bushes, and briars grew among the tall grasses alongside the old lumber track. The four had been following the easier path for about twenty minutes.

Jamal thought his legs were going to collapse. Why did the man want to make sure they were Americans? Were they going to kill them? Was this how it was going to end? He looked at Selma, seeing the back of her head. His sister leaned out, her legs around Victoria's waist, hands on the woman's shoulder, and her head whipping back and forth. A whimpering sound reached his ears. Victoria looked down, ran her left hand through the small girl's hair, and muttered soft words.

Jamal couldn't believe this. They had outrun and lost their pursuers. At least, he thought they had. The last noises of pursuit were over two hours ago. Since then, they had kept a steady pace, heading north away from where he had killed the rebel.

Noise of people working their way through the bushes drew everyone's attention. Two men and a young lad about twelve years old stepped out onto the road. They looked like family to Jamal at first glance. The younger man, about mid-thirties, wearing blue jeans, a ball cap, and a light blue long-sleeve shirt with the sleeves rolled up, held a shotgun. His white face, covered with a rough growth of beard, was bright red from exposure to the sun. Dark sweat stains ran down the inside of his shirt.

The older man lowered his shotgun. Narrowed dark eyes scrutinized George, Victoria, Selma, and Jamal. Wrinkles earned from years of work in the sun wrapped the man's face, reminding Jamal of a trash can near his father's desk filled with wadded-up and discarded paper. The man's face reminded him of the wadded paper, only the face was black.

Then, he shook his head. "Ain't them, Joel," the old man said, spitting to the side, brown spittle trailing the chew all the way to the ground. He wiggled, adjusting his overalls slightly before tilting the ball cap back off his forehead. "Naw, ain't seen these two before."

"You sure, Parker?" the one called Joel asked. "You said you didn't get a good look at all of them."

"That may be true, Joel, but I've been around long enough to know the difference between being mean, being scared, and the difference between a man and a woman. Though Artimecy might argue the latter. These four are scared and exhausted, and we're scaring them more." He reached over and pushed the younger man's barrel down. "Lower that shotgun before we have an accident, Cannon."

Victoria eased Selma to the front of her and lowered the girl to the ground. Then, she leaned forward, her hands on her knees, her breath deep and rapid.

Jamal looked at the boy. They were both about the same age. From his skin color, he suspected the boy's mother was either African or African-American. The boy caught Jamal's stares and stared back. Jamal nodded. The boy returned the nod with a slight grin. George took a step toward the three.

"Hold on a minute, bubba. Who are you?" Joel asked, raising his shotgun again.

George straightened up. "I'm George Coleman. This is Victoria. The boy is Jamal and . . . what's yore name, girl?"

"Selma," Jamal said, watching his sister bury her face in Victoria's skirt.

"We're trying to get to Kingsville."

"Ain't we all," the older man said, spitting to the side.

The older man reached over and pushed the boy's single-shot twenty-two rifle down. The boy started to raise it again so it pointed at George, but the old man cocked his head and shook it. "No," he said. "You and yore pa are determined to shoot someone."

He turned to them and said, "I'm Parker Swafford; this is Joel Grayson and his son, Cannon. Sorry we scared you. Maybe you can tell us how you came to be on this old lumber road. It's not like Joel and me see too many visitors this far off the main road." His voice had that crusty sound with that slight vibration that comes with age.

For some reason, Jamal didn't know why, he trusted these people, even if this Joel and the boy Cannon kept pointing their guns at them. Before George or Victoria could answer, and startling himself, Jamal started talking and once he started, the words flowed like a cathartic purge as he told about Monrovia, his parents' death, the SUV, and the ambush. As he talked, Selma's crying punctuated the story.

He stopped as suddenly as he had started. The adrenaline high was gone. He was exhausted. Twice in less than twenty-four hours they had escaped Lord knows what fate.

"Sounds like the same bunch that raided my place this morning," Parker said, directing his comments to Joel, "and who nearly caught you and the family at lunch." He looked at Jamal. "Was there a thin man leading them with his hair covered with a black turban?" He twirled a finger around the top of his head. "Couldn't talk without screaming?"

"We weren't there long enough to tell," George answered. "It's hard to see someone when you're bent over and running for your life."

Victoria reached down and brushed Selma's hair with her hand.

"When they started shooting, we fought our way into the bush. We heard them chasing us through the woods, and after a couple of encounters, we think we lost them. Boy here," George said, jerking his thumb toward Jamal, "killed one of the fanatics before we were able to lose them."

The sound of voices from farther down the road interrupted their conversation. Someone was coming.

"Quick," Joel said, "this way."

They quickly followed the three up the bank on the other side, and into a small open area where the bushes and grasses had been flattened. *"Something big done that,"* Jamal said to himself. And it caused him to look around, searching for whatever had created the clearing and hoping it didn't decide to come back now.

"This is where my daddy and I come to hunt," the young lad whispered.

"Cannon, be quiet," Joel said, placing his finger across his lip.

Jamal squatted on his haunches alongside Victoria, who held Selma close to her, his sister's face buried in the woman's shoulder. *What kind of name is Cannon?* he wondered briefly.

Jamal had a full view of the overgrown road through the bushes. Several minutes passed before two men appeared around the curve in the road. Jamal recognized them. They had been in the convoy.

George leaned forward and touched the old man on the shoulder. "They were with us when the rebels attacked."

Parker nodded, but said nothing as he turned his attention back to the front. When the two stepped in front of the hunting blind, Parker shouted the same thing he had before. Jamal had a moment of satisfaction as one of the men raised one hand while the other threw both of his into the air. The pleasure was short-lived. One of the men appeared to be Hispanic, while the other was obviously an African-American with a light skin complexion. Africans tended to be a dark-rich chocolate black.

"They've got a baby," Victoria said, seeing the small bundle in the crook of an arm. She pushed her way through the bushes into the road. The others followed.

The two men told how they had darted into the jungle when the rebels overran the SUVs.

Victoria eased the baby from the man's arms, while the African-American youth told how the rebels had jerked the infant from its mother before killing her and throwing it by its feet into the bushes.

Victoria ran her finger along the baby's lips. "Something's wrong," she said, looking at the two men.

The larger hispanic man shrugged.

"He or she's been that way since that man in the long

flowing robe threw it into the bushes. I think it hit its head on something," the youth added.

Victoria moved the baby's head slightly, revealing a large dark bruise on the right side. "Yeah, it may have a concussion."

"Well, come on," Parker said. "We need to get a move on. The wives will be waiting, and the longer we're gone the more nervous they're gonna be. I don't like leaving them alone. Not the way things are." He nodded toward the baby. "Artimecy may be able to help the little one." Parker pointed northeast along the road. "They're with the tractor and wagon."

The small group walked along the old jungle road, staying to the ruts. As they walked, Parker's continuous monologue told how rebels had surprised him and his wife around dawn. They had just sat down to eat breakfast when armed pickup trucks sped into the dirt courtyard of their farm. He and Artimecy had barely made it out the window on the far side before the rebels had torn their way through the locked kitchen door. There wasn't much the two of them could do against all of them, plus it wasn't as if he and Artimecy were *spry chickens*. The men had ransacked the house, stealing everything of value. By the time they left and he and Artimecy thought it was safe to come out of hiding, the raiders had taken everything of value, including all the canned food and all but two tins of his 'bacca.

The good news was other than stealing some valuables and taking their food, the looters hadn't came looking for them and they were still alive. Parker discovered afterward that his truck wouldn't crank. When he lifted the hood, he found the distributor cap had been taken and the spark-plug wires cut. What the raiders didn't know was that Parker kept an old shotgun—the one he was carrying—and a box of shells in the back of the barn near the chicken coop. It was to protect the chickens from *all these damn meat-eaters that throw their weight around the jungle at night*. He and Artimecy had walked four miles to where the Graysons lived. By the time they arrived, the raiders had already attacked Joel and his family, and were gone.

Jamal listened as he walked behind Cannon, watching where he put his feet so he didn't trip over the rough ground.

Joel took over the story. He and Mimy were in the metal barn when the first two rebel vehicles arrived. He had nearly walked out to greet them when a bad feeling made him wait in the shadows. The two had watched as the Africans, under their Arab masters, exploded from the pickups, running to the back screen door and kicking it in. He and Mimy had eased deeper into the barn and with Mimy holding his hand, the two had made a dash for the fields in the rear. Hidden by tall corn, they had run along a path that led to where their two cows were pastured and where Cannon was guarding the cows. The family had hidden in a small floodwater cave in a nearby stream bank for a couple of hours, listening for sounds of rebels searching for them. Joel had squatted under the low-hanging entrance with his gun pointed toward the creek. Around here, you never knew when a crocodile might decide to find out why humans were hanging around its home.

After a few hours when they hadn't heard anyone searching for them, Joel had taken Cannon's rifle and crept back to the house to discover the raiders gone. From what had happened, it looked as if these rebels were on a looting expedition and not a killing one. Unfortunately, what they didn't steal, they destroyed—ruining the inside of the house. Even broke the furniture that had been brought from America. All the dishes lay shattered across the kitchen.

Joel had brought Mimy and Cannon back to the barn, leaving them there while he returned to the house. There, he had shoved a bookcase away from the wall to reveal a hidden gun rack. He had been amazed that in their destructive rage the attackers hadn't discovered it.

By the time he left the house, Parker and Artimecy were coming up the driveway. They could not stay there with any hope of protection. Things were breaking down too quickly. They decided their only hope lay in reaching Kingsville, where Thomaston had his armory. The old logging road above the field offered the best escape route.

"Our place is only about seven miles back that way," Joel said, pointing over his shoulder.

As he finished his story, the group turned a curve to find two women waiting beside an old rust-flecked green John Deere tractor. Hitched to the tractor was a homemade trailer.

Two car tires provided the wheels. Heaped on the trailer was fresh corn, a box of canned goods the families had been able to recover, and several gallon plastic containers of water and fuel.

The older woman, who Jamal figured must be Artimecy, ran forward and took the baby from Victoria.

"What's wrong with your child, honey?" she asked.

"Not hers, Artimecy," Parker said, spitting to the side before he quickly told her the story.

Artimecy shook her head. "The baby is dead, Parker." She turned to Victoria. "I'm sorry, honey, but this child is dead."

Selma started crying again, her shoulders heaving, arms straight down by her sides, tears creating small paths down her cheeks through the dust and grime ground into her face. Victoria wrapped Selma in her arms, and the elderly Artimecy stepped forward and stroked Selma's hair, mumbling platitudes that seemed so strange and out of place in a world gone awry.

Jamal stood to one side, his hand resting on the tail of the trailer. His eyes slowly closed and he jerked awake when his legs buckled. Around him the conversation of the grown-ups with words like "Kingsville," "rebels," "long way to go," and "ammunition" broke the gray haze of his fatigue.

Later, the women fed them, giving each a sandwich. His mouth watered uncontrollably when they handed him the sandwich. The bread had dots of green mold on it, but Jamal didn't care. It tasted so good. His stomach growled as he chewed. The gray haze retreated a bit as he chewed each bite slowly, savoring the taste.

His eyes wandered over the people he and his sister depended on for safety. As he ate, the men dug a hole and buried the baby. In the heat, keeping a dead body would have been impossible. He took another bite of the sandwich, and wondered briefly what the baby's name was and if anyone would ever remember where it was buried. He looked at the wonderful sandwich—two bites to go. The sound of a shovel pounding the top of the grave caught his attention. Would the tigers, lions, and wild boars find it? Would they dig it up and eat it?

Jamal noticed the filth on his hands as he shoved the last bit of sandwich into his mouth. He looked at his sister, who had finished her sandwich and was sitting on the end of the trailer with her eyes shut and head across Victoria's lap. How did Momma expect him to protect his sister when he couldn't even protect himself?

He licked his fingers, feeling the grit of the dirt across his tongue as he tried to save a few specks of bread. He pulled himself up beside Victoria and leaned back on the rough planks of the trailer. He laid his rifle beside him, putting his arm along the barrel, and resting his hand near the trigger guard. Jamal shut his eyes, throwing his left arm across them. He vaguely heard the start of the tractor and felt the short jerk on the trailer as the group started, working their way through rebel-infected jungles toward what they prayed was safe refuge.

The rocking motion of the trailer as the wheels rolled over the uneven surface woke him hours later. He opened his eyes. Bright stars dotted a moonless night. The fresh smell of the forest rode the slight humid breeze. Something bit him, causing him to slap instinctively. When he lifted his hand, several dead mosquitoes and a patch of blood smeared his palm. *Selma!* Anxiously, he raised his head. His sister was curled with her legs drawn up to her chest. Her dress stuck to her. There was a tear running down the left side of the dress, from the armpit to near the waist. Parker, Artimecy, Mimy, the two men from the convoy, all of them walked silently behind the wagon. Up front, the silhouette of George and Victoria walking side by side blended with the blacks and grays of the surrounding jungle. Jamal looked for the other boy, but didn't see him. He laid his head back on the trailer and wondered briefly where Cannon was, the question lost when sleep let loose the chasing nightmares to stampede through his dreams.

On the trailer, Jamal's head rolled back and forth accompanied by soft moans.

"No," Artimecy said softly, touching Victoria on the arm. "Let him sleep. He's been through a lot, but he needs his sleep. He'll be all right, honey."

CHAPTER 8

THOMASTON STOOD RAMROD STRAIGHT, HIS FEET AT A forty-five-degree angle. On this small knoll to the right of the front gate, he overlooked the entrance to the armory. The afternoon heat quickly dried the wet from the African shower, turning the dust that permeated the camouflage uniform into small cakes of dirt. The dank smell of sweat—*an acidic urinary smell*—surrounded him as it did everyone. Body odor was the least of their worries. Thomaston reached up and ran the back of his hand across his brow, wiping sweat away from his eyes. Dark wet stains beneath the arms of the camouflage shirt highlighted the effects of the heat. Sharp military creases so well defined two days ago were gone. Sergeant Major Craig Gentle stood beside him with his hands clasped behind his back, rocking slightly on the balls of his heels.

The armory was two years old, built with funds provided by their *unnamed* U.S. government benefactor. Six-foot-high brick walls encircled the main compound. A heavy-duty steel chain-linked fence, embedded in the center of the brick wall, rose to a height of ten feet. Swaths of razor wire spiraled along the top. Anyone foolish enough to climb the fence would face two feet of jutting razor wire, with another two feet of it on the other side.

He was a Ranger and Rangers thought of defensive perimeters, maneuverability, offensive firepower, and who they could kill. The compound was sufficient to deter the most determined bush gang, but he had doubts it would stand up to an attack by a military foe whose desire to kill Americans was so strong, they were prepared to die in the attempt. He would like them to achieve that goal of death.

He sighed.

"You got that right," Gentle said gruffly.

The armory was never designed to withstand a military assault by trained soldiers. Thomaston had doubts as to how long they could hold out in the face of suicide squads. How much longer before Beaucoup Charlie got the radio back up and running?

A ten-ton truck slowed as it passed the two of them, entered through the gate, and circled the roundabout in front of the doors to the two-story brick headquarters building. Large windows, equally spaced, stretched from a couple of feet above the ground to a couple of feet from the next level. One thing about this construction, Thomaston thought, is they definitely intended it to be a showcase—a showcase for the Liberians and other Africans who visited Kingsville. The armory gave Kingsville a show of permanency. There was an intrinsic value in having something better built than any Liberian fort. It brought influence and prestige to the country as well as this American expatriate community.

"Craig, has everyone returned? Have we managed to move everyone inside?" Thomaston asked, turning to retired Sergeant Major Craig Gentle. Thomaston clasped his hands behind his back like Gentle. He rocked slightly back and forth on his heels. His knees bothered him if he stood or sat in one position too long.

"Most are inside," said Gentle. "Beaucoup Charlie and his radio should be along shortly. Tawela and David Seams are helping him."

"We need to get that set up fast and reestablish contact with Admiral Holman as soon as possible. We haven't talked with him or his fleet in two days. He may be heading south toward the port of Abidjan because when we last talked, we told him we were going to convoy into the Ivory Coast. He may be planning on picking us up there." He looked down at Gentle. "You think our embassy bubbas and bubbettes have told them about the closed border?"

The truck doors opened. On the far side nearest the door to the building, David Seams helped Beaucoup down from the high cab.

"Looks as if Beaucoup is here, Dan," Gentle said.

Thomaston glanced at the truck and the people before turning his attention back to the sergeant major. "How about electricity? How long can we expect the generators to last?"

"I'll check on it, sir. We have moved most of the vehicles into the large parking area to the rear of the building. We can always drain their tanks, if need be."

"One thing we both learned in the Army is always plan for the worst and you'll never be disappointed. Here is what I would like for you to do. . . ."

Thomaston rattled off a series of orders borne of experience. All the food was to be consolidated at one location. A responsible person was to be in charge of it. He wanted a water inventory conducted. Retired Master Sergeant Craig Gentle listened for a few moments. When he realized Thomaston had more than a small list of things to do, he pulled a small red notebook from his shirt pocket and began writing.

It was past five in the afternoon. Another five hours before the summer sun set. The air simmered over the dirt road that crossed a few hundred feet from the armory. August was always the month of long, hot days and sweaty nights. Thomaston was anxious. He was unused to not knowing what was happening; being without information; and being without a trained military force. All he had were these few retired military men and women mixed among this ad hoc militia Kingsville had had for its security force. A three-soldier patrol had been gone about two hours. He had sent it north toward the small city of Tapeta to check local conditions and see if certain medical supplies and drugs were available. They were also to bring back loads of toilet tissue—a commodity few think about until they need it. *But wipe that butt with the wrong leaves and you'd find yourself lighting candles to the great god Toilet Tissue.*

The African Wars had taught him a valuable lesson. When

infrastructure breaks down, disease, chaos, and violence follow. Thomaston had directed the pharmacist, who was one of
only two people trained in medicine, to be a member of the
patrol. The other person was a registered nurse.

He hoped he was overreacting. He recalled during his career that most times every operation was overplanned and
overpowering, but there were those few times when that planning saved their lives. Thomaston raised a hand to shield his
eyes and looked south. Anytime now, American helicopters
would appear over the tall rain-forest canopy and take them
out of here. *Was that a prayer?* On the other hand, never
assume anything to be quick and clean. When you plan for the
worst, always plan for the long haul. Look at the Balkans. Fog
of war and all that bullshit. *We will have our troops in the
Balkans for only one year.* He still remembered the laughter
that greeted the President's statement way back then.

When he had been sent to the Balkans, he had been a young
Army captain. Only be there a year, he was told. Of course,
no one on active duty believed it. Twenty-odd years later and
they still had troops on the ground. The only way to remove
ethnic hatred was educate it out. *Look how Muslim madrassas
educate violence in. Children are the keys to social change.*

"Time to do it again, Craig," he said.

The retired sergeant major nodded and shifted his position
to the left side, slightly behind Thomaston. "I'm ready when
you are, sir."

Thomaston stepped off, moving forward with Gentle in step
to his left. He glanced around the outside of the compound.
The tree line to the rear and the two sides was a good hundred
yards away, while the front was off the road that ran through
Kingsville and continued northward toward the main highway.
Anyone approaching the armory would have to come along
that road. The field to the left of the armory was where he
would put tents if too many refugees arrived. There, they
would be close enough to flee inside when the rebels showed
up. What would he do about human waste? If he failed to
address the disposal problem, then the question became not
"if" an epidemic was going to occur, but "when." Typhoid
lurked around every corner when people crowded together and

sanitation was poorly planned. He had seen the enemy typhoid and it was not a pleasant foe.

The two men walked across the road toward two open double gates that swung inward. He needed to establish sentries and impose a schedule for the troops. He had ceased to think of the citizens of Kingsville as anything other than troops. They had to defend themselves until help arrived. If they didn't, then . . . no need to think of it. They all knew what would happen. Right now, there was not one guard on the gate. Anybody could just walk in.

Since he'd been an Army general, everyone believed, or wanted to believe, that he had the answers. Confidence in leadership was an essential ingredient to victory. A nice rush swept across his conscience. He loved this. Damn! He shouldn't, but this was what he was trained to do. This was what he had done before and done well. It reminded him how much he missed the Army and its traditions. Why did life have to be so short? Where in the hell was a band when he needed it?

"Sir?" Gentle asked.

His mind was wandering.

"Sorry, Sergeant Major. I was thinking about other things we need to do," he said, hoping it sounded true.

They passed through the double gates and continued toward the grassy knoll that occupied the center of the roundabout. A white flagpole surrounded by small white rocks stood in the center of the knoll. Thomaston glanced upward. The American flag hung listless slightly higher and alongside the Liberian flag. It was hard to tell the two flags apart when they hung like that. The fifty stars of the American flag and the one star on the Liberia flag were the only difference between the two.

"It is a beautiful sight," Gentle said, following Thomaston's look. "We raised it when we started moving to the armory this afternoon."

"Do we have anyone who can play the bugle?"

Gentle's eyes narrowed for a couple of seconds before he responded, "Yes, sir. Master Chief Seams plays the trumpet."

"See if he knows how to play taps. We'll institute flag ceremonies while we're bivouacked here."

"Bivouacked? I tell you, Boss, most of these people aren't even going to know what bivouacked means, much less how to spell it." Gentle paused a moment. "Come to think of it, I don't know how to spell it, and I can't recall a United States Army operation where we ever bivouacked. We've ambushed. We've tracked. We've even slept in the saddle of our armor; but no, sir, we ain't never bivouacked." He let out a short chuckle.

"You getting awful talkity in your old age, aren't you, Sergeant Major?"

Gentle scrunched his face for a moment, his lips curling outward as if he was sucking a lemon, and then he smiled. "You know, General, it's a horrible thing to say," he said quietly. "But for some perverted reason I'm enjoying this. I shouldn't, but it makes me miss the Army. Damn. I find me looking forward to the battle that is coming and you and I both know it'll come. It's not an 'if.' It's a 'when.' "

Thomaston threw his hand up, acknowledging a group of men and women who were drinking water from a large Coleman's jug set up near the corner of the building.

"What's worse, Sergeant Major, is that I know how you feel. I doubt those who've never served would understand."

Gentle shook his head. "I don't see how they could. I'm not sure I do."

"Maybe we're looking forward to seeing if the skills that kept us alive through so many close calls during our active-duty years are still fit and tuned?" He shook his head. "Damn, Craig." Thomaston needed to provide focus. The last thing these people would tolerate would be him acting as if this was fun.

"With your knees and my back, I kind of doubt we're the same 'fit and tuned' as you say. Plus, there has to be a better way to find out how old you are."

They stepped onto the knoll. Two ancient Civil War cannons contributed by the Frederick, Maryland, Chamber of Commerce flanked the flagpole. Two pyramid stacks of black-painted cannonballs fused together balanced the tableau. A lot of Army history had occurred since Union forces had used these cannons. Now here they were in Africa. Cement plugs filled the barrels of the old artillery pieces. Of course, Frederick had changed hands so many times during the Civil War these could be Confederate cannons. Either way, the gesture had been nice, and it never ceased to amaze him how native Africans would run their hands over the barrels exclaiming in amazement at the fact that the Americans had cannons. Guess if you've never seen them, then they must seem modern.

Tawela Johnson waved from the top steps where she stood watching the working party unload the truck. The trucks were bringing the food and water from the homes and businesses throughout Kingsville. He knew later the part-time residents would scream and holler when they returned to find the doors to their homes broken from when the townspeople were liberating food, water, and arms.

The young woman raised her M-16 and pushed it into the air above her head several times. *Another person anxious for combat with no idea what she was asking for.* He clenched his fist and responded by jerking it skyward a couple of times. A broad smile, revealing white teeth, stretched across her face for a moment before she lowered her weapon. She straightened, standing as tall as her short stature permitted, and saluted with her left hand.

"Don't laugh. At least she is trying," Thomaston said out of the corner of his mouth to Gentle. He returned the wrong-handed salute.

"I believe I have heard that she shoots better than she salutes."

"I hope that's true for all of them. Let's take a look at the rest of the compound, Sergeant Major. We need to see how they've parked the vehicles. We don't want them so close to the building that if they're hit they'll turn it into a firetrap, and we don't want them so close to the fence they prevent us from defending the perimeter."

"There's not many," Gentle said, pointing left of the building. "I had the men drive the smaller vehicles south into the jungle and hide them. That way if we have to make a run for it—"

"Our Army doesn't run."

"That's true, General. But we don't have our Army here. What we've got is a bunch of civilians looking to you—"

"And you."

"—to turn the tide. You can see it in their faces. They believe that because you're here, nothing can defeat us."

"Don't think I don't know that. But what the two of us know, and probably most of these veterans can guess, is that we have little to defend ourselves with except guts, gumption, and a few weapons."

Rounding the corner, Thomaston touched a nearby windowsill as they walked. The windows went completely around the building. Definitely built for show.

The same brick wall, chain-link fence, and razor-wire construction as at the front surrounded the quarter-acre lot behind the building. Thomaston counted five SUVs, a school bus, and five Silverado pickup trucks, along with several personal automobiles.

"Where are the other buses?"

Gentle shook his head. "Not enough room for them. I had them parked at the edge of the jungle and the distributor wires pulled so they couldn't be used."

"You're right, Sergeant Major. I guess as long as we had them, we had a chance to make a run toward the border, but we both know that our only hope now is the Navy fleet headed this way." He looked at his watch and his eyes cast to the south. "They should be off the coast."

"Probably parked for lunch."

Thomaston stopped and stared at the vehicles. Parked so close that to move any but those at the front would cause all of them to have to shift.

"How many militia do you have?"

"Thirty, General. When the two patrols return, that should raise our numbers back to thirty-six. We should also count the men and women who want to fight."

"Oh, yes! They're going to fight. They have their weapons and they're going to have to use them. What we need is to disperse the militia among those who are untrained. When the fight starts, they need to understand they are to respond to our orders without question and without hesitation. Do you have a muster sheet of those inside?"

"No, sir."

"Then make one, Sergeant Major. Have someone start a roster identifying everyone. Names, ages, and addresses. While you're at it, get their next of kin."

"Yes, sir. If you don't mind me asking, General, what are we going to do with this list?"

"If we have to evacuate in a hurry, Sergeant Major, I want a master list with us so we'll know who we have and who we are missing. Assign someone—a teenager—or better yet, get Marge Sweeney to do it and tell her we need it in alphabetical order. If anyone can manage that, she can. And she'll keep it as accurate as she does our accounts at the store." Thomaston paused for a moment. "Yeah, Marge can do it if she don't lose those Coke-bottle glasses of hers."

"And the bad part of this muster is it will help us track the dead and the wounded."

Thomaston waved his hand as if encompassing the compound and the crisis. "All of this is new. To me, and to you," he said, poking himself in the chest and then Gentle. "We were comfortable American expatriates used to conveniences, expecting an American way of life always to be there, and while we never admitted it, enjoying having the Africans fawn over us. Even here . . ." His thoughts faded off.

He looked up for a moment as if expecting to see aircraft crossing overhead, but only a hot sun filled the cloudless sky—not even a contrail disrupted the sea of blue. No aircraft! Usually you could always see a contrail or two as international flights crossed overhead. His eyes narrowed.

No satellites for their communications, no commercial flights visible, and no contact with the United States force that was headed their way. It was as if he and the others in Liberia had dropped off the map. Would the United States allow this large number of Americans to die without trying to rescue them? What if Admiral Holman has been ordered to turn around? It wasn't something Thomaston wanted to think about right now. He reached up and pinched the top of his nose near his eyes, blinking several times. Africa made everyone appreciate air-conditioning. They always say that if you want something bad enough, that's how you get it—*bad*.

"General, you all right, sir?"

Thomaston looked at Gentle and shook his head. "No, Sergeant Major, I don't think I am. I don't think we are." He took a deep breath and sighed. "If the enemy shows up in the next hour, we'd stand a snowball's chance in hell of stopping them. We have a lot to do."

"Begging the general's pardon, I think we are further along than you imagine."

Thomaston punched him gently on the shoulder. "I would never argue with a sergeant major, and I do know we are where we are because of you, Craig."

Tawela Johnson ran around the edge of the building, her M-16 across her chest at port arms.

"Here comes our one-woman army," he said, causing the sergeant major to turn his head.

It always amazed Thomaston when he saw how a small woman like her carried a weapon. But then he recalled the number of women who worked for him during his career who were still marching when bigger, stronger men had fallen out. Of course, there were those lying alongside the road also. Upper body strength helped, but he truly believed tenacity was the real strength of a soldier. *Give me a person with tenacity over someone with intellect any time.*

She stopped abruptly, shifted her weapon to her left hand, and saluted. "General, you better come out front, sir," she said urgently, turning and motioning him to follow.

"What's the matter?" he asked, his pace picking up as he followed her.

"Well, sir . . ."

One of the militiamen, wearing sergeant stripes on crisp, sharp camouflages, appeared at the corner of the building. The beret sat atop a large Afro hairstyle. The sergeant saluted. "General, there's some people out front who just drove up. You may want to talk to them, sir. They be kinda excited right now, but we calming them down. They from the east—*from Monrovia.*"

Thomaston glanced at the name tag—ROOSEVELT. He was good with names. Seldom forgot a name once he had seen it and pronounced it a couple of times. He thanked the sergeant as he and Gentle walked past. Sergeant Roosevelt, automobile mechanic, and Tawela Johnson, waitress and general worker at whatever job was available, fell in behind the two.

*   *   *

ABU ALHAUL LAID THE PAPER PLATE ON THE TABLE, WIPED his mouth with the back of his hand, and belched. The women provided good meals. Abu Alhaul patted his stomach and wiped his hands on the long white robe that reached to his ankle. He never ceased to amaze himself. He was a legend in his own mind. Pulling the water bowl nearer, Abu Alhaul splashed his hands in it, bringing a handful of water to his lips to wash the food particles from his beard and mustache. The near-worship by those around him was his due because he was empowered by Allah to interpret His word. They should watch, wait, and worship his every action. Their lives were his to give in the service of Allah, and he expected those who followed him to be ready to martyr their lives as he dictated. For he also believed their lives were his to take. He pushed himself up from the floor of the home they occupied. Mumar stood several inches taller. Abu Alhaul looked at the man taken African, and knew he had it in his power to have the man taken outside and his legs chopped off above the ankles. Then the jet-black man would be the same height as him.

"Impressive, isn't it?" he asked, turning for a moment to Mumar Kabir, an ecstatic rush permeating his body. Abu Alhaul sucked in a deep breath—a sharp quick pain struck down his right and left sides. He quickly hid the slight grimace. Allah knew when to remind His followers of their mortality.

Taller and five years younger, Mumar Kabir stood slightly behind and to the left of Abu Alhaul. Mumar was always there. Even when Abu Alhaul would have preferred some solitude. The man acted fiercely loyal. He said the right things about gladly giving his life for him, but he was African and African loyalty, like the Afghanis', ebbed and flowed with the moment. Abu Alhaul touched the dagger on his right side.

"Yes, Great One," Mumar responded, looking in the same direction at the long line of armed pickup trucks. They had liberated several heavy machine guns from the Liberian Army camp in Monrovia.

The voice never indicated the level of mesmerized adoration that Abu Alhaul expected. He didn't fully trust Mumar, but he needed an African lieutenant if he expected the Africans to serve the cause of chaos. Abu Alhaul smiled as Mumar muttered a short prayer to Allah for the ease with which they

had overthrown this heretic puppet government of the Great
Satan. The way of Islam was set with challenges, but someday—*maybe after decades*—the world would become pure Islamic. Other religions twisted and spun Allah's words to
convince many that Islam was a heretic religion—a cult. They
would perish along with the Jewish pigs who occupied the
Islamic Holy City of Jerusalem. His was only one of many
Islamic movements dedicated to bringing true believers into
the fold and to die, like sacrificial sheep, in destroying those
who failed to acknowledge the word of Allah. Abu Alhaul
lowered his head to hide the slight smile he permitted himself.
He was the word of Allah. He was one destined to pick and
choose those who would martyr themselves in furtherance of
Islam. The smile faded and he looked at Mumar Kabir. *And
who better than to die in this cause than Africans? That was
their destiny.*

"Everything is nearly ready, Sheik," Mumar said, his deep
bass voice resonating within the close walls of the room.

Surveillance two months ago had told Abu Alhaul they
would find Humvees, weapons, and Americans at this sore on
Africa's butt called Kingsville. Twenty kilometers from this
small town where he and his commanders prepared for the
advance waited the heretic Americans. Americans who had
brought death, destruction, and disrespect to the Arab world.
He glanced at Mumar. Arab name for an African. *How stupid
the Africans were. They blamed the white man for slavery,
when it was his own people—the Arabs—who'd fostered the
practice, and still engaged it in some parts of the Middle East
and Africa.*

The Americans would die here in the land of their origin.
Abu Alhaul reached forward and took another date from the
bowl in front of him. Stability, educating the youth without
religious influence, and this growing quality of life threatened
the spread of radical Islam. The Americans were the ones doing it. The good thing for him was the jealousy and envy native
Africans felt toward the Americans. It played into his hands.
Even a second-rate mullah knows those two emotions cause
people to rise in revolt. It made it easier to stir them to Jihad
in furtherance of Islam. No, the Liberian experiment must die.

Africa's sparse middle-age population kept the continent

ripe for chaos. The majority of the population was either over sixty or under thirty. Those demographic profiles accounted for over seventy-five percent of all Africans. Allah had truly blessed this continent as fertile ground for pure Islam by killing off most of the one group that could have controlled the youthful emotions of those under thirty. For Islamic radicalism to survive, it required what the West called failed states, and Liberia's success threatened others by showing them the way out. This country needed to return to its former condition. To do that, Abu Alhaul must kill the Americans—the infidels of the Great Satan.

Three Islamic militiamen squatted alongside a second armed pickup truck, sticking on the side of the driver's door a large green flag with the Arabic words ALLAH ALAKBAR written in white on it. From a distance, it looked like the Saudi Arabian flag.

"Mumar, we are truly honored today," said Abu Alhaul. "We are witnessing a turning point in liberating our people who have fallen under the corrupt influence of Christianity. Across Africa, they will see how we met the enemy face-to-face and won victory. It will encourage them to take up arms and eradicate the scourge from their lands. They'll recognize the greatness of Allah and understand my words as emanating from Allah's own lips." His voice rose in tempo as he launched into the familiar vision. A warped vision he deeply and passionately believed was right. A vision to ignite the continent while he still could, for time was his biggest foe now. Several of Abu Alhaul's commanders mingled a few feet behind him. Near enough to hear, but at a respectful distance to allow their leader a small circle of privacy. Mumbles of approval merged with the sound of his words.

"We will destroy the infidels who have usurped Allah's way and who wield an unjust power against the faithful," Abu Alhaul went on. "Destroy those who have opened Africa's borders to Islam's foe." Mumar's eyes glistened. Abu Alhaul saw what he believed to be admiration in the man's eyes, and wondered briefly if it was for show, or was the man truly sincere, for Mumar had heard the same speech repeatedly many times. "They will die also.

"I'm not sure which day it will be, Mumar," Abu Alhaul

said softly. "But one of these days, in this hot month of August, will be known as the day of Allah's wrath. The day when the faithful drove from its shores the heathen seeds of those who would corrupt the will of Allah."

Abdo Almuhedge, the tall, dark Egyptian, approached from the direction of the convoy. The man smiled, raising his hand, palm outward, in a salute as he neared the two men, his gait wallowing from side to side as his heavy weight shifted with each step. The sound of rapid breathing was easily heard.

"Abu Alhaul, we are nearly ready," Abdo gasped, bracing his left hand against a nearby tree while raising his right to touch his forehead. He looked down at his feet for a couple of seconds before forcing himself to stand up straight. He stuck his arms out to the side, and took a couple of deep breaths before jerking a small red bath towel from a pocket on the long, white flowing aba. He wiped his forehead. "Damn heat, my brother. We should be back in Egypt, relaxing in the coffee shops, and enjoying the breeze off the Nile."

Abu Alhaul spit. "Egypt! A land that once was the home of everything we hold dear and now is but a lackey of the Americans!"

"We could always be angry while we drank our coffee."

"It is a hot day, Abdo," Abu Alhaul said, emotionless, his eyes narrowed at the overweight Egyptian. "You should lose some weight before it kills you, my brother."

Neither saw the exchange of glances among several of the Africans and Mumar.

Abdo nodded, running the cotton terry cloth across his face again. It was a futile effort. No sooner did he wipe away the heavy perspiration than fresh rivulets of sweat leaped forward to join the river soaking the neck and shoulders of the Arabic robe. "In this heat, my brother, I will sweat off the pounds." He laughed. "Of course, Allah willing, we will be back in Egypt and once again feel the cool of the Nile breeze upon our cheeks."

Abu Alhaul shook his head. "We have a long road ahead to travel before Allah will permit us to rest."

"You're my brother. I followed you when we were children, and you know I'll be with you when we are old. I would just like for us to grow old together in Egypt. If we stay here much longer, your younger brother will have a neck the size of a pencil and a body of a Saharan jackal." He pointed at Mumar. "In a few weeks, I will be as thin as Mumar."

Abdo fumbled, awkwardly jamming the towel back into his pocket before he continued. "I have good news, Abu Alhaul. We now have ammunition. The trucks brought it from our base across the border. Several of the captured machine guns are mounted on the pickup trucks. This will give us momentum and firepower for wiping the infidels from the land." He raised his arm, twirling the fingers in the air for a few moments before dropping the arm back to his side. "Our patrol says the Americans in Kingsville have an armory with many great and wonderful weapons that we can use."

"If they do, it will delay our overrunning them, killing them, and sending their spirits to Allah as an offering of strength."

"The schools have begun," Abdo offered, ignoring his brother's comment.

"Good!" Abu Alhaul exclaimed. He stretched out his arms, encompassing the scene in front of him. "All of us are but a twinkle in Allah's eye. Our lives are like so many grains of sand in the desert. We are born, we fight, and we die. Even the pickup trucks we arm are only good for a short time. The real weapon to bring Allah's earth into spiritual righteousness is the schools—the madrassas. It is in these religious schools future warriors and martyrs for Islam are molded. For as we know from Muhammad's teachings, this life is a series of devastating horrors in which we fight for the right to die in a holy cause. For to die in this holy cause sends us directly to Allah's arms and the pleasures and rewards for dying in the further-ance of his word."

Mumar's eyes narrowed as he listened to Abu Alhaul con-tinue to discuss educating children to believe that martyrdom was the path of all true believers.

When Abu Alhaul finished his five-minute lecture on edu-cation, Abdo ran the terry cloth across his face again and grinned. "Abu Alhaul, my brother, what good words. Mean-while, I'll wait for one of those martyrs to come to me in a vivid dream and confirm the seventy-two virgins."

Abu Alhaul smiled. "Abdo, why do I put up with such a disbeliever?"

Abdo reached forward and clasped Abu Alhaul on both shoulders. He pulled his brother close and whispered in his ear, "Because we're brothers. You look around and see these lackeys who say they follow you, but in your heart, we both know that regardless of what happens, I will always be here to protect and love you, my brother."

Mumar cleared his throat, drawing the attention of Abu Alhaul and Abdo. Abdo released his brother and stepped back.

"My apologies, Alsheik," Mumar said. "You asked I remind you about the new arrivals."

The smile left Abu Alhaul's face. Mumar was right. Abdo was a pleasant distraction. Many believed the familiarity of Abdo calling Abu Alhaul brother was heretical. The truth was that Abdo was truly his brother. They had been two of eight children of an Egyptian mason who had worked hard to send his two male children to the Islamic madrassa. It was there where Abu Alhaul developed his belief that he was a chosen one of Allah. In private, Abdo was even more sarcastic about some of the tenets of Islam, but in the end, they were of the same blood. Abdo had followed him in Holy Jihad to Afghanistan and to here. He might moan continuously about the climate, but Abdo would forever remain loyal, for nothing was stronger than blood. No, Abdo would remain. But Mumar . . .

TWO HOURS LATER, ABU ALHAUL TURNED TO THE PEOPLE around him.

"Okay," Abu Alhaul said. "Get the ammunition and people loaded on the trucks. It's time to take Allah's word to the American infidels."

"And the women and children?"

Abu Alhaul turned slowly until his dark eyes fixed upon Mumar's gaze. "They die also."

"Yes, Alsheik, but if we keep some, we can sell them."

Abu Alhaul slapped Mumar hard. The slap caused the low-level conversation behind him to stop abruptly. The African grabbed his cheek and stepped back. His eyes blazed at the Arab religious leader.

"Listen to me, Mumar," Abu Alhaul said, his voice threatening. "No one lives. To allow even one child to live means leaving the seed of war to grow; the seed of youth to flourish; and when it reaches maturity, it will come after you. It will come to overthrow Allah's righteousness and glory. The Americans must be eradicated thoroughly. Do you understand?"

Mumar nodded. He brought his hand away from his cheek and fought the urge to turn away. He feared what Abu Alhaul would do if he angered him too much. He had seen Abu Alhaul reach up, jerk the hair of a man backward, and slice the throat cleanly from side to side. Then while the man was dying, Abu Alhaul had slowly sawed the knife back and forth, cutting the man's head off even as he lived. Mumar took a couple of steps backward.

"Of course you are sorry, my friend," Abu Alhaul said. "Just remember we're here for the glory of Allah; not for the glory of money."

"Yes, I apologize," Mumar said, but Abu Alhaul saw the words were not reflected in the eyes.

"Money does help, though," Abdo said softly, wiping the sweat from his forehead.

The commanders standing behind Abu Alhaul tensed, expecting the leader to attack Abdo also.

Abu Alhaul smiled. "And that is another job for you, Abdo. You run the money and the supplies. You leave the victories to me, my fellow commanders"—he swept his left hand back toward the group behind him—"and Mumar, my African disciple." Abu Alhaul faced the African again, reached forward, and pulled the shaking man to him, whereupon he embraced the taller, more powerful Mumar for several seconds before releasing him. A slight pain shot down his left arm.

"Now, go, Abdo. We must move out."

Abdo took a deep breath, looked down at the trucks, and the armed men milling about them. "Yes, my brother. At least it is downhill."

"The rest of you tend to your men. Tell them to prepare to meet Allah's glory."

He waited a minute for them to leave before he picked up his AK-47 from where it leaned against a tree.

*   *   *

ABU ALHAUL GLANCED AT THE BODIES SWINGING ON THE
poles, and a vision of his own body hanging similarly crossed
his thoughts. He reached in his pants pocket and pulled the
prescription bottle out, took out a pill, and slipped it under his
tongue. Time was the enemy.

The pain in his chest diminished, and after several seconds
disappeared completely. He opened his eyes, took a step forward, and when the pain failed to return, confidently walked
along the long line of tables. Discarded plates with half-eaten
food littered the tables and the ground alongside them. Near
the heathen church, a group of young children played tag as
their mothers stood under a nearby cork tree, fanning and talking among themselves.

Tonight, at midnight, they would leave this small town. A
small group would stay behind to guard against an American
or Liberian force coming from Monrovia. Once he had captured Kingsville, he would prepare for the second phase of the
plan. The ship should be in Abidjan within the next seven
days. Then, he would take the battle to the Great Satan itself
while they wrung their hands, rattled their military swords, and
sought to display his head on a stake. Little knowing, while
they focused on Liberia and the American dead here, what
was coming their way. He grinned at the thought, and muttered
a short prayer of thanks to Allah.

Abu Alhaul watched as Abdo eased himself down on the
ground to sit with his huge legs splayed before him. His
brother was watching someone working underneath one of the
trucks. Abu would be lost without his brother. Abdo never
wrote anything down, for he never forgot anything. If only
other members of his staff were as efficient—and as loyal.
Mumar hated Abdo. He could tell by how the African reacted
to Abdo's irreverent comments. He glanced over at the African
lieutenant, who was marching in the other direction with an
entourage of Africans accompanying him. He would have to
watch Mumar. He was becoming too strong a leader of the
Africans. They must never forget that Arabs led them, for who
else could truly interpret the words of Muhammad?

Four men appeared between two trucks at the end of the

parked convoy. Both trucks had M-50's mounted on their cabs, like the pickup Abdo had sent earlier today on a patrol. They had received only one report from the radio in the truck, and it was more fawning than providing information. Without satellite communications, the radios were limited to ground range, so reports from them depended on the patrol keeping within range of the main body. Even the cell phones were useless.

He reached into his shirt pocket, brought out another small white tablet, and slipped it under his tongue. Three of these tablets in less than an hour. He needed to rest, to restore his strength. He was sure Abdo knew the seriousness of his condition, but he also knew his brother would never say anything to the others. As he looked at the back of his brother's head, Abdo turned, saw him, and lifted his hand. No leader could ask for a more loyal follower. No brother could ask for more love from another brother.

Within the next two days, they would kill the Americans in Kingsville. Abu Alhaul had no worries about them escaping to Ivory Coast. His spies had told him the Ivornians, by order of their French masters, had closed the border. This was but a diversion. A pleasant diversion, much like a magician trapping the audience's attention on his right hand while his left hand accomplishes the act. Even if he failed to destroy Kingsville and all who live there, the other plan would continue. Abdo would see to that. A plan that would keep the Islamic revolutionary wheels alive, while the West worried about the next catastrophic act of terrorism.

CHAPTER 9

REAR ADMIRAL DICK HOLMAN LOWERED HIS BINOCULARS. "How many grenades has *Spruance*'s helicopter dropped?"

"Three, sir. One every fifteen minutes, but I don't think that submarine has any intention of surfacing."

He shook his head. "Leo, it's either Russian or French. If it was British, we would have known about it, and if it was ours, it wouldn't have been trapped so easily."

"I would think if it wanted to get away it could, Admiral. All it has to do is go below the sound layer and ease off in any of three hundred sixty degrees."

"Navigator," Holman said. "What's the depth here?"

"Shallow, sir. We have two hundred feet."

"Should be deeper than that," Leo said defensively. "We're thirty miles out."

"Yes, sir," the navigator replied, her voice even. "But the current and wind from the mainland pushes the bottom up in this area. Makes a north-south-running ridge ten miles wide that separates the coastal current from the Atlantic Ocean."

The faint sound of the SH-60 Lamps Mark III helicopter drew their attention.

"There goes the *Spruance*'s sixty again." Upmann looked at his watch. "Right on time for the fourth grenade."

"Wave them off, Leo."

"Wave them off!"

"Yes, tell *Spruance* to hold up on the warning grenades. If the submarine was hostile, we would know by now. They're friendly. Most likely French, and don't want us to know they have been trailing us. The good news is we've done something that will give the captain of that submarine nightmares. We've embarrassed the shit out of him. Of course, could have been worse and we could have caught him on the surface, but it'll be bad enough when his peers discover that he was caught by a surface unit. If *Spruance* hadn't decided to conduct a man-overboard drill, it never would have detected him. The submarine was following in their baffles. We can assume it's been following us for some time—probably a surveillance mission."

"Don't know why he would have nightmares. Current doctrine calls for two destroyers and four antisubmarine helicopters for every submarine you detect. Even then, you keep the destroyers out of range and fight it with the helicopters."

"Did I say nightmares?" Holman chuckled. "The nightmares are the ridicule he'll get when his fellow submariners find out. Submariners are like eccentric uncles. They want to be around the family, but they don't want anyone to know they're there or when they leave."

Upmann lifted the handset of the sound-powered telephone plugged into the circuit on the starboard bridge wing. "Combat, this is Chief of Staff. Wave *Spruance*'s helo off and tell *Spruance* to quit dropping grenades for the time being. They are to remain ready, but hold off until told different."

He held the telephone to his ear listening to the voice on the other end.

Upmann would be speaking to the Tactical Action Officer. The TAO would be Amphibious Group Two's deputy operations officer, but knowing Captain Buford Green, his Operations Officer would be standing near the woman. The information revolution and the sweep of technological advancements in weaponry reduced the time for a warship to react to an attack from minutes to seconds. To respond to this reduced reaction time, the U.S. Navy had in the 1980's authorized commanding officers to delegate to selected, qualified officers the authority to defend the ship and react to an attack.

Tactical Action Officer was the designation given that person.

Holman knew Commander Stephanie Wlazinierz was thoroughly qualified to fight the ship. People usually called her "Stephanie" or "W," which she seemed to prefer. Even he'd had problems pronouncing Wlazinierz. He'd mouthed the name, fumbled it twice, and given up.

Stephanie was probably repeating the Chief of Staff's orders. When a military action was under way and going well, there was always reluctance to back off until the event finished. In this case, he was doing just that—ordering them to stop and hold everything.

Upmann held the sound-powered telephone away from his ear. "W says the French are on NATO red telephone saying they have four Super Etendard fighters en route to do a fly-over."

"You mean requested permission?" Holman asked.

"She said they said they were going to fly over."

"Find out if she inadvertently gave them permission. After our trip yesterday to the French battle group, I'm not gung-ho about them being anywhere near us."

Upmann picked up the telephone and talked with Wlazinierz for several minutes. Holman listened to this end of the conversation, and couldn't believe what he was hearing.

"Sir—"

"I heard. If I'm right, Stephanie told them to wait for permission and they said they already had permission."

"Something like that, Admiral." Upmann looked to the area two miles off their starboard where the SH-60 helicopter hovered in a tight circle.

"Something doesn't smell right. Let's get down to Combat," Holman said, tossing his cigar over the side, stepping through the hatch to the shout of "Admiral on the bridge," followed by "Admiral off the bridge" as he scrambled down the ladder behind the helmsman. Upmann was a few steps behind.

"Admiral in Combat!" someone shouted as Holman opened the hatch at the bottom of the ladder and stepped inside the darkened compartment. No one moved from their consoles and weapon systems. When engaged in operations or standing a watch, sailors might acknowledge the presence of a senior officer, but they never stopped what they were doing. The job must go on.

Captain Buford Green stood behind his broad-shouldered assistant, Stephanie Wlazinierz, watching closely as she tweaked the defense of the task force.

"What have we got?"

"Four Super Etendards inbound and an unidentified submarine bearing one-four-four at eight thousand yards," Buford replied.

Four nautical miles, thought Holman, *pretty close for an unidentified submarine.* The French wouldn't be so foolish as to actually attack an ally, would they? But then, no one thought civilian aircraft would be used as weapons of war before September 11th.

"Let's open up our range to the submarine. Tell *Spruance* to recall her SH-60 and arm her."

Wlazinierz turned around, short-cropped brown hair hung straight down alongside her head, framing a square-chinned face. "Admiral, *Spruance* is prepared. The skipper had two Mark-50 torpedoes moved to the helo deck a half hour ago."

"Stephanie, you tell them to put one Mark-50 on her, but not to launch unless I personally give the order."

"Yes, sir, Admiral," Wlazinierz replied before leaning down to the ASW controller near her and relaying the instructions.

The static sound of the secure communications synchronizing between exchanges mixed with the low background noise within the blue-lighted CIC—Combat Information Center. Scattered amidst the sailors and officers manning the nerve center of the warship were seamen wearing the insect-like helmets of sound-powered telephones. Warships usually had three to four means of communicating throughout the ship. There was the notorious 1MC operated from the bridge, with an alternate switch in CIC. Each battle position had its own internal communications systems, and then there were the sound-powered broadcast systems known as 12MC installed where the warfighters stood. To win in an era where time and information determined combat success, getting the right information to the right person at the right time was the key.

"Get me that Frenchman who calls himself an admiral on the circuit," Holman said through clinched teeth. *Who in the hell did Colbert think he was screwing with?*

Green picked up a nearby red telephone and quickly established contact with the French aircraft carrier *Charles De Gaulle*.

"Slr, Captain St. Cyr is on the circuit. Admiral Colbert is busy and unable to come to the—"

"Why doesn't that surprise me!" Holman jerked the handset out of Green's hand. "Captain St. Cyr, this is Admiral Holman. I am extremely concerned about having your aircraft fly near our task force without prior coordination. We have a lot going on and I would hate for an unfortunate incident to occur."

The speaker mounted above the captain's chair in Combat burst into noise, sending a loud squeal throughout Combat, causing those without headsets to scrunch their faces from the intensity of the sound.

Wlazinierz reached out and quickly lowered the volume.

"Well, that was painful," Upmann mumbled, his eyes squinting as he twisted a finger in his ear a couple of times.

"Admiral, this is Captain St. Cyr. Admiral Colbert sends his apologies and asks that I convey to you that we believe you are right. We should have coordinated the flyby sooner, sir. Unfortunately, the admiral thought that sending our aircraft to help with your unidentified intruder would be prudent ally cooperation."

The static from the speaker showed St. Cyr had released his "press-to-talk" mechanism.

"What the hell can a fighter aircraft do in an antisubmarine action? Wiggle its wings?" Upmann muttered.

Holman pushed the similar mechanism on his handset. "Captain, please recall your aircraft. If we had needed your assistance, you can be assured we would have asked our French ally for it. I am very concerned about the unintended-consequence possibility." He released the button.

Several seconds passed. "Unfortunately, Admiral, it is too late to recall them. May I suggest that you and your task force steam north away from the contact and allow us to handle it. We are much larger. I have already taken the liberty of dispatching the frigates *La Fayette* and *Floreal* toward your position. They are transiting at flank speed."

Holman looked at Upmann, who scrunched his shoulders and looked questioningly at Green, who shook his head. Wlazinierz shook her head, held up one finger, and mouthed the words "First heard."

"Captain St. Cyr, please convey my thanks to Admiral Colbert for his concern. Over and out," Holman said. He slammed the red handset back into its seat on the secure red box.

"What in the hell!" he growled sharply. "I guess that answers our question as to whose submarine is off our starboard side."

"Yes, sir, I think it does," Upmann added.

Holman's face hardened as he reviewed the options available. The most appealing was to shoot the sons of bitches down, but that would make the court-martial of Admiral Cameron look like small potatoes when the government finished with *him*. Regardless of the disagreement he and that French asshole Colbert had had yesterday, the fact remained that America considered France a valuable ally. Personally, if it wasn't for Evian water and French wine, he couldn't see any use for them. Of course, they did give America the baguette. Romance wouldn't be the same without it.

He dropped his head for a moment before raising it to stare at the starboard bulkhead. Out there, four miles away, a French submarine was trapped by his sparse antisubmarine forces. A submarine that had been tailing them for God knows how long. This was not the act of an ally. If the USS *Spruance* hadn't pulled an unexpected man-overboard to recover a lost basketball for the sailors playing on its helicopter flight deck, they might never have known the submarine was there.

He had little choice but to save face and defuse the situation. He felt the eyes of everyone in the darkened compartment on him. Some stared openly, others from the corners of their eyes, and a few would look quickly toward him and then away. A low murmuring told him whispered comments were being exchanged.

"Stephanie, turn the task force north away from the contact. We will leave it to our French ally."

"But, sir . . ."

Holman lifted his hand. "I know, I know, but we have to do it. Turn the task force north, but turn it in such a way that it carries us closer to the Liberian coast." Then in a whisper he added, "Let's take advantage of this to move us closer to doing our mission, rescue Americans."

"Sir, we can drop a Mark-50 torpedo on the submarine. They have violated international law by not revealing themselves and we are perfectly within our rights to attack her," Stephanie offered.

Holman nodded. "We could," he said sternly. "But we know—or strongly suspect—it's a French submarine. I cannot deliberately sink or even attack it just because we have it pinpointed and they refuse to surface. Bottom line is the intruder hasn't done one thing to show hostile intent other than refusing to surface." He took a deep breath, shook his head, and sighed loudly. "No, we'll use this opportunity to close our objective."

"Well, sir, if we show them they can do this and get away with it, then—" Leo started.

"I know, Leo," Holman interrupted, holding his hand up. "I don't like it either, but we're going to do it and we're going to do it my way."

"Aye, aye, sir," Upmann said. "Just, as your deputy, it is my responsibility—"

Holman laughed. "Leo, don't give me that. I've used it too many times myself. Now you, Buford, and Stephanie make this happen. Our mission is to evacuate Americans from Liberia; not fight a war at sea. Let's enjoy the fact the French just got egg all over their faces from an amphibious task force."

The sound of jet engines roaring down the sides of the USS *Boxer* shook the compartment.

"Combat, Bridge; just had those four French fighters fly down our sides."

"Roger, Bridge; we have them on radar."

"That's good. What should we do? Wave at them or shoot them down?"

Holman reached down and pushed the "to speak" lever down. "Wave. It's good for the heart."

"One finger or whole hand?" Leo offered.

Holman patted his pocket. Cigars were in his stateroom. In

his thoughts, Holman was already composing a message to Commander, European Command about the incident. Someone somewhere within his chain of command knew what was going on. It was almost as if they were leaving the decision on how to handle the French to him. If that was true, they why? His head lowered, Holman turned, heading up to the bridge.

He bumped into the back of an officer standing in the shadows near the captain's chair. "What the—"

"Sorry, Admiral, I was watching Commander Wlaz . . . wallz . . . Commander 'What's-her-name,' and didn't see you, sir," the young man stuttered.

"I know you. You're one of those pil . . . operators that's here with Professor Dunning. I thought you left with him."

"Oh, no, sir. He went, but the four of us arc still on board. He didn't want to leave the unmanned fighters and control equipment alone."

"I thought all that stuff went with the technicians." Holman looked at the name tag on the officer's flight suit—SHOE-MAKER.

"Yes, sir . . . I mean no, sir. Some of the lighter stuff and the data drives went off in the tech kit with the professor, but the bulk of the stuff is still aboard. He ordered us to remain with it until it could be off-loaded in Little Creek. It's a little bulky, heavy, and sensitive to move without heavy equipment. The helicopters were busy." Shoemaker shrugged his shoulders. "And it seemed we were low priority."

"Then, you're with us for the duration, Lieutenant Shoemaker," Holman mumbled as he opened the hatch and started up the ladder.

"Admiral out of Combat!"

This was going to send the wrong message to that French bastard of an admiral. Colbert was going to interpret their acquiescence as showing how Holman would react to future French demands. If he only had Harriers embarked. Harriers weren't the best fighter aircraft, but they could stand up to the Super Etendards, and having them would help even on this lopsided playing field. But the harriers were on the ships that had returned to Little Creek.

He stopped abruptly on the narrow ladder leading up the bridge, catching his Chief of Staff by surprise. Upmann's face bumped into his butt, causing Upmann's foot to slip on the metal steps. Upmann's grip tightened on the railing keeping himself from falling.

Holman turned around. "Leo, quit clowning and go back. Hurry," he said, touching Upmann on the arms, trying to turn him around.

Upmann stumbled again before turning around and starting back down the ladder. "I don't understand, Admiral. What's wrong?"

"Wrong? Nothing's wrong, Leo. I think we may have had an answer for our French ally's arrogance and never realized it."

Upmann opened the hatch and stepped through.

"Where is that lieutenant who plays at being a pilot?"

"Admiral in Combat."

He couldn't help feeling a little mischievous glee over the thoughts of what that asshole Colbert was going to do when Holman's joint task force miraculously appeared with fighter aircraft over it. Far be it for him not to repay the French aerial flyby show of respect with his own.

"WHEW!" LIEUTENANT PAULINE KITCHNER GASPED. "THIS is hard work." She wiped the sweat from her forehead, tilted the plastic water bottle up, and took a long drink.

"If it was easy work, someone else would be doing it," Lieutenant Nash Shoemaker said as he intentionally fell backward off his haunches onto his butt. He leaned forward and grabbed his bottle of water.

"How much longer do you think it's going to take us to uncrate these things?" Alan Valverde, the third lieutenant in the Unmanned Fighter Aerial Vehicle group, asked. "Where are the tech reps when we need them?"

"Tech reps ain't military," said Kitchner. "They don't have to stay on board and ride with the systems when their job is done. They can hop on board that helicopter like Dr. Dunning, and be ashore hoisting a cool one within minutes of finishing their job."

"Jurgen!" Shoemaker shouted. "Take a break and have some water. I don't want you dying and me having to explain to your mother that it was because you didn't drink your water."

The three pilots of the Unmanned Fighter Aerial Vehicles raised their water bottles in a mock toast to Ensign Jurgen Ichmens, who stuck his head out of the huge crate in the middle of the hangar deck. Ichmens nodded and started across the deck toward the three lieutenants.

"Naw, leave him alone," Pauline said as Ichmens arrived and threw himself down beside the others. "He's the only ensign we have. I think the three of us lieutenants ought to sit back and supervise Ensign Ichmens while he finishes uncrating the UFAVs. It will give him the benefit of our cooperative leadership while we ensure all safety procedures and standards are followed."

"Yeah, I agree with Pauline," Valverde added, chuckling. "We've only got one ensign and Jurgen's it. Just think of the valuable training he'll get from our supervision."

"Just think of the valuable training I've already gotten from you three." Ichmens chugged the contents of the small plastic container, and then, in an exaggerated hook shot, tossed the empty over their heads into a trash bin located against the bulkhead. *"Dos puntos,"* he said, hooking two fingers downward.

"Now we'll have none of that here," Shoemaker said.

"None of what?"

"You know, *putas*. You want to offend Polly the pilot?"

Pauline reached over and playfully slapped Nash on the back of the head. "Behave before Polly rips your cracker off."

"What's she talking about? What the heck does that mean?" Valverde asked. "Damn, Pauline, speak English."

"You're too young to know. Besides, you're one of those super-secret cryptologic officers from Naval Security Group. I already know everything we say, you're beaming back to some gigantic database so that years later you can blackmail me into wild, abandoned sex."

"Too young? Shoot, Pauline, I'm three years older than you," Valverde answered, ignoring the rest of the hyperbole.

"Age among lieutenants is like virtue among whores," Ichmens added.

"What the hell does that mean?" Valverde asked, raising one eyebrow in a questioning slant.

"That's rank among ensigns is like virtue among whores," Pauline said, "and from the ensigns I've met, the whores have it over them."

"No argument from me," Valverde added. "Why I remember this time—"

"Okay, Lieutenant," Pauline said, letting out a deep breath in mock anger. "Let's don't go down that road."

"I have never understood that quatrain about virtue and rank," Ichmens said, reaching into the ice container and pulling out another water. "Virtue and rank aren't even related."

"Ensigns aren't supposed to understand. They're supposed to stand at attention and accept as the gospel whatever their esteemed leaders tell them. And those crumbs of truth are to be squirreled away like nuts of wisdom until they need them," Pauline rebutted.

"And it's not a quatrain either," Shoemaker added. "It's one of those nuts of wisdom that Pauline mentioned."

"Nuts is right," Valverde said.

Shoemaker pushed himself up, took the white hand towel from his stateroom, and ran it across his shock of dark hair. "Well, enough of a break. Admiral Holman wants the UFAVs ready for launch tomorrow morning. We need to get back to work."

"It would be nice if he could send us a working party to help," Ichmens added. The athletic young man reached up and pushed sweat-soaked strands of blond hair off his forehead.

"He offered, but the last thing we need is to have some well-meaning sailor damage something. Once we have the five UFAVs unsecured and primed for launch, then the ship's crew can move them to the flight deck. That won't take long. What's going to be complicated is getting the data links up and running once we have the control suites operational."

"Take long? Last time it took twelve hours."

Pauline reached into the ice chest and pulled another water out. "Then it should take less time. We've had this experience. We've done this—how many times? Three? Four?"

"This will be the fourth time, but it's the first time we've done this without Boeing tech reps, Dr. Dunning, and someone manning the monitoring station to feed us information on what is going on. Keep your fingers crossed it works when we finish. Admiral Holman isn't a great fan of unmanned aircraft."

"That probably explains why we haven't been invited to sit around his table and exchange hair-raising aerial-combat stories with him."

"I think he's a fan of unmanned aircraft," Shoemaker said. "I think it's the idea of having our great Naval Security Group officer acting as a pilot that grates on his nerves."

"Well, he does have the luxury of knowing that three of us are trained, highly qualified, and with the exception of Ichmens, we have over a thousand hours each in the air," Pauline added. Then she turned to Valverde. "Come on, Alan. Why do we have you along with us? You're wearing a Surface Warfare Officer device along with an Air Medal. Can't say we see a lot of the cross-breeding the fruit salad on your left side implies," she said, referring to the lack of the rows of medals worn on the normal uniforms.

"We won't have someone on the monitor helping us this time," Valverde said.

"Ah, come on, Alan. Quit ignoring our curiosity."

Valverde pursed his lips and threw a kiss at Pauline, who slapped it away playfully.

Shoemaker brought the water bottle down from his lips, nodded, and said, "Guess we will have to become Navy pilots again and do it the old-fashioned way via radio."

"I want to quit being a Navy pilot," Kitchner said. "I want to be like Alan and be a super-secret type of person, longing for the thrill of the warrior ethos."

"Yeah, you're old, all right—what? Thirty maybe?"

"We got radio?"

"Of course, Ensign Ichmens, we have radio. How do you think we talk during our exercises?" Kitchner asked, and before he could answer, she turned to Valverde. "I'm the ripe old age of twenty-nine."

"I thought it was an intercom system."

"Jurgen, you could call it that. Our radios are cables running between the cockpit suites," Shoemaker said, turning as he walked to the nearest crate, which contained one of the UFAVs. "I think the admiral will want us to be able to talk with Combat Information Center once we're airborne. This is going to be a real mission, and we'll have to be able to talk directly to the Tactical Action Officer."

Valverde pushed himself off the deck and stretched. "This heat is hell. Why can't the ship air-condition the hangar deck?"

Pauline pointed to one of the open hangar doors. "Then they would have to shut the doors, and you wouldn't have the cruise advantage of seeing the blue African sea languidly lapping the sides of the ship."

"I can think of other things I would rather have languidly lapped."

"Don't go there," she warned, winking at him, as she pushed herself off the deck and headed toward the second crate in the line. "Come on, Ensign, you've rested enough."

"But I've just sat down," he protested weakly.

"Ensigns should never sit when superiors are standing, which for an ensign is always. If you had worked harder and faster," she cajoled, "your superior officers wouldn't have to be doing this menial labor. Because of you, we are once again forced to regain vertical position." Kitchner exaggerated a shiver. "What a horrible thought. Besides, you're whining, Ensign. Lieutenants do not like to hear ensigns whine. It indicates they may actually understand their low status in life."

"I'm not whining," he replied as he hastily stood and walked past Lieutenant Kitchner toward the crate where he had been unpacking an Unmanned Fighter Aerial Vehicle.

"I think you were," Valverde said, trying to sound serious. "Whining can have a major impact on morale."

"My morale is slipping fast," Kitchner said, her voice shaking slightly.

"Stop it, you two. You're hurting the ensign's self-esteem."

"Uh-oh. The boss is exerting his authority," Pauline said to Valverde. "Hey, Nash, you from California?"

"Sounds like it to me too. Oops! Did you feel that?" Valverde touched his stomach. "My morale fell another notch."

"As the senior lieutenant of this group and therefore the one what's in charge—"

"What's! You mean who."

"Could be who's."

"—I order all of you to raise your morale back to the level

of acceptable standards; to quit picking on the ensign—he's the only one we have and we need him available for further leadership training; and to finish uncrating these UFAVs before dinner. Plus, yes, I am from California."

A chorus of "Aye, aye" sounded through the hanger bay. Within minutes, the banter stopped as the only four UFAV pilots in the United States Navy inventory continued uncrating the aircraft. Even when they finished unfastening the stabilizing straps holding the fuselages, they still had to pull each UFAV onto the hangar deck to unfold the wings.

Shoemaker walked out of the crate. Sunlight blazed across the bay through the open hangar doors. He blinked his eyes several times. Sure he'd told the admiral they could do it, and they could. What he'd neglected to tell the man was they had never packed or unpacked the equipment by themselves. This was the first time, and even with the great level of confidence most aviators possess, he couldn't help but worry a little they would fail to do something right. A vision of the four aircraft taxiing down the flight deck, off the end, and splashing into the water in front of the admiral's eyes haunted him for a moment. Shoemaker imagined how he would turn to Admiral Holman after the four crashed off the bow and say, *"Well, Admiral, the good news is we still have one left."* Might be the last words out of his mouth as the little Napoleon jumped up and throttled him.

CHAPTER 10

RETIRED LIEUTENANT GENERAL DANIEL THOMASTON looked at his watch. The green glow from the hands showed a few minutes after midnight. It was amazing how dark a moonless night was when no electricity flowed to chase back the shadows. "They should have been back by now," he said quietly to retired Sergeant Major Craig Gentle.

"Yes, sir. They were told to be back before sunset." He glanced at his own watch. "They're a couple of hours overdue. Maybe they ran into the rebels?"

Thomaston turned to the side and picked up the M-16 he had leaned against the side of the darkened building. "Could be. I hope they're either broken down somewhere or found a safe place to hole up until morning."

"I hope you're right, Boss, but we've been calling them on the radio continuously with no luck."

"I know," Thomaston added morosely as the two strolled across the compound toward the front gate. "We have to assume the worst." He looked around to make sure no one was within listening range. "Most likely they're dead. Don't want to give up hope, but according to Beaucoup Charlie their last transmission was at 2100 hours—on the dot—as scheduled. They missed the 2130 and 2200 check-in times. No, you're right. They've run into the rebels. The question is whether it was a hostile point patrol or the main force. At the nine o'clock check-in they were fifteen klicks from here."

Thomaston walked around the knoll with the flagpole and Civil War cannons. The flag had come down as planned at eight o'clock. Everyone in the compound had come out, stood respectfully, and watched the militia lower the American and Liberian flags. The young bugle player had done a credible job playing taps. Thomaston had ignored Gentle's cringe when the teenager mangled the high note.

He glanced at the flagpole. A slight breeze rattled the secured flag-line chains against the metal staff. The offbeat clanking sound created a brief vision of ghostly apparitions in Thomaston's thoughts. He hoped the surrealism was not prophetic.

"Sure wish we had some armored personnel carriers, a couple of tanks—" Gentle said, thinking aloud.

Thomaston let a small grunt escape. "And a couple of brigades of Special Forces. It would be one big *hooah* when those assholes arrived."

"Yeah, it would be. Fortunately, we do have a couple of M-50 machine guns, and unfortunately, only limited ammunition for the small arms we have. I hope those sailor boys get here soon with their Marine playmates."

Thomaston stared at the African night outside the front gate. What a cruel continent, he thought. No room or forgiveness for mistakes. *Damn it*. They were told to turn back when they checked in at nine. Instead, they had smooth-talked Beaucoup into letting them go forward for another thirty minutes to see if they could make contact. Why in the hell the radio operator didn't ask *him,* or at least tell him what they were doing, was just another example of the difference between a military organization and one clouded by consensus-building civilians. *"Do a quick reconnoiter and return,"* Charlie had told them.

"You know, we could move those vehicles we got crammed together in back and sparse them out around the perimeter," said Gentle. "Might slow the rebels down if they have to crawl over them."

"Might also give them cover if they get inside the compound. Let's leave them where they are for the time being. It would do little good to move them anyway." They had enough small-arms ammo for the M-16's and enough to make the two old .50-caliber machine guns effective. However, unlike the enemy force headed their way, he had no supply tail to replace what he used.

He ran his fingers along the buttons of his sleeves. He had rolled the sleeves of the jungle-camouflage utilities down when night fell as a preventive measure against mosquitoes. Granted, it made the utilities warmer than he liked, but the threat of West Nile Virus, malaria, and the host of virulent mosquito-borne diseases made the bites deadly. They had started spraying last year, but it hadn't done any good. The slight night winds just imported mosquitoes from those unsprayed areas. Thomaston had been one of the few to argue against spraying. He preferred using natural and preventive methods, for life, once changed or introduced, always found a way to survive and spread.

The two friends stopped near the front gate. The strong steel fence of the gate was closed. It bothered Thomaston. The chain-link gate would allow unfettered weapons fire directly into the courtyard. On the inside of the right gate against the brick wall, two guardsmen manned a sandbagged machine-gun position. The M-50 barrel hovered about six inches above the six-foot-high brick wall, poking under the chain-link portion of the fence that rose above it. That should be sufficient to protect the gate, unless the bogeymen he was preparing the armory for were real and had more than small arms when they arrived.

They had been trying to regain radio contact with this Admiral Holman with no success. The loss of satellite communications and limited VHF/UHF ranges, which were line of sight, meant radio contact would mean U.S. forces were on their way. The only other radios they had were the limited-range radios in the SUVs. He had no way of knowing what was going on except through the hourly BBC news broadcasts on the radio. An hour ago, the BBC had reported both an American and French Naval force off the coast of Liberia. If that was true, then where in the hell where they?

He strained his ears, hoping to hear the noise of an automobile engine mixed with the jungle night sounds. Several seconds of concentration convinced him nothing was there but the nighttime life-and-death struggle within the surrounding jungle.

They had kept scheduled contact with the patrol after it departed the armory. Thick forests, rolling hillside terrain, and unidentified deposits in this mineral-rich nation disrupted radio transmissions. Heightened sunspot activity during the day stopped most radio efforts entirely; especially the lower-high-frequency ranges that had the capability of long-haul earth-bound communications.

Complicating their situation was knowing that Admiral Holman would be operating on the last thing they'd discussed, which was that Thomaston and the Kingsville population were evacuating overland to the Ivory Coast.

That gate still bothered him. "Sergeant Major Gentle, I believe you may be right. Move a couple of those larger trucks up here to this front gate." Thomaston pointed. "Right now, it is like a sieve. Wouldn't stop a BB, much less military small arms. Let's seal this front gate up."

"Yes, sir, General. Shouldn't be a problem."

"Good. We should have insisted this armory be built with a practical military use instead of thinking of it as a ceremonial decoration. This gate would work great keeping demonstrators at bay. Open like it is, it makes the inside of the armory like a pinball machine. Small-arms fire funnels through the front gate, ricochets a few times, and hits someone. While we're ducking, they could mount a concerted offensive that would burst right through it. Trucks across the front would not only block the view from outside, but keep random fire from playing havoc inside here."

"Yes, sir. I'll go take care of that now."

Thomaston watched the back of Gentle for a few seconds as he walked away. The smell of cooked meat whiffed through the air from the back of the main building. The families had been cooking all the fresh and frozen meat. There was no way to preserve it. He spotted a family of refugees emerging from the side of the building, plates of food held near their mouths as they wolfed down the huge helpings being dished out.

Good leadership often meant being consistent even when it

went against personal desires. Civilians were a strange lot, like the lady and her daughter who'd walked into the armory this afternoon. How the hell they'd made it from Monrovia to here was a miracle. But they'd insisted a patrol go to their house in Monrovia to pick up curling irons, hair dryers, and clothes. Shock, he suspected. The lady's husband had been killed during their escape and her two sons were missing. Shock did that to a person. It made your mind focus on minor things to obscure what really frightened you.

He had thirty militiamen if that patrol failed to return. Another sixty men and women capable of firing a weapon, and a host of children and refugees who might find themselves in a battle for their lives. A battle they'd never imagined they would have to fight. He had enough weapons to stop anything within Liberia, unless the rebels brought up the few tanks the Liberian Army had probably abandoned in Monrovia. He crossed his fingers. If they showed up with armor, none of them stood a chance.

"They're moving the trucks," Gentle said as he returned.

The sounds of engines turning over rode the night air. "There they go now," Gentle added, jerking his thumb toward the rear of the compound.

Thomaston nodded. "Thanks."

"May I ask what your thoughts are, General?"

Thomaston sighed. "I am trying to determine what other options we have, Sergeant Major. The failure of the patrol to return helps confirm that an armed force is heading this way. They may show up with heavy weapons, for which we have no defense. Armor would give a small force commanding presence even if they had no ammunition for it." He shook his head. "It doesn't look good. Small arms to small arms, we can hold out for a while, but we can't get into a battle of attrition. They will outnumber us."

"Thank you, sir. Remind me next time not to ask."

Thomaston chuckled. He turned right and with Gentle strolling by his left side, the two walked along the front wall, greeting the two young men manning the machine gun at the front gate.

"Another option," he said as they continued past the gate, "is to abandon the armory and head south, taking everyone with us. But it's dense swamp and jungle. Once inside of it, it'll be hard for the Navy to extract us." He shifted the M-16 from his right hand to his left. "No, they could do it. I've seen it done by us—the Army—on other occasions. This is one of these times that makes me realize what a glutton for information I was when I was on active duty. I'd never engage an enemy with what little we know. We need to have a backup plan. Sergeant Major, maybe you should take a couple of people and see what looks to be the best escape route south into that jungle of a swamp. I'll stay here."

Retired Sergeant Major Craig Gentle rendered a snappy salute. "Yes, sir, I'd do that, but I think we both know if we head into that maze of vines, bushes, and swamps, most of our people are going to die. Some are just too out of shape and too old to make it."

"And if we stay here against a superior armed force that outnumbers us, then we may all die."

Gentle looked south and stroked his chin. "Come to think of it, a brisk walk through that stuff might be just the exercise our town folk can use."

Thomaston watched his loyal friend disappear around the corner of the building before continuing his walk. He needed to survey the perimeter one more time. Others called it management through walking—a talent many leaders had thrown aside for the ease of management through e-mail. Let the troops see you. Let the troops know you're interested in their welfare. It was as important for those serving under you to know you were on top of things as it was for you to have a feel for how your forces were dispersed. No e-mail could substitute for physical presence. Otherwise, you brought your own self-made fog of war into the battle.

Thomaston warned a couple of sentries assigned the night watch to remain alert and awake. He touched each man or woman he passed on the shoulder.

Ahead in the starlight, two rain barrels were braced against the wall with a couple of planks across them. Two people were on the makeshift platform. One was female. He couldn't see her face, but he recognized that energy as he neared.

Tawela Johnson sat with her back against the brick wall, her feet swinging back and forth off the edge of the planks.

That familiar bright-white smile appeared in the faint starlight. Somewhere she had scrounged up an old Army helmet that lay beside her. Sweat matted her thick black hair against her forehead, down the sides of her face, and along her neck. Almost primitive in appearance, but appealing. She stared back. The faint lines visible in the darkness around her eyes betrayed her fatigue. He grinned. She might be tired, but she was enjoying this. She had no idea what was to come, and yet she was looking forward to the fight. He had been around enough soldiers going into combat to recognize the signs, though Thomaston would have been hard-pressed to point them out. Her tired eyes twinkled for a moment, making him realize how close to savagery civilization rested. A young lady should be second—*maybe third*—year in college, flirting with young men and enjoying herself. Instead, she waits with an M-16 assault rifle to fight an enemy she has never seen—and she grins. Civilization was a fragile shell always waiting to burst. All you had to do was remove an essential column of infrastructure and the walls tumbled down. Look how close they had come September 11, 2001. All because of religion— *"Enough,"* he said to himself. *"Leave it be."*

Smiling, she waved. "General, how the hell are you, sir?"

"It was nothing," he said, replying to his thoughts instead of her question. "Tawela, you look bushed," he continued, changing the subject.

She nodded. "Looks ain't everything, General. If it was, I'd be President."

He laughed, drawing a larger grin from her.

He should be chastising her for sitting when she should have been watching the dark outside the wall, but he kept his words to himself. These were not professional soldiers, though by tomorrow they might well be combat veterans. He hoped they were fast learners, for there would be no second chances. He made a mental note to discuss sentry duty with the sergeant major. A perimeter patrol later tonight would be good.

"Tawela, I take it everything is fine." He grabbed the planks and gave them a shake. They didn't move. "Whose idea was this?"

"Mine. I got Roosevelt here to help me, and we moved the rainwater collectors here and threw these heavy planks across them." She stood up, brushed off the seat of her pants, and leaned across the top of the wall and beneath the chain links. "With this, I can stand up and see over the top. Without them, I would have to fire into the air and hope the bullets came down on top of someone."

"See anything out there?" Thomaston asked.

"No, sir. Just darkness," she said thoughtfully, pausing for a moment before continuing, her voice serious. "I never knew the jungle sounded so alive. You hear the crickets? I heard a lion and monkeys earlier." Even through the fatigue, the amazement of discovery emerged. "You know, I've never paid attention to the noises until tonight." She turned her head away to glance again over the wall. "Just never heard them. I'm sure they've been there, but I've just never paid them much attention, even if I noticed them. They blended with our noises."

"That's the sign of a good sentry, Tawela," Thomaston said, reaching forward and patting her on the shoulder. "Now that you have the normal sounds picked out, anything out of the ordinary you should recognize. If that happens, then call the sergeant of the guard—"

"Sergeant of the guard?"

"Yes, sergeant of the guard. Right now, that's Sergeant Major Gentle." Then, he recalled he had asked Craig to do a quick reconnoiter to the south.

"Oh, Craig Gentle. I didn't know he was a sergeant of the guard."

"Never mind, Tawela. If you hear anything out of the ordinary, you call out. If you don't see us, you make sure everyone knows you're hearing or seeing something. Don't worry about false alarms. Between us three, I hope all the alarms are false."

The dark line marking her lips curled back into that everpresent smile. He noticed the right side of the lip went slightly higher than the left. "Thank you, General. General, is there really an army marching against us?"

"No, Tawela, don't believe so. Just a bunch of rabble who believe a bunch of Islamic radical bullshit and want us to help them meet Allah. So, you two, keep a good watch. Okay?"

"Yes, sir," she replied forcefully. She patted her M-16. "And I got just the friend here who can help."

"She means me, General," Samson Roosevelt added.

She slapped him playfully on the leg. "Only if I have to throw you at them."

Craig Gentle ran up.

"Thought you were going to do a quick reconnoiter, Sergeant Major."

"I thought he was the sergeant of the guard."

The two looked at her, Gentle turning his head back to Thomaston. "Sergeant of the guard?"

"He's both, Tawela. When you're good at what you do, you get more titles."

"Well, then what am I?"

"I know what you are," Roosevelt said, laughing.

Tawela slapped him playfully on the side of the arm. "And I know what you'll be if you keep this up," she replied with mock petulance.

"Tawela, Samson; you two keep an eye out there. Sergeant Major Gentle will have someone relieve you before dawn so you can get some sleep."

"Yes, sir," they both said simultaneously.

"Come on," Tawela said to Roosevelt. "Rest your gun on top of the wall and we can lean against it—"

Her voice faded as the two walked away.

"Poor guy," said Gentle. "Hope he can hear something over her blabbering."

"You were going to go plan our backup escape if we needed to do it."

"I did and we don't."

"Explain."

"If we have to evacuate, we only have three exit points. The main gate and two small pedestrian gates along the front. We have no explosives to blast an opening in the south wall, where we would need to escape in mass."

"So, we either do it now or we don't do it at all."

Gentle nodded. "Looks that way, General. We make our stand and depend on our maritime brothers and sisters to come to our aid—"

"—or we round everyone up and herd them into the jungle and rain forest in the dead of night," Thomaston finished.

"Won't happen."

Thomaston nodded. "You're right. My good friend Reverend Hew would hem-and-haw the idea until morning, when it might be too late."

"No idea so small it can't be stopped by excessive attention to irrelevant details."

"Learned that in the Army, did you?"

"No, sir, General. I learned that in Washington."

At the second corner, a green flatbed trailer had been maneuvered against the wall. One of the few militiaman stood on it, his M-16 resting across the top of the wall, its barrel sticking through the small opening between the bricks and chain-link fence. The sound of humming reached Thomaston's ears as they approached. Here was another unseasoned wanna-be soldier looking forward to combat. If they only knew.

Thomaston stopped, talked with him for a couple of minutes, touched the young man's shoulder, and then moved on.

At the end of their tour of the perimeter, Retired Lieutenant General Daniel Thomaston left Retired Sergeant Major Craig Gentle to carry out the few orders remaining. The smell of cooking sent a rumble through his stomach, reminding him he hadn't eaten since breakfast.

The sound of a horn repeatedly blowing drew his attention as he turned the side of the building, heading toward the outdoor grills. His head shot up at the sound, and he began running toward the front. Thomaston rounded the corner of the building just as an SUV roared up to the front gate, brakes squealing as it stopped a few inches from the steel mesh. The horn stopped for a second, then began to blow steadily, drowning out the night sounds. Thomaston shaded his eyes from the glare of the lone headlight as people hurried to open the gates. The glare obscured the view through a windshield that appeared to have bullet holes. It looked as if the driver was slumped over the steering wheel.

MUMAR KABIR STUCK HIS FOOT UNDER THE BODY AND rolled it over. The headlights of the pickup truck cast a long shadow from the body across the dirt road. A second body lay a few feet away. He bent and picked up the M-16, held it at arm's length, and grinned at his good fortune. Now, he had an AK-47 and an American M-16. The smell of cordite whiffed across the warm night air.

"Mumar, is there another gun?" the African, Asraf, manning the machine gun on top of the truck's cab, asked. "I want it. I killed him." The two Africans on each side of Asraf laughed and put their arms around his neck. "Yeah, Boss. We want one too."

"You are stupid, Asraf. You are shit!" Mumar shouted. "I said don't shoot."

"Well, you may have said don't shoot, but they had guns so I shoot, so you go to hell."

The others laughed. "Yeah, man."

"Yeah, you go to hell," Asraf said again, glancing at his friends and laughing.

"I am the colonel, Asraf. You do what I tell you. We are supposed to capture one to take back to Abu Alhaul; not kill all of them. Abu Alhaul will be unhappy."

The laughter stopped. Fear was a great equalizer.

Moreover, they had allowed an American vehicle to escape. Those in it would warn the other Americans.

Mumar looked to where Asraf's voice came from. The headlights blinded Mumar, but the silence told him he had scored. He turned back to the bodies. Asraf made him nervous. Mumar had this itch right down the middle of his back. He knew Asraf was weighing whether to kill him or not. If he was in Asraf's place, he would pull the trigger, for Mumar knew he was going to kill the big man before Asraf went berserk and started killing everyone around him, including *him*. The two Africans with Asraf were petty cowards who would quickly abandon Asraf at the first sign of confrontation.

It had not even been a battle. The Americans had never had a chance. The huge vehicle—*what do the Americans call them? SUVs*—had slowed when it approached the trees pulled across the road. Mumar had stood beside the black pickup truck, hidden among the roadside trees. It had been minutes before two of the Americans had warily gotten out of the vehicle. When they laid their weapons down and grabbed an end of one the trees, he had stepped forward, intending to demand their surrender. Abu Alhaul wanted prisoners. Prisoners he could interrogate before videotaping their execution. Information first, public execution second. Before Mumar could open his mouth, Asraf had fired the machine gun, .50-caliber bullets whizzing so close over Mumar's head, he swore he could feel their wind. Mumar had thrown himself to the ground, rolled to the side, and brought the AK-47 up, aimed toward Asraf. Realizing he wasn't the target, Mumar rolled onto his stomach so he could see the Americans. A stitch of .50-caliber bullets had blasted across the front of the SUV destroying one headlight and shattering the windshield. The driver had done a high-speed reverse, and Mumar watched helplessly as the SUV disappeared into the night. The two Americans lay on the road, blood quickly darkening the light clay.

He should really kill Asraf now. It wasn't as if anyone would object. He was the leader of the Africans who followed the call of Abu Alhaul. He kicked the body one more time. The driver of the SUV was smart. *He* would have done the same. People don't live long with .50-caliber shells passing through them, and to remain because of some self-serving morality would have meant the driver and those inside would have died also.

He thought about sending Asraf after the SUV, but Abu Alhaul had warned that they were to stop moving forward when they engaged the Americans. These were definitely Americans. He leaned down and saw a U.S. Army patch sewn above the right pocket. Mumar spoke and read English. Did this mean American military were here? He shut his eyes for a moment. They could never defeat real soldiers; even he knew that.

Back in the pickup, he lifted the radio and sent word of the incident to the convoy behind them. After intense questioning from Abdo, he was ordered to continue forward, but to check in with the main column in twenty minutes or when they reached ten kilometers, whichever came first. Kingsville was less than twenty kilometers ahead of them. They couldn't get too far forward because the radios would quit working. Why did they have the Africans out front while the Arabs brought up the rear?

Two of his Africans lifted the bodies and threw them into

the nearby ditch. A moan escaped from one of the bodies.

"One of them is still alive," a tall African said to Mumar, drawing his pistol.

Mumar shrugged his shoulders. "Leave him. The animals will get him or he'll die soon. Just leave him to his fate." The idea of lions, tigers, or hyenas devouring the wounded man while he was still alive excited Mumar. He could take him back to Abu Alhaul, but Abu Alhaul wanted a healthy captive who could be tortured and enjoyed before they killed him. This one would die before they ever got back to the main column. Asraf would bear the blame for this too.

Moments later, they were off with Mumar sitting in the cab of the lead pickup. A tall, thin African manned the mounted M-50 on top of the cab of his pickup. Asraf rode atop the second vehicle, and Mumar knew the crazed man, even with all the bouncing from the rough road, would have his finger on the trigger. Hit the wrong bump and the thick trigger finger of the bush warrior would cause the machine gun to go off, probably hitting the truck Mumar was riding in.

Mumar ordered the driver to keep the speed at thirty kilometers per hour. Abu Alhaul's plan was for them to reach Kingsville just before daybreak. The Americans would be in their homes, asleep, believing nothing could touch them. Be some nice women for his troops to enjoy afterward. He would watch, but he would not soil himself with someone else's damaged goods. He grinned for a moment before the thought of Asraf crossed his mind. Asraf's blood lust was too erratic. Eventually Asraf would kill Mumar if he didn't kill the man first. He knew it, and he knew Asraf knew it.

Mumar glanced through the window at the pickup behind them, trying to see the huge man who he envisioned laughing and leaning across the top of the pickup's cab. He touched the handle of the pistol sticking out of the black leather holster treaded through his belt, and then checked the safety on the AK-47 resting in his lap. The only question was when. He pulled the M-16 up from where its butt rested on the floor of the cab and the barrel leaned against the door. He tossed the M-16 behind the seat of the extended cab beside the other one.

*   *   *

"WHAT WAS THAT, DADDY?" CANNON ASKED, TUGGING ON his father's pants leg.

"Shhh," Joel whispered to his son. He put the tractor's transmission into neutral and turned off the engine.

Parker emerged from the darkness on the left side of the tractor. "That was gunfire, Joel," he said softly. "Been around too much gunfire not to recognize it."

"Not too far away," George added from the other side of the tractor. He had his rifle lifted and pointed in the direction the gunfire had originated from. His finger was near the safety.

Joel threw his leg over the seat and hopped to the ground. He reached up and grabbed his shotgun. "Sounded like it came from ahead."

"They may have heard the tractor engine."

"The wind is blowing toward us. Let's hope they didn't," Parker said. He spit to the side.

"If they have, they'll be here shortly," George added.

Victoria stood alongside Artimecy near the trailer. Jamal slid off the rear of the trailer, rubbing his eyes.

"What's going on?" he asked softly.

"There be gunfire ahead of us," Artimecy said.

The men had their heads close together, talking. Jamal wanted to go see what was happening, and when Victoria started toward the group, he went with her. Unconsciously, he scratched the mosquito bites on his arms.

"What is it?" Victoria asked in a whisper. Jamal stood quietly beside her, holding his rifle by the barrel while the butt rested on the ground.

"Gunfire ahead," Parker said, his jaw rotating as he chewed the tobacco that seemed to live and multiply in his mouth.

"We have to know before we go farther. Wait here and I'll go take a look," Joel said.

"Better let me go first. That white face of yours don't hide as well in the night as mine," George said. "You gonna stick out."

"Of course it's so dirty now, you'd blend into Harlem," Parker added.

George pushed around Joel and within seconds, the two men disappeared around the curve in the logging road.

A slight breeze took the exhaust fumes of the tractor and

whirled them around their heads before blowing off into the night. At least the wind was in their favor, even if it stung their eyes. Jamal blinked several times to clear his of the fumes.

Victoria took the end of her blouse and wiped her eyes, revealing for a brief moment the firm mounds of her breast.

The two men from the convoy joined them from the rear of the procession where they had been walking since the group buried the dead child earlier that day.

"I'll go with them," the younger man, called Jose, said.

"It could be dangerous," Jamal said.

Jose laughed quietly. "Hey, man, I don't see how much more dangerous this can get." He reached forward and ruffled the sparse hair on Jamal's head. "Besides, they may need a second set of eyes."

"Well, be careful and don't get yoreself shot coming up behind them," Parker said. "Joel ain't the cautious type, you know," he said, pausing for a second. "And right now, I ain't feeling too cautious myself."

They watched as Jose jogged down the road to disappear around the corner. The other two couldn't be too far ahead.

"They won't be long," Parker said, holding the shotgun in his right hand and resting the barrel in the crook of his left arm. "The highway is just a ways down the hill."

"Are we planning on using the highway?" Victoria asked nervously, concern etched her face. "I kinda like using this back road."

The idea of traveling on a highway caused Jamal's eyes to widen. That didn't sound like a good idea to him either. A tractor wasn't going to get off the highway quick if they ran into rebels.

Parker spit a long trail off into the darkness. "Naw, we gotta cross the highway to get to the other side where this old road continues."

"Good," Victoria said, relief evident in her voice.

"How far does this old road go?" Jamal asked.

"Can't rightly say," Parker answered, his hand stroking his chin, a rasping sound accompanying his words as his hand brushed the two-day stubble of white whiskers. "This is about as far as we ever come. Now, Joel, me, and this young rascal here, Cannon"—he reached over and tussled the hair of the twelve-year-old boy—"have hunted this area, and we know where the two halves of this old road connect. The problem is, we don't know how much farther the old road continues before it peters out or reaches the point where even a tractor can't make it." He spit again, and in a reflective moment said, "We kinda lucky to have made it this far." He brought his hand down. "Been a while since I've been this long without shaving."

Jamal walked past Mr. Parker to the front of the tractor. He put his hand against the narrow end above the two small front wheels, and quickly jerked it back from the heat of the engine block.

Parker chuckled. "Yeah, son, you gonna lean on something, don't do it on a tractor engine. They ain't like the new ones. These will burn you without thinking."

"Where are we?" Jamal asked, shaking his hand a couple of times and then blowing on it.

"About ten kilometers, I reckon, from Kingsville. I figure if this road holds out, it'll take us within a klick or two of the town. Then, we'll have to make a run for it."

"I thought you didn't know where this road leads, Mr. Parker."

The older man looked down. "All roads lead someplace. Some are just better traveled than most."

"I wish this one takes us all the way into Kingsville."

"You and me both, boy. You and me both. We've been making good time. If the road keeps going in this direction, we may find ourselves a little south of Kingsville by morning—probably near their lake. Of course, that assumes whatever Joel and them find down the hill doesn't stop us from crossing."

Five minutes turned into ten, until finally Parker raised his shotgun and looked at the two lads. "Boy," he said, looking at Cannon. "You and Jamal, stay here and guard. I'm going to step out a bit and see if I can see them. They been gone too long for my liking." He looked at the man standing a couple of feet to Victoria's left. "Benitez, you wanna come with me?"

Benitez was a head shorter than George and built almost in

a square, as if chest and hips had absorbed his waist. The small, slightly bowed legs made him waddle when he walked. Benitez's head turned slightly toward Victoria.

"I'll go with you," he said in a heavy Hispanic accent.

All of the men were out there. Hope they don't shoot each other, thought Jamal.

Mimy reached into a brown paper bag and pulled out a plastic bag with biscuits in it. Jamal's mouth watered as he realized how long it had been since he and Selma had eaten. Where was Selma? He hurried back to the trailer. She was curled in a ball, sleeping, her knees nearly touching her chest. He brushed the mosquitoes off her legs and arms, then propped his gun against the side of the trailer, grabbed a nearby table-cloth, and covered her with it. She would have dozens of mosquito bites tomorrow. He patted Selma's head and pulled a piece of trash out of her hair before grabbing his gun and hurrying back to the women.

Mimy handed a couple of the cold, crumbly biscuits to Jamal.

"Your sister still sleeping?"

"Yes, ma'am."

"Then, we'll save a couple for her when she wakes up," Artimecy whispered.

He had never tasted anything so delicious as he chewed the dry, two-day-old bread. He heard a moan from Victoria, and saw the shadow of a smile creep across her face as she chewed. He had this rush of euphoria for whatever great Being looked down because they were alive to enjoy this pauper meal.

"Here," Mimy said from atop the trailer, holding a Mason jar with liquid in it. "Drink this to wash down that dry bread. It ain't much, but it should take the edge off the appetite until morning."

Victoria reached past Artimecy and took the jar from her. "What is it?" she asked as she unscrewed the top.

"That is pure grape juice, honey, made by Parker from our own grape vines." She helped herself down from the trailer. "Or, I should say, nature's grape vines. Parker and me got nearly an eighth acre on the farm where someone years ago must have tried to grow grapes, but they went wild. Personally,

I think juice is a whole lot better when it comes from wild grapes."

Victoria took a deep drink before passing the jar to Jamal.

Jamal tilted the jar back, placing his lower lips over the ridges to keep the juice from leaking out. The taste of warm natural juice rushed over his tongue. He'd never realized how great food could taste. He passed the jar to Artimecy, and by the time they finished eating the biscuits, the jar was empty.

Artimecy and Mimy laughed softly.

"Good, ain't it?" Artimecy asked, brushing the crumbs off her hands. "Cannon, you want something to eat?"

The young boy shook his head. He was crouched near the edge of the road, watching the darkness in the direction where the men had disappeared. Jamal thought maybe he should be up there with Cannon, but the food was so good.

"Artimecy, Mimy, I don't think I've ever tasted anything so good in my life," Victoria said.

Jamal swallowed, the last of the biscuit caught in his throat. It took three swallows to get it down. How could he feel so comfortable, knowing that somewhere out ahead might be men wanting to kill them? Must be the food.

Mimy brought out a plastic container with stale cookies, and they munched on them. Jamal lifted his gun and squatted beside the big tire, taking up a sentry position like Cannon while he listened to the soft talk of the women behind him.

Even as they whispered among themselves, their eyes focused forward, waiting for the men to return. From the questions Victoria asked, Jamal discovered how Parker and Artimecy had inherited the farm from Artimecy's parents, who had come to Liberia years before the dual-citizenship law had been passed in America. Artimecy's mother had passed away quietly in her sleep at the age of sixty-five, ten years ago this coming Christmas. It was a country-folk talk, where everything said had a purpose of ensuring everyone knew as much as possible about each other without revealing anything derogatory.

Joel and Mimy had been high school sweethearts from upper New York state. Their parents had expected them to go off to college, forget each other, marry someone of their own race, and make a good living with lots of grandchildren. Instead, the two had eloped, much to the anger and angst of both sets of parents, who had yet to come to terms with the marriage and the grandchildren.

A liberal elderly aunt on Joel's side thought the whole thing was romantic, according to Mimy—kind of a modern-day Romeo and Juliet. When the two young lovers fled their respective families, who were determined to break up a misguided marriage, the aunt had subsidized their emigration to Liberia with the purchase of an old plantation in the middle of the country. When the aunt died four years ago, she'd left clear title to the five-hundred-acre place in both their names. Joel and Mimy had been trying to reestablish family ties, and his parents had agreed to visit this fall—at least until this happened. Neither set of grandparents had ever seen their grandchild, Cannon, except in photographs mailed or posted on the Internet.

Jamal interrupted. "Someone's coming," he said, his voice high-pitched.

Cannon stepped from the shadows where he had been squatting quietly with his rifle across his knees. "It's Mr. Swafford," he said quietly.

Parker emerged out of the shadows of the pine trees. He hurried past the front of the tractor. "Quick, get a place cleared on the back of the trailer. Joel and them are bringing a wounded man. Cannon, get the Coleman lantern lit. We gonna need some light."

"Won't they be able to see it?" Jamal asked.

"Whoever shot those men is gone."

Artimecy and Mimy quickly shoved aside the corn and a few boxes to clear a small place at the tail end of the trailer. Victoria moved aside more items to make the space wider. Even with the noise and occasional bumping of Selma, she never woke.

"You said 'men.' How many wounded they bringing?" Artimecy asked.

"Only one wounded. There's a second man dead down there."

"How badly wounded is he?" Victoria asked. She stood near where Cannon had been squatting.

"Is he African?" Cannon asked.

"Can't tell how bad. He's moaning, so he's alive, but he ain't complaining and that ain't good. If we hadn't gotten there when we did, he'd be in some critter's stomach by morning."

"Parker, watch what you're saying. We got children here."

"Is he African?" Cannon asked again.

"Their childhood ended two days ago, Artimecy. They need to know what the hell's going on," he said, his voice rising. "And no, he ain't African. He's American, unless we got Africans wearing U.S. Army uniforms."

"Don't use that tone with me, old man. You know what I mean," Artimecy said, reaching up to slap him lightly on the chest.

"The U.S. Army is here?" Victoria asked, hope in her voice.

The noise of feet trampling bushes and the sound of grunts from the exertion of carrying a cumbersome burden announced the return. Benitez had a foot under each arm. Joel and Jose, the African-American youth, had the wounded soldier by the arms. George walked behind the three, holding the guns and continuously looking over his shoulders.

"Over here, Joel," Mimy said, pointing to the back of the trailer.

"Sure is quiet," Jamal said.

"Yeah, when they hear gunshots, the jungle knows to be quiet," Cannon said.

Cannon held the Coleman lantern high, the bright arc light illuminating the night, revealing the greens and brown of the nearby forest. It also highlighted dark red blood bubbling through the bullet hole in the camouflage shirt.

George propped the guns against the large wheel of the tractor before crouching near the front of it, just out of the glow from the lantern. His gun pointed the way they had just come.

The three men laid the wounded American as gently as possible on the rough wooden planks of the trailer.

"I may be able to help. I've had some Red Cross training," Victoria said, pushing her way to the wounded man.

Artimecy looked at the young man. "I think it may take more than Red Cross training for him, honey." She leaned down and touched the man's sweating forehead. "He's too pale, Parker. We gotta stop this bleeding."

Victoria grabbed the red-checkered tablecloth off Selma, ripped a huge piece from it, folded it a couple of times, and pressed it to the chest wound. "If we can stop the bleeding and the other lung isn't punctured, he may live until we can get him to a hospital."

She saw the looks between the adults. "What's wrong?"

"Ain't no hospital out here. Might be something they can do in Kingsville, but nothing we can do here except what you're doing, honey."

"I want my mommy," Selma said, sitting up and rubbing her eyes. She saw the wounded man at her feet, and quickly covered both eyes. Soft murmuring emerged from her slightly opened lips, and tears glistened in the starlight. She sat motionless, her eyes squeezed shut.

Artimecy reached up and patted her on the head. "Now, now, honey. We gonna get you to yore momma. You just hang in there."

"What happened?" Jamal asked.

"We gotta get that shirt off him," Artimecy said, opening a nearby bag and pulling out a pair of scissors.

She leaned forward and quickly cut away the shirt while Victoria leaned on the compress.

"Not sure what happened," Joel offered as the two women worked. "This man and another soldier must have stumbled onto the group that may have raided our farms. There may have been more in the gunfight, because there were several trees across the road. We found a body in the ditch on the far side. He'd been shot. It wasn't until we started back we heard moaning and found this one, still alive. Looked as if he had crawled into the bushes in an attempt to hide."

The man's eyes opened. "Kingsville," he mumbled weakly. "Got to warn them. Got to warn the armory."

"What'd he say?" Joel asked.

"Something about Kingsville and the armory," Artimecy replied.

Parker put his hand on the trailer and leaned across the wounded man. "What have we got to warn them about, son?"

The man lifted his arm for a moment. It fell, coming to rest against Parker's arm. The man's eyes opened. He lifted his head slightly, a weak grip holding Parker's arm. "My wife. My kids. Tell them I love them."

"Sure we will, son, but you gonna be able to tell them yourself."

The man's head rocked back and forth weakly. "No—you got to get to the armory in Kingsville and—" He coughed several times, and a string of blood ran out of his mouth and down his chin.

"You need to rest. We're going to get you to a doctor."

The man shook his head again. "Listen, please. Tell General Thomaston they're coming. You've got to warn him. They don't know," the soldier mumbled, and his head fell to the side. A long escape of air followed.

"Is he dead?" Mimy asked.

Victoria pressed down on the compress and with one hand put a couple of fingers against his neck. "No, he's still alive, but barely." She looked at Joel. "What are we going to do?"

Parker stepped back from the trailer.

"I guess we're going to cross the road to the other side," Joel answered with a lack of conviction.

"That is exactly what we're going to do," Parker said, spitting to the side. "We are going to get on the old road and keep going. What we have to do while Joel is driving is keep this young man as comfortable as possible and hope he lives until we reach Kingsville."

"Another ten kilometers should do it," Joel said.

"And it ain't getting any closer us standing here talking about it. The good news is the armory is on this side of town, so it ain't like we have to go through town to get to it."

"Yeah, if this road holds out and doesn't change direction."

"If, if, if. If it doesn't, then we'll face that when it happens; meanwhile, it's headed in the right direction and I can't see it heading south. Too much swamp and marsh thataway."

Joel grabbed his shotgun and climbed up into the driver's seat. He braced it alongside the controls of the tractor. "It's past midnight now. We don't know how this road is on the other side. This is as far as Parker, me, and Cannon have ever come."

"I'll walk out front," George said.

"We must try," Victoria said.

"Well, you ain't asking, but I'll tell you. I would feel a hell of a lot safer with a bunch of armed Americans around me." He pointed to Joel. "Now, if you can make a couple of kilometers an hour, then we can be there about daybreak and let whoever is holed up in the armory know what this man told us."

"We can do it," Victoria said. She shifted her hand slightly on the compress, and then looked toward Joel. "Please, we have to try. They're in danger and we're the only ones who know it."

"I think Uncle Nathan told them they were in danger," Jamal added.

"He did, but it looks as if danger is creeping closer."

Joel gave a quick nod. "We're going to try. I want everyone to understand that if we arrive and trouble is already there, I'm not going to risk my family. We'll go around and continue on to Ivory Coast."

"No, we aren't going to risk our families, but we need to do what we can to warn those in Kingsville," Artimecy said.

"If they're fighting when we get there, the warning will be a slight too late, Mrs. Swafford," Joel said.

"I'll ride on the trailer and help the soldier," Victoria said.

"Not by yourself, you won't," Artimecy added. "I may not know much about medicine, but I know enough about men." She crawled up and pulled one of the boxes over to lean on. She ripped another swatch of cloth from the torn tablecloth, opened a canteen, and poured some water on it. She then wiped the wounded man's forehead.

"Arty, you be careful," Parker said, a trace of emotion in his voice. "And don't fall off that contraption."

"You watch yourself, Parker Swafford," she replied softly. "I can take care of myself and this wounded man. You just help Joel get us to Kingsville and we'll all be all right. And you be careful. I'm too old to have to train a new husband."

"You boys, bring up the rear," George said. "If anything happens, you skedaddle into the brush and fight from there. Worst case, you run as fast as you can. You survive anyway you can, but you survive."

Jamal nodded. He and Cannon walked to the rear of the trailer and waited for it to start. Selma had not moved. She sat stiff with both hands still over her eyes. Everyone ignored her. What could they do anyway? he thought. As long as she was quiet and stayed where she was, she'd be all right. He wondered briefly if she would ever be the little sister he remembered. Jamal looked around, taking in where each person stood or sat. He never thought he would ever want to have his sister be the same as she was two days ago. It went dark. Someone had turned off the lantern.

Two minutes later, the tractor inched down the hill toward the highway. Starlight lit the way. The sounds of the jungle had returned sometime in the past few minutes, but the tractor drowned out most of them. So far, Joel had turned on the headlights only once on their trek, and that was a few miles back when a swath of overgrowth hid the road where a small stream broke the surface.

The critical time would be the minutes exposed when they crossed the open highway. Several yards from where the old road exited the pine trees, Joel gave Benitez his shotgun and sent him forward to the other side. Instead of dashing across the road, Benitez stopped in the middle of the highway, laid the shotgun down, and put his ear to the paved road. Seconds, which seemed minutes, later, the man stood and waved to the group.

"Come!" he shouted. "No one come."

"What'd he say?" Artimecy asked as she ran the damp cloth around the man's face. "I, for the life of me, cannot understand a word that man says."

Everyone involuntarily crouched as if expecting gunfire at any moment. When seconds passed and nothing happened, Joel accepted the stranger's assessment. He reached forward and shoved the gear into low. The wounded man moaned. Victoria lifted the compress slightly to check on the bleeding. It had slowed.

Jamal saw the dark stain on the bottom of the compress. He wondered, if the bleeding had stopped, would it be because of the compress or because the man was running out of blood? He wondered briefly if the bullet was still inside the young soldier, and figured it had to be there. He recalled Uncle Nathan once saying how bullets made small holes going into a person, but blasted huge holes when they left. More information than a twelve-year-old wanted to know at the time.

With the engine revving, the tractor moved down the last few yards to the highway. It tilted slightly as it pulled up the side of the grassy incline to the road, and then tilted the other way when it went down the other side a half minute later. Within three minutes, the procession was across the highway. This ragtag band of survivors disappeared into the jungle, leaving behind the empty sliver of a road they had just crossed.

Jamal thought of his father and mother, and he hoped they had made it to Kingsville. He shut his eyes for a quick prayer, promising all kinds of things to God if they were safe. When he opened his eyes, Selma looked as if she was peeping between her fingers. The night sounds of the jungle seemed to emerge simultaneously in a cacophony of screeches, light roars, and crashing of bushes. Jamal shivered involuntarily. What was going to happen to Selma and him? He had promised his parents he would watch after her. Tears flowed silently, drawing lines through his dust-covered face, to drip off his chin onto his shirt. Look at her now. They'd blame him for it.

CHAPTER 11

"GENERAL THOMASTON, DICK HOLMAN HERE. I THOUGHT you'd be in Abidjan by now," Admiral Holman said. He released the push-to-talk button in the center of the black handset.

"No, sir, Admiral. Can't tell yo—" came Thomaston's voice through the speaker above the captain's chair in the Combat Information Center spaces. A burst of static garbled the radio transmission.

Dick pushed the earpiece closer hoping to hear the retired lieutenant general over the static that disrupted the communications. The crackling rose and fell with moments of clear voice breaking through.

"—closed the border. Refused to recognize our American passports, saying we were Liberians now, so we needed to stay in Liberia. That closes the east to us and"—a new wave of static burst over the general's words for a few seconds—"here in Kingsville. Can't go south because of marsh and jungle. Passable, but we'd have a lot who wouldn't make it. Everyone's been moved into the armory. Suspect by morning the rebel force will be—"

The static this time rose in intensity, until the general ceased transmitting.

"General, Dick Holman!" he shouted. "I guess the good news is the French, through their Ivory Coast lackeys also refused us harbor permission, so we're still off the Liberian coast. The bad news is the French don't want us to conduct an evacuation."

"What the hell do the French have to do with this?" Thomaston broadcast angrily.

"What the hell do the French have to do with anything that has America in it?" Holman responded. "I said they didn't want us to do an evacuation. I didn't say we weren't going to come to you."

"Sorry, your broadcast was broken up. Say—"

Holman tossed the handset into its cradle and turned to Lieutenant Commander Rachel Grande, the ship's Communications Officer. "What the hell is wrong with this?" he asked, pointing at the handset.

"Sir, it's the best we can do. They're using VHF communications, which is usually line of sight. It's dawn, sir. This sunspot activity is not only hurting our HF communications, but unless we are within direct line of sight of each other, we won't be able to use VHF or UHF comms."

"Admiral, you still there?" came General Thomaston's voice from the speaker. It was a clear transmission.

Holman lifted the handset. "General, I am still here. My COMMO tells me when daylight breaks, this atrocious communications link is going to be nil heard between us. Can you go to HF?"

A few seconds passed, and those in CIC heard the familiar static announcing someone transmitting on the frequency. "It will take some time, Admiral. We're in the armory and Beaucoup, our radioman, moved his VHF and UHF radios with him, but the HF transmitter and the large antenna is across town. I don't think we'll have time to move it before the rebels get here." As he talked, the static reduced in intensity, and by the time he reached the end of the transmission the words were clear. "It's already daylight here."

Holman turned to Grande. "Good job, Rachel."

She looked at Captain Leo Upmann, the Chief of Staff, and shrugged her shoulders. How do you explain electromagnetic phenomena to a warfighter? To them, it was magic. Times like this reminded her of the scene in *Patton* when George C. Scott ordered the chaplain to write a prayer for good weather, and when it happened gave the chaplain credit for it.

"General, what's the situation?" Holman asked. It was the first question he had asked when the two began talking thirty minutes ago. Unfortunately, communications were so bad, he wasn't sure of anything other than Thomaston and his people were barricaded and waiting for Holman to come to the rescue.

"Admiral, hasn't changed since what I first told you. Rebel forces are moving on Kingsville. They could be in the surrounding hills, rain forest, and jungle now. All of the refugees and Kingsville citizens are cramped into the armory. We've limited small arms and ammunition, but should be able to hold until you arrive—if you come today," he repeated, his voice rising in inflection.

"Understand, General," Holman acknowledged, releasing the transmit button for a moment.

"Admiral?" Thomaston asked. "You still there?"

Holman pushed the transmit button. "General, we'll be there. I cannot give you an exact time, but this is one group of sailors and Marines that will not stand by and wait for you to fight your way out. You prepare your people for evacuation." Leo Upmann touched the admiral on the shoulder and held up one finger. "Wait one, General," Holman broadcast. He released the transmit button.

"What is it, Leo?"

"Sir, we need to shift the joint task force south and close the coast to fifteen miles."

Holman's eyebrows arched.

"Otherwise, Admiral, we'll have to refuel the helicopters in flight, and we don't have an aerial refueling capability." He stopped for a moment and then continued. "Ask the general if they have aviation fuel available."

Holman nodded, keyed the transmit button, and asked.

"Sure we have some, but it's at the airport about three kilometers from the armory. I don't have the personnel to secure the airport and defend the armory. Do you need that fuel to conduct your evacuation?"

Holman looked at Upmann and Captain Buford Green, the Joint Task Force Operations Officer, who stood to the left of

Upmann. Captain Green leaned forward. "Admiral, if we do what Leo suggests, we can do the evacuation without the fuel constraints provided it's a straight in-and-out operation and you keep moving south to reduce the flight time."

"Means General Thomaston will have to have his people ready to board when the helicopters put down," Upmann added.

"That's right. Time on the ground should be minimal, and if we're going to carry a full load, then they need to discard everything but the bare essentials."

Holman nodded and keyed the transmitter. "General, we're going to sail closer so we don't have to depend on your fuel as a resource. Means we have to more closer. That will take us a couple of hours before we can launch."

"Add another couple of hours of flight time," Thomaston said.

"That's right. We're talking late morning earliest before we can get there. Can you hold out?" Holman asked, knowing this would probably be their last transmission until he got his Marines airborne toward Kingsville. If Thomaston didn't think he could hold out, then Holman could dispatch a company of Devil Dogs on a one-way trip to Kingsville to help until they changed position.

Several seconds passed before the static preceding a transmission erupted from the speaker. "I think we can," Thomaston replied. "Our last contact with the enemy was four hours ago, and if they run true to form, they'll stop, assess the situation, debate it among themselves, pray to whatever God is in vogue, and eventually move forward. We'll be ready when you arrive."

"Okay, General. If you want, I can dispatch some forces your way until we get there, but if we do, it'll reduce the number of helicopters available for evacuating. That means taking longer to get your people out."

"I would think—" Thomaston started. A burst of static erupted, so loud it hurt Holman's ear, causing him to move the handset away. "Christ! Admiral, we're—" And a loud noise drowned out Thomaston's words before the speaker went silent.

"That sounded like an explosion," Green offered.

"Probably just morning static, Captain," Grande said.

Upmann looked from the Operations Officer to the Communications Officer. "I'm not sure what it was, but it definitely drowned out whatever he was saying."

"Rachel, take this and reestablish contact," Holman said, holding the handset near his ear.

She looked at the handset in her hand and at the admiral staring at her as if expecting her to fix the static. "Sir, I can try, but unless they get HF up, it will be impossible until we get something airborne that can relay their signals. HF is the only frequency band we can reach them without satellite communications—"

"And he did say the HF radio was across town from where they were holed up in the armory."

"That may be, Buford," Upmann said to Captain Green. "But surely he can send someone over there and turn it on."

"What do you think?" Holman asked Upmann, Green, and Captain Jeremiah Hudson, the commanding officer of the USS *Boxer*.

"I think he was saying they could hold out until we got there," Hudson offered.

"He did say that," Green said, "But for what it's worth, that last transmission didn't sound like static to me. It sounded like an explosion."

"What do you think, Jerry?" Holman asked the skipper.

The captain of the *Boxer* jerked his thumb toward Green. "I disagree. I don't think it was an explosion. I agree with the COMMO, but if I was where enemy forces were closing me and had no idea how many or when, I would opt for the Marines."

Holman nodded, biting his lower lip slightly, as he weighed the advice being given. "Leo, get everyone together. I want two plans. One for sending a company of Marines now, and another for holding off and sending them as part of the evacuation operation. Whichever, I want the rescue op to commence in two hours."

"If we send a company of Marines and they land in the middle of combat, we risk losing them and a helicopter. If they arrive before the enemy does, we stand a chance of losing a helicopter and a loss of a helicopter means a longer evacuation," Upmann offered.

Holman nodded. "I know, Leo. Get those two plans worked out."

"I'll work with Colonel Battersby," Green offered, referring to the commander of the landing force.

"Admiral, with your permission, I'll turn the joint task force southeast to close their position," Captain Hudson said.

"Yes, do it, Jerry." Holman looked at his Chief of Staff. "Leo, tell Mary I want an updated intel estimate as soon as possible."

"Yes, sir, Admiral," Leo said. "What about the French?"

Holman bit his lower lip, his eyebrows arched inward as his brow wrinkled. Time to remove them from the equation? "Right now, we don't know if Thomaston is being attacked or not," Holman said, ignoring Leo's question. "That being said, if the terrorists and rebels or whatever you want to call them aren't already in or around the town, they will be shortly."

"We can dispatch Marines within a couple of hours," Green offered.

Holman nodded. "Yes, we can. But Leo's right. We need to know how far the French are willing to go with their thinly veiled threat to interfere with any evacuation attempt." Holman turned to Rachel Grande again. "Commander, have we received a reply to my PERSONAL FOR to Commander, European Command?"

She shook her head. "No, sir, we haven't. I can tweak them, sir, but my only link is via the communicators in Naples, Italy. They would have to call Stuttgart, Germany, to see what the status is of the message. We know it was delivered—I don't have the exact time, but the duty officer in Naples said it was delivered to her counterpart in Stuttgart within a half hour of its release."

He nodded. "It was delivered." His lips tightened as his mind turned to the mission at hand. "Thanks, Rachel. Go back to the radio shack and tweak them. When the reply arrives from EUCOM or from the Joint Chiefs of Staff or anyone who purports to know . . . sorry, anyone senior to me, bring me the message ASAP."

Upmann spoke. "Admiral, I think we should go ahead and dispatch some Marines now."

"Thanks, Leo. But I can't have a helo full of Marines airborne with a bunch of shaky Frenchmen flying fighters around us."

"I don't think he'll do anything."

"If I was him, I wouldn't either, but I'm not him. I'm me. One thing we learned on September 11, 2001 is to accept every threat at face value. A threat made is one responded to. If they say it, then assume they mean it and act accordingly."

"But why are the French doing this?"

"If I knew, Leo, I'd probably be in Washington."

Admiral Holman moved away from the ventilation above his head to the other side of the captain's chair in the center of the Combat Information Center. The hundred-plus degree of heat outside would feel good when he went topside again. A minute later, he turned, a huge smile across his face, which grew broader when he saw the confused expression of his Chief of Staff. *Score another one for the brown shoes.*

"Seems to me, Leo, it's time for what you SWOs do best— a little operational deception."

"Admiral, makes me nervous when you say it's something us surface-warfare officers do best. Deceive them? I suspect you have a plan, sir?"

"Oh, Leo, ye of little faith. Let's play on the national paranoia of France. I have an idea. What I need is help in fattening it out. If we do it right, we'll have the Marines ashore in Kingsville by this afternoon without the French bothering us."

"Sure, Admiral. Whatever you say," Leo said, his voice betraying his lack of optimism.

Holman chuckled, tilted his head, and winked. "Come on, Leo. Have confidence. Didn't I once take an entire carrier battle group through a minefield without a single loss?"

"Yes, sir, you did. The difference is that was a trick against technology and this involves humans—"

"—who seldom listen to their own machines. I know, Leo, I know. Send me that Lieutenant Shoemaker—*I think that's his name*—from those operators of unmanned flying things."

"Oh, the pilot?"

"Leo, he's not inside a cockpit riding a hundred thousand

parts made by the lowest bidder. He's sitting in the hangar bay, playing warrior like some young kid with a new Sony Playstation. Doesn't matter. Time we truly test them."

"I'll get the pilot," Upmann said. "If this idea works, Admiral, you may have to change your views on whether you like or dislike this unmanned flight program."

"That will never happen, Leo. However, disliking unmanned aircraft or not, using them is an entirely different thing. I would prefer heavy fighter aircraft with all their weaponry and pilot capability, but the nearest aircraft carrier is thousands of miles away, and the Air Force doesn't have landing rights in any of the countries around here. We'll make do with what we have and see what happens."

"We going to launch them against the French?"

"Umm. As appealing as it sounds, I don't think so. What I want is to convince the French that an American aircraft carrier has entered the area."

"Be hard to do, Admiral. We can change the lighting on the *Boxer,* but only at night. We don't have the equipment to change our electronic signatures to match a carrier's surface-search, air-search, and fire-control radars. They'll figure it out before we're an hour into it."

"Leo, is this a surface-warfare thing? Half-empty glass of water instead of half-full?" Holman asked, a slight tinge of humor beneath the words.

"Aye, aye, sir. I am sure we can figure out something. And I do see a half-full glass here, Admiral—just the width of it seems shallow."

This could be fun, he thought as he turned to go back up the ladder to the bridge. The men and women manning the various combat consoles around the dark space watched as the admiral departed Combat. The EW operator shrugged and pulled the zipper up on her jacket before returning her attention to the polar display in front of her. A few seconds later, the low murmur of operational activity and exchange of information returned to mix with the sounds of fans inside the equipment working continuously to keep the computers and display units from overheating.

CHAPTER 12

THE EXPLOSION BLEW THE TOP OFF THE ARMORY GATEPOST.
Shards of brick and mortar mixed with deadly pieces of whirling barbed wire ripped along the front of the armory building.
The noise from the M-50 stopped abruptly. Lethal shrapnel
sawed through it and the two militiamen manning the position.
Thomaston's last communication with the Navy had been an
hour ago.

The concussion knocked retired Lieutenant General Daniel
Thomaston to the ground, saving his life as the shrapnel passed
over him.

A moment later he opened his eyes, his vision slightly
blurred. Several blinks cleared them. Something pressed across
his hips and legs. His initial thought was part of the building
had landed on him. He wiggled slightly to see how badly he
was trapped. Whatever it was shifted. Thomaston reached
back, grabbed a handful of cloth, and pulled the weight off
him. He rolled onto his back. A sharp, momentary pain caused
his jaws to tighten. The dismembered torso of one of the defenders lay beside him. A dark swathe of blood covered the
name tag, but Thomaston knew it was one of the machine-
gunners. Both legs were missing from the knees down and

half the head was gone. A single glazed eye stared lifelessly upward.

He turned and pushed himself to his knees, grabbed his M-16, and stood. His camouflage uniform was splattered with blood. Retired Sergeant Major Gentle, at a crouch, ran toward him, glancing toward the wall with his M-16 pointed in the same direction.

"General," Craig Gentle shouted above the gunfire, sliding to his knees beside Thomaston. "Are you hurt, sir?" Bits of brick from the building showered the ground as bullets from the attacking rebels peppered it. "Damn! That hurt," Gentle mumbled, pushing himself off his knees and wiping away brick fragments.

Thomaston shook his head. "I'm fine." Thomaston looked over his shoulder at the building behind him. Every window was broken. The integrity of the building appeared intact. In the basement, far to the rear, noncombatants had taken refuge. He had to move them. The building was too easy a target. A stitch of bullets from an automatic weapon traced along the bricks near the roof, sending more shards raining down on the grass.

The rebels did not intend to take prisoners, unless it was to videotape killing them to inflame the Western world and gain admiration from followers. They also wanted the vehicles parked in the rear as well as the weapons they had. The last thing he intended to give them were weapons to expand their attack against Americans. He glanced at the sky. He wished he knew if Holman was going to send the Marines early, but the attack an hour ago had cut the radio conversation off prematurely.

"Craig, move three of our fighters from the north wall to the front," he ordered, pointing at the area where the mortar round had hit. Dust clouded the area, obstructing a clear view.

Gentle grabbed the barrel of the general's rifle. "Wouldn't use that, sir," he said, nodding toward it.

The barrel bent slightly to the right. If Thomaston had fired it, the result would have been an exploding piece wounding or killing him.

"Here, take mine, General. I'll take that one over there,"

Gentle said, pointing to an M-16 lying unattended on the brown grass of the lawn several yards away.

Thomaston did not have to ask whose it was. He looked along the front wall and, with the exception of the destroyed gatepost, the other militiamen and townsfolk were still fighting. The smell of gunpowder and explosives filled the air, burning his nostrils and causing his eyes to water.

He counted four bodies near the front gate. That left twenty-eight lightly trained militiamen, not counting himself or Craig Gentle. They could not win a war of attrition. The townsfolk with weapons could never withstand a concerted attack by the enemy. He'd even had to show several how to turn the safety on and off. A few figured out on their own how to eject and reload the magazines. Now that they were in combat, he wondered briefly how many remembered how those two simple evolutions worked. Fear was not a great training technique.

Thomaston estimated more than two hundred fanatics facing them. On the plus side, his people were in a strong defensive position if the opposing forces didn't possess too many mortar rounds. Maybe when he surveyed the battleground, he would find most of the enemy dead or dying in the open field between the road and the armory. He sighed. Wishes and hope never win battles.

The attackers had surprised them. He thought they were farther away. The initial attack of four mortar rounds into the armory sent everyone scurrying to their positions. He glanced at the radio antenna, bent in half where shrapnel had damaged it. Then, just as suddenly, the attack stopped and an African waving a white flag had approached the front gate.

The African demanded they surrender and even promised free passage to Ivory Coast. But everyone in the armory recalled what happened to those Americans trapped in Egypt who were offered the same terms and when they walked out of the hotel, they had been captured and tortured, and had their throats cut, one by one. America had never forgotten the power of those videotapes. He shut his eyes for a moment.

Thomaston's hands flexed on his M-16. Nothing would make him feel better than to *martyr* this bunch right here, right now, in Kingsville.

An earlier attempt to bluff this homegrown self-made tyrant who called himself a mullah had failed. This *Abu Shit-for-brains* refused to believe the vehicles were disabled, rendering them useless. The man wasn't after arms and cars. He wanted more videotaped examples to rub in America's face. More videotapes to go into the September 11th memorial in Washington.

Gunfire, rising in intensity, echoed from the direction of the gate. Gentle reached down and grabbed the M-16 as he zigzagged past. Thomaston jumped over the lower half of a leg still encased in a combat boot, joining Gentle in their dash to safety. The two, back first, slammed against the west wall. Thomaston pointed left. Gentle nodded, turned in that direction, and ran toward the corner of the building, bits of masonry flying over him as enemy snipers fired. The retired sergeant major disappeared around the edge of the armory building.

Thomaston ran along the wall, reaching the side of the damaged gate. The light African wind was clearing the smoke and dust away. The right section was gone, leaving an opening big enough for two at a time to enter. Thomaston turned right and hurried along the wall to where three militiamen stood on top of an SUV, firing over the top of the wall. He didn't recall directing anyone to move the vehicle here.

"You!" he shouted to the nearest person. The man looked down at the general. "Come with me!"

The man touched his comrade and pointed at the general. The two jumped down. Thomaston had only meant to take one, but considering the opening near the gate as their biggest vulnerability, two were better than one.

Thomaston ran back toward the front of the gate. The two young men followed. All three ran at a crouch, though the top of the brick wall was high enough to protect them from the angry sound of bullets flying overhead. The thick ozone smell of combat dried the general's nostrils.

When he reached the opening, Thomaston squatted and pointed to the breach. "See that, men?" he said. "If they get through that hole we're going to have to retreat. Once they're inside, it's only a matter of time before they overrun us."

They nodded.

"You understand what I'm telling you?" he asked, his voice

firm as he stared intently into each of their faces. "You can't give up this position. They mustn't get in," he said softly.

The nearest militiaman licked his lips a couple of times and stared at the hole in the wall. He understood. Thomaston saw realization on both their faces. Both had family in the armory. The first's jaw dropped for a second, and then visibly the young man straightened and nodded sharply. "We understand, General. No retreat from this position."

The young man standing behind the first wiped his hands one at a time on his trousers. His eyes glistened with moisture. Thomaston knew the fear they were experiencing, for the most these two could do was buy time, and they knew it too.

"I'll be watching and if it looks as if they are going to breach, I'll try to send reinforcements. You understand?"

They nodded.

"You can't leave this breach undefended. No one, and I mean no one, must get through."

Around the corner of the building, Craig Gentle appeared with four townsmen. About one hundred yards separated the east wall from the lake. Running behind the lake, rain forest stretched down from the hills to join the thick jungle and rain forest to their south.

"Good luck," he said to the two militiamen. He touched each of them on the shoulders as he left, never looking back. Thomaston picked up the pace and sprinted to where Gentle and the others squatted under the protection of the south wall.

Before Thomaston arrived, one of the men jumped at something Gentle said and ran toward the SUV to join the lone gunman there.

Was it his imagination or was gunfire tapering off?

"General, where do you want these three?" Gentle asked.

He looked swiftly around the area where the attack seemed concentrated. "Send them to the other side of the front gate as reserve to the two guarding the breach in the wall. You three, listen to me." He saw the patina on the sleeve of the older man where at one time the black chevrons of a sergeant had been sewn. Fremont Sealey was the man's name. The two bottom buttons of the shirt were open to allow the ample paunch to protrude. He was one of the automobile mechanics of the town. Thomaston never knew he had been Army. "Sergeant Sealey, you keep these two with you. Your job is to reinforce any area of the wall where it looks as if the enemy is trying to penetrate. Watch the front gate. If they get inside the compound, we retreat to the vehicles parked around back."

Sealey saluted. "Will do, sir."

Thomaston detected a slight trace of moisture in the sergeant's eyes. He glanced at the front of the old Army shirt looking for some sign of Sealy's specialty, but saw none. Made a snap decision he was a Desert Storm veteran from his age and gray hair. Been a while since Sealey had seen combat, he thought. "Fremont, the troops are looking to you, Sergeant Major Gentle, and me for leadership. You can do it, soldier. Your job is to make sure no one overruns the breach created by the explosion. I am giving you command of the south and west walls. No one gets inside the compound."

Thomaston saw the man's back visibly straighten. He understood what was happening—the moment in combat when a soldier fully realizes his only chance to live was to fight fiercely and win.

"Yes, sir. We can do it."

"Fremont." Thomaston leaned against the hefty veteran and whispered softly into his ear. "No retreat. There can be no retreat."

"I know, sir. Johnson, Wood," the resurrected sergeant said to the two townsmen behind him. "Let's go." He motioned forward. "Stay with me, and I'll kick yore butts if you try to leave until I tell you to."

"Sergeant Sealey," Gentle said, "be careful."

The old man's face tightened, his jowls and double chin rising, as he replied with confidence, "Sergeant Major; Jason, Andy, and I will be all right. No one is getting inside without coming through us."

Combat was more than a battle of weapons and explosives; it was the measure by which an individual's fortitude was weighed; an individual's ability to fight and win against an overwhelming urge to run. During battle, Thomaston had seen adversity forged in moments from the least likely character, and he had been surprised to discover it lacking in those he'd most expected to rise to the moment when courage was needed. It little surprised him to see it in the sergeant. It mattered little what age you were when it was time to rise to the call of combat.

Soldiers seldom realized the exact moment when they become seasoned combat veterans. One moment they're scared new meat, and the next they're scared combat veterans. There was no universal moment to identify when that transition occurred. One moment they doubted their own capability, and the next they doubted the enemy's. It was also a dangerous moment, when suppressed fear sometimes cost lives.

The whistle of a mortar rode over the noise of small arms. Thomaston glanced upward, tracking the shell by sound as it passed overhead. "Incoming!" he shouted, shoving Gentle. Across the front lawn of the armory, Sergeant Sealey and his two townsmen followed suit, diving to the ground at the same time as Thomaston.

The mortar round passed over the building, exploding near the vehicle park. Across from Thomaston, Sergeant Sealey pushed himself off the ground, slapped the two with him, and the three continued their slow run toward the front wall.

If they started taking mortar fire, the armory building would be fair game to the attacking force. The noncombatants—*the image of the civilians crouching scared in the dark basement broke into his thoughts, and just as quickly he shoved it aside*—must be moved ASAP out of the building.

"Craig, get them the hell out of the building!"

"General, they're safe there," Gentle said, raising to a crouch.

"Not with mortar fire. You know that. If they really want our vehicles, they'll avoid hitting the parking area. The building is nothing to them. It's just a reference point. Use some of the townsmen in back and build a defensive perimeter with those vehicles. It'll give us a place to fall back if they break through. You get everyone out and into the center of that perimeter. Then organize covering fire if we fall back." He paused for a moment. "We both know they're going to break through. I'll lead a fighting retreat and slow them up."

"Sir, why don't I do that? I mean—"

"Thanks, Sergeant Major, but you're needed back there to hold the fort until the cavalry arrives."

"You mean if anything happens to you."

Thomaston nodded. "I would think, after all these years, I should be able to keep from being killed by a bunch of half-trained rabble. They may outnumber us—"

"Outnumber? Damn, General. Now you tell me," Gentle said as he stood.

Thomaston watched for a moment as Gentle zigzagged in his run toward the building, the M-16 gripped tightly in the sergeant major's left hand.

Just as suddenly as it began, the gunfire stopped. Thomaston watched as the townsmen and militia defending the west wall lowered their weapons. From the front door of the armory two women appeared, lugging two boxes of M-16 magazines down the steps. One turned to the right side of the gate, while the other hurried to the other side.

Samson Roosevelt stood on top of the planks braced over a couple of rain barrels. The young African-American with his out-of-date Afro hairstyle looked across the torn-up field in front of the armory at the general. "They're stopping, sir. They're turning back toward the main road." He grinned, lifting his M-16 and shaking it in the air a few times. "Whoa, man!" Roosevelt inhaled deeply several times, shouting "Whoa man!" with each exhale. The man flopped down on the planks, shaking his head.

Thomaston hustled to where Roosevelt stood and pulled himself up. The young man reached down and helped the general the last few inches.

"Where's Tawela, Samson?"

Roosevelt looked up at Thomaston, bit his lower lip, and shook his head a couple of times. "Sorry, General, but she went and got herself shot." He pointed toward the rear of the armory building. "I think she's back there. That's where I saw a couple of men carrying her."

Thomaston nodded, then looked over the top of the wall. The main road, about four hundred yards away, crossed the entrance to the armory like a T. A hodgepodge collection of armed pickup trucks dotted the open field, reaching back to the main force of rebel vehicles parked along the shoulder. The pickup trucks had machine guns mounted on the cabs. Thomaston picked up his binoculars and peered through them—*older version of the modern .50-caliber machine gun, but they'd still kill you.* When he was wounded in Egypt, he didn't ask what type of bullet it was. From the gunfire laid down by the enemy and the return fire his force mounted, he expected to see more than the few bodies he did between the wall and the first line of pickup trucks. He swept the opposing force with the binoculars, inwardly delighted at their over-confidence in not guarding their numbers and their disposition. His people were outnumbered, but the enemy sure as hell had no concept of a military operation. To his advantage, they had no way of knowing exactly how many people—*fighters*— he had. Information was power, and the ragtag rebel army out there was providing him with more than they could imagine. Unfortunately, not all the information in the world would help if he didn't have the forces or time to take advantage of it, but it might allow his people to hold out long enough for those slow-moving Navy folk to arrive. *Damn, Marines! It's time to live up to your self-made nine-one-one image.*

To the enemy's advantage, they knew he only had small arms—basic infantry—to defend his position.

He continued his sweep of the opposing force, soaking up what he saw. It had been an hour since the attack had begun, and this was the first opportunity for him to see the forces arraigned against them. He abruptly found what he was look-ing for. It was located along the highway, three vehicles down from the lead SUV. The enemy vehicles along the highway pointed south, the direction they were traveling when they ar-rived. He focused the lens, brining the load vehicle closer. This was the command vehicle where this self-made Abu Alhaul commanded the attack. The fact that small groups of armed men were converging on the command vehicle confirmed his observation. Damn, what he wouldn't give for an artillery piece or a mortar and a damn good artilleryman right now. He could end this quickly. Most of those approaching were ob-viously Africans, but intermixed among them were the brown-skinned Arabs identified by headdresses and long flowing robes.

He lowered the binoculars and scanned the open ground from right to left. Nothing indicated they were regrouping or shifting forces to the rear of the armory. Not that he could see.

Maybe all this action was a subterfuge to draw attention away from the east wall in the rear.

Thomaston glanced toward the pockmarked building. Every window gone. The eastern corner partially blown away by a mortar shell. He took a deep breath, pulled the handkerchief from his rear pocket, and wiped sweat from his forehead. At least, he had the venerable Gentle in the rear. Without a sense of arrogance, Thomaston knew the two of them were the keys for holding out until rescue arrived. He looked at his watch. Nearly two hours since the African had appeared at the front gate demanding surrender. Thomaston had offered the same surrender opportunity to the African, slightly amused when the man seemed startled by the suggestion. The African, tall, powerfully built, had calmly threatened to kill everyone in the armory unless they surrendered. The threat didn't scare Thomaston—it pissed him off. What the threat told him was the man was one of the leaders. Only one of the leaders could have the authority to make such a threat. A lesser-ranked individual would have hightailed it back to the leadership for further instructions. Thomaston thought for a moment about shooting him—right then at the front gate.

He would have died in the gunfire, but by God, it would have been one less leader against them. This ragtag, dangerous bunch of Africans and Arabs were held together only by the charisma of this religious fanatic. He wondered briefly if the African he had talked to had been this Abu Alhaul.

This shouldn't be happening in the twenty-first century! This was a scene typical of over two hundred years of history in the Dark Continent. Winston Churchill was right when he said that those who ignored history were doomed to repeat it.

He watched the movements along the road and in the town as his mind recalled the initial encounter. Nearly an hour after the surrender demand, scattered gunfire of opportunity peppered the armory. Then, almost on the hour, pickup trucks had surged toward the wall, firing heavy machine guns across the top, wounding several townspeople, before the vehicles had scurried back toward the highway. He tweaked the binoculars. The highway was their main defensive line. Thirty minutes ago had been the heaviest, when the attackers committed ground forces forward supported by the pickups. It was only through the will and tenacity of the defenders that they had repelled the first attack. If he was in Abu Alhaul's shoes, what would he do?

Around the enemy command vehicle, something similar to an American council of colonels was probably advising Abu Alhaul on the next move. He had seen men such as Abu Alhaul in other Third World armies—the North African crusade came easily to mind. He had also seen petty tyrants in his own Army who were soon weeded out before they made lieutenant colonel. Every now and then, one of them made colonel or even higher, but they soon departed from active duty.

If only he could communicate with the outside. If only he had one tank or one APC. If only he had a hundred real soldiers or National Guardsmen. *If* was a big word and a useless conjecture in a fight. A soldier's entire attention was focused on combat, hoping and praying he or she never reached the point where worrying about conserving ammunition affected their fight. When that point arrived, it became the enemy's game. You fought for the moment, and prayed in the real Army that this new concept of focused logistics worked. He always wondered if translating the business concept of *"just in time"* delivery to *"focused logistics"* was something that would work when bullets, bombs, and body parts filled the air.

"General," Gentle said from behind him.

"Yes."

"Everyone's out of the building and in the vehicle park, sir."

The whistling of another mortar round drowned out Gentle's last few words. Along the wall, defenders dropped, burying their heads in their arms. He glanced up at the sky. This one was going to pass over the wall. He looked at the building.

The top of the building exploded as the shell hit, blowing roofing tiles and shattered bricks into the air. Another mortar followed.

"That mortar is going to play hell with us. Craig, tell everyone in the park to stay down."

Gentle nodded and took off running, staying close to the side of the wall. Thomaston squatted with his back against the bricks. He was pleased to see Roosevelt rise and peer over the wall with his M-16 pointed forward. The man had obviously figured out how to tell the path of a mortar round from the whistle . . . or maybe he hadn't.

"YOU MUST BE QUIET, ASRAF," MUMAR FLARED. WHY DID Abdo have the right to choose for this mission? He was in charge.

"Mumar, you carry this machine gun. You fight your way through the brush. You try not to trip, and then you can tell *me to be quiet*, my kaffir countryman," Asraf replied menacingly.

"And I must carry this mortar while Nakolimia carries the shells. They are exceedingly heavy," the man stumbling behind Asraf added.

Mumar's eyebrows wrinkled as he concentrated for a couple of seconds, trying to recall the man's name. His task—assigned by Abu Alhaul—was to place the mortar on the top of the hill overlooking the south wall of the armory. The man had actually touched him on the shoulder, looked him in the eye, and told him how important this mission was. Mumar's upper lip curled. First, it was the Arabs. Then, it was the white man. Then, the Chinese, and now it was the Arabs again. Someday he would rid his continent of these outsiders. This he vowed. Like most Africans, Mumar thought of Africa as the land below the Sahara. He turned and continued his trek up the hill, ignoring the low grumbling behind him.

He touched a small short-wave radio clipped to side of his khaki belt. They had found these nice things in Monrovia. They only worked a few miles. He turned the speaker down, but not so low he couldn't hear the battle commands for the ongoing attack on the armory. Every time someone spoke, a slight click followed by a burst of static erupted before the voices smoothed out the transmission. He wanted to listen to the main attack. Every time he heard another group attacking the American armory, he resented marching uphill. If he had been down there, he would already be inside the armory. Many heads would be strewn around where he stood and everyone would know what a great fighter and leader he was.

He perversely hoped Abu Alhaul's plan to overrun the armory took long enough for *him* to prove his worth. Not for

Abu Alhaul, but for the African foot soldiers who gave their blood for a fight that would never benefit the Africans. When he set this mortar up and lobbed the six shells they carried into the rear of the south wall defenders, he would be a hero. Not to the Arabs, but to Africans. This was important. His only warning from Abu Alhaul was to avoid hitting the vehicles. Mumar knew he must prove his worth if he ever hoped to lead his brothers to freedom, for in Africa only the strong and merciless rose to power. Freedom from the Arabs and freedom from the white man.

Bushes crackled as someone fell behind him. A limb shot forward, whipping across his naked legs and the bottom of his khaki shorts, drawing a short yelp from him.

"Damn you, Mumar!" Asraf shouted.

Unseen, Mumar drew his pistol and turned slightly. He held the weapon alongside his right leg, pointing toward the ground. The dense bushes hid the pistol from view. His AK-47 hung by its strap from his left shoulder.

Asraf lay spread-eagled across the M-50 machine gun. The big man's hands slipped as he attempted to push himself up. "I shall kill you for this. You carry nothing, but walk ahead as if you are better than us." He grabbed a nearby small tree trunk and pulled himself up. Then, still spitting venomous insults at Mumar, Asraf reached down with his right hand and lifted the M-50 by the stock, causing the barrel to sink a couple of inches into the dark humus that made up the rain forest floor. "Or maybe I will just whip you and make you our mule. What do you think, Ougalie? What do you think, Nakolimia?" He glanced back at the two smaller men, who set their loads down on the widening small animal path they were following.

Ougalie, that was the name of the man from Sierra Leone. Ougalie was one of many who were not Liberian. Ougalie spoke Bassa, a regional dialect also prevalent in the Grand Bassa, Rivercress, and Montserrado counties of Liberia.

"It would be fun to see the tall giraffe carry the mortar. Maybe we could tie the shells to him and see how far he could walk," Ougalie offered.

Mumar looked past the two men to the third, Nakolimia. The Liberian rebel from the town of Zorzor was silent, though his eyes shifted constantly following the words.

"Asraf, I am in charge. You will carry the machine gun. You, Ougalie, will carry the mortar, and Nakolimia will take up the satchel with the shells. We will continue," he commanded, his voice low, steady, and more controlled than he thought possible. "And you will keep quiet so the enemy won't hear us moving behind them."

"And how will they hear? Will a clap of thunder ring out across the forests"—Asraf clapped his hands once—"and say, *'Look here, Americans, there are three men behind you'*?"

"They may have spies or patrols to warn them," Mumar offered, aware of the weak argument. "Some are smart enough to know how to fight, not how to shout louder to hide their own stupidity."

The giant glanced uphill at Mumar from beneath furrowed eyebrows bunched over narrowed eyes. Asraf's chest rose and fell in deep breaths as his lips curled upward. Mumar mistakenly decided Asraf's performance was that of a coward who used his size to intimidate and bully. He should have realized this. He smiled.

"Don't laugh at me! You are no better than the rest of us!" Asraf shouted, sweeping his left arm through the surrounding bush to point at the other two men.

"I'm in charge," Mumar said, taking a deep breath and standing as tall as he could. His height could be intimidating. His hand tightened on the pistol. He slid his finger onto the trigger. Not only was Asraf a coward, he was crazy. He was like those who ate the wild berries in the jungle. Only this one never voided them from his system. With his thumb, Mumar flipped the safety off.

"You may think you're in charge. You are but a lover of men. Your butt hole must be this big," Asraf said, balancing the M-50 against his leg to cup the index fingers and thumbs from both hands. He laughed, looking at Ougalie, who laughed with him. "Yes, this big." Asraf laughed louder. "You should have seen this boy," he said, jabbing his finger at Mumar several times, all the while glaring at the taller but lighter man. The recapture of the M-50 by Asraf's right hand didn't slip by Mumar.

Then, in a low, menacing voice, his eyes locked with Mumar's, Asraf continued. "In Monrovia, when we had our choice of women, he refused to enjoy. He walked around the camp, watching us having fun, and when we invited him to sample them, including the American woman and her daughter, he refused. He turned his nose into the air as if he was so much better than the rest of us. Are you, Mumar? Are you better than the rest of us?"

"I don't have to wait for someone to hold a woman down for me to enjoy. I do not have to couple while other men enjoy the spectacle."

"We had two wild women and he wanted no part of them," Asraf said, talking to the other two while his eyes remained fixed on Mumar.

"You talk too much." Mumar tensed, waiting for Asraf to work up the courage to make his move.

"His nose was in the air," Asraf said in ridicule to the amusement of Ougalie.

Mumar kept his left side toward Asraf, keeping the pistol out of sight. Ougalie was thin, as if bereft of substance for most of his life, living off discards of others. There were many like him in the slums of the cities. Africans who would rather beg than work. This one was more of a coward than Asraf. Asraf was a bully, a coward, and dangerous when his confidence overloaded his ego. Ougalie was a true coward who would follow the stronger until the tide turned. Then, the man would flow with the current, rushing away at the first sign of danger.

Mumar glanced at the third man. Nakolimia was slightly larger than Ougalie. The torn green half-sleeved shirt he wore revealed the wiry muscles of a man used to heavy work all his life. Nakolimia stood with his hands hanging by his sides, watching the confrontation and giving no sign of a smile or of revulsion. Nakolimia was a survivor. He would go with the victor, Mumar decided. In Africa, as in Afghanistan, changing sides came easy. It took only seconds for Mumar to assess the two men and realize the true outcome was only between him and Asraf.

"I did not watch," Ougalie said, stepping up beside Asraf. "I too enjoyed the women, but what my brother Asraf says is true, now that I recall it, Mumar. You didn't prove your manhood in Monrovia. Instead, you watched what real men do to women."

"He probably walked off to relieve himself in the shadows so he could watch us without us seeing him," Asraf said. He cupped his right hand and jerked it up and down several times. "Like this."

Asraf took a step forward as if unintentionally changing his stance. The movement was not lost on Mumar. The man was positioning to where with a fast move or leap, he could grab Mumar in those heavy arms of his. If that happened, the game would be over quickly.

"She jerked like a bull with a bee under its tail, screaming for more. . . ."

"If she was having so much fun, why'd you cut her throat?" Keep him off balanced.

The big man's nostrils swelled. His lower lip jutted out and Mumar met the hostile stare.

"When I am done with a woman, she will never find another man like me," Asraf said with a dark smoldering look. Blood vessels along the sides of the man's forehead appeared to swell. "It is better they die than suffer the remainder of their life hoping for a man who can fulfill their desires such as I."

Mumar caught the slight movement of Asraf's hand tightening on the M-50. He glanced down. The humus on the barrel showed the M-50 was no longer buried in the damp forest floor. While he had watched Asraf and the other two, Asraf had slowly edged the heavy machine gun to where he could swing it up quickly.

"What d'you think Abu Alhaul is going to do when we tell him how you offered yourself to us?" Asraf jerked the heavy machine gun up in one smooth movement.

The speed of the big man surprised and nearly caught Mumar off guard. He brought the pistol around and fired before the heavy machine gun reached Asraf's waist. The bullet made a nice round hole in the forehead of the giant before shattering the back of the head as it exited. "I think he will believe you exaggerate too much, Asraf."

The other two jumped back. Mumar moved the pistol slightly so it covered them.

Ougalie dropped to his knees, his hand clasped in front of

him, and cried, "Don't kill me. Please, don't kill me. I didn't mean anything I said. Asraf made me say those things. I would never believe it. Never, never, never. Please don't shoot me."

Nakolimia met Mumar's stare. The Liberian remained motionless in the same posture he had held throughout the confrontation.

"Ougalie, I think I may have to shoot you. You are Asraf's boy, are you not?"

The man fell forward, flat on the ground, stretching his skinny arms forward, hands up. Turning his head so he could look up at Mumar, he pleaded for his life.

Mumar stepped forward, put the gun against the man's head. "You were going to have a lot to say when we returned. Right?"

"No, no. Nothing. I swear. I was never going to say anything."

Mumar smiled. A little begging and pleading was good for the soul. Not necessarily Ougalie's, but definitely *his*. He reached down and pulled the slide back.

"Ahhhh," Ougalie said and passed out. A wet puddle of urine flowed from beneath the body.

Mumar smiled.

"Who is in charge?" Mumar stood, removing the pistol from the unconscious Ougalie's head.

"You are in charge, Colonel," Nakolimia said. The man leaned down and picked up the satchel with the mortar shells. "I am prepared to continue, sir."

Mumar nodded. He kicked Asraf's body. "He had it coming. If I hadn't killed him, someone else would have." He slipped the safety back on and shoved the pistol into his holster.

Ougalie moaned. Mumar kicked him. "Get up, you piece of monkey shit."

The man ran his hand back and forth, rapidly, over his head. Then he jumped up and explored his body in the same manner. His knees buckled for a moment and tears flooded down his cheeks.

"I didn't shoot you, Ougalie. There are no bullet holes for you to find. If you make me angry, or fail to do what I tell you to do when I tell you to do it, I shall put holes in your body and your head and leave you tied down for the ants and beetles to finish you off."

"Thank you, master, thank you," Ougalie cried. "Whatever you want."

"Pick up that mortar. We have a mission to do. Our African brothers are expecting us to save their lives."

He was amused at how fast the Sierra Leone native moved. Someday others would move just as fast, but because of respect instead of fear. Someday he—*Mumar*—would rid Africa of those who would attempt to master his people.

Mumar unzipped his pants and relieved himself on the dead man, ignoring the other two. They were his now. Finished, he rolled Asraf's body to one side to free the M-50, then hoisted the heavy weapon across his own back. The ammunition cache he picked up. Damn, this was heavy. He should have waited until they reached the top before killing Asraf, but nobody was going to ruin his reputation regardless of how big a lie it was. He grinned, aware those behind him wouldn't see it. Nothing like a justified killing to make a man's day. When they returned to the others, he knew the story the two would tell of this would enhance his reputation as a leader with his fellow Africans.

Five minutes passed, and the machine gun grew heavier with each uphill step. Amazing how he came to be here, he thought. It was destiny, he told himself as he moved forward. No one else was as prepared as he was. He had a university degree; how many of the others had one? He had graduated from the University of Lagos. It would be others such as him who would free Africa from the influence and enslavement of the Arabs, the Chinese, and the white man. For that, he must never allow rumors and tales to survive that would affect his stature, for that would affect the larger plan of a free Africa. A free Africa under his leadership. He would have to take another wife. Even these imbeciles failed to understand why he would never sully his manhood with strange women. Never follow another man with a woman. AIDS had devastated Africa. So much so, an entire generation was missing. Few understood the impact of a missing generation, and even fewer appreciated the opportunity it offered for a leader such as him.

Most Africans believed themselves immune to AIDS, but Mumar knew better.

A man of his stature would need a younger, more energetic wife to work alongside the young one he already had. A virgin. Must be a virgin. Age was of little consequence. He needed one who would worship him and do what he said. One who would do whatever act he commanded. When he became powerful, there would be many chiefs who would offer their daughters to be close to him. A wealth of sons would ensure the survival of his line.

Ougalie glanced back at Nakolimia, who jerked his head in the direction of Mumar. Lugging the mortar and the shells, they fought their way through the undergrowth of the Liberian rain forest and jungle with the weapons Abu Alhaul had said would finish off the armory.

Mumar leaned forward as he walked, his breath more rapid as the incline increased. His mind lost in thoughts of future greatness, he stumbled across a vine and felt the weight of the weapon on his shoulder. Recovering quickly, he reminded the two men that once they started firing the mortar, they must avoid hitting the vehicles inside the armory. The SUVs and pickup trucks would be a welcome boon to their army. Combine the victory at the armory with a few smaller victories, and all across Africa fellow patriots would rise up to take their country back. Those same Africans would be the foundation upon which Mumar envisioned his own army with him as its general. It was a great time to be alive and to be African.

The hot African breeze drifting down across the top of the hill did little to cool the trio. But it felt good against his sweat-soaked T-shirt—even where it itched under the arms. Before Mumar's fantasies swirled back to capture reality, voices riding on the wind broke his attention. He held up his hand.

"Ssssh," he said, easing the heavy weapon to the ground. He rotated his right arm, stretching the muscle in his shoulder.

He tilted his head back and forth trying to make out the voices. He motioned Ougalie and Nakolimia to put the mortar and shells down. When they had, he waved them forward and whispered instructions. A few seconds later, they spread out, the two moving forward with their rifles at port arms, and Mumar behind them with his pistol drawn. They pushed the brush away quietly and worked their way silently toward the top of the hill.

The voices became clearer as they neared. Mumar identified several male voices and a couple of women. They were speaking English—American English.

"THE FIGHTING'S STOPPED," JOEL GRAYSON SAID AS HE walked out of the forest, zipping up his pants.

The others, sitting around the tablecloth on the ground, turned toward him.

"Did you see General Thomaston?" Victoria asked, brushing the bread crumbs from her blouse.

Joel shrugged. "I don't know what he looks like and from as far away as we are on this hill, those fighting below look slightly larger than stick figures. All I know is that those inside the arsenal still have control. They've moved the women and children from the building to where the trucks and cars are parked. They arranged a bunch of vehicles in a square. I think those vehicles will be their last stand."

Victoria's eyes darted around the group. "We've got to do something," she pleaded.

Parker Swafford spoke from the far side of the tractor. "I heard a couple of loud explosions."

Joel nodded. "Yeah, the rebels got some sort of grenade thrower or something."

"Probably a mortar," Victoria said.

"A mortar?"

"Yeah, it's like a portable bomb launcher that you drop a shell into it and it fires it up and over obstacles."

"I know what a mortar is," Joel said testily, and then sighed. "Sorry, I didn't mean to be short."

Victoria nodded. "I understand, but there must be something we can do. We can't just leave those people to these terrorists. They will kill them. Those are other Americans down there."

Joel shook his head. "What would you suggest? There's only a few of us and a lot of terrorists. Right now, they don't know we are here, and I would prefer to keep it that way. What I think we are going to do is backtrack. If we continue forward, we are going to come within sight of the armory. Then, both them and the attackers will believe we are with the other side, and most likely start shooting us. Even if those in the armory recognize us as Americans, ain't a damn thing they can do when those rebel fools turn on us."

"You're right, Joel," Parker said as he walked around the back of the trailer. He held his shotgun across his chest. "I just don't like leaving them." He held his hand up to stop Joel from replying. "Ain't like I don't understand what you're saying, but that don't mean I have to like it."

"Joel Grayson, make yourself a peanut-butter sandwich," Artimecy said, pointing to the open jar and moldy loaf of bread on the open tablecloth. "While we pack this stuff up. Ain't much we can do even though you want to, Parker." She looked at Victoria. "I'm sorry, child, but General Thomaston wouldn't want you or us doing anything foolish that won't change the outcome."

Victoria opened her mouth to say something, then thought better of it. She pinched off bread mold from a few places and took another bite of the sandwich.

"Seems pretty quiet now, but it won't stay that way long," Joel added.

"We've got to find help for them," Victoria pleaded, her voice rising around words muted by peanut butter stuck to the roof of her mouth. She leaned forward, coughing to clear her throat.

"How we going to do that? We don't have a radio and the nearest Americans are in the Ivory Coast—*where we need to be headed*," Joel said, poking himself on the chest a couple of times.

Victoria swallowed hard, washing the concoction down with a mouthful of water. "I think we should stay here. Even if we can't do anything now, we may be able to later. Maybe after dark, we can. . . ."

She fell silent. No one answered.

Joel shook his head and spoke up. "I saw another path a mile back on the other side of the hill. We could backtrack and work our way down to it. That will put the hill and the rain forest between the fighting and us. With luck, it will take us toward the border."

Everyone exchanged glances.

"I intend to stay here," Victoria said.

"We don't know who or what is down there," Jose said.

Victoria looked up as Jose spoke.

George nodded in agreement.

"Where are the boys?" Joel asked.

A sharp crack of a gun broke their conversation.

"What was that?" Mimy asked.

"Gunshot," Joel Grayson said, tossing the half-eaten sandwich onto the tablecloth. He grabbed the shotgun from where it leaned against the back wheel of the tractor.

"Where's Cannon?" Mimy asked.

"He's up ahead along the road with Jamal," Victoria said.

Parker walked toward the front of the trailer. "It sounded as if it came from that direction," he drawled, using the end of the shotgun to point down the hill.

"Joel, you've got to find Cannon and Jamal," Mimy pleaded.

"It was only one shot," Jose said. "Probably doesn't mean anything."

Parker looked at the young man. "Boy, in the last few days, everything means something even if it's only taking a leak." He turned his head away and spit a long string of tobacco juice. "Ain't been much that ain't meant something."

"Maybe we should back up the tractor and trailer?" Artimecy offered.

"We can't," Joel answered peevishly. "Whoever fired that shot will hear the engine and know we're here."

"Well, we got to do something," Mimy said, her voice louder than the others.

"Not so loud," Joel said, motioning downward with his left hand.

They argued softly among themselves. After nearly twenty minutes and with no other gunfire heard, they agreed to backtrack when the boys returned. The tablecloth, food, and eating utensils had been wiped and put away. Joel and Parker were heading forward to go search for the two boys when a shout from the left caught them.

"Drop those guns!" Mumar shouted.

The three Africans emerged from the bushes, their guns pointing at the group.

"Don't even think it, old man," said Mumar, motioning his pistol at Parker. "I don't mind shooting you."

Mumar's eyes moved from one to the other. "Back up, all of you!" he shouted, motioning the group toward the rear of the trailer with his pistol. He couldn't leave them here. They would interfere with his bombardment of the armory. His lips tightened. Deciding what to do with this group was easy, and he had no doubt the two men with him would do what he ordered. Killing them was easy, but he also knew Abu Alhaul wanted live Americans to videotape them having their throats cut. Videotapes that would be sent to the news services with the expectation they would be played to help the spread of terror.

"Nakolimia and Ougalie, take their weapons and tie them up. We will come back for them. We don't want them running for help."

Parker guffawed. "You're really stupid, aren't you? Don't you think if there had been any help around, they would have already showed up?"

Artimecy put her hand on her husband's arm. "Don't, Parker."

Parker put his arm around her and drew her close. "Don't worry, honey. We'll be all right. The man is stupid. I know what they intend to do."

"We have so few white men in Liberia," Mumar said, pointing his pistol at Joel. "We will have even fewer soon."

Mumar waved Ougalie forward "Get their guns. You," he said to Nakolimia, "see what's on the trailer."

"There's a wounded black man here," Nakolimia said as he approached the trailer.

Mumar moved sideways, keeping his pistol trained on the group. His eyes returned to Parker every few seconds even as he worked his way to the end of the trailer. The old man was the unpredictable one. Mumar reached forward and touched the unconscious soldier's chest.

"What happened?"

"Found him alongside the road early this morning," Parker said.

Mumar nodded. "Still alive, eh? I figured he'd be dead and some animal would have dragged him off into the jungle for a quick meal by now."

Out of the corner of her eye, Victoria saw Joel take a tiny half step closer to the man who was taking their guns.

Mumar grinned. "Guess Mother Africa didn't have feeding the animals in store for you, boy," he said to the unconscious American. He looked at the others. "I shot him this morning when they refused to stop at our roadblock," he lied, grinning at the shock on their faces. He extended the pistol forward, aiming it at Parker. *If I shoot this old man, the others will stay in line.*

The single shot hit Ougalie in the back, sending him flying into Victoria. A spray of blood shot out of the man's mouth, flooding across her thin blouse as his body hit her. Reflexively, she reached out and shoved him aside. The guns fell in a heap onto the ground.

Mumar jumped to the side as another shot rang out. The bullet caught Nakolimia in the head, spinning him around. Mumar scrambled behind the trailer, leaned up, and fired blindly toward the group.

Benitez leapt toward Victoria, hitting her in the small of the back, knocking her against the trailer, her head striking a piece of the frame. The bullet hit Benitez in the right side of his head, killing him instantly.

"Take cover!" Joel shouted, pushing Mimy to the ground. He jerked up his shotgun, squatting alongside the large tractor wheel.

Two more shots came from the bushes, sending bits of soil into the air where they hit.

Mumar peeked around the edge of the trailer. Everyone had disappeared. Probably at the front of the tractor. Nakolimia was crawling into the brush on the other side of the road. Mumar pulled his head back, but not before he saw a slight movement by Ougalie. The spreading blood beneath the coward meant he was dying. Even if he wasn't, Mumar couldn't do anything to save him. He pulled back, glanced around the other side of the trailer. Saw no one and dived into the bushes, only to discover a steep drop. Somewhere in the tumble through the rough bushes and briars, he lost his pistol. His

AK-47 was ripped off his shoulder. A sharp pain struck the left side of his head, and the last thing Mumar remembered before he blacked out was a cascade of green as he rolled down the steep grade through the African bush.

Cannon and Jamal emerged from the side of the road.

"You okay, Daddy?"

"You two do this?" Joel asked, pointing to the two dead rebels.

"Yes, sir," Jamal said. "We killed them. They needed it."

Artimecy pulled Victoria's head into her lap, lightly slapping her cheek and calling her name. Victoria's eyes opened for a second and then shut again. Several seconds passed before she opened them again. Blood flowed down her left arm.

Parker and Mimy rolled the dead Benitez off her.

"You all right, honey?" Artimecy asked.

Victoria's mouth opened and closed, but no words emerged. "She's bumped her head on the trailer wheel," Artimecy said.

Joel reached forward and touched the side of her head. "It ain't too bad."

"I'm all right," Victoria mumbled, allowing herself to be helped up by Artimecy.

Parker and Joel grabbed Ougalie's legs and pulled him off the road. Ougalie's hands waved feebly in the air. A bubbling moan emerged from the dying African as Ougalie continued to drown slowly from blood filling his lungs.

Parker stood over the wounded African. He spit to the side of the man. "Boy, looks as if you gonna die. Give God our compliments and tell him you be sent by us," he said before turning around and walking back to the group. "One's dead. The other's dying."

A low moan came from the trailer.

It was Selma. She was rocking back and forth on her haunches, moaning as she stared into the sky.

"He saved your life," Jose said to Victoria, pointing to Benitez. "That man shot at you and he jumped between you and the bullet."

Victoria looked down at the body. "Why would he do that?" she asked.

Jose shrugged his shoulders. "Who knows? Maybe he was

trying to dodge the bullets and jumped in front of them."

Jose laid the pistol on the back of the trailer, reached down, grabbed Benitez under the arms, and pulled him to the side of the road.

"I think he's dead now," Parker said, jerking his thumb toward the dying African. "If he ain't, he gonna be."

"Think we ought to take him with us?"

"I think we ought to leave him, Joel. We ain't no ambulance service and he ain't no friend."

Mimy hugged Cannon, running her hand through the young man's hair and holding him tight.

Joel walked over and ruffled the boy's hair. "Good job, son."

"It was Jamal who did it. We saw four men lugging weapons up the hill. I wanted to come back and warn you, but Jamal said we couldn't get here before them. They were ahead of us, so we watched. They had an argument, and the one who escaped killed this big man. Then we followed them. They heard your voices because we could hear them too. When they started sneaking up on you, we just followed, and when it looked as if he was going to shoot Mr. Parker, Jamal shot him. I shot at the other man and Jamal got the one with the guns."

Fifteen minutes later Joel, Parker, Jose, and the two boys had recovered the mortar, the shells, and the M-50 machine gun. Ten minutes later, the weapons that weighed so much and had been carried so far were on top of the trailer beside the unconscious militiaman.

The men took deep drinks of water and wiped sweat from their faces. Tired and unable to argue, they listened as Victoria proposed a plan to help the armory, but Joel and Parker's thoughts were on their family. They sympathized, and although both Jamal and Cannon thought the idea glamorous and exciting, the two older men shook their heads. Jose remained silent.

Victoria's voice rose. She angrily called them cowards, only to apologize. Finally, she insisted they leave her behind with the mortar and machine gun. The men looked at each other. Victoria crossed her fingers and waited. She draped her hand across Jamal's shoulder. He stood straighter, holding his rifle by the barrel with the stock braced against his hip.

He had no intention of leaving and he had no idea what to do with Selma. Jamal had promised his mother to take care of her. Down there was General Thomaston. Down there was the safety his uncle Nathan had promised. So, down there was where they had to go. Maybe—just maybe—his mom and dad were there too.

CHAPTER 13

DICK HOLMAN LEANED AGAINST THE GRAY STANCHION
that encircled the port bridge wing. This was where real Navy
leaders should fight battles, he thought. *I would have made an
outstanding Navy warrior in the early twentieth century—even
during Vietnam.* Today's Navy warriors fought their battles
entombed inside darken spaces artificially lighted to protect
their vision and the fighting scenarios unfolding on giant computer screens. *Shit!* His electrical engineering degree from the
Academy was ancient compared to the information technology
that drove warfare today.

He blew out a cloud of smoke that the wind across the bow
of the ship quickly dissipated. Reaching below the top of the
stanchion, Holman flicked ashes into the brass bottom of a
five-inch 62-shell casing. Once you fired an artillery shell, the
gun ejected the spent casings onto the deck. Boatswain mates,
or deck apes as they were fondly called, used them for everything from storing bolts, nuts, and nails to artistic endeavors
involving elaborate macramé designs. The two casings on the
bridge wings had none of the accoutrements of at-sea art. They
were just two empty shell casings put there by some enter-
prising young sailor who probably was tired of cleaning up
after the admiral. It never occurred to Dick Holman that the

shell-casing ashtrays were tokens of respect from the men and women who worked for him. He made sure he used them. He wouldn't want to clean up after a messy slob like him. He looked at his cigar for a moment before shoving it between his lips. He enjoyed them, but was conscious of public opinion that regarded most smokers as being inconsiderate bastards screwing up the atmosphere and surrounding those nearby with secondhand smoke. He did not intend to be an inconsiderate bastard—*a considerate bastard seems okay.*

The screeching sound of the forward elevator drew his attention.

"That should be them," Upmann said, standing to the right and upwind from the cigar.

A couple of seconds later, the four Unmanned Fighter Aerial Vehicles appeared over the edge of the flight deck.

"How could we ever give up manned aircraft for something like that?" Holman asked.

"Sometimes technology and society don't give us many options."

"And don't forget politics. We got one political party viewing us as cash cows and the other knocking on the door shouting *'We're here to help,'* and ignoring anything we have to say. Sometimes, I don't know how we survive."

The screeching stopped as the elevator reached deck level. A large group of sailors swarmed across the deck, dividing into individual working parties for the four UFAVs.

"If it hadn't been for the war in Afghanistan, we'd be without aircraft carriers today," Upmann added thoughtfully.

Holman shook his head. "Oh, I don't agree with you, Leo. I've always questioned that opinion. Aircraft carriers will be around as long as America needs to control the seas, protect our interests abroad, and project power when needed. What worries me is this idea that unmanned aircraft can replace manned ones. You can't fight a war through the eyes of a camera. You need the man—*or woman*—on the edge of their seats piloting that fighter or bomber, making snap decisions that mean the difference between life and death. Not piping signals back to a bunch of information jocks who will analyze the situation to death."

"And the Air Force?" Leo asked, grinning.

Holman nodded. "Nice try, Chief of Staff. Won't work. I've got enough on my plate here without worrying about what the Air Force is trying to do to the Navy this week. Besides, we need the Air Force. I know getting a bunch of Air Force pilots and Navy pilots in the same room to argue the merits of air-power versus carrier power is like a meeting of the Hatfields and McCoys, but we both know that without their bombers and tankers, we'd've been severely restricted in Afghanistan. Might have taken four months instead of three to conquer the country. Same goes for Iraq."

The first UFAV, attached to a yellow deck cat, moved across the gray flight deck, heading aft toward the stern of the USS *Boxer*. Though it weighed only a thousand pounds, it still needed a runway to get airborne. Beneath each wing, two air-to-ground missiles protruded. Holman did not intend to engage the French fighters. He mentally crossed his fingers. *What gave him the idea that just because he'd fooled a bunch of electronic-configured mines in the Strait of Gibraltar, he could fool a bunch of Frenchmen?* He chuckled. *Because the mines were smarter?*

"What's funny?"

Holman shook his head. "Nothing, Leo. I was just thinking of the thoughts that might go through the head of Admiral Colbert when our little charade begins."

"He's French. Don't have to worry too much about anything going through his head."

"Wish you were right, but I've worked with the French and while they're very nationalistic, they're good fighters. I discovered during Afghanistan that when the French set an objective, they tend to follow it to the end."

Upmann leaned forward, bracing himself against the waist-high stanchion. "If that's right, Admiral, then we won't fool them."

Holman took a puff on his Cubana. "No, you're right, Leo. I don't think we'll fool them completely. But if we keep them confused long enough to land the Marines at Kingsville, then we'll be ahead of the game."

The second UFAV jerked as its wheels rolled across the slight bump between the elevator and the flight deck. The driver of the deck cat spun the steering wheel slightly to align himself about twenty feet behind the first one. The third and fourth UFAVs followed, with the drivers pulling into a parade heading toward the stern of the amphibious carrier USS *Boxer*.

"Has the *Mispellion* reached its position?" Holman asked.

Upmann nodded. "She is thirty nautical miles southwest of us."

"Her team knows what they have to do?"

"Admiral, we gave them a script, but you know it was hastily written and it may be hastily executed."

"All *Mispellion* has to do is give us one hour. If the old ship can give us an hour, we'll have Marines far enough inshore that the French will be hard-pressed to stop them before they reach Kingsville. And they would never dare to act hostile to returning helicopters full of civilians."

Holman turned slightly so he could see the CH-53 helicopters parked along the port and starboard sides aft of the forecastle. Two of them had their rotors turning. Marines with full packs, guided by their gunnery sergeants, boarded through the lowered back ramps. A new whine of engines straining to achieve RPMs joined the cacophony of air operations as the rotors on the other two CH-53 Super Stallions started to rotate. He looked over his shoulder at the two tilt-rotor V-22A Ospreys parked directly across from each other near the bow of the ship.

"They're turning them around, Admiral," Leo said, pointing toward the UFAVs.

Holman looked. Sailors who had walked alongside the procession now crouched between the noses of the twenty-eight-foot-long UFAVs and the deck tractors, working quickly to disconnect the tows.

A blast of gray smoke from the exhaust of an Osprey trailed as it spread toward the stern, wrapping around the forecastle in its passage. Painted parking areas kept them out of the way of flight operations.

Near the UFAVs, the sailors finished picking up the towing gear and tossed it onto the deck cats.

Flight operations should never work. It was an impossible task. You take an 888-foot floating airport with twenty helicopters, two Osprey tilt-rotor aircraft, being operated by many who had never seen an aircraft until they joined the Navy.

Since the Navy rotated its personnel every three years, the ship lost one third of its experienced workforce annually, making the evolution a training continuum where what has been found to work is passed on to those who follow. You could read all the damn publications you wanted, and they wouldn't teach anyone what they needed to know to make an aircraft carrier work. Holman shifted the cigar to the left side of his lips. Complicating the challenges of flight deck operations were things such as fueling aircraft with running engines and Marines boarding. Within feet of these operations, various armaments either waited to be loaded or rested a few inches above your head beneath a wing or along a fuselage.

Holman watched stoically as the working parties aligned the unmanned Navy fighters. This had better work.

A whistle disrupted his thoughts and drew his attention. Holman twisted his head a couple of times before he spotted the yellow jersey of the master chief petty officer in charge of the working parties standing on the starboard side. The man held his whistle to his lips with his left hand, while his right waved the sailors away from the area.

For the uninitiated the noise, equipment, aircraft, oily smell, and intense movement of sailors across the flight deck appeared a disorganized jumble of unrelated events. And it was. Holman tried to recall if he had ever seen or read a book on the management theory of flight deck operations. He shook his head—*only official Navy documents.* Even aircraft and amphibious carriers of the same class had differences in how they conducted flight deck operations. It took experience. Experience on the ship and actually flying off a flight deck, before the epiphany of at-sea air operations fell into place.

"You know, Leo, this scene has to confuse anyone who sees it for the first time."

"I don't know, sir. I think Dante was the first to recognize it," Upmann replied. After a couple of seconds, he continued. "I know it confuses me and I see it nearly every day. It took me nearly a month to figure out different jobs had different sailors wearing different-colored jerseys."

"Kind of reminds me of a beehive."

Upmann chuckled. "I was thinking more along the lines of Dante's Inferno. You could be right. We got workers, we got royalty, and we definitely got stings. Probably a bunch of drones too."

Holman winked at Upmann. "I won't ask who you think the drones are." He turned back, observing the activities below. "When you see all those different-colored jerseys running about the flight deck wearing cranials with different designs on top—"

"Maybe a paintball derby. Yes. That's it; a paintball derby could describe it."

Holman shook his head. "Leo, don't you have something you need to be doing?" Holman asked jovially. "Maybe a few hours working alongside the Air Boss would give you a better feel for the artistic professionalism we witness every day from up here."

"Oh, no, sir. No, thanks, Admiral," Upmann protested. "I've been there and I've watched him. It only took that one visit to figure out why there are no chubby Air Bosses."

Two decks below the starboard bridge wing where Admiral Holman and his Chief of Staff stood, a small compartment jutted out slightly from the side of the forecastle. Windows tilted at twenty-degree angles with windshield wipers locked in place to give the occupants a clear view of every inch of flight deck space. This was the sacred place of the Air Boss. The mystical sorcerer of flight deck operations whose every desire or command produced dread and fear in those singled out by a speaker system designed to be heard over any flight evolution ongoing at the time. The Air Boss, a senior commander or junior captain, was directly responsible for everything that occurred within this nearly three acres of United States real estate floating on this vast expanse of the Atlantic Ocean. For anyone on the flight deck, the Air Boss's word was law, his justice swift, and his punishment irrevocable.

The *Boxer* Air Boss, Commander Scott Proudfoot, native Cherokee, tight end for Naval Academy class of 2001, watched the flight deck. The familiar set of binoculars swung like a pendulum from his neck as he moved from window to window, watching the evolution below him. Around the top of the compartment above the windows, rows of speakers broadcast the walkie-talkie conversations from the flight deck.

Behind Proudfoot, on top of the familiar gray Navy metal

table was a facsimile outline of the USS *Boxer* flight deck and hangar deck. The flight deck got most of his and his team's attention. Hangar decks changed little. But regardless of where a piece of equipment or aircraft was located, nothing moved without the permission of the Air Boss. To do otherwise meant finding yourself back in Kansas for, as Commander Proudfoot enjoyed telling everyone, he owned the power of the red slippers.

On top of the facsimile, scale models of the V-22A Osprey and CH-53 helicopters reflected their true positions. Each model had corresponding tail numbers to help the Air Boss direct deck crews to specific aircraft. Someone had made cardboard cutouts to represent the four UFAVs taking up valuable real estate on *his* flight deck, for Commander Proudfoot wore the wings of a Navy pilot. If they could do this to the fighter jocks, how long before his EP-3E was, replaced by robots?

On the flight deck, every sailor and officer wore a protective helmet with goggles and earmuffs to protect their head, ears, and eyes from the myriad of things that could go wrong in such a confined area. Sailors called the helmets cranials because unlike standard helmets, they were a mixture of cloth and hard plastic built with sufficient flexibility to be folded and carried. The helmets reminded Holman of the heads of beetles. Different colors, stripes, and emblems on top of the cranials told the Air Boss, and anyone else watching from above, the position of authority and skills of the wearer. To the starboard side of the UFAVs stood a tall officer wearing a yellow jersey with a cranial bearing three orange stripes identifying her as an Air Department officer. Proudfoot made a mental note of where she was standing. If she were still there when he came back to her, he'd jerk the handset up and ask her if she knew *what in hell* she was doing. Anyone standing still on a flight deck had no business being there. *If you want to watch, watch from somewhere else and get the hell off his flight deck.*

Sailors, according to their specialty, wore colored jerseys. Purple identified those in charge of fueling the aircraft, while red with black stripes told the Air Boss which ones handled ordnance. Red without the black stripes identified crash/salvage teams. Though all sailors and officers were trained to fight fires, the red jerseys were true professionals.

Yellow jerseys were in charge of the flight deck, aircraft movement, and handling. They were the aviation equivalent of surface force boatswain mates. Those yellows operated the yellow aviation equipment such as the tractors that had towed the UFAVs into place. They also led the firefighting teams when necessary. Fires at sea were scourges for a sailor. Fighting fires took precedence over fighting flooding. At sea you could always refloat a flooded ship, but you couldn't rebuild a burned one.

Green denoted the maintenance personnel in charge of those things on deck that controlled takeoffs and landings. On carriers, they made up the catapult and arresting crews.

Speckled among the profusion of reds, greens, and yellows were the blues who were the plane handlers, elevator operators (white cranial), and messengers. They tied down and removed the chains that held an aircraft to the deck, as well as reaching beneath the turning engines to jerk away the chocks from the wheels.

Safety observers wore white jerseys with a green cross highlighted on the back. The same color jersey with a red cross on the back and the cranials identified the "docs" of the deck— hospital corpsmen. Small first-aid kits were strapped to their waists.

Watching aft, Holman saw the wake bending to port. The *Boxer* was in an easy left turn, shifting the relative wind to bring it across her bow for the upcoming launch. Holman squinted as the sun reappeared from behind the forecastle and the morning shadows on the flight deck disappeared. The African heat rolled across them. Below him on the deck, the long-sleeve jerseys would help keep sunburn down, but already, he knew, sweat was crawling down the sailors' skin, soaking their uniforms. The danger of being blown overboard, cut in half by props, or sucked into an intake was compounded by the danger of dehydration and sunstroke. *Christ! No wonder life at sea is great!* He noticed the safety observers carrying plastic bottles of water with them, stopping along the way to provide drinks to the working parties. *"Umm,"* he wondered, *"who had the foresight to think of that?"*

As if reading his mind, the voice of Commander Proudfoot

echoed across the flight deck speakers. "Okay, everyone, listen up. We're turning into the wind for upcoming launches. I want everyone to be alert to moving aircraft and keep an eye on your shipmate. Watch those propellers! You feel that heat? That's African heat. It ain't heat from home! Every one of you make sure you drink plenty of water. It's only a little after zero-nine-hundred and the temperature is already one hundred. For those of you from Arizona, New Mexico, and Texas, welcome home."

The UFAVs were aligned two by two. They would take off one after the other, down the middle of the deck between loading helicopters and empty Ospreys waiting to launch toward Kingsville. Rotors and propellers turned, hot exhaust fumes mixing with hundred-degree heat, enveloping the flight deck. Inside each idling aircraft, Marines sweated. Suffering through the dehydrating wait. While they sat crammed together, they watched cautiously the mounted ordnance on the wings baking in the heat. This was one of the many critical times aboard a floating airfield. If one of those air-to-surface *what-a-ma-callits* went off, they would never be able to evacuate the helicopter in time.

"Admiral?"

Holman nodded. "Tell Buford to give the go-ahead to *Mispellion*. Let's keep our fingers crossed."

"What do we do when the French discover there is no American aircraft carrier? What if they pursue our helicopters ashore?"

Holman leaned forward and ground his cigar out against the inside of the shell casing. "I'm hoping what we'll have is a lot of French bluster and my fine French counterpart, Admiral Colbert, backs off."

"So do I, Admiral Holman. But what if he doesn't?"

Holman's eyebrows furrowed into a deep V. Being a senior officer meant making hard decisions. What would he do? What he did know, and wouldn't be surprised if Leo Upmann hadn't figured out already, was that Washington and Stuttgart were hanging him out. Why? He didn't know. Every message he had sent requesting clear rules of engagement had been ignored. Effectively, what they were doing was leaving it to him to decide. A wrong decision would affect America's relationship with an ally Washington needed to finish the final terms of the Middle East treaty between Israel and Palestine. Navy officers, more than any of the other services, were forever faced with balancing military actions with geopolitical realities. The tactile authority to spend millions of dollars while deployed, steaming within sight of another country's shores, the presence of an anchored man-of-war in a foreign port; all leveraged American foreign diplomacy.

Washington and Stuttgart knew of his quandary. They were slow-rolling their reply. He didn't spend eight years of his career in the Pentagon without discovering there were many ways to play politics, and using time was a primary one. If you delayed long enough, the problem went away, or someone else had the good fortune of being blamed for the decision.

"Then we fight them," Holman said softly.

Upmann straightened up, a deep sigh escaping. Holman thought he saw his tall Chief of Staff come to attention.

Upmann nodded curtly. "Then, Admiral, may I have one of those cigars, sir?" Leo said after a slight pause.

Below them, the Air Boss's voice reverberated. *"Lieutenant, what the hell are you doing on my deck? If you don't have anything to do, get hell off it."*

SHE GRABBED THE RAG FROM THE POCKET OF HER FLIGHT suit and wiped her hands. "Wow! It's hot," Pauline Kitchner said. She stuck her lower lip out and blew upward. "Damn." Pauline reached up and brushed her wet hair off her forehead.

"Gripe, gripe, gripe," Shoemaker replied standing near the step leading into his UFAV cockpit a few feet away.

"I prefer *bitch, bitch, bitch.*"

"Lieutenant, why haven't we ever met Admiral Holman?" Ensign Jurgen Ichmens asked, looking up from a squatting position near the cables running from the rear of his UFAV cockpit. "I would have thought he would have wanted to see this project. Isn't he a pilot also?"

Shoemaker shrugged. "I am sure the admiral has more important things to do than run down here and hold our hands."

"He could have invited us for lunch—or tea even," Valverde offered, trying to imitate a British accent.

"You have the worst British accent—"

"It's that Southern drawl," Kitchner said, tossing a screwdriver into the toolbox at her feet. She wiped her hand across her forehead. "Damn, I can't take this," she said, reaching up and pulling the flight suit zipper down to her waist. "I'm at least going to be comfortable until they tell us to suit up, take off, and be fighters." She struggled out of the sleeves, wrapped them around her waist, and tied them loosely, leaving her in a sweaty T-shirt easily revealing the low-cut white bra beneath.

Shoemaker and Valverde already had their flight suits at half-mast. Ensign Ichmens stood, wiped the back of his right hand across his forehead, and did the same with his flight suit.

"Told you before we started this," Valverde said.

"Yeah, yeah, yeah. You've told me many things, Alan." She looked over at Nash Shoemaker. "Okay, fearless leader, why don't we go over once again what we're supposed to do."

The screeching of the elevator on the other side of the hangar bay drew their attention. They watched for a few seconds as the Unmanned Fighter Aerial Vehicles and the working parties moving them ascended.

"Looks as if they are getting serious about this."

As if hearing Shoemaker's comments, the hatch leading from the front of the ship opened. Captain Buford Green and Captain Mary Davidson stepped into the cavernous hangar bay. Davidson carried a brown briefcase grasped tightly in her left hand. Shoemaker glanced behind the other UFAV pilots, noticing row upon row of helicopters, mostly CH-53 Super Stallions and four Cobras. These four attack helicopters separated the twenty-foot UFAV cockpits from the troop-transport helicopters.

"Attention on deck!" shouted Ichmens, drawing a stern look from Nash Shoemaker.

"Remind me to kill him later," Pauline whispered as she snapped to attention with the others. While at sea, you seldom shouted attention unless in the wardroom or at some official function, and then only for the commanding officer or a flag officer. These two were neither.

Shoemaker thought he detected a slight smile on the Operations Officer's face. He stopped himself from nodding in agreement.

"Stand at ease," Buford Green said, a broad smile breaking out.

Lieutenant Nash Shoemaker stepped forward as the other three pilots stood still. Green stuck his hand out and shook Shoemaker's.

"Well, Lieutenant, looks as if we're going to launch you and your wingmen in the next thirty minutes. Y'all know Captain Davidson, our intel officer." Green glanced over at the bulkhead and pointed. "Come on, let's take some of those folding chairs and go over your mission. Then, I'll let Captain Davidson brief you on what Intel has."

Through the open hatch, a broad-shouldered senior chief petty officer ducked as he came into the hangar bay.

"Senior Chief! Over here," Mary Davidson called. Turning to the others, she continued. "This is Senior Chief Oxford, my imagery specialist. As you mentioned earlier, Lieutenant, about needing ground support, Senior Chief Oxford has experience interpreting UAV imagery. He'll man the mother system while you're airborne along with a couple of his sailors. They'll be connected to both my shop on the third deck and with Combat Information Center on deck two. This way, we'll be able to see what you are seeing and keep Admiral Holman updated. At the same time, it'll ensure that Captain Green and his warrior buddies are aware of the situation."

The six officers pulled open some chairs normally used by the crew for movie night, and sat down in a semicircle in front of the four cockpits. Senior Chief Oxford remained standing behind Captain Davidson. Fifteen minutes later, the update to their mission completed, they shook hands, and the pilots moved to their cockpits.

Green and Davidson stood watching as the four stepped into the mock-ups and strapped on their headsets.

"Hey, Nash!" Pauline shouted across the hangar. "What's going to be our call sign today? How about something heroic instead of Prototype formation?"

Without waiting for an answer, she slipped her headset on and, in one smooth movement, slid down into the seat.

Shoemaker turned toward Valverde, but the low hydraulic noise of the top closing around his wingman hid Alan's face. From the other side of Valverde, he heard the clicks of Ensign

Ichmens's cockpit closing. Shoemaker looked back at Kitchner. Pauline smiled and waved as she lowered her head to match the closing rate of the cockpit.

Nash tugged the headset down, slapped the red close button, and slid into his own seat. He wondered for the umpteenth time as he clipped himself in why they had harnesses like those on ejection seats. It wasn't as if they were ever going to crash, burn, and die.

He flipped the radio switch. The chatter between Lieutenants Pauline Kitchner and Alan Valverde greeted his entry.

"Black formation, this is Black leader," Nash said.

"Oh, great! We gotta be a color formation?"

"You said—"

"I changed my mind. Let me or Alan pick it."

Across the intercom, came the voice of the Air Traffic Controller located in Combat Information Center. "Lieutenant Shoemaker, this is Petty Officer Watts. Are you going to be Proto formation for this event?"

"No, we'll be—"

"Deathhead formation," Kitchner interrupted, her voice trying to sound low and menacing.

"Sir?" Petty Officer Watts asked.

Shoemaker read the confusion in the sailor's voice. She was probably thinking they had bit the big one.

"Deathhead formation," Nash confirmed.

"Sir, Captain Upmann wanted us to ensure your call signs would be something an F-14 Tomcat would use."

"I understand, Petty Officer Watts, but it's not as if any of our conversation is going to be transmitted anywhere. We'll stick with Deathhead. *It pleases the number two pilot.*"

"One," Kitchner corrected.

"Wait, I'm one," Valverde argued.

"Why don't you two take a lesson from our ensign and keep quiet," Shoemaker said.

"That's what ensigns are supposed to do," Kitchner replied tartly.

"Deathhead Leader, CIC; prepare to launch. Flight deck clear. Waiting for your clearance," Petty Officer Watts announced.

"Roger, CIC," Shoemaker replied. "Deathhead Two, Three, and Four. Request confirm systems check."

The three wingmen answered "check" one after the other.

Ten minutes later, the four UFAVs were airborne at fifty feet heading southwest toward the USNS *Mispellion*.

"THEY'RE AIRBORNE, ADMIRAL," UPMANN SAID, STRAIGHT-ening up from over the air traffic console where he had been watching Petty Officer Watts.

"TAO, Air Warning," the petty officer manning the air-search radar said in a loud voice to the commander who was the Tactical Action Officer.

"Sir," the air-search petty officer continued. "I have multiple bogies inbound from the northwest."

"They're French, Commander," said the electronic-warfare technician manning the AN/SLQ-32(V)6 console. "Their noses are pointed our way."

"Have they checked in?" Holman asked.

Stephanie Wlazinierz, deputy operations officer for Amphibious Group Two and TAO, shook her head. "Not yet, sir. I was going to—"

"Give them a call and ask them what their intentions are."

The commander shut her mouth and nodded. "Yes, sir."

Holman listened to two conversations ongoing in CIC. One was the TAO leading the CIC team in trying to establish contact with the inbound French fighters, and the other was the ongoing dialogue between Shoemaker and his UFAV pilots. *What was his world coming to? French flexing their aviation muscles and American pil—operators sitting on their asses in a hangar bay flying fighters.* Nothing ever stayed the same. No matter how much you wanted to go back to a place you really enjoyed, it was never there. Maybe it was getting time for him to find that mythical piece of God's Green Acre. It had to be located somewhere between West Virginia and Georgia. Let the Navy move toward its future without him stomping his feet and shaking his head like some old bull watching a younger bull work his way through the herd.

"Where are the UFAVs?" he finally asked.

"Fifteen miles southwest of us."

Holman nodded at Upmann. "Go ahead, Chief of Staff. Tell *Mispellion* to start the script."

A couple of minutes later, over the clear-voice ship-to-ship channel, a deep bass voice broke over the low murmur in CIC. "*Boxer*, this is the aircraft carrier *Teddy Roosevelt*. We are one hundred miles southwest of your position. How copy, over."

A shiver rode up his spine. This had better work.

"*Roosevelt*, this is *Boxer*. I read you loud and clear."

"Okay," Holman said, reaching forward and tapping Petty Officer Watts on the shoulder. "Turn those UFAVs around, start bringing them up in altitude so they'll reflect off the French radars, and tell them to activate their package."

"Deathhead Leader, CIC; come to course three-zero-zero. Ascend to altitude two-zero-zero," Petty Officer Watts said over her intercom.

Below in the hangar deck, hidden from sailors who strolled by the four odd-looking cocoons, the four UVAF pilots turned their four-plane formation to the right, in a long semicircle, bringing the unmanned fighters around in a 180-degree turn. Only when they steadied up on course 300 did they start their climb to twenty thousand feet as Petty Officer Watts had directed.

Holman walked over to the holograph display. The information technicians and cryptologic technicians were working the data input for the three-dimensional table. Above the faint white light shining across the tabletop, a green shimmer identified the holograph display. A few inches above the top of the table, images of the USS *Boxer*, USS *Spruance*, USS *Stribling*, and USS *Hue City* rode on virtual waves. The formation was heading southeasterly, closing the Liberian coast. Northeast, a pattern of four French Super Etendards headed toward them. A quick glance at the display numbers showed the French fighters were fifty nautical miles away.

Behind Holman, the CIC operators and those on board the *Mispellion*, nearly one hundred miles from them, acted out the *Mispellion* masquerading as an aircraft carrier. He knew if he was Colbert, he would easily see through the charade. It was up to the electronic simulators on board those unmanned *pieces of shit* to convince them otherwise.

"The fighters are ascending, sir," Upmann said.

"Whose? Ours or theirs?"

"Ours. The French should see them on their radar within the next minute."

"Let's hope this works, Leo. If those fighters see us sitting here with turning helicopters and Ospreys, they'll know we're about to launch."

"Screw them."

"Unfortunately, I don't know them that well. Unfortunately also, I don't know how much they've worked themselves into believing they can attack us and get away with it."

Upmann shook his head. "Sir, for once I have to disagree. Sure, we've our differences, but I can't see the French attacking us. At the very least, who'd buy their wine and water?"

Holman bit his lower lip, his eyes squinting as he thought about it. "You're probably right, Leo, but let's play it out. If the French fighters turn, then they believe it. If they don't, then we'll launch while they watch. Enough of this. Launch our Marines. By now, Thomaston needs them." Even as he gave permission, he knew being out at sea, away from the watchful eyes of the media, meant no one would ever know for sure what really happened—if anything did. He sighed. He wanted to agree with Leo about the French, but for all the bluster they sometimes dished out, they could also surprise you. You never knew whether what they were saying was for public consumption or if they actually meant it. Whatever French diplomacy did, it always complemented some hidden political scheme.

The French blamed the Americans for handing control of NATO's Southern Command to the British, effectively returning the Mediterranean Sea to their historical enemy. They were reluctant partners in the Middle East peace process, throwing up small political obstacles for the Israelis as the agreement gap closed. *Ankle-biters,* Holman called them—obstacles not so large they brought everything to a stop, but small and continuous enough that they created distractions, making sure everyone knew the French were still around. He wondered if this veiled confrontation out of sight of the world was France's way of warning the United States to not ignore this European ally. If so, it was a piss-poor way of doing it. As much as he hated to admit it, the military was sometimes an unwilling cog in the conundrum of foreign diplomacy.

"Commander," the ATC called. "I have video return on our fighters." The ship's air-search radar had picked up the UFAVs.

Fighters, she called them! Damn, this world of the twenty-first century was changing too fast. "Transformation," they called it. *"Amazing,"* Holman thought. Throw a few polished words together. Make sure they complemented something politicians wanted, and you were their golden boy. Probably why Lieutenant General Lewis Leutze was doing so well at the Pentagon. Leutze had been Holman's Joint Task Force commander during the North African crisis two years ago, when the United States Sixth Fleet had been left on its own to rescue American hostages held by Islamic terrorists. Now, the *dynamic* Army officer had moved from being the Director Joint Staff J-3 in charge of Operations to the number-three slot on the Chairman's staff. Even as Holman weighed French reaction to the imminent amphibious landing he was launching, his mind traveled down what most would consider unconnected logic trails. Holman listened to the air-search radar operator reporting the latest contact information, and he watched quietly as his Chief of Staff flittered from operator to operator. The Holograph Display Unit drew his attention as it shimmered for a moment, shifting the icons for the aircraft and ships slightly in response to a computer update on contacts and locations.

"Boxer, this is *Roosevelt.* We're closing your location. I have launched four F-14 Tomcats your way to provide CAP," came the male voice from the *Mispellion.* CAP was short for Combat Air Patrol, and identified a mission where air-to-air-combat-capable aircraft orbited overhead to defend a battle group against enemy aircraft.

"Deathhead Leader, Combat," Petty Officer Watts said, seated to the right of Holman. "TAO said start simulating Tomcats. We have video on your aircraft now. They are bearing one-six-zero, forty-five nautical miles from battle group."

Aircraft! It bugged the shit out of him for them to call those unmanned aerial vehicles aircraft. He opened his mouth to say something, and realized it would sound like whining, but—*shit!*—aircraft have pilots on board. These were nothing but a maze of electronics, computers, and data downlinks. The way things were going in the military, all you needed was a computer degree and *you too could be a fighter pilot.*

It would take some getting used to directing fighter operations via internal communications. Some of the things the young lady was saying to Shoemaker and his bunch would never be broadcast in the clear. Too many operational details revealed.

"Ma'am," the air-search radar operator to his left said to the TAO. "Three of the French fighters have reversed course. They're setting up an orbit halfway between us and their battle group."

"Combat air patrol," Upmann offered.

"What about the fourth?"

"He's still coming—wait!" A few seconds later, the air-search radar operator continued. "He's turning toward our fighters, Commander. He may be heading southwest of us to see if he can confirm the presence of an aircraft carrier."

"Let's call them UFAVs, not fighters." He saw the questioning look in Stephanie Wlazinierz's eyes, but it passed quickly as she acknowledged Holman's command.

Commander Stephanie Wlazinierz, Tactical Action Officer for Commander, Amphibious Group Two, pushed the talk button on her headset and passed the order through Combat. Then she turned to the admiral. Her short-cropped hair was pressed against her head by the headset. She shoved the headset up and off her right ear, pushing her brown hair into a large wing. "Admiral, French fighter approaching the UFAVs, sir. Request instructions."

Holman bit his lower lip. "Turn two of the UFAVs toward the approaching French fighter and let's see if we can scare him off. The other two—the other two, send them to form up on the helicopters and Ospreys once they're airborne."

She nodded curtly, brought the headset back down, and passed Holman's orders verbatim to the Air Intercept Controller, Air Search Operator, and the Air Traffic Controller. Her stout legs were spread slightly to maintain balance. Holman couldn't hear his deputy operations officer's instructions through the intercom, but seconds later he heard Petty Officer Watts relay the orders to the UFAV pilots. *Pilots! Ought to be another word he could find to describe the operators of unmanned aerial vehicles. Maybe drivers. Yeah, he liked that word! Drivers never left the ground. They just motored about!* Seconds later, Watts transferred control of Deathhead Leader and Deathhead Four to the Air Intercept Controller manning the console to her right. The first class operations specialist manning AIC pushed his mouthpiece closer to his lips.

On the holograph display, the four UFAVs split into two pairs. One pair continued toward the USS *Boxer, Spruance, Stribling*, and *Hue City*. The other two turned on an intercept course toward the French Super Etendard fighter. Holman let out a deep breath. Two years ago he would have enjoyed the challenge, but he wasn't the admiral in charge then. What was he going to do once the French figured out there were no Tomcats? What would he do if a French fighter shot down an unmanned American aircraft? It'd be hard to qualify such a thing as an act of war! You throw a piece of new technology on the battlefield not covered by international convention, and someone destroys it! You couldn't very well argue it was an act of war, if they counter with safety concerns for their pilots. *Shit! This was worse than a* New York Times *crossword puzzle. Where was the sage advice from European Command and Washington that usually flooded such an operation? You're damned when you've got it and you're damned when you don't.*

Holman glanced at the large analog clock mounted above the main combat console. Not the accurate digital clock at each computer console or warfighting station, but the twelve-dollar Navy supply variant with huge numbers, two dark hands, and a red second hand. A clock that was in every compartment of a warfighting ship. Ten minutes to nine. How was Thomaston holding out? Had that been an explosion they had heard before losing contact with the retired three-star general, or just an unexplained burst of static arriving with the rising sun?

Leo Upmann turned to Admiral Holman. "Sir, if we are going to do it, now is the time."

"You're right, Leo. This is our window of opportunity. Launch the Marines. Then check with radio and see if they have heard anything from Thomaston. I have a bad feeling about this."

"Thanks, Admiral. That definitely improved my morale."

Holman grinned and patted his shirt pocket, surprised to discover no cigar.

CHAPTER 14

THOMASTON PICKED HIMSELF UP. HOLDING HIS M-16 across his chest, he ran, zigzagging across the compound to kneel beside the destroyed Civil War cannon. Gray dust blocked the view of the front gate. He could see the fighting. Militiamen standing on makeshift platforms fired over the top of the armory wall. To his left, several others lay on the ground, shooting into the dust cloud surrounding the gate. He reached up and slapped his left ear. A ringing sound inside his head seemed to be blocking out the sounds. Concussion, he thought.

A southern gust of wind blew the cloud from the gate toward him. The dark Ford SUV previously blocking the front gate lay on its side, flames leaping from the windows and around the chassis. The front of the armory was exposed. A huge gap lay open where the chain-link fence and car had been.

Samson Roosevelt slid beside him on his right, the young man's M-16 blasting into the cloud of dust. The weapon was firing, but the noise was muffled. Thomaston raised his weapon. He blinked several times, trying to clear the blur from his vision.

Retired Lieutenant General Daniel Thomaston saw Samson's lips moving. He pointed to his ears and shook his head. What if this didn't go away? He stretched his lower jaw, rotating it back and forth. His ears popped.

"—General," Samson said.

There! The noises were slightly muffled, but he could hear them now. "What'd you say, Samson?"

A fusillade of bullets passed over their heads, sending them ducking behind the cannon debris.

What he wouldn't give for just one rocket-propelled grenade launcher—*shit*, what he wouldn't give for some grenades. These rebels only had M-50s and a mortar—which was giving him hell—not to mention they outnumbered him about five to one. Other than that, it'd been a nice day.

"Sir?" Samson asked, touching the general lightly on the shoulder.

"What was that? Sorry, my ears are still ringing."

"General, we can't stay here. The front gate is gone. Mariah and French are wounded. They've been taken to the park."

Thomaston stared at the young man for several seconds. His vision seemed okay now. Moisture ran down his cheeks. He saw the look in the man's face. Probably thinks I'm crying. He reached out and touched Roosevelt on the arm. "It's nothing," Thomaston said, reaching up and touching his eyes. "Slight concussion from that last mortar."

"Roger, General," Samson said in a voice that told Thomaston a slight doubt existed.

Well, Samson Roosevelt wasn't the only one scared. He gripped his M-16 tighter. It was decision time. This was why the Army had paid him the big bucks. The Afro-topped young man waited, his eyes alternating between the front gate and Thomaston. Thomaston looked along the south wall. In several places, mortar rounds had demolished the barbed wire. Mortar hits in three spots had opened the perimeter to the attackers. How many militiamen did he have left? He'd started with thirty-two. Four were dead. He had seen a couple wounded limping to the rear. Some manning the wall had treated themselves and refused to leave. The enemy was going to breach the walls. They could do it any time they wanted. He'd lost count.

Apparitions appeared through the settling dust around the

gate. Samson raised his M-16 and sent a burst across the front. Africans fell.

"Sir, what should we do?"

"Get everyone back to the vehicle park, Samson," Thomaston ordered. His mouth was dry. How long before these assholes overran the armory? He looked up at the clear afternoon sky. Where in the hell were the Navy and Marines? *Damn you, Holman, where in the hell are you?*

Samson raced across the yard to the far side of the south wall where eight or ten, Thomaston could not recall, fought. Spurts of dirt exploded into the air as enemy bullets tracked the youth's run.

Daniel Thomaston fired into the fading dust cloud. If enemy infantry was moving toward the gate, the burst should keep their heads down for a few seconds. He ran forward to where Mariah and French had defended the right side. Pressed against the wall, Thomaston worked his way along, ordering the remaining defenders toward the rear of the burning armory building. Glass exploded from a top-floor window sending shards of tiny fragments raining down on the compound. A piece of glass struck the side of his face, opening an inch-long gash. Flames shot out of the window, sending a fresh wave of dark smoke rolling upward.

Two groups of townspeople dashed past. Samson trailed. He would have made a great sergeant, Thomaston thought, if he'd been in the Army and had a proper haircut. Samson turned, crouched slightly, and fired several semiautomatic bursts into the cloud of dust masking the front gate. The young man reached up, unclipped the magazine, letting it drop to the ground as he slammed in a fresh one. *Yeah, one hell of a sergeant.*

Thomaston looked both ways and realized everyone was gone but him. Looking over his shoulder at the gate, he took off toward the edge of the building, keeping away from the heat of the conflagration. Samson dove behind a slight rise in the ground that stretched from the edge of the building to the north wall. The man rolled once, coming to a stop with his stomach pressed onto the ground. He began firing past Thomaston. Thomaston glanced behind him again as he ran. Rebels were flooding through the front gate. Their weapons were firing blindly into the armory. The dust had blinded them, he realized.

The M-16 jerked as Samson fired at rebels so close together they bumped and jostled in their headlong rush to get inside. Thomaston saw retired Sergeant Major Craig Gentle rushing toward him and Samson from the vehicle park. Another fifty feet and Thomaston would be at the rise.

Gentle dove onto the ground, scrambling on all fours to crawl up alongside Samson. Thomaston changed direction, heading toward the two men from an angle, dodging to keep from putting himself between them and the rebels. A bullet was a bullet, and it didn't matter whether it originated from a friendly weapon or an enemy. If it hit you, it did the same amount of damage. Only difference was you usually got an apology from your own people.

Other men and women started to appear on the rise. God, he hoped none of those defenders on the ridge accidentally shot him. Gentle and Samson swept their weapons back and forth, racking the packed mob that was growing in size as more and more of the combat-crazed fanatics fought through the front gate. About eight other townsmen and militiamen formed a row on each side of Roosevelt and Gentle. A bullet whizzed by his ear, so close he felt the heat as it passed. Thomaston didn't know whether it was an enemy bullet or one from his own men and women. It wouldn't matter where it came from if it hit him.

Thirty feet! *Nearly there*, he said to himself. Suddenly, his whole body slammed forward. He flew through the air, tumbling end over end. The row of defenders passed beneath him. He landed with a thud that rocked his teeth and knocked the breath from him. He rolled a few times and stopped. Through closed eyes that failed to respond to his urge to open them, he heard the shouts of others running toward him.

He was facedown. He wanted to push himself up, but his hands refused to move—motionless, numb. With much effort, Thomaston twisted his head to the side. Two townsmen grabbed him under the arms and started dragging him toward the rear. He heard Gentle shouting orders. The firing line was retreating—a fighting retreat to the vehicle park. His eyes opened partially. They were trapped now. No way out and

nowhere to go. Their survival depended on the Navy and Marines. The men dropped Thomaston at the bumper of one of
the school buses that made up the left side of the defenders'
square. What a dumb move on his part! He glanced toward
the rear of the armory. They needed to blow a hole and make
a run for the jungle and rain forest along the southern edge of
Kingsville. Many, if not most, would die, but it was the only
chance he saw for anyone to live. He should have listened to
his instinct and taken the southern route last night.

Gentle stood with legs apart, facing the enemy. Thomaston's breathing eased, sharp tingling sensations working their
way down his body as feeling returned. Gentle, in his usual
polished sergeant-major style, was shouting orders, reposition-
ing fighters, and cursing the enemy in the fighting retreat to
the parking area. Fire from overlapping M-16's slowed the
enemy's advance. More Africans appeared through holes in
the walls.

Sharp needlepoints of pain followed the tingling sensation
of feeling returning to his arms and legs. The two men picked
up Thomaston again and pulled him into the center of the
perimeter built from SUVs, a school bus, and two pickup
trucks. They laid him on a tarp someone had draped across
the top of the burning-hot pavement. It provided little insula-
tion, and no shade from the mid-afternoon sun. Air simmered
above the gray pavement. The only clouds in the sky were
from the burning building and exploding ordnance. *"God,"*
Thomaston mumbled softly. *"A rain shower would be appreciated—and a thousand Marines."*

The acrid smell of gunpowder, its sharp tang mixed with
the moisture-sapping dryness of the smoke from the burning
building, filled the air around the man-made perimeter.

"Daniel, what have you done to yourself?" Reverend Jonathan Hew asked, easing himself down into a cross-legged
position beside Thomaston. The man had a smile planted
across his face. He lifted Thomaston's hand and ran his own
hand up and down the right arm.

"Nothing," Thomaston said, his voice dry and raspy. "Water, Reverend, would be appreciated. Just a little water and I'll
be all right."

Reverend Hew was up and gone a second or two before

returning with a small plastic bottle of warm water. This time he squatted beside the general. Thomaston shakily turned the bottle up and drank the whole thing in three gulps. Combat and heat. Two things known to kill a soldier who wasn't careful. The sound of gunfire erupted to the right, opposite where Gentle and Roosevelt moved slowly backward, delaying the advance and holding a retreating line.

"General, you lay right there until you feel better," Reverend Hew said, patting Thomaston on the shoulder. "God works in mysterious ways, brother."

Thomaston pushed himself up on his elbows. "It's not God who scares me, Preacher. It's his followers."

"Daniel," Reverend Hew said, putting his hand on Thomaston's shoulder as the retired Army Ranger lieutenant general pushed himself upright. "God's watching over us. He has his own plans, but I think He would feel more comfortable with those plans if you remain alive."

Thomaston rotated his shoulders and stretched his neck, checking his body. Satisfied he was okay, he stared at the shorter, gray-haired man with the familiar spreading middle-age stomach who had led the town in their spiritual needs. He reached over and patted Reverend Hew on the shoulder a couple of times. "Reverend, you tell God, if that's his plan, I concur wholeheartedly."

The sound of combat drew nearer. He wiped his eyes again, clearing away the pollution of combat.

"God will endure, Daniel."

"Reverend, if you expect God to intervene, then you have more confidence than I do." He pushed off the bus. His body ached, but it was nothing a ton of Motrin, a case of beer— *maybe two*, and his hammock wouldn't fix.

Gentle, Samson, and the others backed into the square perimeter. The wounded Harold French, his leg bandaged, leaned against a nearby Ford Explorer, firing his M-16 over the hood. The idea that this giant of a man wanted to die crossed Thomaston's thoughts. There was only French and his son Mahmoud, who was killed yesterday by the rebels. Thomaston's face tightened as he understood that for Harold French, there was nothing left to live for except killing those who had killed his son. Every person has a trip wire that when crossed, sent men to their deaths.

A woman, firing an M-16 from beneath the wheels of the lead SUV, jerked backward several feet. Blood poured from wherever the bullets had hit her. Thomaston could tell with one glance that she was dead.

Short overlapping bursts from the defenders stopped the rebels at the rise along both sides of the building. How long they could hold them there, Thomaston didn't know.

"I need my M-16," he said.

Someone shoved a rifle into his hand. "Here, General, take Seams's. He won't need it anymore," the unidentified townsman said, pointing to several tarps in the rear that covered the dead.

Thomaston joined the defensive fire. The number of enemy on the rise was increasing. There was nothing to stop them from entering the armory, and there was no back door for Thomaston and the others to flee. Few recognized the terminality of life when it was fast approaching, but for Thomaston, he knew this was their Alamo. Somewhere out there, rescue waited. Probably waiting for him to call. A call that would never come, for in the burning building, Beaucoup's radio helped fuel the blaze.

Another defender flew backward as a bullet caught her. One of the ladies ran up and with the help of a young boy, pulled the wounded girl to the rear.

The enemy was going to ground, diving for the sparse cover that being horizontal gives.

"General," Gentle called from a few feet away. He held up an M-16 magazine. "Sir, we're down to two each—maximum." He looked over the hood of the Ford SUV, raised his gun, and fired a quick three-shot burst at an Arab standing near the corner of the building. The man jerked like a puppet as Gentle's blast hit him.

Several windows on the armory building exploded simultaneously, raining more glass down on both defenders and attackers. Black smoke roiled from the building and flames shot from the windows. Even a hundred feet away, the heat from the inferno raised the ambient temperature. The good thing was the terrorists were closer to the fire.

Shooting tapered off as more enemy appeared along the rise, falling to the ground and shooting at the defenders. He could surrender, but he recalled other surrenders to promises of safety. They could die fighting, or they could die like sheep in a slaughterhouse. If they were going to die, then he wanted to take as many of the enemy as possible into whatever after-life there might be.

"Hold your fire," Thomaston ordered, raising his hand. A single shot came from the attackers, as if someone had used his hand as a target. If so, they missed.

Thomaston used the pause in the fight to assess the situation. Across the front of the nearly square defensive perimeter, two Ford SUVs were butted up against each other. A school bus covered the right, and two pickup trucks made the south side. A similar arrangement formed the east side—their rear. The women and children had moved outside the vehicles making up the back line. Behind them were more disabled vehicles, and then the east wall. They were trapped. The east and south walls were intact. What was good in slowing the attackers was just as good in keeping the townsfolk trapped. There was no escape. They had two options to survive. One, the Marines arrive, kick ass, and take names. He looked up at the sun. Mid-morning, he figured. The other was to hold out till night and make a run for it. If he surrendered, none of their lives would be spared. These fanatics lived for the moment when they could kill Americans.

"We can't hold out much longer, sir," Gentle said quietly.

"You think, Craig, you can breach that east wall and fight your way south to the tree line?"

"Why, General? So I can then fight my way to what little protection the jungle is going to provide south of us?" He shook his head, paused, and then added, "Maybe at night I could. But now? Daylight? I doubt it."

"It may be the only chance some of these people have."

Gentle nodded. "I know you're right. But whoever goes that way most likely will die."

"If they stay here they definitely will die." Thomaston pointed to the growing number of enemy in front of them. "You see what they're doing?"

The repeated shouts of *"Allah al Akbar"* replaced the sounds of gunfire.

Gentle looked. "Yeah, they're working up their religious fever to charge. Looks as if they are waiting until—"

"More of them are inside the armory."

"We could blow a hole in the back wall. It would be smaller than the front gate, making it slower for us to get out of here. Then we might be able to make it the quarter mile to the jungle before they run outside, man those armed pickups, and shoot us down. Other than that, it looks good."

Thomaston nodded. "Don't hold back, Sergeant Major. Tell me what you really think," Thomaston said with a trace of humorous sarcasm.

"Not a snowball's chance in hell, General. Most of these folks are out of shape, overaged, and non-combat-able."

"Those are the ones who will have to stay with me to pin down as many of the attackers as we can," Thomaston replied, pointing to the growing crowd along both sides of the burning building. "Or those are the ones who will be sacrificed to save the few who do make it to the jungle."

Gentle grinned. "Only you would think of going on the offensive when you're outnumbered five or six—probably ten to one."

"Yeah, Sergeant Major—but there's two of us."

Gentle laughed. "I've heard that joke, sir. Too many times, and believe it was you who told me. I suspect that between you and me we can keep them occupied long enough for the others to get out."

Thomaston shook his head and placed his hand on his friend's shoulder. "This time, Craig, we separate. I'll remain." He held up his hand, palm out at Gentle. "No, no argument. I've been shot at, blown up, and knocked six ways to Sunday today. You'll have to lead them out and through the jungle to the coast. Hopefully, our Navy and Marine Corps brethren will spot you."

"No, General. I think this time I shall ignore your orders. I think I'm staying here with you, sir. There are others who can lead them out—"

"AMERICANS! THIS IS AMIR ABU ALHAUL!" a bull-horn boomed in sharp accented English.

Thomaston spotted the man standing on the south side of the building. So this was the notorious Abu Alhaul who the United States had been searching for since he massacred those Americans in Kuwait. And those must be his lackeys surrounding him. The bearded man was close enough to see their position. A good sniper could take him out.

Thomaston raised his hand and waved. Talking was time, and time was the thing they needed most. They were nearly out of ammunition, and there was no place to go but a little bit deeper into the vehicle park until the east wall stopped them.

"Craig, get that east wall blown."

A man with a white flag marched forward, his slippers sliding a little on the sloping ground. The messenger wore a long white aba stained with blood and soot. He stopped about thirty feet from the perimeter. He drew back—

"Don't shoot!" Thomaston shouted.

—and threw a container.

"THOSE ARE MY TERMS FOR YOUR SURRENDER, AMERICANS!"

The container landed in the center of the perimeter. Samson ran forward, grabbed the container, and handed it to Thomaston. He pulled two sheets of paper from it. Thomaston read the first one, his anger building as he read the second. The offer of safe passage was there. The same offer made to the holdouts in Kuwait. The other demand was something to which he could agree even less.

"What does he want? Us to give up and have him slit our throats one at a time?" Tawela Johnson asked.

Thomaston looked to the left. It took a second or two to recognize the slim young woman from yesterday. Her hair had been singed off. Dull, dried streaks of blood covered her right arm. The right side of her attractive face was swollen; one eye was completely shut by the swelling. Probably a near-miss mortar explosion.

"Something like that," Thomaston said sharply, his eyes narrowing. "First, we lay down our weapons, march out, and give him the vehicles."

The eyes of the old soldier locked with the eyes of the young woman.

"Y'all ain't gonna do that, I hope?"

"General, we don't have the ammunition or firepower to last much longer," Reverend Hew interjected. "I am sure if we follow his terms and let him have his victory, at least we will live. God is working—"

"If we give him the armory and these vehicles, at least he can't use them," a townsmen said, holding up a handful of spark-plug coils. He drew back and threw, scattering them among the vehicles. He brushed his hands together. "There! They'll play havoc trying to separate them. The vehicles are dead. Screw them."

Craig Gentle handed the paper back to the general. "According to this, General, the women and children can go free. He guarantees to escort them to Ivory Coast and out of the country."

"He's lying. To him, every one of us is a threat to his subjugation of the world into some Islamic caliphate. He knows if he allows the women to live, more Americans will be born. You allow the children to live, and then your children will have to fight them. No, I've already seen what they offer. In their minds, we're heretics. No better than sheep hung up and their throats cut as an offering to their Allah." Thomaston glanced around at the people crammed into the vehicle park. He wished he had time to talk with each of them. "Yeah, God works in mysterious ways," he mumbled.

"Are we going to give the people the choice?" Reverend Hew asked.

Thomaston shook his head. "Reverend, this is war, not a democracy. No choices. We—they made it when we emigrated to Liberia. This country is as much ours as America is." He paused for a fraction of a second. "You disagree, Sergeant Major?"

Gentle nodded once. "No, I don't, General. Well, maybe a little, but I've spent too much of my life following you to decide otherwise at a time like this."

Thomaston looked toward the ridge where more enemy continued to file into the ranks. "Kind of like the Alamo, wouldn't you say?"

"And the Indians are in front."

Thomaston chuckled weakly. "Didn't know there were Indians at the Alamo."

"And there aren't any in front either."

Reverend Hew turned and walked back to a group of townspeople. He began to tell them what Thomaston intended and that they were not going to be able to decide whether to surrender or fight. That this man they expected to lead them to safety was now giving away their only hope to live. God wanted them to live, and to follow God's ways meant they must accept the word of Abu Alhaul.

Thomaston heard the harangue, but ignored it. Without looking, he knew the townspeople were dividing into two camps. Those who would continue to fight, and those willing to throw themselves on the false mercy of this radical believing they would be allowed to go free.

He crumpled the note and crammed it back inside the metal container. He tossed it up a couple of times and turned to Gentle. "Better breach that back wall, Sergeant Major. You're going to need it soon."

Gentle pointed at Reverend Hew. "Don't know if many would follow, sir. Maybe I should remain here and help you implement General George Patton's philosophy of making the other fellow die for his country."

Thomaston laughed. "If he had a country. What should we tell this little asshole?"

"Sir, it should be something that history books can quote."

"So, I guess *'Fuck Off and Die'* wouldn't be something schoolchildren could be taught or politicians could quote?"

Tawela Johnson hobbled forward to the side of Reverend Hew. The crowd around the reverend was growing as others gathered to listen to what the religious leader of Kingsville was saying. Tawela heard the exchange between Thomaston and Gentle, changed direction, and joined the two men.

A white bandage around her arm was covered in fresh blood. "How about 'Bite me,' " she offered.

"You heard?"

"I think some of us did, General."

Those in the rear, out of hearing range, could only hear Reverend Hew trying to raise a rebellion against Thomaston. Reverend Hew, who was convinced the majority of the townspeople would follow him in accepting Abu Alhaul's terms. Why wouldn't they, Thomaston thought. The man has his God, Abu Alhaul has his Allah, and never the twain shall meet.

Thomaston sighed and turned. Everyone seemed to be staring at him. His eyes trailed over the armed defenders crouched around the vehicles. You never knew what the Israelis put up with until it happened to you. *There was another God; Yahweh. Wish the three of those Gods would get together and fight it out and leave their people on earth alone.* His eyes lingered for a moment on those still manning their weapons—those on the front line of this last redoubt. A soldier never chooses who he or she will die with. Bandages, dirt, anger, fear, and blood marked his ragtag militia. They knew. Everyone knew death was swinging his sickle this day. Most had lived what many would call a full life. Every one of them wanted to experience more before *God, Yahweh, Allah, or whatever* clocked them out. He wondered if any understood the historical importance this stand might take on. What they did here today could become either a rally or a dirge for Africa and America.

He propped the papers on the side of the Ford Expedition and wrote his reply. He handed it to Retired Sergeant Major Craig Gentle, who read, grinned, stuffed it back in the container, and tossed the thing toward the rebels.

"What did you say, General?" Tawela and Revered Hew asked simultaneously.

Reverend Hew saw Gentle throw the canister. "Stop him!" he shouted. The reverend ran toward Gentle, his hands out.

"He told Abu Alhaul, 'You have five minutes to surrender your forces to the Army of Free Liberia.' "

Gentle struck out, knocking Reverend Hew's arms down, and causing the elderly pastor to fall to the ground.

Harold French sighed. "Guess that means we won't worry about this heat much longer." The tall, bulky American-Liberian pushed himself onto a knee and wiped blood from his cheek before shakily standing upright and moving to the front of the perimeter.

"Be thankful it's still morning."

One of the rebels ran forward, scooped up the canister, and ran to Abu Alhaul.

Thomaston looked down. Two of the reverend's followers

ran forward, helped the reverend to his feet, and pulled him back with the rest of the townspeople. The general watched for a second, and then turned his attention to the front.

"What is it the Indians say? 'Today is a good day to die.' "

Abu Alhaul opened the container. The Arab threw the container aside, read what Thomaston had written, and then wadded up the papers and tossed them away. The terrorist leader stroked his beard a couple of times before turning on his heels and disappearing around the corner of the building. There would be no further negotiations.

Thomaston looked around the perimeter at the others. Some met his glance, most concentrated on the scene in front, a few sat on the hot pavement, and others surrounded the angry Reverend Hew, whispering in the glare of the hot sun. One made the sign of the cross across her head and chest. Thomaston ran his tongue over his lips, feeling the small cracks caused by the heat and sun. A deep sigh escaped.

Gunfire erupted as the enemy, howling *"Allah al Akbar"* at the top of their voices, rushed the outnumbered Americans. Thomaston raised his M-16, and with the others sent many on to their Maker before they ever cleared the dead grass of the compound or reached the paved parking area.

Around the side of the building a fresh wave of enemy appeared. Company size, Thomaston guessed. He fired a short burst at a group running along the south wall, trying to outflank the defenders and sneak into the vehicle park. If the townspeople could just hold until tonight, which would be a miracle, some of them might be able to escape. Gentle reached over and touched him. "Good luck, my friend." They both knew they'd be lucky to last until noon.

"Be careful, Craig."

The sergeant major nodded and ran toward the east wall. Tawela Johnson ran with him.

The enemy reached the perimeter suddenly. Three African men jumped on top of a pickup truck on the south side, firing at the defenders along the front. The bullets sent three defenders slamming into the Ford SUV parked against the bumper of the Ford Expedition. Harold French took a bullet in his back. Dying on the burning pavement, he raised his M-16 and shot the three attackers.

"Back up!" Thomaston shouted, motioning the remaining defenders to the rear line of vehicles. "To the rear."

They fought a retreating battle, blowing away attackers who seemed to fight for the chance to die as they scrambled over the tops and around the sides of the vehicles. Even as he fought, he waited to hear the crash that would mark Gentle blowing an opening through the east wall.

Roughly ten militiamen remained able to fight as they backed toward the vehicles that created the back line of defense. The enemy poured around the Fords in front. Their firing was erratic as they shouted their prayer and jostled each other for the right to die for Islam or to kill an American. The inside of the perimeter was so crowded with rebels that every bullet found a target. The east wall was closing on them.

Gentle was back there someplace, cranking a vehicle to run through the wall. Unless the sergeant major got it open soon, they would be massacred here. Those without weapons had already fled to the rear. Thomaston looked back. He caught a glimpse of Gentle running from vehicle to vehicle. The retired sergeant major was forcing his way through the mob of townspeople. Thomaston heard a shout, turned in time to see a rebel a couple of feet away with his machete raised. A shot from the side caught the rebel in the side catapulting him aside.

It looked as if the chance to make that high-risk dash to the jungle was evaporating. There was still time, but it was measured in seconds. The key to how many would survive would be how many of the enemy they had tied up inside the armory. Even for the few who would make it out the opening before they were overrun, their only chance would be outside. Maybe more than he thought would make it to the jungle. With most of the enemy inside the armory, they would have to scramble out the gates to their vehicles to chase them down.

Thomaston heard the mortar round coming. For a moment, he thought the rebels had decided in favor of instant death rather than saving the vehicles they wanted. Two Africans charged around the side of the school bus. Thomaston shot one and Samson Roosevelt killed the other.

"Man, oh, man," Roosevelt said aloud, sweat pouring down the sides of his face. "Man, oh, man."

The mortar round passed over their heads. Thomaston

looked to the south, toward the jungles and rain forest. The same direction they had intended to flee. If Abu Alhaul's forces were already there, the flight into the jungle would be the same death trap they were in now, with little chance of survival. Hope of escaping through the east wall was gone.

CHAPTER 15

"PAULINE, QUIT COMPLAINING. AT LEAST YOU WILL GET TO see Africa before we do. So just go with Alan and escort the Marines in. Jurgen and I will intercept the French fighter."

"Deathhead Leader, this is Deathhead Three," Pauline replied formally. "Is this a male thing? Why do you get all the fun? If I recall the last flight, you crashed out of a dogfight. From what I remember—*Hey! Speak up, Ensign Ichmens!* We successfully shot down those Tomcats."

"Hey, don't give Nash a rough time. He can't help it if his piloting skills can't hold an aircraft together in a fifty-G turn," Valverde chided good-naturedly.

"Deathhead Leader, this is Petty Officer Turner. I am your Air Intercept Controller, sir. I have you and Deathhead Four for intercept on bandit bearing three-two-zero from your position at altitude two-eight-zero," Petty Officer Turner broadcast.

Nash's eyes blinked a couple of times, ridding them of that dry feeling caused by forced air circulating through the tight confines of the mock cockpit. Petty Officer Turner had told them that the lone unidentified aircraft was northwest of their UFAVs, flying at twenty-eight thousand feet. Everyone knew it was a French fighter, but until it was visually confirmed, it would remain an unidentified aircraft. So far, only the electronic-warfare technician had verified it as a Super Etendard. Considering there weren't other aircraft carriers around carrying Super Etendard fighters, the process of elimination was easy.

"Deathhead Two and Three, change to channel one. Petty Officer Watts," Petty Officer Turner continued, "will be your Air Intercept Controller with the landing force."

"Well, that doesn't seem too bad," Pauline said on the private line that only the four of them could hear. "May see some action yet." Then, on the connection with Combat, she replied, "AIC, Deathhead Three and Four changing to ATC channel one."

"See you back at homeplate, Pauline; Alan. Take care."

"Alan, join up on my left side. Our link with the UFAVs is line of sight. That means we have to keep gaining altitude the farther we get from the ships. If we lose that data link, then . . ."

She didn't finish, but she didn't need to. Loss of the critical control data link meant the UFAVs would automatically ascend to twenty-two thousand feet and start a circle pattern, five-mile-wide profile. The UFAVs would stay there, waiting for their owners to reclaim them electronically, until fuel reserves reached critical. Then they would put their nose over and dive into the ground, self-destructing all of the avionics, computer systems, and communications equipment on board, protecting the sensitive technology from non-American hands. The downside of this fail-safe mode was it had yet to be tested. The operational assessment of this fail-safe mode wasn't scheduled for another two months.

"Roger, understand," Valverde replied.

Nash listened for a few more moments to Pauline Kitchner and Alan Valverde form up before he mentally tuned them out. He reached over and pushed the data-link diagnostic-check button, holding it for three seconds. The lights glowed green. He and the ensign could have the same problem with their data link as Pauline had warned Alan about, but their aircraft were nearer the ship and had less chance of losing the data link.

If they began to have problems with the control link, their

console's diagnostic lights would change slowly to red like a countdown sequence. Satellite relay would have been helpful, but the military only had limited space resources, and most of those had been relegated to the war in Indonesia.

They had no satellite link available in this area to control a long-range flight, and the sunspot activity had rendered high-frequency control untenable. They were dependent on the very-high-frequency and ultra-high-frequency ranges. Those frequency ranges only worked when transmitter and receiver were in line of sight of each other. There was more to flying an unmanned aerial vehicle than a normal pilot had to know. Every one of them had been at one time or another a communicator, and with the exception of Alan, who was a cryptologist with Naval Security Group Command, all of them were qualified pilots.

What the hell a cryptologist did, none of them knew. When asked, Alan always replied jokingly that he could tell them what he did, but then he was honor-bound to kill them. Or he could tell them a *"wee bit about the dangerous world of Cryppies,"* and then just beat the hell out of them.

Nash smiled. It was unusual for four A-type personalities such as theirs to come together and work so closely as a team. Probably because none of them competed against each other for promotion and none of them were really in charge. Well, technically he was, but he seldom exercised that right.

He glanced at the data-link monitor. Pauline was right. The scientists and other UFAV pilots would understand if they lost contact, but the naysayers at the Pentagon would jump on this as an example of a failed "leap ahead" technology. There was more riding on this than many knew.

No, they had to maintain a line of sight between these mock-up cockpits strapped down in the hangar bay of the USS *Boxer* and those UFAVs boring holes in the sky. There *was* another relay capability they could use. It had had limited testing, but Nash knew it could work, but if he had to use it, it would be the first time in an operational environment. The Unmanned Fighter Aerial Vehicles were designed so that one of them could orbit at high altitude, allowing the others to link through it with their aircraft. This would allow the other UFAVs to operate at a lower, out-of-line-of-sight range. It was a fallback data link when satellite connectivity was unavailable, as it was here. It was also a power-projection capability to extend the range of a UFAV hundreds of miles inland. The downside—*damn, there's always a downside to everything*—was crossing his fingers and hoping it worked outside of the controlled environment.

"Deathhead Three," he acknowledged. "Thanks for the reminder on the data link. Everyone keep an eye on those diagnostic lights. If you see anything that smacks of data-link interruption, tell the others. Talk to you after the intercept."

"Good luck, Nash," Pauline said. Then she added, "Ensign, I hope you know what you're doing. If you had spoken up when I asked, we could be flying as a team again. But nooooo, you had to keep quiet about our success—"

"Good luck, Lieutenant," Engine Ichmens interrupted. "I may be able to recall that dogfight later."

Nash heard the slight click as Pauline and Alan changed to channel one. The four pilots still had their own internal channels, but now they would only interrupt in the event something drastic happened.

The left-side screen showed the edge of Ensign Ichmens's UFAV nose cone entering the field of vision of the camera. Jurgen had joined up.

"Good position, Jurgen."

"Deathhead Leader, Deathhead Four; come to course three-two-zero. Maintain altitude one-two-zero," Petty Officer Turner said. "You will be coming in low and nose-on to approaching aircraft."

"Roger, *Boxer*," Nash replied. He glanced at his altimeter. "Deathhead Four, climb two thousand to one-two-zero, maintain position on my left. Coming to course three-two-zero now." He put the UFAV in a slight turn, correcting the course by a few degrees, and then pulled back on the stick, bringing the nose up. Motion on his left screen caught his attention. He watched for a brief moment as the nose of Jurgen's UFAV reappeared and crept up until the Deathhead Four UFAV was flying alongside him in tight formation. Then Jurgen's UFAV eased back as he assumed wingman position to Nash's lead UFAV.

"*Boxer*, Deathhead Leader; one-two-zero altitude, steady on course three-two-zero."

"Roger, Deathhead Formation. I hold bandit course one-four-zero, descending, passing two-five-zero. Intercept in five minutes."

Nash clicked his transmitter a couple of times, acknowledging the transmission. The French fighter was descending toward them, passing through twenty-five thousand feet.

"Why do you think he's descending, Lieutenant Shoemaker?"

Nash pressed the private-line button. "No chatter, Jurgen." Wasn't the time for them to start a separate chat. Remain focused and let the AIC do his job.

"Deathhead Formation, *Boxer*; Admiral Holman says intentions are to try to keep you out of visual of the French fighter as long as possible."

"Roger, understand." Once the French saw they weren't F-14's, then the dance of the titans would stop, freeing the French to do whatever they decided. It was inconceivable to Nash how the country directly responsible for America's independence, and which America helped free in World War II, could reach the point where it felt threaten by America.

He smiled, recalling Pauline's response to such a question. "I mean, how can they be upset? Don't we have French companies like Kentucky Fried Chicken, McDonald's, and Disney World scattered all over America?"

"Deathhead Formation, *Boxer*; come to course three-five-five. Maintain current altitude. You are on course toward *Boxer* task force, distance twenty nautical miles."

Nash reached up and touched the focus of the cameras on the UFAV. The ships should come in range shortly.

"Deathhead Formation, Deathhead Formation," Petty Officer Turner said urgently. "French fighter is not alone. Video return shows two fighters. I repeat, two fighters. They must have been riding close up, one over the other to fool the radar, but they have broken apart."

"Roger, understand, Petty Officer Turner. Where are they?" Nash asked, his head twisting as he searched his screens for any reflection or movement that would reveal the French fighters.

"Yes, sir. I have them from you, bearing three-three-six, range twenty-five. Still descending, passing altitude two-two-zero. They may have you painted, sir."

Nash nodded. If the French aircraft radars had them *painted,* as radar operators say, then his electronic-warfare suite didn't show it. "Seems to me, Petty Officer Turner, that those aircraft are intercepting us rather than us them. I think instead of us trying to make the task force, we should engage them. If nothing else, we can confuse them for a few more minutes. I believe the secret of this operational deception is to buy time."

"Roger, sir. Wait one."

Nash knew the young Air Intercept Controller was discussing the proposal with the officers in Combat. Most likely the admiral was up there, but at a minimum Captain Green or Captain Upmann would be there.

"Deathhead Leader, come to course three-three-zero, ascend to altitude two-four-zero."

"Roger, Boxer. Understand."

"Deathhead Four, this is Deathhead Leader. Turning your way, shipmate. Steady up on course three-three-zero, maintain wingman position, and follow me up. Appears we are going to force them to either follow us above the few clouds in the area, or give us the chance to attack them from above."

"Roger, tallyho!" Jurgen shouted, using aviator terminology that he was about to engage the enemy.

"Deathhead Formation. Be advised, weapons free not authorized at this time."

"TALLYHO!" HOLMAN SAID ALOUD. "TELL THEM THEY AREN'T authorized to engage."

"Admiral, the French are on an intercept course to them!"

"Yes, they are, Leo, but they are on an intercept course to *two unmanned aerial vehicles.*" He'd be damned if he was going to call them aircraft. "What am I going to do? Authorize the shoot-down of manned French fighter aircraft to protect unmanned aircraft? Can't do it. Not yet. They're still our allies."

"What do we do if they fire on them?"

"They evade, they jam, they twist and turn, and avoid. But they don't fire on those aircraft. They maneuver like real pilots know how to do."

"They can't engage anyway, Admiral. They only have air-to-ground missiles on them."

"I thought they had guns."

Upmann's eyebrows bunched. "They do, but I don't think they are loaded," he said, his voice trailing off.

"Don't think, Leo," Holman said harshly. "Find out. If they're armed, tell those pi1-operators to lock down their firing mechanism." The last thing he wanted was to be responsible for setting an international precedence for UFAVs to shoot down manned aircraft. The United States had only used them against enemy forces to protect American lives. As much as Colbert pissed him off, being pissed off was not a good argument for following the rules of engagement that gave him permission to shoot down hostile aircraft.

"ROGER, *BOXER*; WE UNDERSTAND, BUT BE ADVISED OUR cannons aren't loaded and we have air-to-surface missiles; not air-to-air. We can intercept and engage, but we have no defense. And if we should lose these two UFAVs, then you are limited to one UFAV to escort the Marines to Kingsville because the other one is going to have to act as a relay."

"Roger, I will pass this information to Commander W."

"Lieutenant, I have the Frenchmen visually," Jurgen said. "They're at our ten o'clock, below us about four thousand feet. I think they are circling for a left-to-right pass."

Nash looked where Jurgen said he saw the French fighters. A brief reflection of sunlight highlighted the French aircraft. The two were in a similar formation to his and Jurgen's. A lead aircraft with a wingman slightly back on the left side. The two aircraft were in a turn that would carry them behind and beneath the two UFAVs.

"*Boxer*, Deathhead Leader; we have visual on the bandits. Request permission to engage."

"Wait one."

*   *   *

"ADMIRAL, THEY HAVE THE FRENCH FIGHTERS AND WANT permission to engage."

Holman bit his lower lip. Time was the key element here. "Where's our landing force?"

A few seconds passed. He walked the two steps to the holograph display. The lieutenant manning the console hit the "refresh" button. The holograph display simmered slightly for a couple of seconds. Icons moved as positions were updated. Four CH-53 helicopters followed by two Ospreys were reflected several miles from the coast. At a higher altitude, Pauline and Jurgen's UFAVs followed. The display showed the two UFAVs closing the landing force formation. Northwest of the task force, two French fighters merged beneath the two UFAVs. The landing force should be safe. They would cross the shore in the next couple of minutes. Northwest of Joint Task Force Liberia, three French Super Etendards orbited in a standard racetrack combat-air-patrol formation.

"Permission denied. Divert the two UFAVs away from the French fighters and head them toward Kingsville to help the landing force."

"DEATHHEAD FORMATION, *BOXER*; PERMISSION DENIED. Turn to course one-six-zero. Maintain altitude. New mission is to join support elements for evacuation operation."

The front of Nash's screen blacked out for a moment as a French Super Etendard blew past it, heading up with afterburner on. The view on the screens bounced as turbulence knocked the smaller UFAV around in the air. The stick shook in his hand. The altimeter showed him losing altitude. He glanced at the screen to his left, afraid for a moment he and Jurgen's UFAVs would collide. Nothing there but a few clouds zooming past him.

"Too late, *Boxer*. Just been buzzed by one of the bandits. They know we're here."

"MEANS THE FRENCH KNOW WE HAVE NO AIRCRAFT CARrier and no Tomcats," Holman said, biting his lip lightly.

"May still take them some time to figure it out, Admiral."

Leo Upmann glanced at his watch. "They may be having their lunch. By the time the French pilots relay their information back, the operations people interpret it. Pull straws to see who has the pleasure of taking the news to their pompous French admiral—it could be ten to twenty more minutes."

"If that's true, then they are less professional than I have known the French to be. We have to assume they *have* figured it out."

"Aye, sir. We have ordered the UFAVs south to join the landing force."

"Ma'am," the Air Search Radar operator said to Commander Stephanie Wlazinierz. "The three French fighters to our northwest have left pattern and are now on intercept course toward the landing-force formation."

Holman looked at Leo, who shrugged his shoulders. "Guess I was wrong. We got those three up north and two to our southwest. Those two southwest of us are nearer the landing force if they decide to head that way. I would suggest, Admiral, we need to keep them occupied. Those three heading on intercept course with the landing force won't reach them before they pass over the coast. It'll be hard to track them with that mess of jungle and rain forest cluttering up their radar capability. Those southwest of us, though, could be on top within five minutes. I recommend we treat them as hostiles, Admiral. Have Lieutenant Shoemaker and his wingman engage them."

Holman shook his head. He patted his shirt pocket like a security blanket. "We could." He nodded. "Okay, Captain Upmann, they have permission to engage, but do not have 'weapons free' authority. Unless the French fire on our landing force, I will not authorize unmanned vehicles to return fire regardless of what those French pilots do."

"Sir, they have nothing to fire," Upmann said, referring to the UFAVs

"Bullshit, Leo. If I was a pilot and got jumped by an enemy and all I had were air-to-ground missiles, I would fire them just to keep them confused and pray for a lucky hit. Thank God they don't have their cannons loaded."

*   *   *

"JURGEN, YOU OKAY?"

"Roger, Lieutenant. I have you slightly above me and to my right."

"Where are they?"

As if listening on their private line, Petty Officer Turner spoke. "Deathhead Formation. You may engage, but with weapons tight. You are not authorized to fire even if fired upon."

"Let ourselves get shot down?"

"Sir, your orders are to engage and keep them occupied while our forces continue toward Kingsville."

"But—" Jurgen broke in.

"Roger, understand. Doesn't really matter since we only have air-to-ground missiles on board," Nash said, interrupting his wingman.

"Deathhead Four, switch to tactical channel twenty-two. Your controller will be Chief Petty Officer Cooper. Deathhead Leader, remain this channel."

"Roger," Ensign Jurgen Ichmens said.

A click followed almost immediately. Nash reached up, moved his helmet slightly, and ran his handkerchief across his forehead. They were separating the UFAVs for the engagement.

"Turner, tell the boss up there to get the other UFAV ready for launch!" Nash said urgently. "If we lose one of these, we can reconfigure—"

"Deathhead Leader, come right NOW! Descend immediately two-zero-zero!" Petty Officer Turner shouted.

Nash shoved the stick down and to the right, putting the UFAV into a spiral spin. Déjà vu thoughts from the incident in North Carolina crossed his mind. He looked at the G-force meter: ten Gs. Nash eased back on the stick. The UFAV started to vibrate, shock waves transmitted back through the data link to the controls of the mock-up cockpit. He jerked his head to the left and saw the underside of the French fighter as it passed. That was close.

Nash pulled the stick to the right and brought the nose up.

"Contact two miles, separation one thousand feet, right-hand turn."

He's coming around for another pass. Nash wondered

briefly if the fighter had fired on him. He bit his lower lip. As long as the French fighter used cannon, the only sign the UFAV was being fired upon would be him seeing flashes from the cannon or the UFAV being hit. Otherwise, it was practically impossible for him to know.

Well, a manned fighter could take a few Gs. The UFAV was capable of much more. At least, it was supposed to be capable of more. The crash in North Carolina had reduced Nash's confidence slightly in the turn capability of the Unmanned Fighter Aerial Vehicles. He pulled the stick back and watched the heads-up display on the front screen while he glanced at the G meter: 13—14—15—16—the controls began to vibrate. He eased back, bringing the G meter to 12.

"Fire-control-radar switch on."

A second passed before Petty Officer Turner spoke. "Deathhead Leader, turn off fire-control radar, sir. You are authorized to use air-search mode only."

"Air-search mode only! If I don't use the fire-control mode, Turner, I won't be able to engage him at close range. It'll all be smear because he'll be inside the minimum range."

"Yes, sir, I know. Orders are no fire-control radar."

"I'm in a slight spiral, heading down toward the sea. I have a fighter on my tail. They won't let me turn on my fire-control radar so I can have a better look at what I am fighting."

"That's because we're not being allowed to fight!"

"OKAY, ALAN, PUSH THAT FIGHTER OF YOURS A LITTLE FARther out. You're making me nervous being this close," Pauline told Jurgen.

"Roger, madam."

"Quit that. Makes me either sound old or a manager of a whorehouse."

"Let me see—old or manager of a lively business establishment? Decisions, decisions, decisions. I don't think you'd do good 'old.'"

"I think you're doing that on purpose."

"Deathhead Two, *Boxer*; you should be able to see the helicopters, Lieutenant," Petty Officer Watts said. "They should be below you at six thousand feet at your three o'clock."

Pauline leaned toward her screen as if she could look below the frame. She searched the view, knowing a movement or flash of sunlight off the helicopters would catch her attention. There it was!

"Got them, Watts. Alan, you see them?"

"Yeah. Got 'em."

"Deathhead Formation, descend to seven thousand. Come to course zero-eight-five."

"Follow me, Alan. Keep wingman position." Pauline pushed the stick forward and slightly to the right. The front view shifted as the UFAV turned right and began to descend. She turned her head left for a moment, and saw Valverde's aircraft maintaining the same distance and position. He was good. Had to give him that.

The digital readout on the altimeter sped by. *Too fast*. She pulled up slightly on the stick to slow the descent. A quick glance showed that her wingman had adjusted his descent automatically to compensate for the change.

She pulled the stick back to the centerline. The UFAV leveled itself, but continued descending. Ahead, the helicopters grew in size. Pauline saw movement to the right and the left of the four CH-53's, and for a moment a chill went up her spine before she recognized them as Ospreys. Somewhere behind them were French fighters.

"*Boxer*, Deathhead Two here. What happened to those French fighters?"

"Wait one, Deathhead Two." A few seconds passed before Petty Officer Watts replied. "Ma'am, two French fighters are currently engaged with Deathhead Leader and Three. We've lost contact with the other three aircraft. Their last course had them on intercept toward your position. Air Search is reporting multiple contacts overhead the French battle group. Commander Wlazinierz believes they are launching more aircraft."

"What does that mean?" Valverde asked over their internal communications link.

"Means multiple aircraft orbiting over the French fleet and three French fighters disappeared heading our way," Kitchner replied with a deep sigh. "News just keeps getting better and better."

Pauline clicked her transmit button twice acknowledging

Watts's report. She reached over and alternated her hands on the stick as she pulled her flight gloves tighter. Reaching over to the intercom system, Pauline nearly switched on the private channel between the four mock-ups, but didn't. She wanted to. She wanted to find out what in the hell Nash and *her ensign* were facing. Maybe they needed her and Alan? Then again, maybe they didn't.

The data-link contact light blinked red a couple of times before steadying up on green. "What the heck!" She reached up and hit the lamp check switch. All the lights glowed green.

"Deathhead Two, this is Deathhead Three; Pauline, just had a data-link-interrupt light flash a couple of times."

"So did I, Alan." She bit her lower lip, her eyes turning toward the data-link console where a green contact light shined steadily. "We must have passed through an electromagnetic phenomenon," she offered.

"Yeah, they have those out here? As much as I hate to say it, I think we are reaching the limits of our line of sight. That quick flash was probably the transmit system changing frequencies, searching for a better data connection."

"If you're right, Alan, then we'll see another flicker in a few seconds. Let's steady our altitude." She glanced down at her altimeter. "Here, six thousand feet."

"Maybe one of us should ascend to ten thousand feet? Then if we lose contact, the lower UFAV will lose it first. Then we can link through the higher-flying UFAV."

"I knew that," she said. "Petty Officer Watts, need to keep one of us at a higher altitude so we can maintain our electronic links between *Boxer* and the UFAVs. We may be reaching the edge of our transmit range on these frequencies."

Before Petty Officer Watts could reply, the red light on the data-control console came on, and this time it burned steady. "Pull up! Pull up!" she shouted just before the screens went dark. "Shit! Alan—"

"I've lost contact, Pauline."

She reached down and slapped the switch for the private circuit. "Nash!" she shouted.

"Pauline," he said through clenched teeth. "Get off the circuit. Jurgen and I are trying not to get our asses shot down right now!"

"We've lost our links with our UVAFs. I think we passed our line-of-sight capability," she continued, ignoring Nash's order.

She heard the click as Nash disconnected her. Must be bad if he couldn't talk to her.

"Deathhead Two, *Boxer*; Lieutenant, we show you and your wingman in a stationary orbit and ascending."

"Pauline, the UFAVs have gone into automatic mode, heading toward twenty-two thousand feet."

She felt foolish. "Roger, Alan."

As if on cue, the red data lights changed to green as automatic electronic links readjusted and reconnected. Her screens flickered a couple of times before steadying up. She looked to her left to see where Alan's aircraft was. The nose of the wingman's UFAV was pointed directly at her.

"Jesus Christ!" she shouted. Pauline pushed forward on the stick, sending the UFAV into an emergency dive.

"Alan, pull up! Pull up!"

"I don't have contact yet. Wait a minute! Here it comes. Shit! I've lost it again."

Pauline's controls shook as the angle of descent grew. She drew up involuntarily waiting for the collision. The renegade UFAV passed overhead. It disappeared for a moment, to reappear on the right screen in a sharp turn to begin another orbit.

She pulled back on the stick. Nothing happened. She tried with all her strength, but the stick refused to budge. Kitchner pushed down hard on the left flap, putting the UFAV into a left turn, reducing the drag for a moment. She pulled back, and like a large bucket rising from deep water managed to slow the descent. She fought the unmanned aircraft back to a level course. The digital compass showed her on a course of one-nine-zero, heading out toward the empty Atlantic. She pulled around, steadying up on course zero-three-zero. The red light on the data-link readout flickered.

"Alan, I'm about to lose control again."

"Deathhead Two, I have you on course zero-three-zero, altitude eight-zero. The landing force has just crossed the coast. They bear zero-two-five, altitude four-zero. Admiral Holman would like for you to return to ordered position."

"Roger, *Boxer*. I know where I'm supposed to be, but we

lost contact for a bit with our UFAVs. We'll rejoin now. Request you provide ground-control-intercept guidance for us."

"Pauline, I'm getting intermittent contact with my UFAV."

"Lieutenant, I show you have plenty of fuel," Senior Chief David Oxford, the intelligence specialist manning the mother console above the four mock-up cockpits, said.

"Fuel ain't the problem, Senior Chief. The problem is we can't maintain data link with our unmanned aircraft unless we have another UFAV orbiting at high altitude to act as a relay."

"Uh . . . that sounds . . . not so good, ma'am."

"Nope. You're right. I can see why you're in Intelligence, Senior Chief. It ain't good. It means we've got an aircraft that will orbit until it runs out of gas, and we got a fighter aircraft that can't go much farther because it doesn't have the radio range to do it."

"YOU HEARD?" UPMANN SAID TO REAR ADMIRAL HOLMAN.

Dick Holman nodded. "We need to break off Deathhead Leader and Four and vector them toward the landing force."

"What about the French fighters?"

Holman's eyes narrowed, and then he grinned at Leo. He leaned over and touched Commander Wlazinierz on the shoulder. "Stephanie, get me Admiral Colbert on the circuit."

Captain Upmann looked at his boss, his expression questioning.

Holman nodded curtly at him. "Time to see if we can ease the tension here so we can redirect those aerial vehicles toward our landing force."

"Good luck, sir. Admiral Colbert doesn't strike me the type to have a great sense of humor."

"Sir, I have Captain St. Cyr on the black telephone," Commander Wlazinierz said, pointing toward the black handset resting in its cradle beside the captain's chair.

Holman picked it up and pressed the "push-to-talk" button. "Captain St. Cyr, this is Admiral Holman."

"Bon jour, Admiral. How may we help you?"

"I'm trying to help *you,* Captain. Please pass along my respects to Admiral Colbert. What I would like to know is why are your fighter aircraft dogging our target drones?" Target drones were aerial targets usually pulled behind an aircraft so ships at sea could practice their surface-to-air-missile firing and the ship's antiair gunfire.

A few moments of silence passed before the circuit broke open again. "I am sorry, Admiral. We have never seen drones like these before. They do not have American markings on them."

"What are your intentions, Captain? We are preparing to fire on those drones, and we can't do it with your aircraft in the area."

Holman held the handset away from him and looked at Commander Wlazinierz. "Stephanie, bring up the fire-control radars on the USS *Spruance* and USS *Stribling* and have them paint our UFAVs. It should cause the electronic-warfare alarms on the Super Etendards to alarm and hopefully scare the shit out of those French pilots."

He brought the handset back to his ear.

"Admiral, this is Captain St. Cyr again, sir. Our early warning aircraft—one of your own manufacture—an E2C, has detected what may be helicopters heading into Liberia. I have been instructed to send aircraft to intercept and turn them back."

"Captain, do you also see two aircraft orbiting between my battle group and the coast?"

A few more seconds passed. "Yes, sir, I do."

"Those are F-14 aircraft from the USS *Theodore Roosevelt*."

"Admiral, I think someone is pulling—*how do you Americans say*—your legs. According to our intelligence, the USS *Theodore Roosevelt* is in the Indian Ocean and cannot possibly make it here before next week."

"Things just keep getting better," Upmann said.

"What now?" Holman asked, holding the black handset by his side as he looked at Leo.

Upmann shrugged. "Don't know, Boss. I would suggest that arguing with the French uses time. Time in which we can redirect the UFAVs toward the landing force. If the French decide to intercept, at least we'll have three-and-a-half fighters between them and the landing force. Possibly four, if they reestablish that data link."

"Stephanie, take Lieutenant Shoemaker and his wingman and vector them toward the other two unmanned aerial vehicles."

Upmann shook his head, putting his hands on his hips.

"What's your problem, Chief of Staff?"

"Why don't you just say UFAV or unmanned aircraft; or better yet, just aircraft."

Holman wrinkled his nose and winked. "You say it your way and I'll say it the Naval Aviation way." He tapped the stars on the collar of his khaki uniform. "Besides, I've looked over the manning of Joint Task Force Liberia and discovered I was in charge."

Holman lifted the black handset. "Captain St. Cyr, you could be correct. I'll have a talk with our intelligence officer and ask her to confirm what you've told me. I wonder who would benefit from trying to fool our Joint Task Force."

"Admiral, your fire-control radars have locked on our fighter aircraft. Admiral Colbert demands that you shut down your fire-control radars immediately."

"Tell Admiral Colbert to go take a flying leap," Upmann recommended in a low voice.

"Captain, tell Admiral Colbert that we're vectoring our target drones away for the firing. The only radar we have available to keep track of them are our fire-control radars. They should be off your fighter aircraft shortly, or if you vector your aircraft north away from the drones, then they will be outside of the fire-control-radar zone. I'm too far along in the exercise to shut down the fire-control radars at this time. As a precaution, I recommend you recall your fighters immediately. I have a lot of young Navy officers who're still too young to resist pushing every button they see. I would hate for an unfortunate incident to happen."

Holman turned to the deputy operations officer. "Stephanie, where are the unmanned aerial vehicles?"

"Sir, Deathhead Leader and Four are on intercept course with the other two fighter aircraft—"

"Stephanie!" Admiral Holman interrupted.

"Sorry, sir—the other two UFAVs. In two minutes, they will be five nautical miles south of us at altitude six thousand feet on a course of zero-nine-zero, Admiral."

"Tactical Action Officer!" the Air Search Radar operator called. "I show the two bandits southwest of us on a north-easterly course heading away. Current course will take them back to the French battle group."

"That's good news," Upmann offered.

"Yeah, they could have vectored them toward the landing force."

Holman took the handset away from his ear. The French must be discussing the situation, trying to decide what course of action to take. Why did it have to come down to two of the mightiest democracies on earth having a Naval confrontation off Africa? He knew the answer was politics. Politics on a global scale, and what better place to iron out some of the finer points of American-French foreign relations than at sea? History had shown that Naval confrontations ran less of a risk of escalation than those ashore. Holman knew it was because out at sea it was easy for statesmen to put a more positive spin on events that permitted both combatants to back away from a full war. War? *Hell of a thought.* Could never see America and the country most responsible for its freedom in a military conflict. But here it was, and he was being left out on a limb with no advice from senior leadership on what to do. Just go rescue the Americans in Liberia and return to the United States. Well, he would do that. Those were his orders and orders were to be obeyed, unless they were illegal, and there was nothing illegal about rescuing American citizens in danger of being killed.

"Commander, I have bogies—four—heading toward the or-biting UFAVs southeast of us."

"Where did that fourth one come from?" Holman asked.

"TAO, Electronic Warfare here; I have hits from Super Etendard fighter aircraft," the young petty officer manning the AN/SLQ-32(V)6 electronic-warfare console announced.

Holman looked past the captain's chair at the glowing green screen of the EW operator. The AN/SLQ-32(V)6 was the latest in early-warning technology. In the automatic mode, the system could take over the electronic-warfare defense of the battle group. This new EW defense included jamming enemy radars and filling the skies surrounding the ships with small bits of aluminum to confuse enemy missile-seekers. This EW system also had a transformational capability of interjecting small bits of radar return that made the enemy operator see multiple targets and inbound missiles. This new technology also caused the enemy radar returns to flicker and change positions so rapidly that it confused the operator. It intentionally slowed computerized analysis of radar and electromagnetic signals.

"Go automatic, Commander," Holman said to Stephanie.

"Aye, sir," she acknowledged. Then she pushed her button down on her sound-powered telephone. "EW, turn on automatic defensive measures. Link with the other EW systems on the other ships and turn the computers loose."

She looked at Holman. "Activate the black program, sir?" she asked, referring to the most top secret of technology the United States military possessed. Technology only authorized in time of war.

He shook his head. "No, let's hold that unless we have to do it."

She pushed her headset against her left ear. The wing of hair flopped down alongside her head. Wlazinierz acknowledged whatever was said and turned to Holman. "Sir, the four UFAVs are together."

"Admiral Holman," said the voice of Captain St. Cyr over the speaker.

He picked up the handset and pushed the talk button. "Yes, Captain, go ahead."

"Sir, we are confused by your actions. Those drones were not shot down, and now they appear to be orbiting with the two to your south."

"You're right, Captain. After what you told me, I had no choice but to investigate your claims about them not being F-14's."

Several seconds of silence passed before Captain St. Cyr replied. "And what did your intercept reveal."

Holman thought for a moment, and then pushed the talk button. "The intercept told me you were right, Captain St. Cyr. I will have to do some royal ass-chewing within my task force. Seems one of the other ships launched drones also. Now, I have to find out how come we believed them to be F-14's from one of our many aircraft carriers."

"You can say that again," Upmann added.

*   *   *

"PAULINE, I HAVE YOU IN SIGHT," NASH SAID OVER THE PRI-
vate circuit.

"I have you too, Nash. Never thought I'd like to see you
two flying over the horizon at me." Pauline spent three minutes
bringing Nash up to date on what happened and the course of
events that occurred.

"Deathhead Leader, this is *Boxer*; orbiting UFAV is at altitude two-two. Come to course zero-one-zero. Target is five
miles."

"*Boxer*, this is Lieutenant Shoemaker. What are we going
to do once we get there? Shoot it down?" he asked with a
slight hint of anger over being vectored toward the wayward
UFAV. When no reply came, he added, "Just leave it alone
and keep a radar watch on it."

"Sorry, sir," Petty officer Turner said. "I just thought—"

"Never mind, Petty Officer. Give us some time down here
to discuss it. We are as close as we need to be right now, and
the orbiting UFAV has sufficient fuel for another couple of
hours. Why don't you put the four of us on one traffic controller?"

"Roger, sir. Change to channel one. Petty Officer Watts will
take over. New directions before you go. Admiral Holman
wants you to catch up with the landing force. We have four
French Super Etendards heading toward the landing force."

"Well, if they are any kind of pilots like the two we just
played with, they'll get lost on the way."

"Roger, sir. I will pass that on."

"Wait a minute, Petty Officer Turner. Don't pass everything
we say on to the admiral. We have enough problems without
having flag testosterone bouncing all over the place. Just stay
off the circuit for a couple of minutes and let us see if we can
fix the problem."

"What are you going to do?" Alan asked.

"We need to recycle the avionics," Nash offered.

"Means that you are going to have to shut down while that
intelligence specialist, Senior Chief Oxford, brings the system
back on-line. Kind of like restarting your computer when the
blue screen of death appears."

"That may take some time."

Nash mentally shrugged. "I don't see much of a choice, Alan."

"Deathhead Formation, *Boxer*; sorry, sirs and ma'am," Petty Officer Watts interrupted. "I have control of Deathhead Formation. Deathhead Leader, Deathhead Two, and Deathhead Four, prepare for vector to the landing force."

"What about me?" Alan asked.

"Alan, we're going to need you right where your UFAV is now, once you regain control. Climb to twenty-five thousand and act as data relay. Alan, work directly with Senior Chief Oxford and get control back. You may have to vacate the mock-up, get on the mother-board, reactivate the avionics, and the data-link systems. The senior chief doesn't have any experience in doing this. You're going to have to do it. Check each one as you do it, and run diagnostics on the data-link systems before you reactivate them."

"Roger, will do."

"Petty Officer Watts, this is Deathhead Leader. We await your command."

"Roger, Deathhead Formation; come to course zero-four-zero, max speed. Maintain altitude two-zero-zero."

CHAPTER 16

THE INCOMING MORTAR ROUND EXPLODED ON THE GRASSY
area of the compound killing several of the enemy. A second
round, followed by a third, screamed through the air. Thomaston slowly stood as he searched the sky, trying to follow
the whistling sound of the mortar. Each one was exploding
into the attacking charge. If Abu Alhaul terrorists were firing
that mortar, they were piss-poor in their aim, thank God.

The Africans were the first to break and run. The Arab
leaders in their midst hit out at them with the butts of their
guns, trying to force them to turn around and continue toward
Thomaston and the trapped townsfolk. Thomaston watched as
an Arab shot a fleeing African before turning his gun back
toward the townsfolk just as a group of Africans knocked him
down and trampled him as they fled. The whistling sound of
another mortar pierced the noise of the gunfire, and drowned
out for a moment the cries of the attackers as they ran in
disorganized retreat. Another African fell, or was shot. Those
behind trampled him as they continued their pell-mell race
away from the incoming rounds.

The fourth mortar round exploded near the edge of the
building. A new sound joined the foray—Thomaston tried to
place it, but the whooping noise mixed with mortars, screams,

and gunfire was too faint to stand out alone. Along with the noise, huge clouds of dirt and dust from the explosions, bodies, and body parts filled the air. Many of the enemy were sent tumbling across the ground, only to discover themselves unharmed when they stood. Those ran harder toward the front gate of the armory. That fourth round must have changed the Arabs' minds, thought Thomaston as he watched them join the Africans in the mad dash to safety. They were in full retreat. Thomaston held up his hand to stop his people from firing. They might need the few remaining bullets they had. He stood straight, and watched the flight for a few more seconds. More time bought, he thought. The whistle of a fifth mortar round flew overhead. The round clipped the east side of the armory building, the explosion sending bricks flying into the air. A sixth round passed over the building and exploded somewhere in front.

"Listen," he said.

From the front of the building and out of sight came the new sound of heavy-machine-gun fire accompanied by screams of pain. The *whoop-whoop* sounds from earlier rose in intensity. Another explosion outside of the armory rocketed debris skyward. Sure sounded like a helicopter to him, thought Thomaston. He glanced at the tree-encrusted hill to the south. The noise of large-caliber machine guns reached his ears. More than one.

"Sounds like fifty-caliber," Thomaston said.

"Guess those Arab allies don't like their African brothers running for their lives," Roosevelt said.

Craig Gentle ran up beside the general, touching Thomaston on the shoulder. "Never thought I would see this. Christ! What lousy shots those assholes are. Ought to give that A-rab mortar-er a Bronze Star!"

"Thought you were going to make a hole in the east wall."

"Would have, but Lincoln's disabling of the vehicles was very thorough."

An explosion from behind knocked Thomaston into Gentle, throwing both toward the ground. Thomaston threw his arms out, saving his head from slamming against the pavement. These explosions were going to kill him, and he had yet to be hit by one.

The two men rolled apart and raised their M-16's toward the east wall.

"Well, there's our hole, General."

A ruse! The enemy was behind them and the rebel force had now closed their only chance of escape.

Thomaston rose to a crouching position. One knee on the hot pavement and the other bent so his left foot could push him upright at a moment's notice. There was no other place to go. At least the miscalculated mortar fire had eaten into the forces making the frontal assault. He had not believed this disorganized force of rebels hell-bent on reaching their cult version of heaven could mount a two-prong attack. A cloud of dust obscured where the explosion had destroyed the wall. The sound of gunfire rose in intensity out of sight from the front of the armory. If this is a small force unaware of what happened to their comrades in front, then Thomaston and his people might still have a chance.

Bricks rolled to the side of the wall. Strands of sharp barbed wire swung, bouncing up and down, from where they hung by single strands to the remnants of the wall. He raised his M-16 to fire. Figures appeared out of the cloud. His finger tightened on the trigger. The camouflage utilities of a United States Marine emerged. Behind the man, additional Marines ran into the compound. Thomaston lowered his weapon. A patch displaying the United States flag was prominent on their right shoulders. The Marines flowed past the survivors and surged forward, charging after the fleeing attackers. Other Marines rushed into the makeshift defensive perimeter along the edge of the pavement.

A CH-53 appeared suddenly overhead, the noise of its straining engines filling the air. Then two of the strangest flying machines Thomaston had ever seen crossed east to west at about one hundred feet, heading toward the fight out front. White, about thirty feet long. As he watched, each fired a single missile. The missiles arched for a moment and then, with white spiraling contrails following, they disappeared in front of the armory building. Two large explosions quickly followed as the missiles hit their targets. Two huge white clouds burst into the air, followed immediately by dark roiling smoke. No cockpit. The things wiggled their wings as they circled overhead for another pass and disappeared toward the front, weaving right to avoid the dark smoke rising from the building. *What in the hell—*

The cheers from the townspeople drew his attention. Thomaston counted twenty Marines before he stopped. An unexpected emotional surge caused his eyes to well for a moment. The U.S. Marines had arrived. *Damn! Why couldn't it be Army? HOOAH!* A second and a third CH-53 roared over the armory, lower this time, sending stinging clouds of dirt and rock into the air. The heat from their engines raised the temperature while they passed overhead. The acrid smell of exhaust fumes enveloped those below. The CH-53's passed over the south wall. Both noses of the helicopters angled into the air slightly as the two large troop carriers changed their forward momentum to a momentary hover. Then, they quickly disappeared behind the wall, landing in the field between the armory and the rain forest. Combat landing!

Two Marines stopped and exchanged a few words with one of the women in the rear. She pointed toward Thomaston and Gentle. The two men ran toward Daniel Thomaston. People along the way reached out to touch them. Most stood—laughing, crying, family members hugging each other, celebrating the appearance of U.S. Marines. Thomaston smiled. The helmet had the black but familiar spread-wing eagle of a colonel in its center. This would be the leader of the rescue party. Behind the two men, Reverend Hew stood alone.

The men slowed to a walk and saluted as they neared.

"General Thomaston, I am Colonel Charles Battersby. Sir, hate to be a killjoy and interrupt your fun, but Admiral Holman insisted I pass along his compliments to you, sir, and apologize for the delay. Seems he had to work out a little disagreement with one of our allies before we could deploy."

Thomaston returned the salute and shook hands. Damn! He wanted to hug this big son of a bitch. His throat constricted slightly. Thomaston smiled, cleared his throat, and replied. "Colonel Battersby, it's about time you showed up," he said, hoping his voice didn't sound as shaken as he felt. Thomaston coughed. "We thought we were going to have to whip their asses by ourselves." He turned to Gentle. "Colonel, this is my sergeant major—Craig Gentle—late of the Eighty-second Airborne."

"Sergeant Major," Colonel Battersby said, nodding at the noncom. "General, I would like to tell you that you are relieved and we will finish the mopping up, but I respectfully ask your permission."

"Colonel, you have my permission."

"Colonel, great job with that mortar. We thought they were coming through the rear," Gentle said.

"Mortar?" Battersby looked at the lieutenant colonel standing to his left. "We didn't fire any mortars, sir," Battersby said. "We were making a low-level assault from the east when those rounds were fired. We marked the spot on the hill south of you where they originated, but when we saw they were targeting the enemy, we left them alone. Figured they were part of your elements." Ignoring the questioning looks exchanged between Thomaston and Gentle, Battersby continued. "This is it for Marines, though. We have two Ospreys inbound," he said, and as if hearing him, the two tilt-rotor aircraft appeared over the armory, their rotors tilting as they approached the makeshift landing zone in the south field.

"Everyone we have is here that we know of, Colonel. If it wasn't you firing that mortar, then we've got enemy fighters to the south of us," Thomaston offered.

"Not according to the UFAVs, sir. They did a reconnoiter minutes before we landed."

"You mean UAVs, Colonel?"

"No, sir. Unmanned Fighter Aerial Vehicles. But they have cameras, and if there are enemy fighters in that direction, then it's not a large group. General, we need to start evacuating your people to the *Boxer*. If you would start moving your people through the gap and toward the Ospreys, we will start the evacuation."

Thomaston looked toward the gap in the east wall. If Marines could come through it, they could go out of it.

A couple of men stepped over the remnants of the wall into the armory. One of them was white. Both wore civilian clothes. *Where did they come from?* he wondered.

"General, I have to join my Marines, sir. If you would—".

Thomaston reached out and shook Colonel Battersby's

hand. "Sure thing, Colonel. You go whup ass, and I will take care of getting everyone out of here."

Battersby saluted and the two Marines took off, jogging toward the burning armory building. The sound of fighting in front of the armory continued.

"Who's that?" Gentle asked, pointing to the two men standing just inside the hole in the wall.

Thomaston shrugged. "Don't know. Probably more refugees."

"One's white."

"Not everyone has the luxury of being black, Craig."

"You know what I mean. I bet he's CIA."

Thomaston thought for a moment. He did have an agreement with the Company. "If they are, they'll let us know." He turned his attention away and smiled. "Sergeant Major, let's start everyone moving." When he looked back at the gap, three women and two young boys had crawled through the gap.

The slender woman with the shorter skirt was carrying a young girl. The young girl curled against the woman's chest with both of her small hands wedged into her eyes. Even from here, he saw spittle running out of the girl's mouth.

This group of newcomers was pushed aside as the crowd surged forward at the direction of a couple of Marines who were shouting directions.

Thomaston turned and leaned against the SUV. In another time, another era, another life, he would have rushed forward to the sound of gunfire. The term *LGOP* came to mind—a combat rule that meant command and control had broken down. In this case, he was the LGOP—"Little Group of Paratroopers." When you had a bunch of LGOPs running around, many times you were in as much danger from them as you were from the enemy. LGOPs subscribed to the combat order to soldiers that when you are lost and don't know where you're supposed to be, march toward the sound of gunfire and kill everyone you encounter not wearing your uniform. The sound of gunfire in front seemed to slacken, and then suddenly stopped altogether.

*   *   *

ABU ALHAUL STARED FROM THE EDGE OF THE JUNGLE TO the west, trembling with rage at the devastating effect the Marines' superior firepower had on his force. The Africans were useless as fighters. Look at them run. Look at the cowards run instead of standing up and fighting until death for the honor of martyrdom.

"Abu Alhaul," Abdo said softly. The overweight and taller man reached forward and tugged on his brother's shirt. "We must go, Abu. There will be other days to complete this mission."

Abu Alhaul shook his head. "One more hour and we would have overrun the Americans." He raised his fist and shook it. "Why am I surrounded by cowards? Why cannot I have the fruit of the madrassas here to rush forward to give their lives for Allah?" he asked angrily, referring to young men and women taken as toddlers and trained in religious schools for the purpose of martyrdom. "I will show them how to do it," he said, and stepped forward.

Abdo grabbed him, his massive arms reaching easily around the smaller man. "Ah, Abu Alhaul, if I allow you to sacrifice yourself, then your other plan will fall apart. Your chance to show the world the vulnerability of the Great Satan. I don't think you want that to happen. Do you?"

After a few seconds, Abu Alhaul stopped struggling. Abdo was right. "You may release me. You are right. Allah has a greater purpose for me before I join him." He felt the massive arms relax. Abu Alhaul reached up and pushed them gently aside. Then, he turned. Behind him not only stood Abdo, but also his retinue of Islamic guards who had sworn an oath to give their lives for him and Allah. If he had charged forward toward martyrdom, every one of them would have come gladly to their deaths with him.

Abdo reached down and picked up the AK-47, Abu Alhaul's personal weapon of choice. "Here, my brother." Abdo pointed deeper into the undergrowth. "We must go."

"And we must ensure the ship is ready for America."

Abdo nodded in response. "It is nearly ready. Only a few things to do before it sails."

The two walked through the bodyguards and followed the three men hacking a path deeper into the rain forest. The last man bringing up the rear overheard the comment about the ship. He had to find out more about it. Langley would want to know.

GEORGE REACHED OVER AND PULLED VICTORIA BACK BE-side him. "Don't want you to get trampled as they leave."

"I think we should have stayed outside," Jamal whispered to Cannon.

"We didn't know Marines were going to show up," Cannon said, his head going back and forth as he watched the people leave. He pointed toward the two men talking near the SUV. "That's General Thomaston. He's the one who founded Kingsville."

Jamal looked at the smoke rising from the houses in town. The big place on top of the small rise in front of the armory had flames licking through the windows. "Don't look like much of a town now." As he watched, the roof of the community center caved in, sending embers high into the air.

"What you think, Parker?" Joel asked.

Parker spit away from the crowd. "I think we should have stayed outside. Just my luck to get where I want to go to find everyone leaving and us at the end of the line."

Joel laughed. "Someone always has to be at the end of the line."

Parker grinned. "This time it'll be you, white boy."

"You two stop that," Artimecy said, taking Parker by the hand.

A Marine Corps corporal walked over to them. "Excuse me, if you follow the line, we are starting the evacuation."

"Wonder where they're taking us," Jamal said.

Cannon shrugged. "Don't know, but I hope they got food."

Victoria reached over and tussled Jamal's hair. He looked up. "Selma?" he asked.

"What?" she replied softly, her voice muffed against Victoria's shoulder. His sister kept her fists pressed against her eyes and her head pushed down onto Victoria's bosom.

"We may be going to find Mom and Dad."

She shook her head. "No, we aren't. Mom and Dad are

dead. Even I know that," she said, and then began to cry. "Even I know that."

Somewhere deep inside, he knew that Mom, Dad, and big brother Abdul were dead. He just didn't want to admit it. He fought back the tears. Jamal didn't want Cannon to see him cry.

Cannon looked at his new friend for a few seconds, and then walked over to his father. "Dad, we going with them?"

The Marine motioned to them.

"I don't think we're going to have much choice," said Joel.

Jamal looked up as the two strange aircraft passed overhead. *How did the pilot see?* he asked himself. There're no windows in the thing. Victoria's hand pushed lightly against his back, urging him toward the hole in the wall. Ahead walked Cannon with his family and the older couple. He hoped this adventure ended soon. When it did, he knew the only good news would be that he kept his promise to his mother and led Selma and himself to safety.

IT HAD BEEN TWO DAYS SINCE THE BATTLE. HOLMAN STOOD on the flight deck. Thomaston turned as he put one foot on the steps leading into the CH-53 Sea Stallion. He waved, and in two quick steps was inside.

Holman and his Chief of Staff, Captain Leo Upmann, stood near the hatch leading into the main part of the forecastle, watching the helicopter carrying General Thomaston and the others lift off the flight deck. The helicopter was taking him back to Kingsville, where other evacuees had returned earlier in the day. The helicopter turned left, and then circled the USS *Boxer* before steadying up on an easterly course away from Joint Task Force Liberia. The noise on the flight deck returned to its normal level of loud clanging, running feet, and the straining engines of flight deck equipment.

Holman led the way as they reentered the forecastle. "Hope he knows what he's doing," he said.

"I suspect he does. Or like most general officers, thinks he does."

Holman gripped the railings of the ladder leading up. "Is there a hidden comment in there somewhere, Leo?" He both pulled and stepped his way up the ladder to the next deck.

"*Moi?* I would never say such a thing about you, sir."

Holman waited a second or two for Upmann at the top of the ladder before he continued down the passageway, heading forward. "Here he is, a retired three-star general who could go live anywhere in America and on his retirement pay probably be in the top income bracket, and instead, what is he doing? He's out here in Africa, leading a bunch of expatriates in trying to establish their own little America."

"Who knows why, Admiral. When I left last night after dinner, did he give any indication as to what his intentions are? I mean, with the exception of the ten or eleven families who elected to return to America with us, the rest are returning with him."

Holman shook his head. "No. He just believes that African-Americans, unlike their white countrymen, and even like native Africans, have a right to a heritage. A right to know where they came from."

"His DNA library has received a lot of attention in America," Upmann offered. "And before this insurrection, Liberia was well on its way to being the showcase country for Africa. I was a little surprised when he said they would be returning."

"I wasn't."

"I don't understand. You come out here to this inhospitable part of the globe and nearly lose your life for a speck of ground. Well, me for one, I would have packed up long ago and headed back home to the land of McDonald's, Burger King, and Chuck E. Cheese. There's no government now."

"There will be. Thomaston intends to go to Monrovia and establish his own interim government until new elections can be held. You saw what the State Department said during the video teleconference yesterday. They'll recognize him as long as he keeps his promise. I can't imagine an American military officer not keeping his promise."

"That should keep America happy as long as Thomaston doesn't have something to hide and decides to keep power for himself. That would be something, wouldn't it. A retired American general who takes over a country and becomes its dictator." Upmann chuckled at his small joke.

Holman stepped up as they passed through a watertight

hatch in the center of the passageway. Upmann followed, having to duck his head to keep from bumping it on the overhead, and taking an exaggerated step up so as not to trip on the metal knee-knocker at the bottom of the hatchway.

"Leo, everyone has a hidden agenda. Come to think of it, he did say some things that might provide insight as to where this small piece of America will go from here."

Leo reached forward and opened the door to the flag wardroom. "What was that, Admiral?"

"He said that he believed Liberia was where Texas was when it won its independence from Mexico. He even referred to the Battle of Kingsville as their own Alamo. Talked about the relationship between Liberia and the United States, going all the way back to when Liberia was originally established. Even pointed out that the only difference in the Liberia flag and the American flag was forty-nine stars. Oh, yes, he has plans, and while he didn't share them, I think I know what he intends."

Upmann pulled the door shut behind them and headed toward the coffee urn. "What does he intend?" He pulled out a couple of cups from the pantry.

"I think that in a few years, our Congress will have more on its agenda than just approving dual citizenship for those of African descent. I think they may be faced with the prospect of another independent country like Texas applying to be a state."

A knock on the door drew their attention. It opened and Captain Jeremiah Hudson, commanding officer of the USS *Boxer*, entered.

"Jerry, come on in and have a cup of coffee with us," Holman said, motioning the commanding officer into the flag wardroom.

He shook his head. "Admiral, Admiral Colbert is on the radio and wishes to talk with you."

"You mean the French Admiral who would never answer any of my calls?"

Hudson bit his lower lip and nodded a couple of times. "Same one, Admiral. Seems the French fleet has been recalled to the Mediterranean."

Holman turned to Upmann. "Leo, you want to take this one

for me? Express my regrets but tell him I'm unavailable."

Upmann's eyebrows arched. "Nothing would give me greater pleasure, sir." Three steps later he was out the door.

"These are for you, Admiral," Jeremiah Hudson said, handing a couple of sealed envelopes to Holman.

Holman looked at one, then the other. "How about that? PERSONAL FOR messages from Commander, European Command and from *our very own* Chairman, Joint Chiefs of Staff." He tossed the unopened envelopes on the table. "I am sure you've read them, Jerry. Let me see if I can guess what is in them." Holman put the back of his right hand against his forehead and shut his eyes. "Ah, it's coming to me." He lifted one of the envelopes. "This one feels as if it's from European Command." He tossed it into the air a couple of times. "It is a 'well done' from General Shane, telling me what a great job we did and how impressed the world is with our success." He tossed the envelope back on the table and picked the other one up. "Ah, this one is easy. It references General Shane's message and tells me how great and wonderful we are. How much we are loved in Washington for a successful operation against the terrorist hordes and saving American lives."

He opened his eyes and tossed the envelope on the table. It landed on top of the other one. He picked up his cup of coffee and took a sip. "So, how close was I?"

Hudson grinned. "It's almost as if you wrote the messages yourself, Admiral."

Holman nodded. "If we hadn't been successful, there would have been only one message. It would have come from the Department of Navy and started off something like: *'Effective immediately, you are hereby ordered to turn over command, et cetera, et cetera, et cetera.'* There are multitudes of good things about being a professional military officer, regardless of which service you are in. There is also the other end of the sword where, regardless of why or how well you're trained to do something, when you fail—you fail. Failure is not an American trait taken well."

"Yes, sir, but it's not as if they provided any guidance to you," Hudson offered.

Holman took another sip. "Oh, they provided ample guidance, Jerry. They said, *'Go evacuate the Americans and don't fight the French.'*" He pushed the coffee cup away. "We did our mission and we did it effectively. Now, Jerry, I think I will go up to my favorite bridge wing and have a cigar. Call me when we reach Little Creek. I'm sure my staff at Commander, Amphibious Group Two has missed me and are already waiting on the docks with iced beer and nibblies."

Jerry laughed and followed the admiral through the stateroom door. "I am sure they are, sir."